Review

I0593951

This is a must-read novel involving an international trail of investigation, historical cover-ups, some damning evidence about the Catholic Church, and a whole lot of action guaranteed to make readers rethink Dan Brown for gripping drama. The wealth of background research and information certainly adds to a story that spans a few thousand years and draws the reader back into centuries-old theological battles without overwhelming the plot. An interesting, compelling novel, I recommend it highly

Readers' Favorite

2013 Readers' Favorite silver medal winner
2013 Eric-Hoffer finalist

Books by Stefan Vučak

General Fiction:
Cry of Eagles
All the Evils
Towers of Darkness
Strike for Honor
Proportional Response
Legitimate Power
Autumn Leaves
All My Sunsets
F/X-26
28th Amendment
Night Sirens
Broken Rose

Shadow Gods Saga:
In the Shadow of Death
Against the Gods of Shadow
A Whisper from Shadow
Shadow Masters
Immortal in Shadow
With Shadow and Thunder
Through the Valley of Shadow
Guardians of Shadow

Science Fiction:
Fulfillment
Lifeliners

Non-Fiction:
Writing Tips for Authors

Contact at:
www.stefanvucak.com

ALL THE EVILS

By

Stefan Vučak

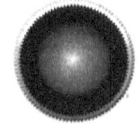

ALL RIGHTS RESERVED

No part of this book may be reproduced or transmitted in any form or by any means, electronic or mechanical, including photocopying, recording, or by any information storage and retrieval system, without permission in writing from the author, except in the case of brief quotations embodied in reviews.

Note:

This is a work of fiction. All names, characters, places, and events are the work of the author's imagination. Any resemblance to real persons, places, or events is coincidental.

Stefan Vučak ©2010
ISBN-10: 0-9942923-9-2
ISBN-13: 978-0-9942923-9-1

Dedication

To Irena ... and a fulfilling journey

Acknowledgments

The Vatican's spy service, the Holy Alliance, was formed in 1566 by order of Pope Pius V, renamed The Entity in 1930. The sister counterespionage service, the *Sodalitium Pianum*, was founded in 1913 by Pope Pius X.

Information about The Entity was sourced from the Internet and by permission, *The Entity* by Eric Frattini; published by JR Books, Great Britain, 2009.

Cover art by Laura Shinn.
http://laurashinn.yolasite.com

"For they eat the bread of wickedness, and drink the wine of violence."

Proverbs 4:17

Prologue

A hot sun beat down on the small parking lot. Peroni squinted despite his dark shades and glanced at the black Rado on his left wrist: 12:20. Watching people make their way out of the building, he figured it wouldn't be much longer. After observing him for two days, Vanetti's movements were predictable and the reporter should be emerging at any moment. Peroni could have made his move earlier, but he never took unnecessary chances.

Cardinal Belconi did not tell him why he wanted the reporter silenced, and he didn't need to. Peroni knew how to read. The last two issues of *Panorama* were less than flattering to the Institute for Works of Religion, otherwise known as the Vatican Bank, and in particular, it's Vice President, Morgan Farrugi, and his alleged money laundering for the Sicilian Mafia. After the collapse of Banco Ambrosiano in 1982, he thought the Holy See would know that crime does not pay, but apparently not.

Peroni looked around the shimmering parking lot, switched on the engine, and started the air-conditioner. After an initial blast of warm air, a cool breeze played across his face and chest and he sighed. He endured far worse in the parched Iraqi desert, but saw no reason to suffer unnecessarily here. Belconi might not agree with him, having said that suffering was man's divine lot, but seated in his opulent Vatican office, easy for the wily old cardinal to say.

Another hour and he should be able to wrap up the assignment and catch the three o'clock flight to Rome from the Milan Linate airport. Not a bad way to make a hundred thousand dollars, his target not a professional, unlike some he'd tackled. The

1

fact that Vanetti annoyed The Entity to a point where his articles on the Vatican Bank's dealings threatened to spill over into another national scandal didn't worry him. He never worried about the why, only the how and the when. If God was happy to sanction what Belconi did, Peroni felt certain He would forgive him his little trespasses. If not, that's how things went.

The tall, spindly reporter emerged from the *Panorama* headquarters. After a glance at the harsh blue sky, he walked quickly toward a red Fiat. Peroni watched the little car turn right onto Via Mandadori and eased his BMW rental after it. He smiled when the Fiat turned right onto Via Rivoltana and stopped outside the popular little Thetoria da Carlo restaurant. He slowed as Vanetti got out of his car and disappeared inside. Peroni parked the BMW on the Fiat's driver's side, climbed out, and headed for the café. Cars whispered along the highway behind him.

Being lunchtime, the place full and noisy without being overcrowded. He spotted Vanetti at a table next to the tall plate glass windows and took a seat beside the serving counter. Wearing formal suits, office workers on either side of him hardly gave him a glance.

A vaguely pretty thing dressed in a green blouse and skirt, chewing gum, stood on the other side of the counter and waited, eyebrows raised in expectation. The coffee machine hissed and gurgled and the cash register clanged. Peroni ordered an espresso and slid a five Euro note toward her. She smiled briefly and the note disappeared. By moving his head left a little, he could watch Vanetti without being obvious about it. Moments later, a waitress brought the reporter a plate with a bulging sandwich, french fries, and a can of Coke. After a brief chitchat and a nod, Vanetti dug into his sandwich with gusto. When his coffee arrived, Peroni took his time sipping it.

Seeing the reporter almost finished, Peroni pushed back the small cup and saucer and walked out of the restaurant. When he got to his car, he opened the trunk and pulled a small black leather valise toward him. He unzipped it, took out brown calf leather driving gloves and slipped them on. He grasped the Glock 17, chambered a round and screwed on the silencer. Vanetti appeared beside him, glanced at him and nodded.

"Buon giorno."

"Likewise," Peroni said with a smile. "Hot day."

The reporter unlocked the door to his Fiat and shrugged. "They're predicting rain in the afternoon."

Peroni merely shook his head. Vanetti prepared to close his door when Peroni stepped toward him and raised the handgun. The reporter's eyes bulged, but before he could yell, Peroni sent two bullets through his heart, the soft *thufts* hardly audible. He slammed shut the Fiat's door, leaving the reporter staring vacantly at nothing. He strode toward the BMW's open trunk and shoved the Glock and gloves back into the valise. Closing the trunk, he got into the car, started the engine, reversed, then slowly drove toward the exit and turned left onto Via Rivoltana. By the time somebody discovered the body, he'd be long gone.

At the airport, he parked the BMW in the Avis parking lot, wiped it down, retrieved the valise, and headed for the terminal. The air smelled of jet fuel and car exhaust. Cars and taxicabs made a steady stream in front of the building. People crowded the sidewalk, dragging luggage or simply hurrying to get away or catch that flight. An Airbus A300 cleared the roofline and lumbered into the sky, its engines warbling.

Peroni paused beside a stormwater drain, bent down, placed the valise next to the open drain and fumbled with the strap on his right shoe. He straightened and gently shoved the bag into the black pit. Satisfied, he strode into the terminal, welcoming its air-conditioned coolness, and headed for one of the fast food restaurants, tables and chairs arrayed in front of them. Hungry, he had plenty of time to eat something before his flight boarded.

Sitting at a small round table waiting for his order to arrive, he pulled his BlackBerry cellphone out of his jacket. Secure behind a blanket of background noise and milling people, he typed in his ten-digit PIN and made a connection to a special number. It only took two rings.

"Cardinal Belconi."

"It's Peroni, Your Eminence," he said coldly, repelled by the cardinal's heavy voice, keeping his dislike from showing. He didn't care how the head of The Entity did business as long as he paid promptly. "Target eliminated. I don't have immediate confirmation, but I imagine the *Il Manifesto* and other media will carry the story by day's end."

"Excellent! Balance of your fee will be paid upon confirmation. Go with God, my son," Belconi said and hung up.

Peroni stared at the BlackBerry and smiled. *Somebody* would be walking with God. He simply wasn't sure it would be him.

The waitress brought his tray and he nodded to her. All in all, not a bad day.

Chapter One

Garbaldi stepped out on the sidewalk, paused, and automatically squinted. Still early, dark shadows cast sharp outlines across the cobbled street. Where it touched, buttery sunshine warmed his face. Overhead, clear azure skies heralded another fine spring day. Crisp cool air, laden with scents of pollen and flowers, caressed his cheeks and he breathed deeply. Branches and leaves hung limp in the stillness. The street empty and quiet except for the whisper of traffic, an occasional car horn and squeal of tires on the nearby Via Luigi Settembrini, momentarily piercing his bubble of serenity and satisfaction. However, the distraction passed quickly. God smiled on his creation and Garbaldi reveled in a feeling of well-being. Eager and ready to start a new day, he marched purposefully toward the intersection.

Around him, Rome stirred.

A block up, he turned right onto Via Giuseppe Avezzana. Most of the condos along the street had a worn, used look, with tired façades and peeling paint, reflecting the weary tenants inside. Much of the inner city had been like this for as long as he could remember; something stable and comforting to cling to in a world fast changing. Some twenty meters from the corner, he pushed open a creaky door beneath a gaudy neon sign jutting out above a grimy stone entryway, announcing the entrance to Torano's. The place had seen its share of years and some of the paint and décor could do with a facelift, it served excellent food, and stood a prime location.

Several familiar faces, early risers all, looked up as he walked in, briefly interrupting the serious business of eating, and nodded. To an Italian, eating did not merely sustain a necessary bodily function, but provided a cheerful social occasion and a source of intense pleasure to be savored accordingly. Interruptions were not welcome. Breakfast smells hung heavy in the air, coffee and freshly baked bread predominant. The patrons lounged around square, cloth-covered tables, their voices creating a spirited atmosphere. The wide frosty glass doors that led to the formal dining area were closed. They would open for dinner, and Garbaldi fleetingly contemplated eating there tonight, but probably not. Although the Vatican Secretariat of State subsidized his apartment and paid him a modest salary, the stipend hardly sufficient for him to indulge in dining out. 'Cast your eyes to heaven with poverty and charity in your heart', one of his portly seminary professors used to intone ponderously. 'Material possessions are a road to sin and damnation.' Judging by his bulging stomach, a source of much earthy amusement among the students, everyone figured the horrible man already well down that road. A mean old bigoted coot, no one missed him when he retired. Unfortunately, it took hard Euros to eat, sin or no sin. Heaven did not provide for him as it did for birds of the air. Garbaldi walked to the checkout counter, waited for a customer to pocket his change, and leaned against the warm, dark wood.

A young woman, short black hair framing a fresh pretty face, closed the cash register with a clang, looked up and smiled flirtatiously in a promise of love.

"The usual, Father?"

"*Si*, please," he said absently and bobbed his head.

The way she always looked at him made him wonder if she actually saw his priestly garb. Did she think him forbidden fruit and therefore considered a challenge? He thought he saw a look of resignation before she shrugged and stepped to the coffee machine. When the contraption finished its hissing and gurgling, she fixed a plastic cap on the cup and placed it on the counter.

"One decaf cappuccino. For you, Father, that'll be one Euro twenty," she said sweetly and beamed at him, teasing him with a saucy look beneath long eyelashes.

It was one Euro twenty for everybody, Garbaldi mused wryly, returning her smile. Here, no one got a discount, not even a priest. Ignoring her inviting look, he fished coins out of his trouser pocket and placed them into her waiting hand.

"*Grazia*, Filippa. I'll see you tomorrow."

"Any time, Father. Any time. *Ciao*!" she called after him, the cash register clanging.

He knew if he looked back, he would see her watching him like she always did. He grinned to himself and couldn't resist a quick backward glance. She *did* look at him, slowly shaking her head in amusement.

Outside, Garbaldi popped the lid and took a thirsty sip. The rich flavor tasted just right as always and he savored the brew before swallowing. Although he usually made his own coffee with breakfast, it simply wasn't the same thing as a brewed cup. His coffee maker at home never seemed to get it quite right. After two years, buying his morning coffee at Torano's had become something of a ritual, as had Filippa's thinly veiled seduction gambits. He could not afford to think along those lines, no matter how enticing. His heart happened to be already taken. Besides, she was merely a child. His inner voice laughed at him with derision, reminding him that children were not built like that, certain her boyfriend did not think of her as a child. Amused, he pushed the disturbing thoughts away.

Holding the warm cup as he made his way toward Piazza Giuseppe Mazzini, the coffee helped him prepare mentally for the day's work. Glancing at fellow pedestrians equally absorbed with their steaming cups, his was not the only addiction. It wasn't as though he sinned by deriving a modicum of enjoyment from his indulgence. Although some fellow priests knew bemoaned indulgement in all pleasure.

He took a left from the treed square onto Viale Giuseppe Mazzini, enjoying the view of slanting yellow sunbeams where they plunged between tall trees planted along the avenue. It felt good to be alive on a morning like this, enjoying God's handiwork. He picked up his steps. Two more weeks and his current cataloging program would be completed. A welcome milestone in itself, it also heralded the start of a two-month sabbatical. A mixture of rest, research and writing. Off to Cairo's Museum of Egyptian Antiquities, where after months of wrangling, the authorities finally relented and gave him permission to read a number of second century Coptic scrolls and codices.

The Roma Tre University sponsored the visit, which would culminate in a book titled: *An Anthropological View of Early Middle Eastern Christianity*. It should be a page-turner and would no doubt cause a stir among theologians of all persuasions, as had his previous books and papers. He did not seek to deliberately provoke or inflame established doctrine, but fact rarely sat comfortably with accepted 'truth'. The manuscript outline had already landed him in some trouble with the Congregation for the Doctrine of the Faith's censor, but Roma Tre was an independent campus and promised to publish. He respected the Church's position on preventing the release of blatant falsehoods, but he resented its attempts to stifle genuine scientific scholarship, regardless of any inconvenience or irritation it caused. Being a scientist and a priest meant walking a tightrope of learning that hung over a chasm of dogma—an intellectual and emotional challenge he had yet to resolve and cross.

He turned left when he reached Via Giunio Bazzoni and headed for Viale Angelico. The main boulevard busy with traffic going both ways, and the noise here more than a mere background disturbance. At the corner, he turned left again. In the distance, far down the straight avenue, he fancied he could see a segment of the Largo del Colonato that bordered the round Piazza di San Pietro guarding the entrance to the famed basilica.

He could not, of course, but he did see it in his mind. Michelangelo's brown-tinged dome loomed proudly above lesser structures, making them look mundane. Every time he saw that perfect architectural majesty, his heart skipped a beat. He had observed it since childhood, and even as he grew older the feeling of awe, reverence, and the centuries of turbulent history it represented never diminished. To be ordained by Pope Benedict XVI himself beneath that wonderful dome a profoundly humbling and proud moment in his then young life. The awe and reverence still remained, but he was no longer young, or naïve. Then again, everything had to age a bit before displaying its true character, didn't it? That dome may be perfect, but sadly the people who stood beneath it were not.

Crosswinds of change whispered through his soul and he gave an involuntary shiver.

As Rome slowly woke around him, pedestrians hurried toward the Vatican and surrounding office buildings. Cars provided a constant cacophony of background noise. Oblivious to it all, Garbaldi allowed his mind to drift. Thinking about nothing in particular, the fifteen minutes it took him to reach Piazza del Risorgimento passed quickly. The inward sloping wall of the old city along Viale Vaticano, with its large squared blocks, stretched away to his right. History of ages lay written in those gloomy gray stones, if only they could be read. As a scientist, he thirsted for that knowledge. Eager sightseers were already lined up in a long queue waiting stoically for their turn to enter and marvel at the undisguised opulence of the two Vatican museums open to the public; a small fraction of riches the Church draped itself with, lamenting all the while a shortage of working funds, and pass around the gold plate. It just didn't seem right.

Even though not yet eight o'clock, locals and visitors filled the sidewalks, the park, and surrounding cafes, sitting around tables sipping their latte or espresso before getting down to the day's business. About them, pigeons fluttered underfoot and pecked at scraps. Although a somewhat dubious tourist attraction, they were real pests, but seemingly impossible to remove; a plague like the tourists themselves. Well, they were also God's creatures and deserving of life.

He crossed the plaza and entered the Via di Porta Angelica. Several foreign embassies still lay in dawn's shadow along its length on his left. He stopped at Porta di Sant'Anna and gazed for a moment at the double gray colonnades guarding the entrance on either side of the narrow street. Recognizing him in his civilian attire, the two Swiss guards, dressed in plain royal blue uniforms, came to attention. Garbaldi nodded to them and took the three steps that led into the church of S. Anna dei Palafrenieri. As the Vatican's private chapel, although tourists were allowed in, he always made it a point to stop here on his way in for a quick prayer or two. It became something of a ritual since his appointment to the Archives as a special researcher. That his hurried prayers were now almost rote disturbed him. Was that all his faith meant? Reduced to blindly following ritual and reciting hollow dogma meant for children?

Inside the cool, echoing interior, sunlight streamed in soft shafts through ornately patterned stained glass windows. He slid into one of the back pews and knelt. His eyes fixed on the subdued lavishness of the altar, flanked by two yellow columns that joined the dome, he found himself unable to start his prayers. At the altar, an elderly priest in white garb wearing a red belt just finished Mass. No altar boy stood in attendance. Garbaldi had never seen one here, which typified what was happening to the Church. Staring at the altar, his thoughts wandered.

He remembered fondly his days as an altar boy at another church, the small, but stately Santa Maria in Vallicella, dubbed the Chiesa Nuova by the locals, in the Piazza della Chiesa Nuova, a stone's throw from the Tiber with a grand view of St. Peter's. Hemmed in by other buildings, the grubby marble façade with its narrow double colonnade entrance did not look like much from the outside, but its magnificently painted arched ceiling and grand altar transported the visitor into another world.

He did not mind attending the morning Mass, even though he had to get up early. In wintertime, it had not always been easy having to contend with icy winds. He particularly loved Mass on the warm, lazy summer evenings when the air had a dreamy, soft quality made living a joy. The church then always full, reverberating to powerful organ music and enchanting, melodious hymns sung with gusto. There used to be keen competition among the boys to serve each Mass. Afterward, they would help with the cleaning up and collect coins left by the parishioners, sometimes helping themselves to a few to buy chewing gum or ice cream. Sadly, that too had now faded and few boys these days thought of serving behind an altar as being cool. PlayStation and other electronic distractions were their gods now.

Since his ordination, he had returned to the old church once and regretted going. Only frail, black-garbed old women, waiting for death and promised salvation, now frequented its cold, echoing interior. Even the wall and ceiling frescos seemed darker as though God had removed the light from his house. He walked away dejected, wondering where all the people had gone, where faith had gone.

He jerked back to reality when he heard discrete coughing and shuffling of restless feet. The priest stood up, crossed himself, and slowly walked down the red carpet laid down the center aisle, his heavy footsteps unnaturally loud in the thick silence. Garbaldi hardly noticed him, his concentration absorbed by the small crucifix on the stone altar. Being in the rear, he could hardly see it, but he didn't have to see it to understand its meaning: suffering, betrayal at many levels, disappointment and hopelessness.

Faithful to St. Paul's version of faith, Church dogma said that Christ died for the remission of man's sins, Jew and gentile alike. For the flock, it brought comfort, a release from the hardship of living, and hope of an eternal afterlife of bliss and ease in the sight of God. If only it were true. As a scientist, Garbaldi appreciated the depth of gulf that lay between truth and fact. No matter how much he tried to deny it to himself, the inescapable reality he faced, he doubted the truth of his faith. Too much undeniable concrete evidence refuted gospel history as written by early Christian fathers long after Jesus' death. As a priest, it caused him much soul searching; definitely something to be discussed with his confessor. Then again, perhaps not. Unfortunately, nothing was sacred anymore, not even a confessional. The realization did little to dispel the shadows of doubt or ease the burden on his soul. Anyway, he didn't need a confessional to make peace with God. He only needed a place where he could bare his soul and pray for guidance. He prayed, but God had not listened, or perhaps he already knew the answer to his dilemma and afraid to admit it.

His eyes strayed from the altar, taking in the beautifully painted frescos and decorations, and marveled at the product of man's genius. He couldn't help wonder how many artisans and craftsmen had slaved with hardly any pay or reward to produce them, while the Church profiteered by selling red hats to the vain rich and sin Indulgences to the gullible poor in the forlorn belief that the piece of paper would bring them closer to heaven. There had to be something wrong with that picture.

I weep for thee, my Church.

He gave a weary sigh, crossed himself, and stood up. With a last glance around empty pews, empty church, he hurried out, hoping that work would distract him from dwelling on questions to which he already knew the answers and give him a measure of inner peace. He was hiding and knew it, not quite ready to face the harsh consequences his answers demanded.

At the end of the short street, he turned right at Cortile del Belvedere, past the Hall of Bramante, and walked quickly into the yellow three-story building that housed one of the Vatican Secret Archives complexes. Not bothering with the elevator, he took the white marble stairs to the second floor directly beneath the Leo XIII Hall reading room. His footsteps echoing on the hard floor, he walked to the third door on the left, slid a large old-fashioned key into the keyhole, and turned it. When the lock clicked, he pushed open the heavy door and walked into the cramped workroom.

As he stepped in, he reached with his right hand and flipped on a light switch. Four bright fluorescent strips fixed to the high ceiling flickered and flooded the windowless room with harsh light. Tall oak bookshelves lined three of the walls, most filled with cardboard boxes, old codices of various sizes, their faded spines cracked and gaping, and bound manuscripts. The air smelled slightly musty, a characteristic of libraries everywhere. Something new stood in the room, a small plain table on which stood two standard 500mm by 750mm removals cartons. Those were not there yesterday and he frowned.

Absently, he removed his brown corduroy jacket and hung it on a wall hook mounted beside the door. He glanced at the cartons again and closed the door with a backward push of his foot. Obviously, after he left yesterday, someone had brought the stuff, and that implied more work for him. If this meant delaying the start of his sabbatical, he wouldn't do it! There were limits. He looked away, shook his head and sighed. Whatever secrets the cartons held, first things first.

He pulled back his cloth-covered ergonomic chair, leaned across the wide desk tucked hard against the corner and pulled a little cord that hung beneath the green glass reading lamp. Still leaning over the desk, he switched on his laptop. He dragged a keyring out of his trouser pocket and unlocked the cabinet under the desk. Opening the middle drawer, he lifted out a blue hard-cover A4 book. Actually an old diary he never got around to using, but more than adequate as a pad for his working notes. He slid the diary on the desk and turned to the wide 49cm LED screen connected to the laptop. The brown round *Archivum Secretum Apostolicum Vaticanum* logo stared at him. Using a keyboard and remote optical mouse—he hated the laptop's touchpad—he quickly logged on and swiveled the chair, looking thoughtfully at the two cartons.

Well, it wouldn't hurt to take a *little* peek. The emails could wait a few moments.

He stood, walked to the table, and fingered the packing. Each box had the Archives seal stamped on its side, but that meant nothing. None of them were taped, implying the contents were repacked. He pushed open the flaps of the closest and peered inside, already knowing what he would see—more old codices, dusty papers and files. Instead, he saw three white cardboard packages laid vertically side-by-side. His breath caught. These were not standard commercial packs, but carefully prepared containers used to transport old manuscripts, every one being of different thickness. He reached for the middle pack and began to pull it out when a knock on the door stayed his hand. Still frowning at the carton, he took two steps and opened the door.

The tall, gaunt figure dressed in a plain black cassock with a broad red belt, smiled urbanely and nodded pleasantly. Bald, except for a ring of white hair around the sides and back. The face long and narrow, the dark yellow skin marked by thousands of little wrinkles. Not a kind face, time having worked on it, but it wasn't severe either, just old.

"*Buon giorno*, Father Garbaldi. May I come in?" the figure asked smoothly, his voice soft and ingratiating, hiding the steel beneath.

Garbaldi extended his arm and automatically stepped to one side. "Of course, Your Excellency. You're always welcome here."

"Thank you, thank you. I won't keep you long." The Most Reverend, Monsignor Giovani Giacomo, the library Prefect, smiled again and slowly walked in. He glanced at the packed shelving and gently shook his head. "So much knowledge hidden in those volumes. Dangerous knowledge."

"For mankind, Your Excellency?" Garbaldi ventured as he closed the door, aware of Giacomo's extreme conservative views. Everybody knew, had he the power, the Vatican Secret Archives would be permanently closed to all outside scholars and its eighty-four kilometers of corridors and shelving sealed. Also known, and Giacomo probably appreciated the irony, he would never be the Supreme Pontiff, giving him the ability to implement his obsessive views. From what Garbaldi understood, the realization had not embittered the man. On the other hand, it did not stop him from pouring sand into the Vatican's political machinery either. Progress had always been forced on the Church and never embraced willingly. God's will or man's machinations? What a contrast between the goings on within the gilded St. Peter's and a humble parish church. Which of them more truly represented the Christian faith? Two sides of the same coin? Garbaldi not entirely sure.

"For the Church, my son, the Church!" Giacomo retorted sharply, emphasizing the point with a raised bony finger. "You couldn't have forgotten that our work is the preservation of dogma among the flock, not the evangelical dissemination of faith as is commonly assumed."

"I understood, Your Excellency, that saving souls was our work."

Garbaldi enjoyed sparring with the monsignor, always pushing the limits of discourse and, of course, the unspoken boundaries of Church tolerance. Rather than rebuke his moments of verbal rebellion, the old priest tolerated his outbursts and seemed to find the exchanges amusing. More than once, he startled the Prefect with some of his ideas, who even expressed admiration for his original thinking.

Giacomo's tolerance, however, came with a warning. Garbaldi knew that his propensity to cut straight to the issue would need to be curbed if he were to rise in the Vatican's faction-ridden cauldron. Unfortunately, just because something was right and should be done, did not mean it would be done. Giacomo might tolerate his honesty, but that also did not mean others would be as forgiving. Young and idealistic, he realized he lacked sophistication and had still to learn guile. The Church had enormous historical inertia, not counting vested personal interests, which required massive effort or a pivotal event to shift. What he came to learn, the Church abhorred change, seeing it as a malignancy to be excised. If only they could return to the halcyon days of the Dark Ages.

Giacomo chuckled. "It is, it is, but we have to have priorities, my son."

Garbaldi didn't say anything, but his face creased in disapproval. He extended an arm toward his chair. "Would you care to sit down?"

"Kind of you, but no. I just came to explain that," Giacomo said firmly in a voice weighed down with years of authority, and waved a hand at the two cartons. "I see your curiosity has already been at work."

Garbaldi smiled. "A temptation I couldn't resist."

"Understandable. Everything is in a lengthy email, when you get around to reading it, but under the circumstances, I thought I'd give you a personal explanation. You have done exemplary work sorting through your portion of the Diplomatic Archives. The cataloging, indexing and cross-referencing is necessary and invaluable in deciding what can be released for external scholarly examination and what should be withheld."

"I am pleased to hear it, Your Excellency."

"Like I said, dangerous knowledge, my son, and the Church must always be on guard against blasphemous writing. Your doctorates in Middle Eastern languages and early Common Era anthropology made you ideal for the task, although it did take you away from your posting at the Section for General Affairs."

"I serve the Church, Your Excellency."

Garbaldi did serve the Church, but when he released his *Ancient Eastern Religions and their Influence on Early Christianity*, he could not help feeling that his Church had exacted vengeance by sending him back to the Secret Archives as an ordinary researcher. They dressed it up as a special assignment, but the Congregation for the Doctrine of the Faith left him in no doubt of their feelings when they expressed deep displeasure at his work and conclusions, stating that it endangered the faith, which the Congregation had the task of promoting and safeguarding. They also chose to leave a black mark on his record for his trouble. The Church tolerated freethinking, even encouraged it, they said, but it must be tempered with their version of wisdom and prudence. Giacomo had reminded him more than once that he should have sought guidance from Church authority before rashly allowing the book to be published. His period of penance lasted two years, but if the Curia anticipated that working in the Archives would in any way change him or temper his writing, they would be disappointed.

"And because you do it so well, you're being punished," Giacomo added and gave a barking laugh, looking amused at Garbaldi's puzzled expression.

"Punished? I don't understand."

"Exemplary work is always rewarded with more work, my son, and these boxes are your reward. You're aware that the Archives General Secretariat has a program to secure material from all dioceses around the world, at least as much as they are willing to part with. And you don't have to tell me the headache we have storing all that extra material. That is not your concern. Sometimes we receive works from other Catholic churches, as is the case here. Your task is to examine the contents of these boxes, catalog them, determine each category, or *Fondo*, where they should be stored, and make a recommendation on what can be safely released to outside scholars. This will take priority over your existing work."

Garbaldi could not hide his dismay. "Your Excellency, this could take a week! My secondment—"

"Will be extended," Giacomo said with finality, ending the discussion. Seeing Garbaldi's alarm, he relented. "My son, this work has been approved by the Substitute for General Affairs, Cardinal Enrico Fontini himself. Your position at the Secretariat of State will not be jeopardized, nor will any plans you may have for your sabbatical. This work is important, more important than you realize. Consider it a minor extension of your current assignment."

Garbaldi bit his lower lip in an attempt to mask his frustration. Minor extension? He spent two long years sifting through dusty volumes and brittle manuscripts, and jumped at the chance for a change when a posting became available in the Section for General Affairs at the Secretariat of State. He needed to get the stale smell of old books out of his system, if only for a while. Not entirely the whole truth, of course. He was weary of eternal bickering over what material could be released, and what should be locked away forever, being deemed too damaging or embarrassing to the Church. Nonetheless, the Church held invaluable historical texts that cast a vastly different light on its early history than was commonly known or believed by the masses, although much was lost or never returned when, in 1810, Napoleon removed a great deal of material from the Archives to Paris. The Vatican still negotiated with France for the return of that material.

His own research into books on what used to be the *Index Librorum Prohibitorum* had led him to question the Church and some of its motives to maintain secrecy. Not exactly the kind of reading the Curia expected when they sent him to the Archives. He wanted to do genuine anthropological research, hence a trip to Cairo and his new book. Garbaldi pondered again his commitment to the Church and his choice of vocation. Perhaps his calling did have more to do with family expectations and neighborhood dynamics than a genuine voice from God to serve. He had still to resolve that one, for it would force him to review his deepest motives, something he did not care to do right now, although he knew he would have to confront them sometime, and probably soon.

As he found early, having faith and following dogma not enough if one wanted to survive and thrive in the Vatican machine. Even being an ordinary parish priest no longer an option, although superficially attractive. He stood contaminated, cursed with too much knowledge to be content in a simple pastoral setting, not that there were many of those anyway. There was always missionary work, but that had never been a passion tugging at his soul, however commendable the vocation.

Well, if Cardinal Fontini himself approved the assignment, it looked like he would simply have to endure. Resigning himself to the inevitable, he inclined his head at the table.

"What are they?"

"Manuscripts from the Coptic Orthodox Patriarchate of Alexandria," Giacomo said simply.

For a second, Garbaldi simply gaped. To lay his hands on texts not previously seen by anyone! It would complement perfectly his own research. Was this reward for the hard work he had already done? It didn't matter. Despite his initial misgivings the scientist in him yearned to know more.

"The Coptic Catholic Church?"

Giacomo smiled knowingly. "I see the prospect is not without some attraction."

"I cannot deny it, Your Excellency. I know the 2003 International Joint Commission for Theological Dialogue between the Catholic Church and the Oriental Orthodox Churches have achieved some success in bridging gaps with the Holy See, but I did not know it extended to an exchange of material."

"A dribble admittedly, and union with the Coptic Church will not come about in our lifetime, if at all, but progress is being made to improve communication and reconcile important theological differences. In time, the Patriarchate will see the error of their ways."

Garbaldi wondered how much of that was true, or merely propaganda for his benefit. As far as he knew, the fundamental theological schisms were as deep today as they were when it all began. Before the Rome faction gained ascendancy, the Christian movement was a fragmented affair with much squabbling among largely independent bishops over theology and emerging dogma. Dredging his memory, Rome and Egypt became divided through a culmination of internal political infighting, punctuated by three principal events.

In 318 CE, Arius, an Alexandrian presbyter, maintained that Jesus was not coeternal with God the Father, and before begotten, did not exist. Understandably, the emerging mainstream Church was not happy with that interpretation. In 325, to resolve the dispute, Emperor Constantine held the Ecumenical Council of Nicea, which produced the Nicene Creed, declaring Jesus a god. The declaration not entirely made on pious grounds or accepted by everyone. A clever move by Constantine to quell growing unrest and make the new Christian religion more palatable to ordinary Roman citizens by incorporating Jesus into the existing pantheon of gods.

A modification by the First Council of Constantinople in 381, attested that Jesus was incarnate by the Holy Ghost of the Virgin Mary. In 428, Nestorius, the Archbishop of Constantinople, rejected the addition, preaching that the Virgin Mary was Mother of Jesus, not Mother of God. It led to Pope Cyril I of Alexandria to issue the famous Twelve Anathemas, excommunicating anyone who followed the teachings of Nestorius. In 451 the Council of Chalcedon repudiated the idea that Jesus had only one nature as maintained by the Egyptian Church, and stated that he had two natures in one person. The Egyptian Church, which later became the Coptic Orthodox Church, rejected the Council canons and remained split with what eventually became the Roman Catholic Church.

Garbaldi was not about to get involved in a sensitive theological debate, not with Giacomo. "Then these cannot be the original packing cartons?" he ventured, pointing at the seals.

"Hardly. The contents were repacked after clearing the da Vinci airport. Despite letters of approval, Immigration and Customs insisted on confiscating the originals, afraid of biological contamination or some such nonsense. If I hadn't been there personally, those clowns would still be fumigating and stamping forms."

Garbaldi had to smile, being all too familiar with Italian quarantine obstacles and petty officials. "Your Excellency, I would love to get on this right away, but Father Zamatini is expecting a preliminary catalog from me by end of the month," he lamented and swept a hand at the surrounding shelves.

"There is no need for concern. I already discussed the matter with him and the necessary change in your priority. Send him what you have."

"As you wish."

"Good. In that case, I shall leave you to it. *A piu tardi.*"

Garbaldi opened the door for the older man and nodded. "*ArrivederLa*, Your Excellency."

"To work, my son. To work!" Giacomo announced briskly and, without a backward glance, ambled down the empty corridor.

Garbaldi closed the door, leaned against it and chuckled. Easy for the Prefect to say, he would not be the one doing it.

* * *

Garbaldi leaned against the chair, rubbed his eyes and gave a long sigh. He rolled his head to get the kinks out and stretched his arms. After four solid hours behind the screen, his eyes were burning and he needed to loosen up. Right then, he really wanted a caffeine fix. With priceless manuscripts all around him, that was of course, impossible. The thought of spilled coffee over one of them made him shudder. Better to be excommunicated! Besides, a brisk walk down the street to Piazza del Risorgimento would do him good and there were plenty of cafes there to indulge his craving.

At least the spreadsheet entries for the two cartons were done. Three days, that's how long it took him to unpack everything, give each item a quick peruse, properly number and label the volumes, catalog every piece into its appropriate category and shelve the folios. A different color sticker identified each *Fondo* where the codices would be eventually stored. Somewhat tricky as some volumes could easily be cataloged in several different *Fondos*, hence the reason for the cross-referencing spreadsheet entries. Without meticulous referencing, the material could be, and was undoubtedly lost in the dark corridors of the Archives. That constituted part of his current job, physically examining the Diplomatic Archives and laboriously checking every item against old card indexes. At least with the Coptic material, it helped that whoever packed the manuscripts knew what he was doing, and properly labeled the contents. Everything still needed close examination and reading, but at least he knew roughly what he faced.

What astonished him when unpacking the second box, and he immediately wanted to look more closely at the collection, he found a complete copy of the four gospels in Sahidic script. Clearly not an original, although written on papyrus, if authentic, it would make an astonishing addition to the Vatican Archives, and an important comparison baseline for study of the New Testament. He knew that fragments of Fayumic and Sahidic versions were today held in private hands and public institutions such as the British Museum, Berlin Library, Bibliotheque Nationale of Paris, and the Imperial Library of Vienna. How the Coptic Church managed to preserve an apparently intact set, and willing to part with it, was beyond incredible.

As an anthropologist, a copy of the Gnostic Gospel of Judas captured his attention. One version of the text, discovered in the 1970s near Beni Masah in Egypt, dated to the late second century. Only bits and pieces remained today due to poor handling and storage, the surviving material now held by the Maecenas Foundation. Why the great museums failed to bid for the papyrus when it came on the market was unfathomable. Garbaldi also knew the Vatican owned a complete copy from a different source, but the tractate was never released to outside scholars. Given the controversial nature of the material, he wasn't altogether surprised. Could he get his hands on the thing for comparison? He would have to talk to Giacomo about it.

Why the Patriarch of Alexandria would send the Vatican a copy of Zoroastrian sacred texts, the Zend-Avesta, a diverting curiosity. A sense of oblique humor? His Holiness Pope Shenouda III did include for the Holy Father five personally signed books on theology out of the one hundred or so he had written. Something for the Holy Father to ponder during winter evenings? The remaining material, the Rite of Constantinople, the Agpeya—Book of the Hours, and several liturgies were known texts, but would nonetheless make interesting additions to the Archives.

Blue skies greeted him when he stepped out. An occasional gentle warm breeze ruffled his shirt. Far too pleasant to be wearing a coat and he had left his inside. Past noon, the sun cast dark shadows, islands of refuge from the heat. Via di Porta Angelica was noisy, busy with traffic, hurrying locals doing odd chores over their lunch break, and gawking tourists sporting digital cameras, camcorders and bulging money belts, to the delight of prowling pickpockets. The sounds and background noise a familiar protective cocoon, something part of Garbaldi's nature. They washed over him and he hardly noticed them. Children ran carefree in the Piazza del Risorgimento, absorbed in their games. He bought coffee and a salad roll from one of the stalls and sought an empty bench. This time of day, with the plaza full, an empty spot would be hard to come by. Just as he prepared to make himself comfortable on the lawn, a mother and a little girl got up from a bench and strolled off. He didn't dally claiming the spot.

Enjoying a shell of privacy, he munched his roll, only absently aware of the people around him. Across the way, the queue to the museums looked as long as it had in the morning and he felt mildly sorry for those patiently waiting, having to endure a two or three-hour crawl before being able to get in. A tour leader, holding high a yellow umbrella, led a large group straight for the entrance, to the ill-concealed stares of annoyance and hostility from those in the queue.

He finished his meal and sat back, perfectly relaxed, and allowed the city to cradle him. A world he knew and understood, uncomplicated and superficially simple. As he studied the passersby, he wondered if they were enjoying the pleasure of being alive as much as he enjoyed it, or whether some cloud of worry shadowed their day. He longed to linger, but like Giacomo said, there was work to be done. He stood up, brushed crumbs off his trousers, and walked slowly toward Porta di Sant'Anna. The break just what he needed to lift his steps.

Once again in his workroom, despite the bright lighting, it felt gloomy and austere after the dazzling sunshine outside. There were no decorations, plants or paintings to lighten the atmosphere, only shelving and smelly old manuscripts. This is what he did, but as he walked toward the far shelf, he wondered if this would still be him in the years to come if he didn't toe the line. Absently, he reached for the bound volume of Coptic gospels and pulled it out with one hand. Even as the heavy codex slid out, Garbaldi realized his mistake. He would never be able to hold it with one hand. He lunged with his left arm, but the volume was already slipping from his grasp. It landed on the dark polished oak floor with a jarring thud and his heart skipped a beat. Luckily, it only fell a meter, but still an unforgivable blunder on his part. He knelt beside the codex and lovingly cradled it in his lap. After a quick scrutiny, he felt satisfied that he had been lucky and muttered a silent thanks. What if the thing was damaged? God! His skin crawled at the awful possibility.

He carried the book to his desk and opened the front cover. He then noticed a loose page, a small corner that protruded from the rest. Had the binding been torn after all? Hardly daring to breathe, he opened the book at the spot...and stared as a hot flush diffused through him. The deep yellow papyrus page had ragged edges, revealing typical cross-grained strands of its manufacture. Clearly not one of the book's original bound pages. At first glance, the faded brown text looked like old Sahidic, some of the lettering barely legible. Without touching it, the anthropologist in him recognized the extreme age of the tractate. If genuine, the thing was priceless. What was it doing in a copy of Coptic gospels? While the codex itself might not be third or fourth century, still obviously old, perhaps a twelfth century copy, and valuable nonetheless. And the papyrus? The possibilities were endless and the simplest explanation probably true. Centuries ago, someone put it there temporarily and the thing forgotten. The Alexandria librarian had not known it was there. Or perhaps planted deliberately just to see the Vatican run around in circles. Oddly enough, he prepared to believe that of the Church, but not the Coptic Orthodox Patriarchate. So much for faith in human nature.

Still studying the papyrus, he opened the top drawer and absently dragged out a large magnifying glass. He positioned the page under the reading lamp, set the magnifying glass and peered closely at the text. The odd mixture of Roman and Greek characters were instantly familiar. He didn't have to compare the writing with authenticated texts to realize what he had was genuine. After a moment, he straightened and frowned.

What now? Advise Giacomo and have the thing returned? It would not only be the honorable and correct thing to do, the gesture would also go some way toward fostering a warmer relationship with the Coptic Church. If he suspected the Coptic Church of planting the papyrus, wouldn't they suspect the same thing of Rome? After all, they didn't know the tractate existed in the first place. He was realistic enough to appreciate the potential for a rise in political tension between the two churches instead of the reverse by having the papyrus revealed. This needed to be handled very carefully. Thoughts racing, his eyes naturally began to follow the text since he already had the thing in front of him. It bore no title, a fragment of a larger work perhaps?

And it came to pass when John baptized, preaching repentance and deliverance of the tribes by him who was to come after him. Rejoice, for a new kingdom is at hand. Prepare you for the way of the new king and make his path straight.

He is said to be from the tribe of Levi, son of Zachariah the priest and Elizabeth. He preached, healed the sick and performed mighty deeds.

They sent to him from the land of Judea, even the Pharisees and the Sadducees, all of Jerusalem, and were baptized. He wore a garment of camel's hair and a leather girdle about his loins. And his meat was wild honey, which tasted like manna, and locusts formed into cakes with oil. And he told them: 'And now will also an axe be laid against those who bring evil, and will be hewn down, and cast into the fire. Repent and you shall be saved.'

Priests and Levites came from Jerusalem to ask him: 'Who are you?' And John replied: 'I am the voice crying in the wilderness, making the way for the one who will speak for the people. There will come one mightier than I after me and I am not worthy to stoop down to his shoes. He shall liberate you and rule a new kingdom in the sight of God.'

Then they asked: 'Are you Elias?' And he answered: 'I am he who was foretold by the prophet Esaias.'

And they said to him: 'Why do you baptize if you are not the Messiah or Elias?' John replied: 'I prepare the way of the spirit for all, and baptize with water, but there stands one among you who you know not, who shall prepare the way of deliverance with the sword from the oppressors.'

The people having been baptized, it came to pass that Jesus, with his followers, also came from Galilee to Jordan to seek his blessing.

The next day, John saw Jesus coming to him, and after lifting his arms, cried: 'This is he of whom I spoke, that he should be made manifest to Israel and lead you to salvation.'

Seeing the anointed one, Jesus cried: 'Master, for what I am to do, I have need to be baptized by you.' And John replied: 'Follow in the way against our enemies and I shall suffer you.' And so it came to pass that John baptized him, proclaiming: 'The spirit is with you and you shall establish a new kingdom for all Israel, for you are beloved of God.'

Staggered, Garbaldi felt his whole body turn to stone as the enormity of the text's meaning sank in. Jesus was John's disciple and *John* the anointed one, the Messiah! He might doubt the Church and its practices, past and present, but he *believed* in Jesus the Lord. The essence of the gospels *had* to be true. Shaken, head spinning, he groped for the chair and sat down heavily. Everything he knew, everything he believed in, might all be fabrication and a lie. Didn't he suspect that all along? Weary and disillusioned, he buried his face between his hands as the comfortable, predictable world he knew crumbled around him. His breath came in ragged gulps and his stomach knotted. After a while, he slowly lifted his head and gazed at the small wooden crucifix fixed to the wall above the desk. St. Matthew's words burned bright in his mind.

Eloi, Eloi, lama sabachtani: My God, my God, why hast thou forsaken me?

He didn't know how long he stared at the simple crucifix. Time had no meaning and he a hollow shell waiting to be filled and renewed. Out of momentary despair and darkness, a light of reason slowly dispelled the questioning demons. The figure on the cross seemed to nod at him and he felt warmth steel through his body, a warmth of comforting realization and hope. He had taken on a calling to serve God, not the Church, and it looked very much like he might be guilty of misguided loyalties. Given his scientific training, he easily saw how he strayed. Perhaps his seminary friend, Carlo Noris, had it right when he said that he would also face his test of faith. Was this his moment of liberation, his real calling, to bring truth to the faithful?

After another moment, he pursed his lips. Very well. If it be God's will.

He would seek out the truth, and if it contradicted the Church's version, so be it. Living a convenient lie to maintain a comfortable existence would be a real road to damnation. Could this innocent piece of papyrus be truth? What was truth, someone once asked, and he asked it now. Before doing anything, he needed to find out, not only for himself, but every Christian in the world. And if the tractate *was* truth? The Church held awesome secular power, and the millions of believers represented an enormous social and political force. It would not be easy to sway them, no matter the validity of evidence. Most would continue to believe. Perhaps, but that did not invalidate the reason for revealing evidence. As a scientist, he should approach the problem with all the tools science made available.

Somewhat relieved, he sat up straighter and looked closely at the faded papyrus sheet. The text bore close resemblance to the Gospel of St. Matthew with a mixture of St. Mark, the earliest narrative gospel written as a cohesive whole. The other gospel writers all used his material and added their own interpretations and embellishments. There was indisputable proof the author of St. Mark's gospel himself had access to earlier versions, collectively known as the Q or *Quelle* document, meaning the 'source', now lost, with hints of its presence buried in the synoptic gospels. As a scholar, he discounted St. John, the gospel being a political document to appease the Romans, shifting the blame for Jesus' death on the Jews. Could the papyrus be one of the pieces of Q text from which the synoptic gospels were written? That would immediately date the scroll to before 70 CE and subsequent destruction of Jerusalem by Rome. If in fact it was that old. Given how it had been handled, it had survived remarkably intact.

As a scientist, he knew that little remained of early Christian writing that might differ from the canonical gospels. The Church always maintained that its creed was a unique, miraculous and supreme revelation without predecessors or outside contributors. The early fathers could not accept that their movement comprised of disparate doctrines, teachings and ideologies, borrowed from Buddhism, the Egyptians, Babylonians, and the Assyrians. He should know, he researched it in depth.

Shortly after the Council of Nicea, the bishops embarked on a program of total destruction of all texts that contradicted the Church's version of the New Testament as literal history. They declared Jesus a god and couldn't afford to have it otherwise. The burning of the Library of Alexandria in 391, the sum accumulation of man's knowledge at the time, a hideous culmination of that program. In 642, the Muslims finally sacked what remained of the Royal Library and the Daughter Library at the Serapeum. Some historians claimed that the centuries of Dark Ages that followed were directly attributed to the Church attempting to keep the minds of the faithful in servitude and ignorance, obedient to its will. Wearing his secular hat, Garbaldi tended to agree. They hadn't managed to destroy everything.

Stefan Vučak

In 1945, peasants unearthed papyrus scrolls in sealed jars at Nag Hammadi, discovering what was at best only a tantalizing fragment of early Christian writing. The Church fought long and hard to suppress the material, but no longer the Church of old, couldn't keep the scrolls from being published. The release caused a flurry of consternation among the learned, but the finding hardly generated a ripple elsewhere. The faithful were simply not interested.

In 1947, a Bedouin shepherd boy, wandering the barren cliffs of Qumran, found broken jars that contained rolled leather scrolls, which with later finds from a total of eleven caves became collectively known as the Dead Sea Scrolls. The tortured release process of the scrolls and cries of a Church conspiracy still held a morbid fascination with the public at large, but little else. Again, few bothered to really study the material and understand the implication it held for the Church. A lifetime of indoctrination and blind obedience represented a potent force that only a shattering revelation could sway. Except for the monks tending them, who knows what lay undiscovered in far away monasteries where time did not march and foreigners were discouraged? But should anything ever rear its head, the exterminators would be alerted.

How could he reconcile what the Coptic papyrus sheet said from what the seminary lecturers taught and what he learned from personal research? If Jesus was John's disciple, it pointed to the existence of two Messiahs. Not exactly news, as Zechariah and the gospels of Matthew and John hinted as much. There were certainly no doubts in the minds of the Dead Sea Scrolls writers. They clearly told of two Messiahs, a priest and the warrior. The Messianic Rule and the Manual of Discipline scrolls stated plainly that the priestly Messiah would be born into the tribe of Levi, as John the Baptist indeed was. The second Messiah would be born in the house of David, overthrow the Romans and rule over the lost tribes of Israel. Jesus' genealogy a torturous concoction of two versions, and his stated claim to the house of David dubious at best.

They put Father Roland de Vaux, a Dominican monk, in charge of the international team responsible for translation and publication of the Scrolls when they were stored in the Ecole Biblique in Jerusalem. Controversy still raged as to whether he in fact took a number of scrolls from Cave Four the Church deemed contradicted its version of history, and later transferred them to the Vatican Secret Archives. As part of his first doctoral thesis research, Garbaldi sought access to the Archives of that period, repeatedly denied. He still wondered what those dusty shelves contained to be so dangerous to the Church.

The cold truth was, far from being divinely inspired, the gospels were written by men to lay a common foundation for an emerging religion under a single established authority. Material that didn't conform, ruthlessly purged. Over the centuries, even the accepted writings were subject to ongoing changes and 'corrections'. The most profound change took place with the translation into English by John Waycliffe in 1384, followed by William Tundale's version in 1524, which formed the basis of the King James Bible, issued in 1611. The Council of Trent in 1545 decreed that no further changes or additions were to be made, but by then the damage was already done. Garbaldi had a copy of the Vatican's *Codex Vaticanus* dating from the mid-fourth century. Together with the British Museum's *Codex Sinaiticus*, they constituted the oldest complete manuscripts of the New Testament. Comparing the *Vaticanus* with today's versions, he easily identified doctored changes and twisted meanings to fit the gospels within Church dogma. He could only shake his head at the human misery and warped mindsets heaped on the West by incorrect translation and liberal interpretation in the English version.

Still deeply disturbed, beset with questions and doubts, Garbaldi nonetheless felt better. He may be in a crisis of faith, but God created man with the ability to solve problems using reason and logic. Very well, he would treat the find like any other, applying reason and scientific methodology against a hypothesis. Before he could consider reporting the find to the Prefect, he needed to formally authenticate the papyrus and ink used. If this was an elaborate fraud perpetrated by the Coptic Church, he didn't intend falling for the gag or embroil the Vatican in a controversy because he got swept away with emotional fervor. Fortunately, his training put him on solid ground here. He conducted dating of old manuscripts before and knew exactly how to go about it.

Papyrus tractates had always been a pain to authenticate. First, the papyrus itself had to be reliably dated. In the old days, one would snip off a sample, to the painful howl of the archeologist or anthropologist concerned, send the thing to a recognized laboratory and have it carbon-14 tested. The results were usually reliable to between plus or minus twenty to fifty years. Even if his papyrus turned out to be from the late first or early second century, that would not validate the text itself. Using correct ink and an appropriate period writing style, someone who knew what they were doing could have written the thing yesterday. No need to forge and age a papyrus sheet when getting hold of an authentic first century sample did not pose an insurmountable obstacle. Museums and libraries around the world held countless scrolls gathering dust in basement annexes that would never see the light of public display. Most of those had leading or trailing blank sections. Given the right connections, appropriating one or two sheets would be childishly simple.

These days, getting the ink right presented a more challenging difficulty for any forger. As early as 2500 BCE, eastern civilizations uniformly used carbon inks. These were made by burning oil or tar to produce soot, which was mixed with water and gum in a suspension. The problem with carbon ink, it smudged and deteriorated over time. The difficulty was solved, when in the first century the preferred method used iron-gall ink. They mixed Gallic acid with water and vitriol, to which was added gum from acacia trees to act as a suspension agent. Depending on the exact ingredients, the ink ended up as either ferric gallic acid complexes or iron pyrogallol, which over time faded from its original red to a durable dull brown. Iron-gall was perfect, as it did not rub off documents. The major downside, if the ink became too acidic, it tended to react with collagen in parchment or cellulose in papyrus. He had seen documents with holes where the ink had eaten right through the material.

He looked more closely at the innocuous piece of papyrus on his desk. There existed clear evidence of some acid penetration, but the text looked quite intact, although some of the words and lettering were badly faded. By using x-ray fluorescence, or better still, proton induced x-ray emission analysis, he could test the thing without having to remove a sample. Unless a forger had a bottle of ink from the first century stashed somewhere, he was out of luck.

But whom could he trust to do the testing? The Laboratory for Cultural Goods (LABEC) in Florence, part of the National Institute of Nuclear Physics, did excellent carbon-14 accelerator mass spectroscopy analysis. He had worked with them before. There was also the ENEA Bologna Research Center, but they both required a sample. More troublesome, they would want paperwork, letters of introduction, questions, queries to the Prefect, which would all result in premature disclosure. He needed an independent facility where analysis could not be traced to him or the Vatican. It had been a while, but he knew the person to call.

In his last year at the seminary, already planning to take postgraduate courses at the Pontifical Lateran University, his closest friend and confidant had suddenly dropped out, disillusioned, his trust in the infallible Church shattered. They used to devour old philosophers like Spinoza, Percy Shelley, George Eliot, Immanuel Kant and others; hotly debating morality, ethics, the evolution and purpose of religion and man's place in it, especially in the current Western version of pluralism, while decrying the stupidity of politicians, bureaucrats and dogmatic clergy everywhere.

Officially, Carlo Noris left voluntarily to pursue secular studies, but later, Carlo told Garbaldi they kicked him out for holding views and philosophies inconsistent with Church doctrine. Garbaldi had found that difficult to comprehend or believe. His friend was pious, a respected scholar, widely read and an expert on early Church history. No one was more devoted to the calling. Between playing pranks on the faculty, something they all indulged in, Carlo sometimes irritated his lecturers, launching questions and making observations not entirely consistent with the serious pursuit of priesthood, but everyone did that from time to time. The students were learned men, not impressionable teenagers, and their minds roamed, straining against the fettered views of their lecturers. His friend merely laughed at Garbaldi's confusion and naiveté.

Taking him by the arm, Carlo led him to a café on campus grounds and offered a dose of reality into seminary life, the Noris version.

"You know what they did? They sent stooges from the Congregation for the Doctrine of the Faith to test our beliefs. Not our beliefs in the faith, but Church canons. They had seminary staff make reports on everyone to determine our suitability for priesthood and be obedient little lambs. They issued a questionnaire with sixty-four points, and each dealt only with dogma. Nothing about the faith, the Savior, or the New Testament. Students were graded on how they answered."

"How do you know that?" Garbaldi demanded, hardly able to believe as he never saw such a document, but Carlo's sincerity had the ring of truth. He knew the Congregation was nothing more than the old Inquisition under another name. It could no longer compel secular authority to torture or burn people at the stake, but its charter still demanded pursuit and elimination of all those who opposed or questioned the Church and its authority. If what Carlo said was true, seminaries now pursued elimination from within, a sobering and disturbing thought.

"Because, my simple deluded friend, I saw the records. I had access to Admin files, don't ask me how, but I saw them. Don't think they're doing it because this is Rome and the Vatican rules. It's being done at every seminary around the world. You needn't worry. You're just the trusting, wide-eyed type they're looking for. I know that your reading and anthropology studies have raised doubts in your mind, questions you don't really want answered. Your lecturers are not entirely pleased at the direction of your secular pursuits. When they approach you, under whatever pretext, hide your thoughts well, my friend, or you'll end up like me, disillusioned and broken—and perhaps freed," he added bleakly, then lifted his espresso in a salute. "Don't be concerned about me. It isn't the end of the world. On the contrary, I have seen the true light and I am now liberated. That's my version anyway. My parents will be distraught for a time, given how they slaved and scraped to put me here, but I was never truly cut out to wear black, too morbid, my friend. I suppose they'll get over it. They'll have to. In time, Paulini, you too will face a stark choice, walk in darkness or open a door to enlightenment. I don't envy you that moment of soul wrenching."

Garbaldi never forgot the incident and the event had forever scarred him, casting a shadow over his once flawless Church. They had to give Noris his master's in Middle Eastern Anthropology, but not his licentiate degree. He went on to the University of Rome at La Sapienza for his PhD, while Garbaldi did postgraduate work at Tre, to the thinly veiled dismay of his Lateran professors. They wanted his studies to have a theological bent, not trusting the impartiality of a freethinking secular institution. At the time Garbaldi failed to see any conflict, pointing out that Lateran didn't offer the subjects of his interest, only later coming to realize the reason for their concern, why they wanted him isolated and controlled. Perhaps he was innocent and naïve as Carlo hinted. For truly, shape the mind of a child and he will forever be yours.

Afterward, they still kept in touch and shared an occasional espresso, but his friend became a changed man. A man who had lost his faith, searching for something else to believe in, and someone in danger of losing his soul. Three years later, Carlo went to America to take on a posting as an assistant professor at Harvard's Center for Middle Eastern Studies, a prestigious appointment, and keeping in touch became harder. Now an associate professor, published and widely respected, and Garbaldi was glad. They still exchanged emails and an occasional phone call, but both knew they lived in different worlds now. There is something sad when friends part, for whatever reason.

Wearing a mischievous smile, he glanced at the watch on his right wrist and nodded. Two-thirty here would make it nine-thirty in the morning Massachusetts time. He reached for the phone and stopped. Did he truly want to do it? Did he want to bring this into an arena where an inevitable accounting would have to be made? Why set into motion something which could potentially have profound repercussions not only for the Church, but the upheaval of the Western civilization as a whole? Who was he to set himself up as an arbiter and judge of what was right? Would it be such a bad thing to continue living a lie for the greater good of all? How many lives would be affected and perhaps destroyed by his revelation? And whom would it serve if truth were revealed, if it was truth? Could this be merely hubris on his part, a desire for personal revenge, or an act of rebellion? Holding his hand on the phone, Garbaldi warred with his beliefs, his teaching and what the Church represented and meant, not only to him, but to the faithful everywhere. As a priest, he was beset by doubt, but as a scientist, he knew without reservation what needed to be done.

He picked up the receiver and began punching in numbers. He could condone what the early Church fathers did. Although misguided, that's how they did business in those days, and maybe even today. What he found difficult to accept was the hypocritical duality the Church maintained merely to perpetuate its position and power. Clearly, the commandments were only meant for the masses, not the Vatican Curia. He thought the one about not bearing false witness particularly apt.

Before getting the connection, something else occurred to him and he replaced the receiver. He took the papyrus sheet and put it into the photocopier, cum printer/scanner capable of taking A3 sheets. On the touch screen, he selected Scanner. The screen changed to show a settings menu. He selected 1200 dpi and pressed the Enter key. The machine then prompted him for his email address. He typed it in and waited. The blue-green light slowly ran the length of the scan surface and the machine returned to the menu. He touched the Cancel button to erase the image from the buffer and took out the confirmation sheet from the printer tray. The still warm paper had date/time stamp statistics, his email address, and the reduced image of the tractate. After staring at it for a second, he slipped the sheet into his diary. It wouldn't do to leave the thing lying around. He removed the papyrus sheet and put it on the desk.

It only took a moment to log onto his personal email service provider's website and check his inbox. He smiled when he saw the message from the scanner and opened the file. He positioned the cursor on the Forward icon and pressed the Enter key. He quickly typed in a new email address and subject message on the new screen and erased the scanner details. His own message a single brief sentence, but Carlo was worldly, experienced and would know what to do. Reassured, he pressed the Send icon and redialed the phone number.

It took three rings before the familiar nasal voice answered. "Dr. Noris."

"*Come sta*, my heretical friend," Garbaldi replied with a grin, feeling a rush of nostalgic warmth and closeness to Carlo he had not felt for some time.

"Ah, if it isn't Cardinal Garbaldi!" Noris replied with a chuckle in Italian. "They still have you digging through the Archives?"

"Better than spreading blasphemy to innocent undergrads."

"Not blasphemy, my misguided padre, but truth!"

"Truth according to Dr. Noris, no doubt."

"What other is there?"

A game they played, although lighthearted, it did reflect their personalities and respective convictions, but perhaps no longer. For Garbaldi, the trip had simply taken a little more time, but nonetheless still wrenching.

"Truth, a fickle mistress, my rebellious buddy," he mused. He could still put the phone down and walk away. Could he walk away from his image in the mirror every morning? "How have you been? We haven't spoken since—"

"I know. It's been some time," Noris finished soberly. "The spring semester is finally finished and so am I. It will be good getting back to some solid research without being bothered by classes. I tell you, Paulini, I don't know how some of those kids graduate. Not an original thinker in the lot. They don't know anything except how to regurgitate text."

Garbaldi reflected on his own experiences and gave a short laugh. "It's the weight of the dissertation that counts, not the scholarship in it. Original thought and clear thinking just get in the way. I thought you knew that one by now."

"It doesn't count with me, as many a hopeful have already found to their dismay." Noris paused, then sighed. "I know, I'm only venting spleen. Enough of that. How are things with you?"

"Enjoying an early summer—"

"I know. I've seen the weather reports. And your latest book? Also hot?"

"It will be, once I get the material I need from Cairo."

"You're going over there next month, right?"

"I'm already packing, but…"

"I detect a fly in your cheer somewhere."

Garbaldi took a deep breath. "Carlo, I don't want to burden you with my problem, but I'm in serious trouble and I need your help."

"What can I do?" Noris said without hesitation, his voice somber.

In a few short sentences, Garbaldi told him, comforted by his friend's immediate readiness to help. Regardless of any differences regarding their beliefs, a characteristic that always endeared him to Carlo. "I need the papyrus sheet and ink reliably dated. I don't want it done here. Too many questions."

"I don't blame you."

"I need to know what to do. It's tearing me apart and I'm deeply troubled."

For a moment, Noris didn't say anything. Then, "My friend, I'm sorry this had to happen to you and I know what you must be going through. Believe me, I do, because I went through the same thing myself. I always knew that sooner or later you would face your own trial of faith."

"I cannot deny it will take some hard thinking on my part, and I thank you for your words, but before I despair completely, I need hard facts."

"Paulini, even if the papyrus is authentic, it may not mean anything. Hundreds of scrolls were written in that period and all of them probably wildly contradictory. You could be working yourself into a state for nothing."

"You're right, but we both know one other thing. Many of those scrolls, and the people who wrote them, were hunted down and destroyed if they didn't conform to official dogma."

Noris gave a long sigh. "I can't argue with you there. Like you said, the first thing to do is get the thing dated. Some universities here do good work, but it's mostly AMS spectroscopy. What you want here is PIXE analysis."

"I know. Do you have a place that could do it without asking too many questions?"

"Our Physics Department has a nice lab where we could do the test. I have done business with them before and I know the director in charge."

"It means bringing the papyrus to America."

"That would be the general idea, yes. Unless you want to mail it to me," Noris quipped.

"Your famed wit is operating at half strength, my friend," Garbaldi drawled dryly and Noris laughed.

"And you don't have any sense of humor. When can you come over?"

"I wish I could do it today, but this will have to wait until my sabbatical. I'll be finished on July 13 and flying home from Cairo the next day. I can be in Boston on Saturday the 16th."

"Sounds good, but July 16 is a long way off. I'll be gnawing my fingers to the bone until then. You wouldn't care to give me a peek at the thing in the meantime?"

"Check your email," Garbaldi said smugly, pleased at having pulled a fast one on his friend.

"Using your Vatican service? Tell me you didn't!"

"Take it easy, Carlo. I may not be worldly-wise like you, but I'm not completely stupid. I used my personal email address."

"Well, thank heaven for small miracles. Sorry for snapping at you, but you must know that what you have is explosive. Watch your step here, my boy. You could get yourself into a lot of trouble if they ever got wind of what you're doing. Serious trouble."

"You mean Archives Security?"

"Them too, but I meant the counterintelligence service."

"The *Sodalitium Pianum*? Why would they be interested in me?"

"You can't be that dense. Wouldn't you want to suppress a document that could undermine everything the Church stands for?"

Garbaldi didn't know much about the Vatican's intelligence service, the Holy Alliance, commonly known as The Entity, or its sister counterintelligence service, nobody did. Officially, they weren't even supposed to exist anymore, but Carlo could be right. He *was* being dense. What he contemplated wasn't simple theft to be dealt with by Archives Security, but a threat against the Church body itself. Like any living organism when stung, the Church would retaliate. He disagreed with Carlo's insinuation at the gravity of that retaliation.

"I hear what you're saying, but I don't see how they could know what I'm doing."

"Keep it that way, okay? I don't want to be reading your obituary or contemplating mine."

Something he hadn't thought possible and the implication chilled Garbaldi. "They wouldn't—"

"They would and they already have," Noris told him bluntly. "Take it from me. These people play for keeps. The Curia may not soil their hands, but they would nevertheless make sure the job was done while clutching crucifixes and praying for absolution. By the way, are you calling from your office?"

"Yes. Why?"

Noris gave a low hiss. "Probably nothing, but from now on, use your cellphone and do it from outside. Walls have long ears, my friend."

Garbaldi thought it over and didn't like any of it. This shadowy side of the Church not something he ever contemplated, or thought existed. What was he getting himself into?

"Under different circumstances, Carlo, I would dismiss your natural cynicism as paranoia, but I'll be careful."

"You always did have your head up in the clouds," Noris complained with a trace of bitterness. "But we shouldn't talk on this line. Call me if anything changes. In the meantime, I'll look at your email and get things organized at my end. Man, are we going to have fun. You'll enjoy Boston."

"As much as I'd love to see the sights, it will be a working visit only, I'm afraid. I can't stay long."

"Why the rush?"

"I have a deadline to finish the book, and Roma Tre is already on my back about it."

"Ah, you're a spoilsport, but I understand. A rain check, then." There came a short pause. "Tell me, what will you do if the papyrus turns out to be genuine?"

It was Garbaldi's turn to pause. "I don't know. I'll have to think about that one."

"We'll discuss it when you come over. Paulini, I'm glad you thought you could call me. It was good to hear from you again." A click and the line went dead.

Garbaldi gently replaced the receiver and stared vacantly at the PC screen. His friend's words about The Entity had disturbed him more than he cared to admit. Would they in fact go after him, or worse? The more he reflected on what he planned to do, the less certain he was of the righteousness of his cause. Skulking around, secret rendezvous, trench coats and black hats just wasn't him. He was a priest and a scholar, not some undercover gumshoe. His inner voice sneered at him. Easy to be morally outraged when nothing was at stake, eh? But when he had to follow through on his convictions, his indignation turned out to be hollow bluster—another pontificating armchair hero.

Somewhat chastened, he logged off and looked at the tractate.

Sandwiched inside the codex, the sheet had withstood the centuries remarkably well. Ordinarily, the Archives' Conservation Laboratory would handle such a manuscript where it would be treated and preserved, something like laminating an ordinary piece of paper. In this case, definitely not an option. He could imagine the look on Father Reoni's face if he saw the papyrus. On the other hand, he couldn't simply stick the thing into his diary and walk out. Or could he? The walking out part would not be a problem. He had taken work home before and the guards never bothered him. Before he did smuggle it, the manuscript had to be protected from accidental damage.

He bent down and opened the bottom desk drawer. From the mess of odd stationery, he pulled out two pieces of beige A4 cardboard and an ordinary transparent plastic bag. He also took out a thin pair of cotton gloves and pulled them on. Working quickly, he sandwiched the papyrus between the cardboard sheets and slipped the whole thing into the bag. He patted it down to squeeze out the air and slid back the sealing tab. Relaxing, he admired his handiwork. It would do until he got the thing home where he would do a better job, something that would withstand rough handling and aircraft travel. After this discovery, returning to a semblance of normalcy would be a letdown.

Removing the tractate from the building somewhat an anticlimax, much to his intense relief. His imagined heart attack mostly self-induced, as were images of a heavy hand on his shoulder and an authoritative voice requesting he accompany the waiting men. Phantom shadows followed him to Porta di Sant'Anna. He had willfully stolen something and broken one of the commandments. Getting caught would be a relief, a release from damnation. Didn't Proverbs 28:1 say that the wicked flee where no man pursueth? He knew exactly what that meant. Holding the high moral ground, truth did not necessarily a shield make against the forces of evil. The closer he came to the two Swiss guards standing on either side of the gate, the more terrified he became, but they merely nodded as he paused beside the church of S. Anna dei Palafrenieri. After a moment of uncertainty, he strode up the steps and walked into the church through the open doors.

Inside, it was cool, almost chilly. Tourists wandered about, cameras and recorders going, talking despite clear signs for silence. Many of the forward pews were occupied and someone was saying Mass. He took a seat next to the right side chapel alcove and composed himself. Hands clasped in his lap, he groped for the right words.

Father…give me strength for what I am about to do and don't let me falter. Your glory is for all time, but it should not be tarnished by man's wickedness. If what I do is wrong, tell me, before I stray from your path. Bless me Father and forgive me my trespasses.

A load seemed to lift off his shoulders and he breathed easier. When a group of tourists walked by along the central aisle, he got up and followed them out. No phantoms haunted his footsteps.

This time of day, pedestrians packed the sidewalks, anxious to get home, and Viale Angelico carried its usual rush hour load of noisy, smelly traffic. Garbaldi was used to it and hardly paid any attention, absorbed in thought. Walking on automatic, head full of the day's events, he was surprised when he found himself at Via Luigi Settembrini. Taking a corner, the gray three-story apartment building loomed on his left, the street already deep in shadow. As usual, he climbed the stairs to his second floor condominium. One of his third floor neighbors leaned over the railing and waved at him. Garbaldi waved back and hurried down the tiled corridor. Once inside his apartment, he laid the diary on the dining table, walked to a large west facing window, and pulled open the drapes. Low sunlight streamed into the stuffy room. He extracted the long piece of dowel blocking the slide and opened the window. A refreshing breeze came through and he took a satisfied breath. City noises came flooding in, but he didn't mind the intrusion. A comforting familiarity. He stood there for a while watching the sun, then turned toward the small kitchen to make dinner.

As he waited for the spaghetti to cook *el dente*, he quickly prepared a simple sauce: fried onions, diced bacon, a can of chopped tomatoes and spices. He drained the spaghetti and mixed in the sauce. A glass of chilled red Chianti completed the preparation. Table set, he gave thanks and turned on the 108cm Samsung LED television in time to catch the evening news.

Garbaldi twirled the spaghetti around his fork and sighed at the misery man insisted on inflicting on himself. Always the same: senseless road deaths, involving the young mostly, murders, political scandals at home and abroad, and gutter journalism about celebrities of all types.

He noted with interest that President Walters still held firm on his commitment to complete the Afghanistan pullout by end of the year. NATO countries were no longer so willing, and America became tired wasting lives and pouring billions down that bottomless hole when faced with trillions of domestic debt and blatant Afghan corruption.

Another clip on the worsening currency wars between America, China and Europe made Garbaldi groan. Hadn't the near collapse of the world's financial system in 2008 sobered everybody?

The most depressing were scenes from the West Bank where the Israeli army were forcibly removing illegal settlers. Families fought for their homes, women screamed invectives at stone-faced soldiers while children stood by helplessly, not understanding what was going on, simply crying. In the background, tanks and armored personnel carriers brooked no interference as families were herded into buses and trucks, dragging suitcases and meager possessions. A house stood by the roadside engulfed in flames, the owner preferring its destruction rather than have it fall into Palestinian hands.

God should not allow such misery, he thought. Of course, God had nothing to do with it. Man had free will. No use lamenting to Him for the evils of man's own making.

At least Israel had followed through on its commitment, made on the floor of the United Nations. Not exactly an expression of Israeli altruism, but pragmatism. After Mossad sabotaged an oil refinery in Galveston, making it appear an act of Iranian terrorism, the United States exacted a heavy toll. Israel could either tackle the Palestinian problem seriously or become an international pariah, ostracized from American support.

Garbaldi tried to recall the two people responsible for uncovering the plot, and then he had it, an article in the *Il Manifesto*: Thomas Meecham from the FBI and Mark Price from the Department of Homeland Security.

He finished his meal and washed up. Glass in hand, he stood by the window and watched as dusk fell and night slowly blurred everything.

Later that night, with the city quiet and subdued, hands clasped behind his head, it took Garbaldi a while to fall asleep.

Chapter Two

Comfortable in his brown leather chair, Monsignor Giovani Giacomo slowly sipped his lightly sweetened chamomile/lemon tea. Holding the warm mug between his hands, enjoying the aromatic bouquet, he allowed his mind to drift. A pile of loose-leaf folders on his desk waited to be read, applications to access the Archives awaiting approval or rejection. To look at them meant having to make decisions and initiate inevitable action. Right now, he couldn't be bothered. Although idling like this had a sinful flavor to it, he didn't think God would mind his lapse just once. Perhaps God would not, but Cardinal Gulio Albani probably would, he mused wryly.

A stickler for detail and exactitude, unfailingly devout, the current Archivist was nonetheless a driven man. Only forty-eight—the Holy Spirit himself must have hovered over him to become a prince of the Church at such a young age—an emerging modernist, Albani wanted to open *all* the Secret Archives. The very thought made Giacomo shudder and reach for an aspirin. The Church may be founded on a rock of righteousness and the pontiff was Christ's vicar on Earth, but sadly, as history all too vividly demonstrated, the Church was also a procession of men, sinful and all too fallible. It simply wouldn't do to parade centuries of that fallibility before all. The sanctity of the Church had to be protected at all costs, lest it lose its authority in the eyes of the faithful masses. Sometimes, this required protecting it from itself. Unfortunately, the Archivist had the pontiff's ear and pursued his program of revelation, as he called it, at a pace Giacomo did not approve of at all. Still, he did have resources, and

the sheer disorganized vastness of the Archives provided a veneer of credibility to his obfuscation and delaying tactics. God
may work in mysterious ways, but Giacomo certainly did not.

He derived comfort from the thought that in another year or
two, Albani would most likely be promoted, moved to another
post inside the Curia, and Giacomo would quietly undo the damage done. Ambitious, Albani saw himself as the next Cardinal
Secretariat of State, whereas Giacomo was a realist, content to do
God's work in a more unassuming way. He would never make
cardinal, but the realization had not diminished his spirit, faith or
belief in the inviolability of the Church. He was a custodian of
Church secrets, white and black, his work important, he took his
duties seriously. Besides, he was past the age when ambition and
a desire to strive and dominate ruled his life, although he had
been there and reached for power. Very early in his ministry, he
realized that change came from a select few who had vision and
drive to overcome obstacles, whatever they might be. He had
achieved a measure of seniority and respect, sufficient for him to
do his work. Along the way, of course, he made enemies; regrettable that such a thing was possible among men of cloth. After
all, they *were* only men. These days, he valued accomplishment,
contentment and a measure of personal satisfaction as yardsticks
of achievement, and he considered himself fortunate to have
them. If along the way, he needed to curb childishly dangerous
idealism in a superior, he accepted that this too was part of his
work. He just had to be careful how he managed Albani.

Giacomo gave a little burp, muttered a 'pardon me', and patted his stomach. The last few minced ravioli he had for lunch had
undone him. Sinful overindulgence and he now paid for it. Soft,
lazy sunshine made golden pools on the dark wooden floor. A
light breeze stirred the partly opened striped gauze curtains that
covered ceiling-high windows, allowing him a view of the gardens
in front of the *Casina* of Pious IV. Beside him, a screensaver image of the Matterhorn, with the small village of Zermatt nestled

in the valley below, made him wish he were there. The only thing he had was a cramped office, a wall full of books, periodicals, folders and metal filing cabinets. He placed the mug on the desk, pushed back the PC keyboard and, with a sigh, bent over the paperwork spread in apparent confusion before him. He was doing penance and knew it.

A knock on the heavy oak door broke his concentration and he looked up.

"What is it?"

The door opened and Sister Valentina's elfin face peered in. "Excuse me, Your Excellency, but Captain Markus Allard is here to see you. He says it's rather urgent."

Giacomo frowned. To the head of Archives Security, everything always urgent.

"Show him in." He would get no peace until he satisfied the man, but more importantly, the interruption provided a welcome diversion. Today his heart just wasn't in his work.

Valentina opened the door wide and the tall Swiss walked in past her. Blond with clear blue eyes and tanned complexion, dressed in a dark gray suit, Allard projected an aura of total competence impossible to miss, a source of mild irritation for Giacomo. Nobody should be that sure of himself. Almost sinful, but the man was annoyingly efficient and there was no getting around it. He pursed his lips to mask his dislike and extended a hand toward a vacant chair.

"Please sit down, Captain."

"Thank you, Your Excellency," Allard said in a surprisingly soft voice. His eyes flickered at a print of Pope Paul VII that hung on the wall.

Giacomo waited patiently as the young man eased himself into the seat without a trace of self-consciousness. Allard had been head of security for eighteen months, and although his duties were always executed with flawless efficiency, the young man displayed a certain level of disdain for Church protocols and his duties. He also sensed that Allard harbored disdain for him. A product of his military training and secular upbringing. A career officer, he probably saw his present tour as merely another line in his resume. Anyway, at the next May rotation, he would be out of here and into Brussels as a major, a NATO liaison posting. Giacomo would not be sorry to see the last of him.

He glanced at Valentina and nodded. "Thank you, Sister. That will be all."

She flashed him a small smile and closed the door. Giacomo folded his arms over the desk and blinked.

"All right, Captain, what's the urgency?"

For the first time, Giacomo saw Allard actually looking uncomfortable. The young man shifted his legs and cleared his throat.

"It may be nothing, Your Excellency, but procedure requires that I bring it to your attention. Have you heard from Father Garbaldi lately? We cannot get in touch with him."

Giacomo frowned. "Garbaldi? No, I haven't. He is on a sabbatical in Cairo and due back on the weekend, I believe. What's the trouble?"

"I'm not sure," Allard said thoughtfully and reached into his left jacket pocket. He pulled out a folded sheet of paper and slid it across the desk. "Your Excellency, that's a log printout and message attachment downloaded from our document scanner email server. Father Garbaldi scanned something on June 15, using equipment in his office."

"So he sent himself an email. What's the big deal? He takes work home all the time. We all do."

"But this was sent to his personal address. You know we monitor all emails coming out of Secret Archives computers—"

"As per my order. And…"

"At first glance it didn't mean anything, until one of my people examined the document text as a routine check. I'm told it is Coptic Sahidic. He called Father Garbaldi for clarification, but when he couldn't reach him, he took it to Father Reoni at the—"

"I know where Reoni works," Giacomo snapped, wishing the man would get on with it.

"Yes, sir. My analyst thought it might be a tractate the Conservation Laboratory worked on for Father Garbaldi. That's why he took the log printout there. When Father Reoni read it, he immediately called me and ordered that I bring it to you. He seemed to think you would understand. If I can add, Your Excellency, he looked extremely agitated and upset when he spoke to me."

Giacomo remained unmoved by Reoni's apparent reaction. The little bird-like man was high-strung and always twitchy, but a superb technician nonetheless. He unfolded the sheet and began to read. Sahidic, all right, and looked like a fragment of St. Matthew's gospel. By the look of it, a different and possibly older version…

As he read, his frown deepened. When he reached the last verse, the hair on the back of his neck stiffened. A wave of cold goosebumps ran down his body and he gave a sharp hiss. No! What he read was impossible. A cheap fake, a lie, and darkest blasphemy. That such evil could be perpetrated here. His whole body trembled and he knew his face was red with moral outrage. He swallowed hard, took a deep breath, and gently placed the sheet on the desk, then clenched his fists.

"Who knows about this?" he demanded with steel in his voice, his eyes fixed on the security chief.

Allard blanched, clearly startled by Giacomo's reaction. "Only the four of us, Your Excellency."

The Prefect nodded. Perhaps the damage could still be contained if he acted swiftly. And it *had* to be contained. If the document ever leaked out, fake or not, the Church could face disaster. The detractors would seize on it as proof of a tottering dogma, the evangelists would be making protest marches in St.

Peter's square and the faithful, as always, would stoically pray for guidance, uncertain what was going on, but unsettled. He wondered how young Garbaldi came into possession of the thing. It could all be completely innocent, but he needed to know what Garbaldi had done with the tractate. More importantly, why hadn't the young fool reported this immediately? The fact that Garbaldi had not, clearly showed he understood well the explosive nature of the damning words. Where *did* the perishing thing come from anyway, and what did Garbaldi plan to do with it, if he hadn't already done so?

Giacomo knew Garbaldi's academic qualifications had tarnished an otherwise promising vocation. There was such a thing as too much knowledge and he feared that Garbaldi's faith and obedience to the Church were perhaps irrevocably stained. If he put himself in the young man's shoes, what would *he* do? It took no time at all to figure out. As a scientist, Garbaldi would want to authenticate the document. If that were the case, why didn't he simply take it to Father Reoni? Knowing its sensitivity, perhaps he wanted external validation before revealing it. If the thing was a fake, he'd be guilty of raising a false alarm, no matter how well intentioned his action. Something else occurred to Giacomo, something more sinister. Did Garbaldi plan to release the contents of the tractate independently? He did not want to contemplate the awful possibility, but could not very well dismiss it either.

His eyes bored into the security chief. "I want you to go down to IT and have them delete the log of this email."

Allard stiffened. "Your Excellency, I'll need formal authorization from Cardinal Albani before I can do that. Your order violates several security protocols."

Giacomo wanted to rage at him for being a stupid obstructionist, but refrained. Allard simply followed procedure and could hardly be blamed for that, regardless how personally irksome at the moment.

"Very well, Captain. You shall have it within the hour. In the meantime, make all necessary preparations."

"You realize, sir, because the email was generated over a month ago, this will also require wiping backup and archive records."

"Whatever it takes, but I don't want a trace of that thing anywhere. As far as you and your analyst are concerned, this email never existed. Is that clearly understood?"

"Completely, Your Excellency. And Father Reoni?"

"You leave Reoni to me." Giacomo tapped the paper with a stiff finger. "Tell me, Captain. Why did it take your people more than a month to dig this up? Looks like negligence to me."

Allard shifted in his seat, acutely embarrassed. "It's being looked into, sir."

"Once you've finished looking into it, I expect you to take appropriate corrective steps. Is that understood?"

"Of course."

"We can now return to your first question. Since you don't know where Garbaldi is and I don't know where he is, given the contents of his email, it behooves us to find him. Wouldn't you agree?"

"With respect, Your Excellency, I don't know the contents of his email, or why it appears to have such importance to warrant complete erasure. I cannot then say why it is necessary to locate Father Garbaldi."

Giacomo glared, then gave a stiff nod. Allard was quite correct, of course. He merely delivered a message from Reoni. In some ways, handling Reoni was actually more important and had to be done quickly.

"Take it from me, Captain, it's crucial that you locate him as a matter of highest priority, using whatever resources are necessary. I don't know his flight details, but you should be able to find out. Park your men at the Fiumicino airport and his apartment. I don't care what. Just find him."

Allard raised an eyebrow. "And once we locate him?"

"Tell him to report to me at once. He is also to bring the tractate. He'll understand."

"Are we to detain him?"

"Of course not! He's not a criminal. Just tell him to report."

"Very good, Your Excellency." Allard stood up and came to attention. "If that's all, sir?"

For a moment, Giacomo stared at the young man, then waved a dismissive hand. "You may go, and thank you, Captain."

Allard nodded stiffly and walked out. When the door closed with a soft click, Giacomo ground his teeth.

Hellfire and perdition! What a mess. One thing to keep Albani in check, making sure the Secret Archives *remained* secret, another to get embroiled in a scandal over dogma. He didn't need such excitement or exposure. Why in damnation hadn't Garbaldi just come to see him instead of going off on some misguided personal crusade, regardless of his intentions? If that is actually what he had done. The Church had wiser heads who could properly assess the material and take appropriate action. Appropriate for everybody concerned, especially the Church. As far as Giacomo was concerned, that meant quietly burying the thing in the Archives, real or fake. Now, the young idiot had brought on himself the full weight and authority of the Church.

He swiveled the chair until he faced the computer screen. Opening a temporary Word document, he quickly typed in a rough translation. A warm copy slid from the printer and he closed Word without saving.

Mouth set, he grabbed his beige phone and punched in numbers. It took two rings before Sister Angela picked up.

"Good afternoon. Cardinal Albani's office."

"God bless you, Sister," Giacomo said gravely. "Is His Eminence available?"

"Monsignor Giacomo! I think so. Please let me check."

There was a click and the haunting strands of *Ave Maria* came through. Listening to the enchanting music, Giacomo marveled at man's devotion and intellect able to produce something so magical and perfect.

"I'm putting you through now, Your Excellency."

"Thank you, Sister."

"Giovani! Haven't heard from you in a while. How are those access approvals coming for Princeton?" Albani demanded, on top of things as usual. Giacomo glanced guiltily at the pile of papers on his desk and winced.

"They will be able to send their team in September as scheduled, Your Eminence."

"Good, good. Now, what can I do for you?" Albani's voice throaty and rich, gave the impression of joviality and suppressed laughter.

Outwardly, the man *was* engaging, and at times charming, articulate and a polished conversationalist. As Giacomo knew from personal experience, the cultural veneer merely a façade for an accomplished political manipulator. He had nursed his career by cultivating a circle of influential supporters and played by all the unwritten rules. The tactic obviously worked as it got him the red hat. Sadly or otherwise, these days no one wore the red hat because of piety and devotion alone, if they ever did.

We are all God's tools in the execution of His work, Giacomo consoled himself, *and we do it in our own unique way.*

"I need to see you, Your Eminence, on a matter of the gravest urgency."

There was a moment of silence. "Now?"

"This cannot wait."

"You cannot tell me over the phone and save us both some time? I'm rather busy right now."

"The matter is too delicate for that, Your Eminence."

"Very well, then. Come on over," Albani growled and hung up.

"Thank you," Giacomo said into the dead phone and cradled the handset.

He placed both hands on the desk and stood up. Clutching the offending pieces of paper, he stepped to the door, opened it, and nodded to Valentina sitting behind her desk, guarding the entrance to his office. She looked up and flashed him a warm smile.

"Is there anything you need, Your Excellency?"

"Yes. Please leave a message for Father Reoni to see me at his earliest convenience. I should be back shortly."

"Very good, Your Excellency."

Giacomo strode from the outer office into the dark, wide corridor, part of the old building's architecture whose designers subscribed to austerity and plain functionality rather than aesthetics or comfort. Hung paintings broke what otherwise were plain white walls. At the end of the corridor, he paused and opened an elaborately carved entrance. When Sister Angela saw him, she immediately stood and opened a heavy dark paneled door beside her desk.

"His Eminence is expecting you, Your Excellency."

"Thank you, Sister. I must say, you look becoming today."

A faint blush highlighted her cheeks and she dropped her eyes. "Your Excellency, you do go on."

Chuckling, Giacomo stepped through the doorway. He liked playing the flirting game with her and neither thought further about it.

A tall window on either side of Albani's ornately carved desk provided a warm and sunlit working environment. Winter was something else, though, as the building's heating system didn't always work as advertised. Suffering was good for the soul, Giacomo mused. The soft brown and yellow hews of the worn parquet floor added to the cozy atmosphere. The left wall held a floor-to-ceiling bookcase filled with all manner of material, ranging from magazines, literary and religious works to volumes on social and philosophical commentary. Above a gray marble fireplace set into the right wall, hung a huge, exquisitely woven Persian rug, supposedly handmade, depicting a battle. Whoever did it must have spent two years on the job. From what he heard, the rug had adorned the wall for centuries.

Cardinal Albani looked up from his paperwork and waved at a stately French visitor chair, dispensing with the ring kissing routine. He had a thick crop of black hair framing a ruggedly handsome face. His dark brown eyes shone with penetrating intelligence. He looked like a man on the rise and knew it. A product of a wealthy Venetian family, social standing and powerful political connections, Albani seemed to have it all. Giacomo did not begrudge him his successes. They were all equal before God…but you had to be in heaven before that really became true.

"Make yourself comfortable, Giovani, and tell me your troubles," Albani invited soothingly, locked his fingers and beamed.

"Unfortunately, they are no longer my troubles alone, Gulio," Giacomo said heavily as he sat down. He leaned back and crossed his legs.

"Oh? And why is that?"

"Take a look at these." Giacomo shifted and slid the two papers across the desk. "The first is an email log of a tractate young Garbaldi dug up somewhere."

"Garbaldi? Isn't he the one here on secondment—"

"That's him."

"Brilliant mind," Albani said approvingly and picked up the printouts. "But those books he has written, questionable…very questionable. Still, he is young and we should nurture and channel an inquiring spirit, not punish it." He glanced at the first page and frowned.

"It's Coptic Sahidic," Giacomo explained. "Apparently a very early version of St. Matthew's gospel, or more likely, part of the Q document."

"And? You know I can't read that stuff."

"Read the second document. It's a fair translation."

Albani shuffled the sheets and began to read. After a moment of stunned silence, he slowly looked up, mouth gaping.

"Holy Christ! According to this, Jesus was John the Baptist's disciple. Incredible that something like this should have survived. I would have thought the Christian fathers had rid us of such heresy."

Giacomo's smile was grim. "Clearly not. The idea has been contended before, as has the notion of two Messiahs; a spiritual one represented by John, and a conquering one who would overthrow the Romans and reunite the tribes of Israel. But you knew that already."

"Essene sacrilege!" Albani hissed and threw the papers on the desk. "And this is blasphemy, pure propaganda. A fabrication. It has to be."

Giacomo shrugged. "I'm not here to argue about the Essenes or early Christian dogma. But Garbaldi's papyrus? I don't know. The Church fathers were quite liberal in their interpretation of Jesus' life and very selective when choosing gospels that fit the emerging doctrine, St. Paul's dominating influence notwithstanding. Our own Archives have documents that remain secret for a very good reason, even from our own researchers."

When Albani shifted in his seat, Giacomo knew the Archivist was uncomfortable venturing into those waters. Despite Albani's belief that all the Secret Archives should be opened to accredited scholars, given his position, he had to know the dark side of the Church hidden in the kilometers of shelving and dusty codices lying dormant, waiting to one day shred the faith if brought to light. The archives might not be opened in his lifetime, but nevertheless, Giacomo feared that one day they would. He wasn't talking about Inquisition atrocities or keeping the populace in ignorance during the Dark Ages.

He feared revelation of truly secret texts that could utterly shatter the Vatican and all priestly authority. Christianity might survive in some form, but the Church he knew would be swept aside in the ensuing social turmoil. Would that necessarily be such a bad thing? Do not lie or bear false witness. Wasn't that the eighth commandment, something the Church had been breaking for almost two thousand years? Perhaps, but he did not want to carry the guilt for the sins of his fathers. The hypocrisy of that thought brought him up short as his conscience rebelled.

The Church simply *couldn't* reveal all. Lives of the faithful would be torn apart, political institutions disrupted and the stability of Western civilization itself threatened. Over time, he told himself, in bits and pieces, as the social climate permitted, all *would* be revealed; preferably long after he was dead. Albani's program to open the archives would continue, but responsibly and with care if Giacomo had anything to do with it. Much damage could be done in the blind name of truth, and he had worked too hard to attain his position simply to have it swept aside for some nebulous revelation, however deserving.

The faithful were the flock and the Church their shepherd. Like children, they had to be cared for and nurtured...and taught to obey the Church—without question. Thinking of Garbaldi, the parable of the lost sheep came to his mind, but in this instance, more like bringing a lamb for the slaughter. Still, the silence of one was worth the price to save the many. Wasn't it?

"Who knows about this?" Albani demanded somewhat more calmly.

"Reoni and whoever Garbaldi may have brought into his confidence."

"Wasn't Garbaldi due back from his Cairo research?"

"This weekend, I believe. I directed Captain Allard to track him down and have him see me. Then we can have an explanation."

"He's not answering his cellphone?" Albani looked incredulous.

"Apparently not."

"That new book he is writing, more heresy, and now this. The papyrus, does he have it?"

"I don't know. It's possible he removed it from his office."

"Mmm. This might be nothing. On the other hand, depending on what he proposes doing with the thing, it could spell calamity for the Church. Regardless of his questionable scholarly leanings, I cannot believe he intends us any harm. Nonetheless, you were right to bring it to my attention." Albani frowned and pulled at his chin. After a while, he set his mouth and his look burned into Giacomo. "Given the potential ramifications, I think Cardinal Marati is probably the best person to deal with this."

At the mention of the former Patriarch of Venice, Giacomo involuntarily squirmed in his seat at the thought of confronting the formidable cardinal. He knew the Prefect's background, everyone did. A doctorate in Christian Philosophy from the Universita Cattolica del Sacro Cuore in Milan, followed by another doctorate in Fundamental Moral Theology from the Pontifical Lateran University, appointed Professor of Theological Anthropology at the Pontifical John Paul II Institute and worked with Cardinal Joseph Ratzinger while both were in Munich. Giacomo figured that is where Marati developed his more conservative views. Under John Paul II, he was Consultor to the Congregation for the Doctrine of the Faith, and when Ratzinger became pope, Marati received promotion as the Congregation Prefect, continuing the uncompromising policies on dogma set by his predecessor.

Giacomo had hoped the Garbaldi matter could be handled quietly between Albani and himself without involving anybody else, especially Marati, and resented Albani passing on the responsibility. Getting the Congregation involved always meant an uncomfortable time for someone, innocent or not. They had a way of digging into things that insinuated guilt even where there was none. Then again, he could appreciate Albani's position. Should Garbaldi do something foolish and the matter became public, no one would be thanking him for sitting on it. Instead of heading the Secretariat of State, he could very well end up running the La Paz diocese in Bolivia instead. But then, Albani always had a keen political sense, adept at managing the Church's interests as long as they didn't conflict with his. Pragmatic and coldblooded as that might be, Giacomo could hardly fault the man for it.

"I suppose it's necessary," he said with resignation and sighed, still not entirely comfortable with the idea as it meant having to bare *his* soul to Marati. He did not relish the thought of needing to reveal some of his dealings, no matter what the reason.

"There is no supposing about it, Giovani. When Garbaldi comes to see you, I want both of you here. Is that clear? We need to have a hard talk with our young reactionary."

"Shouldn't we alert Inspector General Emanuo—"

"This is not the business of the *Corpo della Gendarmeria*! The last thing I want is them meddling in a matter of Church doctrine. It's bad enough having Allard involved, although unavoidable."

"As you wish."

Albani tapped the printouts. "Are these the only copies?"

"The translation is. I asked Allard to delete the email log, but he requires your authorization."

"Leave Allard to me. You can leave the material with me as well. However, be prepared to face Marati. He'll want a detailed background briefing…as will I. Have a talk with Reoni. He is to keep his mouth shut."

"Already arranged." Giacomo stood up and looked closely at Albani. "Let's not overreact here, all right? Garbaldi may have a legitimate reason for sitting on it."

"Perhaps, but we cannot take that chance. He should have reported the find to you immediately. His action reckless and ill-advised at best."

"Weren't *we* foolish when we were young?"

"Not with something like this! Garbaldi may have a brilliant mind, but a stern censure now might straighten him out. He does not dictate policy for the Church!"

Giacomo made for the door, then paused and turned. "Be careful with Marati, Gulio. He is a hatchet man."

"So I've been told," Albani said gravely. "*Ciao*, my friend."

When the door closed, Albani picked up the translation and slowly read through the verses again. *Of all the things to happen now!* The Church was riding another financial scandal involving the laundering of money for the Venezuelan president, and the god-less man was a communist. He thought the Vatican Bank mess had been cleaned up years ago. A festering sore still existed about pedophile priests in the New York and Frankfurt dioceses, among others. He would have had them stripped and handed to civil authorities for prosecution under the full weight of local law. The former pontiff's policy of merely having them transferred where they could resume doing their evil work was incomprehensible. Benedict XVI had made a public apology on behalf of the Church, several of them, but hardly enough for the victims. A millstone around their neck and cast into the deepest pit is what they deserved. Trying to simply cover up the problem had turned into a public relations disaster, causing great damage. The Church had sinned and it should confess. Punish your own and do penance. Wasn't that the right thing to do? At least the current pontiff had the fortitude to take positive action and weed out the vermin.

Now the mess with Garbaldi, something he didn't need laid at his feet right now. Cardinal Enrico Fontini was stepping down in January as Substitute for General Affairs and Albani had positioned himself to take on the post in a final step to assume the

Secretariat of State. With the pontiff sympathetic to the idea, he considered his chances were good. However, should Garbaldi do something foolish and the papyrus somehow became public, it could seriously undermine those plans. Although not directly responsible for the young researcher, his enemies would seize the incident to undermine him, a move that might very well work and scuttle his ambitions. That, of course, was something he could not permit. No, his initial instinct was correct; pass this on. Regardless of what happens now, he would walk away snow clean.

He picked up the phone and dialed a direct number. On the fourth ring, the familiar heavy, clipped voice answered.

"Cardinal Marati."

"It's Gulio."

"Ah, the redoubtable Archivist himself. It must be something weighty for you to call me from your vast corridors of moldy books. You never do otherwise."

Albani winced at the veiled barb, aware that he had neglected his close and powerful friend, despite the eleven years difference in their ages. Without Marati's strong endorsement, he doubted that his elevation to the rank of cardinal-priest would have gone through. He had never forgotten, a debt still being discharged.

"My apologies, and I shall try to make up for the omission."

"Hah! By letting me hear your confession?" Marati quipped and laughed.

A snort escaped Albani and he grinned. "Hardly! I don't want you setting the Inquisition on me."

"Wise, wise. And it's not the Inquisition anymore, you know. Now, why the call, or did you just want to chat?"

"Both. Something has come up which needs your delicate touch and must be discussed privately."

"A mystery, eh? Okay, I'm game. I'll drop by your office. I was about to go out anyway. Ten minutes?"

"See you then." Albani replaced the receiver and leaned back.

He did not want Marati involved, but the Congregation was nonetheless the appropriate instrument to handle this. He had no trouble rationalizing the move. Young Garbaldi had been irresponsible in the extreme not to come forward with the tractate the minute he found it, and now faced some serious questioning and another black mark on his otherwise fine record. Whatever happened next, he will have brought it on himself.

He spent time going over papers, but didn't remember what he read, his thoughts on the damned translation.

A knock and Sister Angela opened the door wide to admit his corpulent visitor. Although not tall, the senior cardinal bore himself with dignity and authority, accustomed to deference and instant obedience. Given his position, he usually got it. Considered a theological conservative, nothing stood in his way when it came to protecting the Church, from within or without. Naturally, as Congregation Prefect, he was also rightly feared and inevitably resented by some. All that might be true and Marati did not hesitate to use his position to exert considerable influence on his brother cardinals and the pontiff himself, but Albani knew that beneath the stern, formidable exterior also lay a deeply religious and caring individual who could be gentle and sympathetic. However, not many got to see that side of him. Well, each had his own cross to bear.

"Cardinal Marati, Your Eminence."

"Thank you, Sister. Come on in, Renaro."

Angela softly closed the door as Marati walked to a visitor chair, ran a hand through his fading hair, and sat down without being invited, his black robes swishing around his legs. Neither stood much on ceremony.

Without saying a word, Albani held out the translation printout.

"No small talk, no coffee?" Marati quipped.

"Later. Read that first."

Marati raised an eyebrow in admonition, took the document and began to read. When done, he flicked the page onto the desk, his wrinkled face expressionless, but his eyes were hard.

"This is bad. I suggest you shred it."

"Of course."

"Fill me in," the older man ordered, all trace of levity gone.

This was serious Church business, as Albani well knew, convinced it was something that fell under Marati's responsibility. In a few short sentences, he sketched out the situation. When he finished, Marati pulled at his chin, his concern clear on his face. Bad on so many levels.

"Where is the papyrus?"

"We don't know. Father Garbaldi may have taken it home for his research. That's only a supposition, of course."

"Search his office and sift through everything, including his apartment. We must find it."

Albani stared, shaken by this blatant violation of privacy. "His apartment?"

"Discreetly, of course. The young fool! He has no idea what he started."

"Let's not jump to conclusions here, Renaro. Garbaldi may have been rash by not reporting his find and I don't condone what he has done, but the fact that he didn't go to Giacomo also tells me he clearly understood the implication."

"Perhaps, but I'll feel a whole lot better once we have the papyrus in our hands. This is not to be discussed with anyone. I know you understand why and I apologize for having to remind you."

"Your duty," Albani said a little stiffly. He did understand. That is why he didn't resent his friend's reminder too much. Marati remained an inquisitor in the old mold and did not mind throwing his weight around.

"We need to deal with this quickly," Marati said and glanced at his wristwatch. "Please have Monsignor Giacomo come to my office this afternoon at four. There is obviously more to this than you told me and he is the man with the answers. At least I hope for everybody's sake that he has some of them." His mouth twitched in a small smile. "Of course you know, you've ruined a perfectly good day for me."

"This doesn't rest easily on my shoulders either," Albani retorted crisply, maintaining a façade of concern for the welfare of the Church, but still shaken by Marati's hardline approach. "What do you intend doing if we don't recover the papyrus?"

Marati stood up, his features grim. "Whatever is appropriate, but I agree with you. Let's talk to Father Garbaldi first. Still, I fear the portents, my friend. Set your house in order, and God be with both of us, Gulio."

Albani did not care for the portents either. He watched Marati close the door and sighed, wondering whether God *would* be with them. The look of set determination on his mentor's face worried him. Whatever happened, his conscience was clear, he had done the necessary thing. Did he do enough, or perhaps too much?

* * *

Warm sunshine streamed between the tall poplars, birch and cypress of the papal private grounds, the trees maintaining a protective wall from the noise and turbulence of the world outside. Sitting on a stone bench, contemplating the manicured lawns, elegant patterns of bright flowerbeds and a small fountain in the center that whispered softly as it tossed a thin stream of water into the air, Marati's soul was troubled. He had faced scandals, within and outside the Church, but nothing like what he potentially faced now. Curbing the rash enthusiasm of young South American priests whose liberal views openly threatened the authority of the Holy See, and by extension the oppressive secular regimes of that region, an ongoing headache. Lifting restrictions on stem cell research, abortion and the use of birth control measures, not only during normal sexual intercourse—God forbid that in holy union a couple should derive a degree of pleasure from the act—but as a mechanism to protect against HIV, were some of the most festering. They were God's creatures in flesh, made that way. So why should the Church condemn sex as impure? He had to acknowledge, though, that the Holy Father had eased his stance and allowed the use of condoms, but the Church still had far to go to pull itself out of the eighteenth century. Given the appalling living conditions of people in South America, the priests there sought practical solutions for local problems, and throwing dogma aside while doing it. Getting involved in the political process of those countries was but another side of the same coin. The priests in Africa faced equally daunting issues for exactly the same reason.

The Church had failed in the West as the faithful simply ignored papal edicts. Like tobacco companies, it needed to seek out fresh customers. That, however, was a policy of diminishing returns. There were only so many ignorant people left in the world the Church could woo and convert. Sooner or later, Third World countries would be better educated and would start to think, to question, something supremely dangerous for any religion. Deny the faithful absolution of sins at confession? No longer a threat either, as compulsory confession was effectively abolished in favor of collective reconciliation during Mass. In his opinion, a grave error when introduced, further eroding Church authority. As was the ululation meant to represent speaking in tongues that had excited popular scorn and numerous jests. Many saw the practice as comical and ridiculous, providing yet another reason to avoid attending Mass that had degenerated into hollow ritual, weary sermons, and reading of the parish balance sheet.

For the moment, he kept the radical priests in line, but the signs were already there. The populace of Africa and South

America were no longer prepared to blindly follow Rome's dictates when those dictates clearly caused harm and suffering. The older generation would continue to faithfully pray and suffer, they didn't know any better, but the young abhorred Church hypocrisy and were ready to follow the radical priests, or abandoned the Church altogether as an irrelevant and nostalgic anachronism. Privately, he understood what motivated the young and sympathized, he had been there himself, but until the Holy Father decreed otherwise, Marati would enforce the will of the Church on all, on pain of excommunication, or worse.

Taking in the drowsy afternoon warmth, he faced the possibility of such punitive action now.

The translated words of Garbaldi's papyrus blazed vividly in his mind, searing through a comfortable veneer of established dogma. There were populist books by the score that played loosely on early Church history, the life of Jesus and his disciples, some of them coming uncomfortably close to a truth not meant to be revealed. Knowledge could no longer be suppressed like in centuries past. The scholarly works were the worst, openly pointing out inconsistencies and blatant errors in the scripture, refuting with archeological evidence the Bible's fictional history. With both problems, the Church had two enormous advantages that negated, in part at least, published material. The devout simply ignored the evidence, and the poorly educated were never given an opportunity to access such books. Even for the sophisticated, few were prepared to invest the time and intellectual rigor required to study and critically evaluate reputable scholarly works. Should a common person be prepared to question even a little, the Church could cease to exist. Sheer historical inertia, and habit ingrained from childhood, worked in its favor, but for how long? He feared the sands in the hourglass were already running out.

A lot could be said for denying the faithful access to the printed word. When the Guttenberg press and devices that followed became prevalent, Church authority had forever been gravely wounded. The ordinary parishioner should never be allowed to think for himself. The Church had been more interested in enslaving the poor in serfdom and lining its own pockets than dealing with the emerging threat. It pained Marati to admit such truth, but history nonetheless.

Did Garbaldi intend to publish the tractate? And he could be overreacting as Albani said? He did not know much about the young scholar, except for notations of disapproval when he insisted on going to Roma Tre instead of remaining at the Lateran University in pursuit of his academic interests. Despite questionable publications critical of the Church, the Prefect had spoken highly of him, as had Cardinal Fontini. Clearly, Father Garbaldi was a very capable and intelligent man, which also made him that much more dangerous. Marati wondered to what extent his scholarly pursuits may have diminished his faith and conformity to Church will. By not handing over the tractate the moment he came across it meant that Garbaldi was indeed corrupted, perhaps irretrievably. To be fair, it could also mean he might be gathering evidence before revealing the thing, like the scientist he was. Marati sighed, knowing he was only making excuses for the young priest. The new generation of priests, learned, sophisticated, idealistic and critical, impatient of authority…and so dangerous to the faith. He had seen it before and fought to crush every one of them. And now Garbaldi…

Marati knew very well what motivated the rebellious young and how they thought. An intellectual rebel himself, following in the footsteps of the then Cardinal Joseph Ratzinger, Marati had produced six definitive works on faith, adherence to Church dogma, and ethics in a modern society. Most recently, two hotly debated books on social dislocation, dissolution of family unity, and decline of morality caused by technology and the materialistic Western lifestyle. His open criticism of the Church's failure to make itself more relevant in today's success-oriented society and the inclusion of female priests had drawn the ire of several conservative cardinals, but he was far too senior and powerful for the criticism to concern him. Moreover, his views were tempered by years of authority and encyclopedic knowledge, offering options to address the problems, not merely serving criticism out of spite. In his view, for the common man on the street, struggling with a mortgage, maintaining a family, managing a career, or merely trying to hold down a job in uncertain economic times, the Church should be the one he could turn to for solace, guidance and spiritual fulfillment. Instead, drugs, television, pornography and alcohol were the preferred options in the vacuum the Church continues to ignore and should fill.

Despite his writings and personal clashes with his brothers over dogma, he was nevertheless the custodian and guardian of Church doctrine and faith. Anything perceived as a threat to that doctrine had to be excised like a malignant tumor before, like cancer, rogue cells multiplied and spread through the body of the faithful, eventually killing it. A clean surgical strike now could avert much suffering later. It might already be too late.

Marati smiled wryly, knowing why Albani had thrown this hot potato in his lap. He was aware of his protégé's ambitions and happy to further them. The Church needed young, modern thinkers, but a rather transparent ploy. Albani could have handled the matter himself, as he rightfully should have, but being an astute political operator that he was, he immediately sensed potential danger for himself if things fell apart. To be fair, his friend did not have the necessary apparatus to deal with it, or the moral resolve. On reflection, perhaps Albani had done the correct thing after all.

Bemused, shaking his head, he stood up and made his way along a brick path that led toward his office. He strode up the broad flight of stairs to the third floor, paused before a white-painted door opposite the staircase, and stepped in. Father Teleman automatically looked up and stood. A diminutive, bald individual, the old priest a perfect personal secretary. Unfailingly polite, he was nonetheless utterly pragmatic and devoid of any pretensions. Marati hated to think how many times he not only sought, but followed Teleman's suggestions and sage advice. They made an ideal complementary pair—power and wisdom.

"Anything urgent come up?" he demanded offhandedly and Teleman shook his head.

"Some routine papers from Paris, Your Eminence. Otherwise a quiet day."

"The abortion thing?" Marati queried quietly and Teleman nodded.

A teenager had been attacked and raped by a Muslim youth, leaving her with child. Her parents approached their local priest to allow an abortion. He refused, of course, stating the usual line about the sanctity of all life. Unsatisfied, they took the matter to the Archbishop himself, who upheld the priest's decision. Disgusted, the parents went to the papers with the whole sordid story, claiming if the Church wanted the child, they could care for it once it was born, but hollow platitudes did not make up for the girl's mental suffering and social embarrassment. Marati sympathized. She had an abortion at one of the free clinics and the Church probably lost a few more parishioners.

That family's plight typified a major problem with the Church's outdated policy. One thing to disallow abortion and birth control on theological grounds, but it did nothing to help the victims emotionally or materially to help raise an unwanted child. Even the threat of hellfire only raised scorn. No wonder people ignored the Church. What the Vatican should be doing is building orphanages, offering financial support, working with victims to solve the problem, rather than pontificate from an opulent office removed from reality, deluding itself it was obeying God's commandments. It wasn't really, as not surprisingly the

Bible had nothing to say on the matter. Abortion had been common practice throughout the Roman world. Talk about Pontius Pilate washing his hands. Marati had said as much to the Holy Father and gotten nowhere. The pontiff still to exert his full authority after demise of Benedict XVI, and unyielding on some points of dogma as Marati. In the meantime, the faithful suffered and silently rebelled.

"A mess, all right. Please check if Cardinal Belconi is available to talk to me. If he is, put him through."

"Of course. Anything else? Coffee, tea?"

Marati waved a hand in dismissal and walked into his office. The papal gardens looked much better seen from the third floor. He just managed to sit down in his faded old yellow leather chair when the phone rang. He picked up the receiver.

"Cardinal Belconi is on line three, Your Eminence."

"Thank you," Marati said and pressed a glowing button. "Avero, it's Renaro."

The head of The Entity gave a suffering groan. "I've had a very pleasant day so far, Renaro. Why do I get the feeling that you're about to spoil it?"

"You're bored and I have just the thing to cure that, but we shouldn't talk on the phone. Can we meet?"

"Not even a hint?"

"Can we meet?" Marati repeated, not in the mood for games.

"My office. I can see you now."

"I'll be a moment."

* * *

The tires of the Alitalia Airbus A340 scraped the runway with a shudder and the aircraft swayed left against the crosswind. Several passengers gasped in alarm and clutched their armrests. Garbaldi's stomach tensed, but he wasn't overly perturbed. An understandable reaction, as motion always seemed exaggerated in the confines of the claustrophobic flight cabin. The pilot shut off reverse thrust and the aircraft slowed rapidly. It turned right onto a taxiway and headed for the da Vinci-Fiumicino international terminal lit by golden afternoon light. He peered out the small window and watched aircraft taxiing out to get in line for their shot at a runway or jostle toward an assigned spot among the already parked gaggle.

As soon as the Airbus stopped, everyone immediately got up and began reaching for the overhead lockers. Having retrieved their bags, they stood in the aisles waiting stoically for the first and business class passengers to alight. Eventually, a flight attendant unclipped the curtain that led to the main cabin and the line began to move. Garbaldi dragged out a small brown leather case containing all his notes and research from under the seat in front of him and eased himself into the aisle. An elderly woman shot him a surly look and allowed him to get in front of her. He gave her a wan smile, not understanding her reason to be out first, but for some those few seconds obviously meant a lot. He wondered if she would have reacted the same way had he worn his black shirt and white collar.

The departure gates were hot, noisy and crowded with travelers waiting to board their flights. Ignoring the crush, his fellow passengers hurried down the broad corridor that led toward Immigration and baggage claim, flanked by duty-free stalls, wanting to beat others through the tiresome passport control. Garbaldi sympathized, an aspect of air travel he could easily dispense with. After long hours cooped up in a plastic and metal tube, he didn't look forward to waiting in line simply to have his passport stamped and then more waiting for his luggage to be regurgitated—if it hadn't been misdirected to God knows where.

"Father Garbaldi?"

Garbaldi was startled to hear his name, turned and looked for the source of the voice and blanched. Wearing a slight frown, Captain Allard walked quickly toward him. Dressed in a dark blue lightweight suit, he bore an unmistakable air of power and authority that seemed to surround military officers and senior executives. They knew they had it made and the world lay at their feet. Garbaldi understood immediately why the chief of Archives Security was here and fought hard to suppress his dismay, hoping his expression would be mistaken for natural curiosity.

"Captain, an unexpected encounter," he said smoothly even though his heart raced, dreading what was to come. Allard came alone, so perhaps things were not as bad as they seemed.

Allard stopped before him and cleared his throat. "I apologize for jumping on you like this, Father, but I have orders from Monsignor Giacomo and I wasn't able to reach you on your cellphone."

"Ah, sand in the works, literally," Garbaldi said truthfully, intimidated by the man's presence.

"Egypt will do that," Allard agreed with a nod. "The same thing happened to me in Tunisia. His Excellency requests that you see him at your earliest convenience, and you are to bring with you a certain tractate. He expected you would understand what he meant."

Garbaldi clenched his teeth in apprehension. Giacomo knew about the papyrus, but how? He hadn't left any clues of its existence, none! When he saw Allard's look of concern, he managed a small smile.

"I do understand, Captain. A bit of personal research on a Coptic scroll that seems to have surfaced prematurely."

"Whatever it is, sir, it made an impression. When he read your email—"

"My email?"

"A routine check of our internal email traffic revealed that you scanned a papyrus sheet and sent it to your private address. That in itself didn't mean anything to me, but Father Reoni seemed very disturbed when he saw it and ordered me to bring the matter to His Excellency's attention."

Garbaldi nodded, understanding completely. Of course Security would have taken the email to the Conservation Laboratory, to Reoni. He could picture all too clearly the little man's consternation at seeing the Sahidic text and Giacomo's subsequent reaction when he read it. The annulling fact that the Prefect had summoned him for an explanation rather than being summarily hauled away, not that Allard had authority to arrest anyone, only a *Corpo della Gendarmeria* officer could detain him, suggested that his plight might not be dire—yet. Still, not the homecoming he expected, and he felt more than a little unnerved.

"I see. Well, thank you, Captain. Please convey my respects to His Excellency and inform him that I shall call on him sometime tomorrow morning. I need to unpack and unwind."

"I understand, Father," Allard said and touched his temple in a brief salute. "Can I give you a lift home?"

"That's kind of you, but it will be a while before I clear Immigration and collect my luggage. I don't want to detain you unnecessarily."

"It would be no trouble."

"Thanks, but I'll be fine." Garbaldi waved a hand in dismissal and resumed his walk down the corridor, his mind churning, oblivious to people around him; any relief he might have had at being home totally shattered.

His palms were sweaty, but he dared not wipe his hands, afraid that Allard would see and infer the obvious, that he was indeed guilty of something, which unfortunately would only be the truth.

The scanner email! It never occurred to him that IT would be monitoring such routine messages, presumably from everyone working in the Archives. Only Giacomo would have the temerity to order something like that. The man must be completely paranoid. To be fair, the Archives contained legitimate secrets the Church did not wish revealed. Still, where was trust and the Christian spirit? He gave a bitter smile, being the last man to ask that. What now? Cancel his plan to see Carlo? He needed to think about that. And seeing Giacomo tomorrow? He needed to think about that too.

After waiting forty minutes in a winding line, he finally cleared passport control, collected his battered and scratched dark blue Delsey suitcase, and took a cab downtown underneath a gray sky, dusk fading fast. His withdrawn manner discouraged conversation and the drive home spent in silence. Garbaldi was startled when the cab pulled onto the sparsely lit Via Giovanni Nicotera and slid to a stop next to his apartment building. He paid the driver, who immediately got out and retrieved the case from the trunk, leaving it on the sidewalk. Garbaldi watched the cab drive off, picked up the Delsey and walked to the glassed entrance. He typed the access code into the security pad and the door clicked open.

After a warm day and being closed for a week, his apartment stuffy. He quickly opened the window to let in fresh air. The surrounding red-tiled rooftops glinted under yellow street lighting, pale compared to the city's glare around him. He understood Rome. Despite its failings, it was far preferable to Cairo's stifling pollution, incessant noise, milling populace and mad traffic. His third visit to Egypt, he could still not get himself inured to the squalor and poverty under which most of the population suffered; definitely a different world compared to the evident material luxury of Italy. He could not reconcile seeing children in the streets, dressed in rags, scrounging through rubbish, with the pomp and opulence of the Church. *If you don't have charity, you are nothing*, the words came to him unbidden. After watching the city for a few moments, not actually seeing it, he turned and picked up the remote phone from its wall mounting. He sat down at the small kitchen table and dialed. Carlo answered after three rings.

"Dr. Noris."

"*Come sta*, my friend," Garbaldi said heavily, his mood introspective and gloomy.

"Ah, my favorite cardinal! I planned to call you, but you obviously managed to escape the clutches of the mad Arabs. How was Cairo? You still coming over?"

"Cairo was bewildering as always and I'll tell you all about it. And yes, I'll be flying out on Saturday morning as planned."

"Glad to hear it. Paulini, you sound tired. Is anything the matter?"

"It's been a long day and I just got home. Flying would not be so bad if they could figure a way to dispense with all that Immigration and Customs nonsense."

Noris chuckled. "I know what you mean. They seem to be making things more difficult all the time while telling us it's for our protection. You can't take more than a hundred mills of liquid on board for fear it might be an explosive, but you can tuck away two liters into your luggage. Go figure."

Garbaldi sympathized, but this was hardly the time to discuss airport security. Anyway, he wanted a shower and something to eat, perhaps a quiet dinner at Torano's? He hadn't had dinner there in a while and felt like indulging, not in the mood to cook.

"Carlo, we have a small development."

"Oh?"

"Monsignor Giacomo found out about the papyrus and I'm ordered to see him."

"Don't tell me! They bugged your phone after all?" Noris sounded outraged and Garbaldi grinned.

"Nothing so sinister, but close. They saw the document scanner-generated email when I scanned the tractate."

"I cannot believe it! They're checking scanner emails? Giacomo must be obsessed."

"Carlo, I'm not worried, not much anyway. If Giacomo talked to Albani, the worst they can do is haul me before the Congregation for the Doctrine of the Faith for breach of procedure. That might not be so comfortable for me and I could find myself on the short end of the career straw, but I doubt it'll come to that. Scanning a piece of papyrus and emailing myself a copy is not a crime. I've done it before."

"This isn't an ordinary piece of paper and we both know it. Besides, you stole the thing."

"They don't know that. They may suspect it, but they don't have any proof, and I've got the thing in a safe place."

"They don't need proof to act, you fool. Giacomo must know what disclosure of the papyrus would mean. He'll take steps, or Cardinal Albani will."

"You don't mean The Entity?"

"Damn right I do."

"But I don't intend to publish. At least I don't think so. I only want to date the thing before making up my mind what to do."

"They don't know that."

"You're making too much of this. Look, if they were after me, they would have grabbed me the minute I stepped off the aircraft."

"Ah, you still refuse to take them seriously. They haven't grabbed you because they're not sure what you're doing. Ordering you to see Giacomo gives everybody a chance to settle what could be a simple misunderstanding."

"Carlo, listen to me. Even if The Entity is involved, once I'm in Boston, I'll be beyond their reach."

"You hope!"

Garbaldi was silent for a few seconds. "You're right. Given this development, you may want to reconsider the whole thing. I would never forgive myself if something were to happen to you."

"Back out? Not on your life, but you listen to me, Paulini. This could still turn ugly. Perhaps you're the one who should think about backing out. Give them the papyrus and walk away while you still can. Tell them you took the thing home to study it. They can't prove otherwise and you'll be in the clear. Think of your future!"

"It's a little late for that, don't you think? And I have thought about my future. I cannot pretend I didn't see it and simply walk away. This is no longer merely about me. You understand, I've got to see it through."

Noris sighed. "I understand all too well, my friend. I've been a driven man myself. You intend to see Giacomo?"

"Are you kidding? Tomorrow, I'll dig in and pretend I'm not home…in case someone comes knocking. By the time he realizes I'm not coming, I'll be over the Atlantic."

"Wish you luck. See you in a couple of days, then. Paulini, you take care of yourself, hear?"

"With God's help, we'll see it through, Carlo."

"Yeah, but keep in mind that God helps those who help themselves."

When Carlo hung up, Garbaldi shook his head at his friend's irreverent attitude, dwelling on the possible consequences of his decision. In the end, he shrugged. Whatever Giacomo knew or suspected, fundamentally, nothing had changed, not where it mattered. He had come too far to give up now. Staring at the phone in his hand, he fervently hoped his resolve was not misplaced—or his faith. What he contemplated was dangerous at so many levels, not least of all to his soul.

He had already obtained a BA, majoring in Middle Eastern anthropology and history, before embarking on his theological studies for the Licentiate of Sacred Theology and the priesthood. Ancient religions had always fascinated him, as well as the enormous influence they exerted on the formation of today's three dominant faiths. At the time, it seemed a natural progression into priesthood. His decision delighted his aging mother who always hinted rather loudly to everybody in sight that her little Paulini was destined to serve in Christ's footsteps.

His much more down-to-earth father, on the other hand, thought it a wasted life of ease on other people's labor and misguided charity. A building construction site manager, he had a tough outlook on life and people. His father would have made a great Roman Centurion. According to his unshakable belief, a man should struggle for his bread and provide a roof for his family, not spend his time in idleness pretending to serve a higher calling. God only needed reverence, not a self-serving Church. Perhaps he had something there. His father also maintained it was a woman's place to be at home, rear the children and look after her husband. Given today's turnstile marriages and divorce rate, that may not have been such a bad philosophy. His father had not protested when Garbaldi announced his intention to pursue the priesthood, but he didn't have to. His deep scowl and heavy frown were clear marks of disappointment and profound displeasure. But then, his father had always considered him his mother's boy. Garbaldi still found it hard to admit that entering the seminary perhaps had more to do with meeting a mother's expectations than a result of true calling. He *had* felt a calling, in the beginning anyway.

It came back to him as though it were yesterday. Already into his second year of BA studies when he wandered into the old Chiesa Nuova church during one warm, cozy summer evening. He could never explain what brought him there on that fateful day, but he could not deny the compulsion. It was before Mass and the church still empty, his footsteps echoing on the marble floor as he walked in. Taking a seat in a rear pew, his gaze wandered over the lofted ceiling and settled dreamily on the altar, not seeing it, letting his mind wander. After a while, he felt prickly warmth suffuse his body and his skin tingled like he glowed. On the cross above the altar, the drained body of Christ pulsed and brightened. Garbaldi stared at the figure and felt a connection with the thorn-crowned face. He knew then what he had to do.

Looking back on it, that moment seemed to have happened to someone else, in some other realty. Perhaps he should have a sober talk with his old man. His father knew how to cut through trivia and lay bare the problem.

He slowly replaced the phone in its cradle.

* * *

Peroni waited patiently as the elevator lurched to a stop and the single doorway sighed open. He turned left and walked casually down the dimly lit corridor, checking apartment numbers. At 608, he paused, extracted a lock pick out of his pocket and slid it into the keyhole. After a little fiddling, the lock clicked. He reached into another pocket, dragged out a pair of fine brown calf leather driving gloves and pulled them on. Only then did he grasp the door handle.

The single bedroom apartment modest, but tastefully furnished. He could not expect Father Reoni to do better on a Vatican stipend. Working quickly, he kicked in the 81cm plasma TV screen and ripped out the DVD player/burner out of its rack. He pulled out drawers from the TV stand, giving the contents a cursory glance. The bedroom received similar treatment, but there, he found 360 Euros in a plastic sandwich container. He pocketed the money and left other contents scattered on the floor. He hardly expected to find anything in the kitchen and didn't. The last thing he did was return to the living room and throw the LED screen off the computer table. Before doing the same thing to the tower PC, he delicately pulled at the main power cord. There was a yellow flash within the box, followed by a smell of burnt wiring, the short effectively cooking the motherboard and the hard drive, wiping any stored data. He then heaved the tower to the carpeted floor.

He sprawled into a settee facing the TV, took out a Beretta 86, 9mm semi-automatic, screwed on the silencer, and chambered a round. Holding the weapon, he rested it on his lap and closed his eyes. Nothing more to be done except wait for his target to show up. He didn't know how long he waited, but probably less than twenty minutes. When he heard a key being inserted into the lock, his eyes snapped open and he lifted the weapon, adrenalin shooting into his bloodstream.

The door opened and Father Reoni walked in. He automatically reached for the light switch mounted on the left wall and flipped it on. Closing the door after him, he took a step in when Peroni shot him in the chest, the silencer making a soft *thuft*. He controlled his instinct to make it a double tap, but that would not be consistent with a break-in. Reoni looked surprised, staggered and folded, dead before he hit the floor. Peroni quickly turned him around, making it appear he was shot while opening the door. He rummaged through the pockets, extracted forty-eight Euros and some change.

He unscrewed the silencer and slid it into his right pocket. He slipped the automatic into a shoulder holster on his left side. Without looking back, he opened the door, stepped into the empty corridor and closed the door after him.

* * *

From his seat, Garbaldi looked down with interest as the lumbering Boeing 747 extended flaps, sank through Boston's blanket of brown smog, and lined up to land at the General Edward Lawrence Logan International airport. The city below, divided by snaking waterways, could have been anywhere. From the air, they all looked the same, a sprawl that ate up the landscape. At least the flight was on time. Getting up at three a.m. to shower, clean up and check his documents one last time, then calling a cab for the twenty-minute drive to Fiumicino airport by four-thirty a drag, especially after having come from Cairo the day before. Cairo had been a short hop home, less than four hours, and not too much of a strain. The Boston leg far more taxing, and he longed for landing, a luxurious shower and sleep. With a short layover in Amsterdam's Schiphol airport, the twelve-and-a-half hour packed flight had become weary even as the aircraft headed toward the northern Atlantic. He could have taken a direct flight, but the cost too prohibitive, at least for him. His seat felt like a concrete slab before they touched down in Amsterdam and had not gotten softer afterward.

Doing laundry, repacking and going over his notes, his phone went off twice yesterday, and around three-thirty, someone banged loudly on his apartment door. Garbaldi didn't have to guess who, waiting with baited breath for a pair of footsteps to recede. He worried all day that Allard or his men would break in and haul him away. A senseless fear, but it haunted him and made the day one prolonged mental torture. He had not slept well last night and having to get up early this morning didn't help.

As the 747 sank along its glidepath, wings level, he gave a quick prayer for the safe flight and hopefully, a safe landing. The nose came up a fraction as the aircraft crossed the threshold and the runway suddenly a rushing blur. The wheels touched down with a gentle jolt and the pilot immediately engaged reverse thrust, causing Garbaldi to lean forward slightly. He glanced at his watch: 1:12 p.m. local time. He automatically unbuckled his seatbelt despite the fasten seatbelt sign still being lit. Judging by the clicking noises around him, he was not the only one violating safety procedure. Even though the flight came in on time, it took another eleven minutes to taxi in and park. He didn't look forward to the coming Immigration and Customs formalities. With a seat in row 35, he would at least beat the crush of the flight's other coach passengers.

To his surprise the formalities were mercifully quick, having filled in his green entry card during the flight. He didn't enjoy having his photo and thumbprints taken, but made allowances for the paranoid Americans. He located the baggage carousel for KL1596 and waited stoically for his suitcase to show up. His fellow passengers all had the same look of weary suffering and a desire to get to wherever they were going. The conveyor belt started moving and everyone perked up. It only did two circuits before his worn suitcase tumbled out. He rolled the bag through the Nothing to Declare doorway and was in the United States of America. Technically, he committed a felony by not declaring the papyrus, but the Customs card didn't have a category to cover it. A moot point anyway, imagining all too clearly the reaction from U.S. authorities to the thing and subsequent furor it would cause.

Outside, people waited for arrivals and relatives hugged loved ones. Those without anyone forlornly pushed through the crowd to disappear in pursuit of their particular destinations.

"Paulini!" an excited voice cut through the general noise and Garbaldi eagerly searched for Carlo's face.

Then his friend came and they embraced. Garbaldi found the contact comforting and reassuring. Still holding his shoulders, Carlo stepped back. The warm smile faded and his dark brown eyes probed.

"It's good to see you again after all these years of misspent youth," Noris said in Italian.

"I trust it hasn't all been misspent," Garbaldi admonished in English and Carlo gave a broad grin, revealing even white teeth.

They were both the same height, except that Carlo carried a few extra kilos. His dark olive complexion radiated health, confidence and accomplishment, and Garbaldi was glad. Carlo certainly did not bear the scars of someone haunted, searching for a new faith or someone in danger of losing his soul. Ironically, that had now shifted to him.

"Ah, those were the days. We had fun and we believed. Now, knowledge has robbed us of our innocence." Without being asked, Noris snagged Garbaldi's suitcase and began the brisk trek toward the exit.

Garbaldi somewhat surprised by his friend's somber statement. Given the circumstances of his visit, it rang uncomfortably true. That was Carlo, always on the edge.

"Remember when we crazy-glued Father Calabrini's slippers to the floor?"

Noris chuckled fondly at the memory. "And he failed every one of us at the next exam when no one owned up."

Calabrini was an intolerant, constipated disciplinarian, the very antithesis of what a loving and caring priest should be, hardly a role model. He taught ethics with a strong personal bias and you had to have a ready stack of authoritative references if you wanted to disagree with him. Even then, he tended to be dismissive. Definitely a personality everyone loved to decry, but the practical jokes they pulled on him made up for his abrasive manner.

"A hard man, all right," Garbaldi agreed with a smile. "Anyway, he had it coming."

"Did you confess?" Noris demanded, giving Garbaldi a sidewise look.

"Confess what? We didn't commit any sin. Did you?"

"Hardly! Ah, we enjoyed ourselves there. Wait till I get you home. Then we'll reminisce. How was the flight? You look beat."

"Long, and I am somewhat tired," Garbaldi admitted. "It's early afternoon here, but my body thinks it's already evening. Five-hour difference, remember? And I didn't sleep much last night, expecting to be hauled away at any moment by Archives Security."

Noris laughed and slapped Garbaldi on the shoulder. "That's what a guilty conscience does to you. You hungry? We can stop somewhere if you like."

"Thanks, but I'm okay. They served us lunch on the flight."

"Plastic mush," Carlo snorted derisively.

"It wasn't all bad," Garbaldi said defensively.

And it wasn't. His chicken dish, fried potato cubes and mushrooms, tasty, and the cheesecake dessert delicious. A small bottle of some nameless French red wine complemented the meal nicely. He didn't know why people decried airplane food.

"If you say so. Let me know if you want anything. I have a house in Cambridge. It's close to Harvard, which is convenient, but it's somewhat awkward going to the airport, having to go through downtown and the Ted Williams Tunnel to get to Apple Island. It'll take us about forty minutes to get there. After you freshen up, we've got some serious catching up to do."

"I'm betting that my life is nowhere as interesting as yours," Garbaldi said, amused at his friend's take-charge approach. "From what I remember, you were never a conformist."

Noris gripped Garbaldi's arm hard. "I'm not so sure about that. Damn, but it's good to see you."

Once in the car and out of the multi-level parking lot, Noris drove his brown Pontiac Coupe out of the airport onto the I-90 with confidence and ease, pointing out the sights. Across the harbor, the North Boston skyline a jagged collection of skyscrapers obscured by haze. Garbaldi sat back and relaxed, happy to be with his friend again. They hit the tunnel and everything became dark and noisy. Carlo gave him a quick glance.

"Your research in Cairo, productive?"

"Very, and I have everything I need to finish my book, but it will take a while to consolidate all my notes. To be honest, my mind was preoccupied by something else." Garbaldi didn't have to elaborate. Both knew what that preoccupation was. "I'm still wondering if I did the right thing not reporting the tractate right away."

"They would have buried it and you know it," Noris said firmly. "Or destroyed it more likely. I only have the scanned image you sent me, but I can tell you one thing with certainty. The text is absolutely authentic first century Sahidic, right down to the style of writing, how the characters are formed, even the little idiosyncrasies typical of the period. I'd stake my reputation on it, and believe me, at Harvard, it's pretty high. That's not ego talking either, my friend."

"I know. I've read some of your papers. Your *Coptic Church, the True Faith* was a showstopper. Although I don't believe all of your sacrilegious conclusions."

Noris smirked. "You wouldn't, seeing how your mind is still fettered by Church dogma and its version of history."

"You may have a point," Garbaldi acknowledged candidly. "Fettered or not, I'm trying to get at the truth. No, I didn't mean that. I'm after facts."

"I'm glad you amended that," Noris said seriously, glancing at Garbaldi. "Truth is an agreed opinion, whereas fact is demonstrable, repeatable science. While we're on the subject of science, what do the Vatican powers think of your upcoming thesis? They must be a little ticked off at Roma Tre for agreeing to publish without prior review by the Congregation for the Doctrine of the Faith."

"They already carpeted me about it and I'm required to submit a draft manuscript to them before publication. It changes nothing. They may not like some of the things I'll say on theological grounds, but they'll not be able to deny archeological evidence."

Noris clicked his tongue and shook his head. "Ah, you're being naïve again. Of course they can deny evidence, or ignore it. They've done it before. They will demand that you remove anything that might contradict dogma. If you refuse, they can make your life as a serving priest very difficult. Any career aspirations you may have will effectively be at an end. The best you can look forward to is some quiet rural parish where you'll have plenty of time to contemplate what might have been."

Garbaldi peered at his friend and grinned. "Ignoring your cynicism, that might not be such a bad thing, and you can step off your pulpit now, Father Noris."

"I guess you never lose it, do you?" Noris agreed and snorted. "But seriously, things could get grim for you."

"I've thought about it, a lot. If that's what they want to do, then perhaps I'm not fit to be a priest. Not in their mold anyway. Being with you right now may have set the wheels into motion already."

"Ah, the circle closes. We shouldn't get all morbid, not now. Business will keep until tomorrow."

Easy for Carlo to say, Garbaldi reflected. His friend wasn't the one carrying the burden. Still, he was right. There would be enough time for business later.

Out of the tunnel, the city rose up around them. Garbaldi stretched his legs and watched traffic streaming both ways along I-90. Carlo had to do some tricky maneuvering to get to I-93 and onto Monsignor O'Brien Highway. What struck him was the preponderance of large cars and gas-guzzling four-wheel drives; SUVs they called them here. The Americans have always been in love with their powerful vehicles, so different from the Italians and their efficient little compacts. He tried to visualize a lumbering Cadillac trying to negotiate Rome's congested narrow streets and grinned.

Noris caught him at it and smiled in return. "What's so amusing?"

"Just watching the traffic," Garbaldi said.

"This is a cakewalk. You should see it during rush hour, wall-to-wall cars. Then again, perhaps you don't want to. It can be frustrating. Thankfully, I'm spared that daily nightmare."

"With your semester finished, are you doing any private research?"

Noris smiled. "As a matter of fact, I am. It's called the John the Baptist scroll."

Garbaldi chuckled. "Funny man!"

"Seriously, ever since you emailed me the thing, I couldn't get it out of my hair. Now that you're here, there's nothing stopping us working on it. Damn! You've got me talking business again."

"Sorry about that."

"Yeah. But I do have some pleasant personal news. The University has offered me tenure."

Garbaldi looked at Carlo and noted an expression of intense satisfaction. To be tenured by an institution like Harvard at such a young age, an enviable achievement.

"That *is* great news. It's about time, and you have my warmest congratulations. This calls for a celebration."

Clearly pleased, Noris nodded. "When we get home. Come January, I'll be a full professor at Harvard's Center for Middle Eastern Studies. Provided I don't do anything dumb, like getting mixed up in Vatican intrigues." Noting Garbaldi's look of dismay, he laughed. "Just kidding, my friend."

"You have a low sense of humor, did you know that?" Garbaldi growled, not at all amused. The last thing he wanted was to cause Carlo problems with the university.

"Yeah, so my students tell me. You'll get used to it. They do."

Garbaldi studied his friend. "You still living alone?"

"Still a bachelor," Noris confirmed and cocked his head. "You trying to marry me off to be fruitful and multiply?"

Garbaldi laughed at the notion. "Hey! It's your life. It's just that you don't look like someone who is pining away the hours."

"I didn't know it showed. As a matter of fact, there is someone, an assistant professor at the School of Medicine. She is into applied psychology. We've been seeing each other for a while now."

"She applying some psychology on you?" Garbaldi queried with a raised eyebrow.

"We're just friends," Noris said, but his voice hinted at something more, and Garbaldi was glad for him.

Once they turned off Monsignor O'Brien Highway and entered the old part of Boston along Cambridge Street, everything narrowed and sidewalks were lined with birch, maple and elm. The colonial architecture gave the mostly terrace buildings a pleasing character. Garbaldi watched with interest as Noris steered the car past elegant stately homes and small apartment buildings. No one seemed to be about.

"During the semester, the place is packed," Noris commented, "but right now, everyone's fled for their vacations, except those attending summer sessions or remedial classes."

He rounded a corner, turned around and parked before a red brick terrace. Creepers covered the entire frontage. Moss hid in corners of speckled gray-black tar shingles.

"Welcome to my home, Father Garbaldi," he said simply and unbuckled his seatbelt.

"Wow, that's not bad," Garbaldi murmured, studying the old house.

"It's a quiet neighborhood and I like it." Noris got out and walked to the rear of the car.

Garbaldi stepped out, stretched his arms, and slammed the door shut. Standing there, he breathed deeply of the fragrant air. Warm and quiet, the sun felt good on his face. A couple of sparrows chirped on the sidewalk and flew off. A gray squirrel peered at him, twitched its tail and scampered up an elm.

"Do you own this?"

"Every brick," Noris said proudly as he pulled the suitcase from the trunk. "I'm still paying in installments, property values in Boston are murder, but when the world financial system melted down in 2008, I picked this up for half of what it was worth a year before. An elderly couple just finished renovating it, got into a liquidity squeeze, and had to sell. I know all this as I rented a room upstairs before they started work."

"And how far are you from Harvard?"

"A six minute drive. I've been thanking God ever since this thing fell into my lap. If I ever leave Harvard, it will still be a great investment."

"And the elderly couple?" Garbaldi asked as he followed Carlo to the front door.

"Doing fine. I took out a loan when money was still available and paid cash on the spot. The bank didn't see me as a risk. Would you believe it?"

"Careful, Carlo. Your halo is showing."

Noris laughed, opened the door wide and pushed the suitcase against the wall. "We'll take care of that later," he said briskly and walked through a double sliding doorway on his right. "Your room is upstairs, first door on the right. It has its own bathroom, so I don't have to worry seeing your naked butt. My den," he said expansively, waving an arm. "Take a seat and I'll fix us a drink. You're still a bourbon man?"

"Still, and thanks," Garbaldi said and walked into the spacious, tidy living room.

Noris disappeared through another doorway, and from the layout inside, the kitchen. The 'den' had tall, double windows that reached to about thirty centimeters below the ceiling. Polished oak flooring glinted in the afternoon sunshine. Directly in front of him, open bookshelves framed a large flat screen TV, surround system speakers, a DVD and CD player. An open fireplace stood tucked neatly into a corner of the kitchen wall. A two-person sofa and a soft leather chair guarded a wooden coffee table. Looking at the comfortable layout, Garbaldi raised an eyebrow. His friend had clearly done well for himself. An associate professor's salary probably paid Carlo something like ninety-five thousand a year and the advances on his books helped maintain this. Not having a family didn't hurt either. A far cry from his own humble rented apartment.

Noris walked in carrying two crystal tumblers with ice. He held one out to Garbaldi, who took it and raised it in a salute.

"To our yesterdays."

"To our tomorrows," Noris replied seriously and they clicked glasses. After twirling the ice and taking a sip, he eased himself into the leather chair, obviously his favorite, and waited for his friend to take the sofa.

Stefan Vučak

Garbaldi sat down, gave a contented grunt, and took another pull of whiskey. Smooth and went down like oil. He nodded and glanced around the room.

"This is nice, Carlo."

"It's comfortable. You sure you don't want anything to eat? I had a casserole done this morning. It won't take a minute to bring it to a simmer."

"Thank you, but I'm still digesting my airplane lunch."

"In that case, drink up. On Monday, we'll go down to the nuclear physics lab and run the tests. Allowing an hour or so for preparation, the tests themselves will take a little while. We won't have the results for another twelve hours after that."

"At the lab, no one can see the entire papyrus sheet," Garbaldi warned.

"Not a problem. It's all arranged. Like I said, I know the director and he'll be supervising the whole thing himself. Besides, both of us will be hovering over his shoulder to make sure nothing goes wrong."

"Sounds good. What did you tell him I had? He must be curious."

"He is, and I told him he'll get an exclusive from you before you publish. Academics have done this type of thing before and it's nothing unusual."

"And how much will the test itself cost?"

"For you, I'm running a special. Nothing."

Garbaldi sat up. "Now just a minute. If you—"

"Paulini, this is covered by my grant. It doesn't cost me anything either."

"I did bring money, you know," Garbaldi protested, uncomfortable at being treated like a charity case.

"And I can imagine how long it took you to save it," Noris quipped. "It's legitimate research, my friend. Besides, you're not getting this service entirely free. I want my name with yours when you publish. You will publish, won't you?"

In the academic world, writing papers and getting published was everything. Publish or perish, the old adage said, something Garbaldi knew well, even though not directly subject to it. His output woefully inadequate, but after all, he was a priest, not a full-time academic. He lifted his tumbler and nodded.

"We'll publish. But I thought you said you didn't want to get involved in murky Vatican intrigues?"

"Are you kidding? For a paper that will rock the world? We'll be famous forever."

"Infamous, more likely," Garbaldi drawled and drained the last of his bourbon. "Excellent whiskey, just what the doctor ordered." He searched his friend's honest eyes and extended a hand across the coffee table. "I cannot tell you how much your unreserved support means to me, Carlo. After all the years that we've been apart…"

"Tomorrow, after you're rested, and take as much time sleeping in as you want, we're not on a schedule, I want to take a look at the original tractate. Then we'll talk." Noris clasped the offered hand between both of his and smiled warmly. "We should collaborate like this more often. If the Vatican ever gets too uncomfortable, Harvard could use a man like you. Now, tell me how you found the papyrus. I want to know everything."

Chapter Three

"The first target has been eliminated, Your Eminence," Peroni said coldly and pushed a folded copy of the *Il Manifesto* across Cardinal Belconi's desk. He sat down without waiting for an invitation and crossed his legs. Even in a chair, he projected coiled power ready to be unleashed.

Belconi frowned at this impertinence and glanced at the paper. At the bottom of page four, a small column announced the wanton murder of Father Estonio Reoni, a case of apparent vandalism and robbery. The column went on to decry lack of security in the apartment building and others in the northern Prati district. The columnist hoped this occurrence of yet another senseless death would prompt the authorities to take action.

He didn't need to read further. He had seen the piece already in the *Il Messagero* and watched a brief thirty-second clip during breakfast news. His black eyes gave nothing away as he regarded his visitor. He could have used one of the reliable Knights of Malta or Jesuit Order operatives for the job, but he did not want more people involved than absolutely necessary. In his opinion, too many were involved already. Besides, the Society of Jesus members were fanatics, undesirable meddlers. Their maxim, 'The end justifies the means', extreme even for his taste. Ever since its sanction by Pope Paul III in 1540 as 'a new battalion in the spiritual army of the Catholic Church', the Jesuits had enjoyed a turbulent history.

Meant to be a spiritual order, its Spanish founder, Ignatius Loyola, took its charter as an army literally. During the war against Protestant Reformation, assistance from Jesuit knights was accepted, but with their insidious and ongoing program to usurp local authority, Rome had enough. In 1773, Pope Clement XIV abolished the Jesuit Order, citing interference in secular affairs and internal administration of governments. Following the Papal bull, fifty European countries, England and America, expelled the order. Only a first wave of expulsions. In 1818, the Society was again banned from Belgium and the Netherlands for undermining the governments. In 1901, they were expelled from Portugal for the third time. Since then, England had expelled them a total of seven times and France nine, but the Society always managed to work its way back into the social fabric, a product of fortuitous legislation that protected churches. The Jesuit Order today was more sophisticated in applying its 'Articles of Faith', but Belconi knew they had never abandoned their Constitution and objective to make the pontiff the spiritual and temporal ruler on Earth. God help everyone if they were to succeed.

Spiritual failings or not, the Jesuits were efficient, but using them also meant owing a favor, something he did not want hanging over him. They *always* got their money back. With an outsider, strictly a business transaction without any accompanying emotional baggage.

Sometimes, though, he did not have a choice, and this was one such instance.

Of course, none of this would have been necessary if that fool Giacomo had simply brought Garbaldi in. Now, the young priest had slipped through their fingers, leaving a dangerous mess to be cleaned up. Worse, he wasn't advised that Garbaldi was gone until Monday, thinking all along that Marati had the matter in hand. His fault, in fact. He should have kept a tight rein on the whole business himself, a lesson he thought he knew.

At least one potential security leak was now plugged.

"The balance will be paid into your Swiss account today. Computer records?"

"His PC is destroyed and any data it may have contained is wiped," Peroni said tonelessly.

"Satisfactory. Now, on a more delicate matter of Father Garbaldi…"

"Apart from not keeping his appointment with Monsignor Giacomo on Friday, Garbaldi made no attempt to cover his tracks, Your Eminence," Peroni said, reciting bare facts.

His dark eyes were chilly, devoid of light, as was his expression. Of medium build, the noticeable things about him were his weightlifter shoulders and arms. Every time he moved, muscles rippled beneath his navy, lightly striped jacket.

"And?" Belconi prompted.

"He landed at Boston's Logan airport on Saturday afternoon and disappeared. Tracking him down took better part of a day as I had no leads, except for an email he sent to a Dr. Carlo Noris, an associate professor at Harvard."

"And you found that how?"

"Accessing Garbaldi's email service provider's database."

Belconi did not want to know how that was done. "You checked his apartment and computer?"

"Nothing…in both."

"Go on."

"Once I had that information, locating him was relatively routine. All I need now is your authorization, Your Eminence, and I'm ready to commence the second phase of the operation. I have a direct flight booked for Boston leaving tomorrow at ten a.m."

"You have it. As usual, one hundred thousand American dollars will be deposited into your account—"

"For each target," Peroni prompted and Belconi nodded, annoyed at having to be reminded. With mercenaries, always money first.

"Of course. Half will be paid today. Recovery or destruction of the papyrus will earn a bonus of fifty thousand dollars. Destruction should only be considered as a last resort. Recovery is by far the more important. A further fifty thousand will be paid on erasure of any and all computer records made by Father Garbaldi and Dr. Noris."

"That might not be possible or easily done, Your Eminence."

"Make it possible, my son. That's why the bonus." Belconi reached into his drawer, rummaged around and held out a card. "Your contact in Boston. Use him. Whatever you need to get this closed, your contact will get it for you. When the operation is successfully concluded, you will notify me in the usual way. The balance and bonuses will then be paid."

"Understood," Peroni said and stood up. "There is one other matter…"

"Yes?"

"You should consider a diplomatic option for my extraction should I be apprehended by American authorities."

"Are you out of your mind? The Church cannot afford to be implicated. You're being paid, and paid well, for your work. It's adequate compensation for any risk you might face."

"Your Eminence, I won't be hanged on a cross of expediency singing glad hosannas merely to protect you or the Church. Unless I have your word that you will extract me, we have no deal. In case you harbor any thoughts of reneging if I need to call on you, I'll divulge everything to the local authorities."

Belconi placed both hands on his desk and slowly rose. "You wouldn't dare!"

Peroni stared at him, his eyes hard. Belconi knew he could not afford to falter now. This job had to be treated as a simple business transaction like any other. One sign of weakness before this repulsive man and he was dead.

Belconi didn't want to use the man, but he had a time constraint. In the end, he broke eye contact. He sat down and cleared his throat.

"Very well. You have my word," the cardinal said harshly and nodded.

Peroni didn't look fooled, certain the matter would come up again—once he got the job done—and he was right.

"Thank you. If that's all…"

"Go with God, my son."

Peroni grimaced. "I am one of his instruments, is that it?"

"God's will is done in many ways," Belconi retorted sternly, his revulsion clearly written on his face.

"And rest assured it shall be, Your Eminence." Peroni ignored the extended hand and ring to be kissed, and walked out.

* * *

With barely a glance at the dried up, prim matron clicking away at her keyboard in the reception office, Peroni marched to the door, opened it, and slammed it shut after him, glad to be out of there. Holier-than-thou hypocrites, all of them. Ready enough with their money when they wanted a messy job done, which otherwise offended their starched sensibilities, but they never let you forget that they've been somewhat tarnished by having to step down to his level. God's will indeed. He was an instrument, all right, but not God's. Like any clandestine intelligence service, The Entity regularly used external floaters, part-time assassins, in execution of covert black operations. After all, it was not the CIA with limitless resources.

As Peroni walked down the echoing corridor, he wondered what the papyrus contained to make its disposal worth fifty thousand, three hundred actually. He might be curious, but his only concern was the probability factor of carrying out the mission successfully. Worrying about the why of it would only impede his efficiency and he didn't care to know.

He understood men like Belconi, unscrupulous operators who cloaked their shady activities under the umbrella of Church work. Colonel Rozari had fitted the same mold. The nature of the job. He didn't know much about the current head of The Entity and didn't particularly care to. Under Monsignor Luigi Poggi, in charge of all Vatican espionage services during the reign of Pope Paul II, Monsignor Belconi had run the counterespionage arm, the *Sodalitium Pianum*. In 2005, Pope Benedict XVI appointed him to head The Entity. He knew something of the Vatican's clandestine intelligence dealings and the caliber of men who carried them out. Security services world round attracted certain types of men and The Entity not any different; perhaps more vile as it hid behind black robes and a red hat. To kiss Belconi's ring would be the ultimate in hypocrisy. These days, Peroni did not concern himself over the whys or the morality of his work. He did once, but then, he'd also been young and idealistic.

From a peasant background, his parents ran a sprawling fifty hectare farm among the rolling hills of Tuscany, trained at the prestigious Accademia Militare at Modena, his dissertation paper on rising Muslim terrorism as an economic weapon, brought him to the attention of the Italian Military Intelligence and Security Service, the *Servizio per le Informazioni e la Sicurezza Militare*. Although not serving in a regular Army unit, he still underwent rigorous platoon and company leadership courses, coupled with intelligence and counterintelligence indoctrination. He became a troubleshooter, quickly gaining a reputation for quietly handling tricky assignments. In Iraq, SISMI, his own outfit, with an Iranian backed Shi'ia counterinsurgency group, betrayed him while delivering cases of M-16A2 automatic rifles and ammunition to Sunni fighters. The whole sordid ops had nothing to do with helping the Sunnis. The Americans wanted a level of corrupt Sunni leadership eliminated, and having the Shi'ia do the dirty work for them seemed an ideal way to go about it. It's how their thinking operated.

When the Shi'ia sprung their ambush, the Americans set off theirs. Three Apache helicopter gunships swooped in and sent volleys of Hellfire guided missiles into the buildings, followed by strafing runs. Those who survived the initial attack were gunned down mercilessly. By chance, Peroni and the Sunni warlord chose the same bombed building to hide in. The Sunni's shot missed, Peroni's didn't. Before the Muslim died, Peroni demanded to know who betrayed him. Perhaps the warlord figured neither would be getting out of there alive and saw no reason to hold back. He may even have thought he inflicted torture on Peroni by giving him a name. He died with a smile on his bearded face.

When the troop helicopters landed, soldiers spilled out and fanned to search the smoking remains for survivors. He emerged from his hideout, hands raised, blood dripping from a gash on his left wrist, and was immediately clubbed unconscious. It took a while to verify his identity. In the end, the Americans let him go, but only after Colonel Rozari from SISMI himself intervened—the name given to him by the dying Sunni leader.

For his part in the action, Peroni received promotion to major and given a decoration. However, he was no longer the trusting captain willing to risk everything on a glib explanation and an order. His world had darkened and so had he. From that moment, he wrote his own rules. Determined to revenge himself, he cornered Rozari right in the secured part of Baghdad. He even told the colonel why before sending a bullet into his heart, but it brought him little pleasure. Then he resigned his commission, citing psychiatric reasons. The Army felt real bad about letting him go, offering him a posting in Rome, but eventually they did when he remained unmoved.

With his special training and intelligence connections, he became a gun for hire. It did not matter for which side, as there were no sides. Bitter experience had taught him that everything could be rationalized. He simply skipped that step. Anyway, it was always about power or money, on a personal, corporate or national level. It made no difference. Once *Sodalitium Pianum* contacted him to remove a banker who threatened to expose the Vatican Bank's Colombian money laundering operation, his conversion complete. When the Holy See itself sanctioned terminations, the games others played were reduced to irrelevancy.

What he did was not a bad life. It paid reasonably well, which enabled him to live comfortably and indulge in some of life's luxuries and pleasures. He lived alone, studied the arts, music and history, and how to more efficiently carry out his job. When he wanted a woman, there were plenty who were available to satisfy his needs. His belief now only in himself, his precision, and mastery of the craft. So far, his skill had never failed him. Sooner or later, though, he knew he would have to retire or be retired by somebody else. Statistics always caught up with you if one overstayed playing the game. He had heard of colleagues, if that was the right word, who faded out of sight through one means or another, determined to avoid the same fate. He still had plenty of time before he would seriously consider bowing out. Perhaps those others also thought the same way and pushed it beyond prudence, secure in their own infallibility. The idea brought a wry grin of amusement to his face.

As he walked through the Porta di Sant' Anna, the bright afternoon made everything alive and exciting, his mind automatically went over details that would not only ensure satisfactory completion of his contract, but also his extraction. He reached into his jacket pocket and switched off the composite plastic, spring-powered mini recorder. He only needed to leave the tape with a trusted source, just in case. Mercurio Peroni never left anything to chance.

* * *

"Look at it!" Noris declared as he tapped the printout with the back of his hand, his face radiating excitement. "The papyrus is dated at 68 CE, plus or minus five years, and the text is right on 69 CE. Paulini, my boy, you've struck it big here, real big. You know that."

"I don't know whether to be relieved or disappointed," Garbaldi said morosely, his expression glum.

"Hey! Why the long face? I'd have thought you'd be jubilant."

Garbaldi picked up the papyrus sheet off the coffee table and scanned the ancient text; so much potential for harm in so few seemingly innocent words. What right did he have to set into motion something that could have a profound impact on the entire world, the faithful and nonbelievers alike? But he had wrestled with that question already and made his decision. The tests only confirmed the validity of his choice.

"I'm still wondering whether to take the matter to Cardinal Albani and let proper Church authority deal with it."

"Take off your white collar, Father Garbaldi, and face reality," Noris told him sternly. "You came to see me to help you determine the authenticity of the tractate. We've done that. Our next action is clear. We write a paper and figure out how best to publish. If you had any doubts, you wouldn't be here now. I know you. You cannot sit on this and you know it. So quit your breast-beating and let's get on with it."

"You're right, of course. And you do know me," Garbaldi acknowledged with a wan smile. "But doing this, as a priest, I have betrayed the Church. That doesn't rest easy on me, Carlo, no matter how much I believe in the righteousness of my cause."

"I know, Paulini, I know," Noris said more gently. "My own confrontation with Church dogma equally wrenching. Being the man you are, I would be disappointed had you felt and acted otherwise."

Garbaldi sighed and wiped his brow. "I don't know who I am anymore," he whispered tragically. "Am I a priest with a passion for anthropology, which has caused me to doubt my faith, or am I a scientist who should never have become a priest?"

Noris nodded. "I see the internal struggle on your face and sympathize completely. It is terrifying having to confront one's demons, but they had to be faced some time or there will never be peace. Knowing it doesn't help much, though, but I suspect you already have your answer. Your problem is that you don't want to accept reality, as it would mean stepping out of that comfortable, sheltered life you've been hiding in, and the world outside is cold and unforgiving."

Garbaldi laughed without mirth. "You don't go out of your way much to make this easier, do you? But I don't resent the truth of your words and I'm not feeling sorry for myself either. Well, perhaps a little."

"If you are, there is plenty of bourbon to exorcise it," Noris said wearing a broad grin. "Seriously, when you get back, expect an explosion. Albani won't be pleased with you for disobeying Giacomo and fleeing the country."

"I know. It's not going to be pleasant, but with the papyrus safely locked up at Harvard, they won't be able to do a thing."

"I wouldn't be so sure about that. Once they realize you're likely to publish, they'll be after you. They'll be after both of us. We're playing for high stakes here, my boy, and you know it."

"You're just being paranoid," Garbaldi growled.

"Perhaps, but you know what they say. Even if you're paranoid, it doesn't mean they're not after you."

"Fool! About our paper. How do we pitch this, and are you sure Harvard will publish? This is not something I want dragged through a peer review process. We'd be plagiarized and damn the furor afterward."

"Good point, but Harvard will publish, trust me. When Professor Renauld sees what we have—"

"Your faculty director may go for it, but once Harvard editors see this, they might decide it's too hot for such a respectable institution. They'll know it's controversial."

"Okay, let's say they don't publish. As a last resort, we can release it ourselves on the Internet and newspapers. Let's not get ourselves tangled up before we have to. As for the paper, I'm thinking of a straightforward dissertation. We put in elements of early Christian writing, destruction of nonconformist gospels, throw in existing Bible verses where John the Baptist questions Jesus as the leader and then we tack on your tractate. It will be all solid, verifiable material."

"Except for the tractate," Garbaldi added.

"Not after we add the dating data."

"Harvard might not like it having been used like this."

Noris waved a hand in dismissal. "Nothing to worry about there. They've done anonymous tests before. Plenty of archeologists and anthropologists want validation before rushing to publication to avoid possible subsequent exposure and ridicule."

"Sounds like you've been there yourself once or twice," Garbaldi said with a twinkle in his eyes.

"Believe it. It only takes one careless mistake to ruin a reputation and a rising academic career, my friend. I've had my detractors. Some of them were reasoned and their comments well researched, but for the most part, simple professional jealousy, or annoyance at having holes poked through pet theories. Don't tell me you haven't come across this yourself?"

"Sadly, I have."

"I know you have. Your *Ancient Eastern Religions and their Influence on Early Christianity* raised more than one scholarly eyebrow."

"And the Vatican's," Garbaldi added with a grin. "You know, now that I think about it, shortly after its release, I found myself cataloging the Secret Archives."

"You see? They punish and segregate what they don't like. Didn't the Congregation try to stop the second printing?"

"That they did, but Roma Tre stood by me. I'm glad I studied with them."

Noris snapped his fingers. "Tre, now there is an idea. If Harvard refuses to publish, perhaps Tre will."

"That *is* an idea," Garbaldi mused in appreciation. "But like you said, we're not there yet. About tomorrow…"

"It's all set. Renauld is all clued in and you'll be able to look over our faculty at will. When he learned you were here, he was most anxious to talk to you, as are some of my colleagues, at least those still at campus. Many of them took off for the summer to pursue individual research. There'll be some gnashing of teeth when they learn they've missed you. You've got quite a reputation, you know; a priest and an acknowledged scholar whose academic works haven't been tainted by his sectarian beliefs."

"Now you're making me blush."

"Seriously. Your output is respected, even though not everyone agrees with your conclusions. Renauld has organized lunch and the afternoon is yours."

"Thanks, I appreciate it."

"You'll find Vince somewhat standoffish and intimidating at first, but he's actually a nice guy once you get through his shell. Don't let his manner put you off."

Garbaldi smiled as he pictured a stern, white-haired, frowning figure glowering at his students over a lectern. "I'll try not to."

"Great! And while we're talking of lunch, let's have ours. I promise not to submit you to another of my culinary experiments."

"Hey! Did I ever complain?"

"Never mind. There is a particularly fine Indian restaurant just around the corner on Hampshire. Unless you prefer Italian?"

"Indian is fine with me."

"Good. Afterward, we can talk about our paper in detail. You're still determined to leave on Saturday?"

"I must, Carlo. I'd love to stay longer and sightsee, but I need to go through my research notes and finish the book before September. I'm fighting a deadline, which I'm afraid I'll probably miss. You know how it is."

Noris sighed. "Unfortunately, I do. Well, if that's how it's got to be…We'll have to agree how to correspond. I wouldn't use your computer at home. Get a free Gmail account and use an Internet café whenever possible."

"You *are* being paranoid," Garbaldi chided, "but I'll humor you. I'll use Tre's facilities under an alias. I already have one, a safety against inquisitive faculty members. You must have something like that yourself."

"Better believe it. In our business, you cannot trust anyone." Noris clapped his hands and stood up. "Right! Let's get lunch."

* * *

"It's Peroni. Are you secure?"

"Secure," the American contact responded.

"I'm on a Delta Air Lines flight DL8120 due at Logan International at one-fifteen p.m. Meet me."

"Everything you asked for is waiting for you, Mr. Peroni," the voice answered, a subordinate talking to his superior.

"Surveillance?"

"A watch is keeping an eye on the residence at all times. Confirm two occupants."

"Don't let your teams be noticed," Peroni warned, wary of having to rely on hired help, preferring to work alone. The more people involved, the greater the risk someone would screw up, compromising the entire op.

"My men know what they're doing," the voice answered primly. "And it's not a hands on surveillance."

Peroni did not care what it was as long as done right. He could not afford to worry about wounded sensibilities, not when he could be placing his life on the line, or worse—capture and incarceration. He figured he had a certain out for that one. Even if Belconi baulked at a diplomatic option to extract him, revealing the existence of the taped conversation, to be released should something unpleasant happen to him, Peroni felt certain his return to Italy would be affected with a minimum of official entanglements. He should have asked the cardinal for a diplomatic passport, that would have been best, but again, not enough time to arrange that; something to keep in mind for future operations perhaps. At any rate, he would renew his current passport once he got home, like always. Not wise advertising to everybody where he had been. He firmly believed a person could never have too much insurance.

"Very well, I shall see you tomorrow," Peroni said and switched off his BlackBerry cellphone. He appreciated he ran a slight risk using a cellular phone. The Italian domestic Intelligence and Democratic Security Service, *Servizio per le Informazioni e la Sicurezza Democratica*, SISDE, routinely recorded all electronic communication made by visitors and the blissfully ignorant citizens. The telco providers were obliged to disclose the GSM encryption key to them—all in the name of public safety, of course, citing the standard line that if you did nothing wrong, you had nothing to fear—always a good precursor to a police state. In his case, the risk of an intercept almost negligible. There were no trigger keywords to alert filtering computers to get a human analyst involved, and he had an additional scrambler application loaded on his cellphone. Once in the States, though, he would need to be extra careful not to alert NSA's monitoring network.

As long as he stayed in the anonymity of millions of daily messages the NSA computers routinely processed, he should be relatively safe.

Although late afternoon, he had no trouble picking up a cab to Nomentano where he owned a comfortable two-bedroom apartment. He had plenty of time to rest and get ready for the morning's nine-hour non-stop flight. He would carry a briefcase and garment bag only. The briefcase simply to maintain appearances. It only had a John Grisham novel, in English, if anyone got curious, and some toiletries. Except for the handles, both were thoroughly wiped for fingerprints. Traveling business class would avoid the check-in crush, something he detested, but could not always avoid.

With the sun low in the sky, he did some warming up exercises and then practiced his karate and aikido moves. Loose and comfortable, he took a brisk jog around the Piazza di Siena. A shower, followed by a shot of ice-cold aquavit, he dressed conservatively and strolled to Gabrielo's for a quiet dinner.

After a refreshing sleep and a light breakfast, he got to the da Vinci airport forty-five minutes before boarding time. He collected his boarding pass and cleared baggage security without fuss. Ordinarily, he would use the premiere class lounge while waiting, but he had timed his arrival to perfection. He spent ten minutes eyeing duty-free stalls when they called boarding for his flight. A pretty young attendant beamed at him, tore the stub off his pass and wished him a pleasant flight. He barely noticed her, or the long line of waiting economy class passengers impatient to check in. Inside the aircraft, another pretty face showed him to his seat and handed him a menu and a hot face towel. While he looked over the selection, he ignored the streaming passengers pushing by on both aisles, eyeing his comfortable wide leather seat with envy. A harried woman carried a crying baby passed him and he felt mildly sorry for those who would be crammed around her. Their problem…

Delayed another nine minutes, the aircraft finally pushed back. He paid no attention to the safety video, sipping his glass of crisp Riesling as he stared at parked aircraft outside. An attendant collected his tray and he relaxed. Another delay while they uncoupled the little push truck, then the aircraft spooled up its engines and began rolling toward the taxiway.

Flying was a bore, and doing it business class merely made it marginally comfortable. At least the flight being non-stop, it avoided tiresome layovers. Boston looked clean and fresh in early afternoon light as the pilot brought the heavy jet down on its final approach. No unnecessary banking or wobbling of wings, the professionalism pleasing Peroni no end. The Boeing 777 touched down smoothly, with barely a shudder when the wheels hit the runway. With no luggage to collect, he cleared Immigration quickly and was free to go.

In the crowded arrivals terminal, he ignored the waiting hopefuls and scanned placard-holding individuals for his name. He spotted a Scandinavian type, tall, blue-eyed and blond, with his name card and nodded to him.

"Mr. Peroni, welcome to the States," the Scandinavian said and lowered the card. He didn't offer to shake hands. They were not buddies and this was strictly a business deal. "I'm Martin Swens. Let's get to my car and settle you in at the Holiday Inn Boston at Somerville. It's only about a ten-minute drive from the Harvard campus."

"Fine, but I'd like a drive by the target residence first," Peroni replied in smooth American English.

"No problem. I wanted to suggest the same thing, and Cambridge isn't far off our route," Swens said amiably, steering them toward the multi-level parking lot.

"Anything new from surveillance?"

"Yesterday, Garbaldi spent most of the day at the university, returning to the residence late in the afternoon. Noris never left the house."

"We'll do the hit at nine-thirty tomorrow. We've got to do it tomorrow as Garbaldi is flying out on Saturday."

"Why not do it tonight?" Swens countered. "That way we won't be rushed."

"We shouldn't be rushed at all," Peroni snapped. "I don't want to do it tonight because people are at home and the street could have unwanted pedestrian traffic. In the morning, those who are working will have left, and those at home generally mind their own business. If we do this right, we'll be in and out without exciting anyone."

Swens glared, swallowing his resentment at being dismissed so casually. "Okay, it's your show. I understand you want to question both targets before we make the hit. That's always messy, especially if they refuse to talk."

"We'll be playing one against the other. Given the relationship between them, one of them will talk."

"I wasn't aware of any relationship," Swens remarked sourly, hinting that he should have been.

"No reason for you to know. It had nothing to do with your side of the operation."

Swens gave a tight smile. "You're treading pretty hard, Mister, and if you're not careful, you'll get stomped on. I'm getting paid to do what's a pretty simple hit, which me and my boys could have done without you. Rearranging a few of your teeth first, I'd be happy to do for free. Got it?"

Peroni did not bother answering him, but watched the streets, memorizing the layout.

When they got to Cambridge's residential section, Swens slowed down the Saturn Astra, presumably to give Peroni an idea how the streets were laid out. He turned off Hampshire onto Norfolk and slowed even more. Trees lined the narrow nature strip on both sides of the road, providing shade and softened the sun's bright glare. He passed a stately double-story building on their right and nudged Peroni's shoulder.

"That's the one."

Peroni looked at it carefully as they drove by. It appeared elegant with its front covered in creepers, but nothing to distinguish it from similar dwellings along the deserted street.

"Where are your watchers?"

"In a rented room a block from here. Probably having coffee," Swens said, looking pleased. "We installed a miniature video camera transceiver in the branches of an elm across the target's house. We'll remove it tomorrow night. We can't do it during the day for obvious reasons."

Despite himself, Peroni was impressed. Simple, neat, and avoided men on the ground with a chance of being made. Technology was handy if you knew how to use it.

"Excellent. Very well done."

"We know our business, Mr. Peroni," Swens mused, turned right on Broadway and stopped the car. "I was just thinking. We could do the job right now. The equipment is in the trunk and both targets are at home. The conditions won't be any better in the morning."

Peroni hated last minute changes. They usually led to mistakes, sometimes fatal ones. In this instance, Swens' suggestion made a lot of sense. Besides, conditions *could* turn tomorrow which might jeopardize the operation. Slightly tired from the flight and could use nine hours of sleep, but not that tired, and the prospect of action had his body primed. Had he overlooked something? Offhand, he could not think of anything. If something did go wrong, he still had tomorrow to clean it up.

"Mmm. Normally, I don't deviate from a plan, but on this one, you may have a point. Confirm targets are in there."

Pleased, Swens dug a cellphone out of his jacket and tapped in numbers. "It's me…Yeah…Targets still inside?" He switched off and glanced to Peroni. "Still tucked inside."

"Okay. Let's go somewhere quiet and check the equipment," Peroni ordered, still worried he had missed something.

"You got it!" Swens beamed happily. "And I know just the place."

He drove down two blocks, turned right on Prospect Street, crossed Hampshire and slowed before the Alhoda Market underground parking garage. About to pull in, Peroni grabbed the steering wheel.

"Drive on."

Swens bit back an angry retort, continued past the small shopping center, and stopped before reaching Cambridge Street. He turned and glared at his passenger.

"What the hell was all that about? If you don't trust—"

"Did you notice the surveillance camera above the entrance?" Peroni remarked softly and Swens' expression changed. "If there is a camera outside, how many are inside? You'd have given store security an open invitation to tape what we were doing."

"Who cares about a lousy camera! We've been here before. It's no hassle."

"In this car?"

"Sure. So what?"

"Then you've been compromised. That's what," Peroni snarled, liking the American less and less.

He should have handled the job alone, like he did all his hits, but getting what he needed in a country he wasn't familiar with took time, and time was one element he didn't have. He needed Swens and his boys.

"Once we make the hit, what do you think the Boston Crime Scene Investigation unit will do? I'll tell you. They will look for connecting evidence and supermarket surveillance tapes are something they're likely to look at. Perhaps not right away as sorting through all that information will be laborious, but why dangle a pattern for them by going there repeatedly?"

"So they make the Astra," Swens said with a smirk. "Big deal. It's stolen."

Peroni sighed and shook his head. "You're driving a stolen vehicle? What happens if you're pulled over? The cops do a check and the game's up."

"No shit, Sherlock! You think I don't know that?"

"Perhaps it's a good idea to make the hit now after all. We might not make it until tomorrow," Peroni grated sarcastically. "Let's get back to the supermarket and get this done. I don't want to be around when the local cops catch up with you."

"Didn't anybody tell you that you're a real jerk?" Swens demanded angrily and Peroni smiled fleetingly.

"It's been mentioned once or twice."

"I'm not surprised. You've got nerve pissing on a deal where there hasn't been *time* to get everything the way we both would like it. Because I've been hurried and I recognize the risk I'm taking, I wanted to get this done quickly, rather than wait until you're all comfy and powdered. Clear?"

"Okay, you've made your point and I apologize. It's only—"

"Yeah. You're a professional and you don't like mixing it with amateurs. Right?"

"Something like that."

"Don't let that hang you up. My boys and I are also professionals. I don't like my competence questioned by some raw spaghetti. I've seen action behind the lines in Iraq as a SEAL, and I've tangled with Colombian drug lord heavies. Pussies really, when compared to some of New York's Mafia operators. I'll show you how business is done in the 'ole U.S. of A." He pulled away from the curb and made a U turn. "If we mess up, we'll clean it up. Your ass won't be hanging out there. Are we on the same page?"

"For now," Peroni said calmly.

He winced when the car drove under the entrance camera mounted directly above them and lifted his left arm to make sure his face would not be taped. Swens snorted with derision at the gesture and steered the Astra toward an empty corner. He backed against a wall and switched off the engine. They were in a gloomy spot and Peroni could not see any cameras pointing their way. He waited for Swens to get out and quickly wiped the steering wheel and the seatbelt buckle with the palm of his hand, reminding himself to get his suit laundered once he got to the hotel to remove any contaminants from the car seat. He opened the door latch with his index finger, making sure any print got smeared. Once out, he closed the door with a shove of his elbow. The parking lot smelled of burnt gasoline, and somewhere ahead of them, footsteps made muffled echoes.

He watched closely as Swens opened a blue canvas duffel bag and pawed through the contents. Without thinking, he reached into his coat pocket and pulled out leather driving gloves. While he got them on, Swens held out a spare clip and a Hi-Point C-9, 9mm polymer frame handgun fitted with a silencer. If everything went smoothly, he wouldn't need that clip, but it was insurance. Peroni pocketed the clip, took the weapon, tested the weight and balance, ejected the clip and pulled back the slide. The chamber was empty. He replaced the clip, chambered a round and flicked on the safety. The weapon felt uncomfortable behind his hip, and his tight trouser belt made it more so. He let it ride. The discomfort would be momentary anyway.

"The handguns…" he prompted.

Swens slid his behind the small of his back. "Untraceable. I'll get rid of 'em once we're done. Satisfied?"

Peroni did not say anything, noting that Swens wasn't wearing gloves. If this was an example of American professionalism used by Belconi, he had little taste for it. The sooner he finished this and safely on his way home the better he would feel. The wise thing to do would have been to decline the American leg of the job in the first place. Swens could have done the hit without him. If he were wise, he wouldn't be in this business anyway. Then there was the money…

"Right, let's get going," he said and got into the black hatchback, automatically noting the license plate number. One can never tell when such an item could become useful.

As they drove to the house, he insisted that Swens do a final check to ensure the targets were still inside. Swens parked the car opposite the house and Peroni immediately got out, making sure the camera in the tree above him could not see his face. He waited until Swens came up behind him and walked across the street, not pausing as he made for the front entrance. Before pressing the doorbell, he scanned the street both ways. Apart from parked cars, it was empty. The door chime went off with tubular bells. A few seconds later, he heard footsteps and immediately pulled out his gun, flipping off the safety. The door opened and Noris wore the curious expression of anyone seeing someone he didn't know. Peroni lifted his handgun and pointed it at Noris' chest.

"No noise or you're dead," he said in soft northern Italian. "Move back."

Noris paled and stepped back. "It seems that Vatican hasn't wasted any time, and you look far too composed to be ordinary burglars."

"I'm only after the papyrus," Peroni told him calmly and inclined his head for him to go into the living room.

Framed in the entrance, Swens walked in and closed the door behind him, his gun drawn.

"Who is it, Carlo?" a voice queried from the kitchen.

Peroni immediately lifted his left index finger and placed it across his lips. Noris apparently got the idea and said nothing.

"Carlo?"

Garbaldi appeared in the doorway carrying a glass carafe and Peroni shifted his handgun to cover him.

"Run, Paulini!" Noris yelled.

Garbaldi dropped the carafe and leaped aside. The container hit the floor tiles and smashed, spilling hot coffee. Swens was good. His two shots splintered the doorframe where Garbaldi's head had been a fraction of a second before.

"After him!" Peroni snapped, covering Noris, but Swens already bounded into the kitchen.

"Who sent you? The Entity?" Noris spat with a sneer.

"I'll ask the questions, Professor," Peroni said coldly. "Actually, only one question. Where is the papyrus and any copies?"

"That's two questions."

Peroni dropped his right arm and squeezed off a round. The heavy bullet struck Noris' right kneecap, shattering bone and cartilage as it exited behind the leg and lodged in the floorboards. Noris screamed and fell, clutching the destroyed knee. Blood pooled on the polished boards.

"Do you want me to repeat myself?" he offered softly.

He hated doing this part, preferring a clean kill, but he had to recover the papyrus. His victim showed courage by resisting, but it was misplaced loyalty and stupid. Also illogical human nature.

Peroni could see tears glistening in Noris' eyes. The professor shook his head and smiled faintly.

"Fuck you."

Peroni shrugged and shot him in the left knee. Noris jerked and passed out momentarily. When he came to, he writhed on the floor, keening softly, his arms cradling one knee, then the other, hands smeared with warm blood.

Swens appeared in the kitchen doorway, his gun arm hanging. "He got away. Jumped over a neighbor's fence."

Peroni could not believe it. "Fool! Why didn't you go after him?"

"And have a neighborhood shootout? Are you crazy?"

"He's unarmed, you idiot," Peroni snarled in disgust. "I can't believe you didn't cover an escape route."

"It was meant to go clean," Swens protested weakly.

Peroni sighed, suddenly weary. The whole business had now gone horribly sour. He didn't blame Swens. He blamed himself. He should have gone to the hotel as planned, checked every detail, and tackled the job after a refreshing sleep; certain that he'd missed nothing. Instead, he had allowed himself to be persuaded by a seemingly easy opportunity to do it quickly. Swens wasn't the idiot. *He* was!

"We don't have much time. Garbaldi is probably calling the authorities." He looked down at Noris and his eyes hardened. He could not afford to waste any more time here. "Last chance."

"You can shoot me," Noris growled, "but I have the satisfaction knowing that Paulini is safe. You'll never get your hands on the papyrus."

Without blinking, Peroni shot Noris once in the heart. Even as he lowered his arm, he sensed movement in front of him and threw himself back. Swens' round went *wheet* past his left ear. On the floor, his right arm already up and he squeezed the trigger. A poor shot by his standards, getting Swens low in the left lung, but enough to make the large man stagger and clutch at his chest. Peroni's second shot was higher, at the level of the fifth rib, which snapped Swens' head back and he fell through the doorway into the kitchen with a heavy thud.

Arm extended, ready to shoot again, heart racing, Peroni watched for any movement from anyone, not that he expected any, but his training had reduced some of his responses to reflex. Satisfied, he lowered his arm and sat up. No longer a mystery why Belconi wanted him to eliminate the two targets personally, and it had little to do with his familiarity of the case. No one needed to know Garbaldi or Noris, or understand what the tractate meant to do the job, as Swens just demonstrated. No, the wily old cardinal wanted to remove him and *his* knowledge of the papyrus. The contents must be such that simply being aware of its existence constituted a deadly threat to the Church. Belconi had forgotten why he preferred Peroni to do his dirty work for him,

Stefan Vučak

or more likely, overestimated the skill and proficiency of his American people. It didn't matter which. The cardinal had shown his hand. Very well.

Peroni would report the elimination of Noris as arranged and failure to locate the papyrus, for now. He still needed to remove computer records, if any, but terminating Garbaldi had now become far more problematic. Not impossible, simply more troublesome, thanks to Swens' bungling. He would report that as well. Given what happened, it was unlikely that Garbaldi would be leaving the country anytime soon, and okay with him. He needed time to track him down and plan how best to take him out. He could not afford too much time in the effort.

What Belconi would make of someone supposedly dead still engaged in the operation was something Peroni would like to see as a fly on the wall. If the fact caused the old bastard indigestion and some loss of sleep, so much the better. Peroni had no intention of seeking revenge. Unprofitable and emotionally exhausting, and he engaged in neither. He would simply demand more for his services. As a professional, he understood what Belconi had done and why, something he might have done himself. Too bad, or fortunate, that the plan had backfired. What was nice, he now had another lever over the old man, always useful in his line of work.

But right now, he needed to extricate himself from the scene before the local authorities came swarming. To think that Swens had not covered an escape route. Such an absurdly simple thing to have undone a straightforward hit, always the little things. Peroni sighed and in a single fluid motion got to his feet. Served him right for breaking his rule to always work alone. He patted down Swens' blazer and extracted a cellphone. Peroni ran up the stairs, taking two steps at a time. He quickly checked the first bedroom and found nothing. The second room outfitted as an office and guest bedroom. He gave it a cursory check only. There were too many holes in a house this size to hide a piece of paper and he didn't have time to fool around. He stepped to the computer tower and placed two rounds down the box, effectively shredding the DVD player/burner and any hard drives mounted beneath it. If Garbaldi and Noris had copies of the tractate or anything else related to it on the PC, the information now gone. Not a completely satisfactory conclusion as there could be photocopies somewhere else, but he would extract the papyrus and any copies once he found Garbaldi. Even if he could not find the papyrus, eliminating the priest now came first.

He tucked the handgun against his hip and bounded down the stairs. Without hesitating, he opened the door, keeping his head down from the prying camera across the street. He strode to the Astra, extracted his briefcase and garment bag and began walking up Norfolk with long, sure strides toward the Hampshire Street intersection. He wanted to get back to Alhoda Market and pick up a cab to another hotel. Going to the Holiday Inn now would not be wise.

Swens' surveillance team would wonder why he came out alone, but without a warning call from their boss, they wouldn't become suspicious immediately at seeing him. There could be any number of good reasons for coming out. After all, Peroni had not taken the car. So, how far can he get? He relied on that acquiescence to complete his disappearance. He did not want Belconi's hitmen after him with the job only two-thirds done. Still, it was possible that Belconi might identify him to his American operatives and finish what Swens failed, but he doubted it. The cardinal presumably knew how to cut his losses. Anyway, he still had the recording.

Peroni did not break his stride as he neared the intersection. At Hampshire, he turned left.

* * *

Garbaldi held the carafe in his right hand and frowned, the

enticing smell of freshly brewed coffee momentarily forgotten.

"Carlo?"

Who could be at the door and why didn't Carlo answer? He stepped to the lounge doorway, saw two strangers brandishing silenced handguns and froze. Burglars? But would burglars be dressed in suits? It all flashed before him in a split second: Carlo's warning, his skepticism and blind trust in his Church, which could not possibly do what his friend had suggested. Faced by two armed men, he realized it was all unbelievably, but shatteringly true. His insides twisted as everything he thought sacred collapsed around him.

"Run, Paulini!" Carlo screamed in desperation.

Carlo's shout galvanized him into action. He dropped the carafe and leaped aside. There were two soft popping noises in quick succession and the doorframe splintered where his head was a moment before. His mind still in turmoil, he ran through the kitchen, pushed open the door to a small laundry, and clawed at the back door handle. Before leaping through, he pressed the deadlock button and slammed the door shut after him. The rear fence a meter and a half of chicken wire held in a frame of steel piping. Heart pounding, expecting a bullet to smack into him, he covered the short backyard in eight frantic bounds and jumped for the fence, throwing himself over onto freshly cut lawn. Garbaldi landed with a thud that momentarily knocked the breath out of him. He scrambled to his feet and ran toward a white door sheltered beneath a small veranda, hardly noticing the slim cypress and neat flowerbeds planted on either side of the yard.

He grasped a bronze-colored doorknob, turned it right and pushed. Thankfully, the door opened in and he fell through. A sharp crack above his head, followed immediately by another. When he looked up, two little black holes made jagged tears in the wood. He hastily pushed the door shut and found himself in a gloomy little room filled with shoes and outdoor clothing mounted on hooks. He grasped a doorknob beside him and slowly opened the door, only to face a middle-aged woman standing behind a kitchen sink, gaping at him. His impression was of a trim, tallish person dressed in a beige sweater and black slacks. When he entered, she screamed.

Breathing heavily, Garbaldi slowly extended both hands before him, palms up. "Please, don't be alarmed. I'm not here to hurt you. Call the police. Some men are after me and want to kill me."

He saw a small table tucked against the wall, took a hesitant step toward it and pulled out a chair. Heaving a sigh, he slumped into it. Then the cold shakes started and he hugged himself. Part of him wanted to rush back and help Carlo, but he recognized the futility of that option. What could he do unarmed? Even if he had a weapon, he realized he could never use it against another human being. The realization did nothing to ease his guilt. He should have confronted the armed men, not Carlo. Illogical, but he couldn't help feeling he had somehow let Carlo down.

Perhaps seeing her chance, the woman picked up a large slicing knife and held it toward him, point up. "You make a move and I'll cut you!" she warned him uncertainly, clearly unnerved by his sudden appearance, and not sure if she was capable of acting on her threat.

"I mean you no harm," Garbaldi repeated, desperate that she not waste time on him. "I'm a priest. Call the police, please. The men who are after me might try to follow me here and you could be in deadly danger."

She still hesitated, then apparently made up her mind. With one last searching look at him, she placed the knife on the sink bench top and stepped toward a wall-mounted phone set near the refrigerator. Looking at him, she punched in three numbers.

"Hello…Please send someone at once…Gladys Turner…26 Tremont Street…No, I'm not hurt, but a man burst through my back door claiming someone is after him and that I might be in danger…No, he hasn't made any threatening moves. Please hurry." She replaced the receiver, then slowly pulled out a chair opposite him and sat down. She brushed back her short brunette hair and gave a nervous little grin.

"You know my name, what's yours?"

"I am Father Paulini Garbaldi. I work at the Vatican—"

"Where the pope lives?" she said in wonder, eyes round, her fear of him fading.

He smiled. "I'm afraid my work is nowhere as glamorous as his."

"Who are those men you say are after you?"

"Please, I can't talk about it. I don't want you getting involved more than you already are, for which I apologize."

"But—"

They heard a squeal of tires as a car pulled up outside. Moments later the doorbell chimed and someone pounded on the door. "Police! Open up!"

Gladys drew in a sharp breath and scrambled to her feet. "Goodness! That was quick. Ordinarily, when you want them they're never around," she muttered and disappeared through the doorway.

Garbaldi heard the front door open and Gladys say, "He's in there!"

Two grim faced uniformed officers stepped into the kitchen, handguns drawn. When they saw him, the shorter man wearing sergeant stripes immediately crouched into a shooting position.

"Don't make a move, Mister!" he snapped. "Rob? Frisk him," he ordered without moving his head.

His slightly taller partner holstered his weapon and slowly advanced on Garbaldi, motioning him to stand. The patting down quick and efficient.

"He's clean, Kurt," Rob said and placed his hands on his hips.

The sergeant relaxed and took a normal standing position, but still held his gun leveled.

"Okay, start with the explanations."

Although he had a gun aimed at him, Garbaldi felt some of his tension ease. At least the police here were not about to shoot him on sight.

"I am Father Paulini Garbaldi—"

"A priest, eh?" Rob commented and raised an eyebrow.

Kurt frowned, but his gun never moved, a professional. "So you're a priest. What gives?"

"I am visiting a friend who lives opposite the backyard of this house—"

"Hey! That's Carlo, right?" Gladys said and brightened.

"That's right. Two armed men entered the house and one of them shot at me. I'm gravely concerned about my friend. I fled across the fence and came here where I asked Ms. Turner to call the police. If you open the rear door, you will see bullet holes."

"Bullet holes, eh?" Kurt remarked and jerked his head at Rob. "Check it."

Rob walked to the door, jerked it open and peered inside. When he stepped back in, he turned and nodded to Kurt.

"Bullet holes, all right."

"My veranda door!" Gladys squeaked. "Who's going to pay—"

"Father Garbaldi, you said two men entered your friend's house?" Kurt prompted, waiting for the rest.

"Yes. Both were armed with semi-automatic handguns fitted with silencers."

"You're pretty observant, for a priest. Okay, you stay put while we look into it." He glanced at Rob who took out his gun and both walked out.

Gladys placed her hands on her hips and stared at Garbaldi. "You were serious when you said that somebody was after you, weren't you?"

"I am only sorry I had to get you involved," Garbaldi said gravely, worried for Carlo's safety. If something happened to him, he would never forgive himself. When Allard confronted him at the airport, he should have ended it there and then. But, no! He had a moral duty to save the world and his moment of righteous arrogance might have cost Carlo his life.

"Well, I needed a new door anyway. Water had gotten to it," Gladys muttered sourly and walked to the percolator. "Care for some coffee?"

Garbaldi wiped clammy hands against his trousers, feeling himself go numb. "I could use a cup, thank you."

"How do you like it?"

"One sugar with a touch of milk, please."

"We call it cream here. You speak pretty good English, like a New Yorker."

Garbaldi smiled. "Thanks. A product of my education."

Kurt appeared in the doorway, looked at Garbaldi, and shook his head. Garbaldi's stomach tightened and his mouth went dry. The look on Kurt's face didn't herald good news.

"Excuse me," he mumbled vaguely and stood up. Gladys stared at him, mouth open, her face tragic.

Outside, Kurt cleared his throat and shifted his feet. There was no sign of Rob.

"Father…"

"What happened to Carlo?"

"We found two dead men. One had bullet wounds through both knees and chest. The other received two shots in the chest. It suggests a second shooter like you said. Otherwise the place is empty. Rob is calling for backup and the forensics team will sort out what happened. I'm real sorry about your friend, Father."

"Carlo!" Garbaldi sobbed and buried his head between his hands.

Something heavy rolled across his chest and he sagged. Carlo was dead and all because of him. He should never have involved him. The papyrus was not worth his death, two deaths. Pain twisted his insides and he moaned as it rippled through his guts. Carlo probably got shot through the knees. They most likely tried to make him talk, and when he wouldn't, they just killed him. No, the gunmen didn't kill him, the Church did! The gunmen were simply mindless tools. His world reeled and he felt like he stood at the edge of a fiery abyss. He wanted to hurt whoever ordered this. It would only take a small step to give into hate, but even if the men behind this hideous horror were without principles or conscience, he could not betray himself by descending to their level. There had to be a way to make them pay.

He made a silent plea for Carlo's soul and prayed for his own deliverance. When he looked at Kurt, his face was hard.

"I want to see my friend."

"I sympathize, but that isn't possible. It's pretty messy."

"He deserves to have the last rites!"

"Perhaps, but I've got to consider what this could do to you. This is a crime scene now. I don't want you disturbing evidence. Sorry."

Garbaldi knew Kurt was right, but he still felt a need for release, a need to vent his rage and frustration. Carlo! Helpless, utterly weary, he nodded.

Kurt looked at him closely. "Father, I've got to ask you. Why were those men after you and your friend?"

Garbaldi sniffed, wiped his eyes and blinked. "I'm sorry, Sergeant. I cannot tell you that."

Kurt snorted and stepped back. "You cannot tell me? I've got two bodies back there, a second gunman on the loose and you cannot tell me? Which diocese are you working for? Maybe you want to talk this over with them first?"

Garbaldi chuckled, something torn from the depths of his soul, and left behind a black hole of despair.

"Diocese? Rome."

The policeman stared. "You mean as in the Vatican? Then you're not an American?"

Garbaldi shook his head. "I was visiting—"

"A friend, I know. You said that. But, you don't have an accent. I assumed…Ah, shit. You know the paperwork I'll have to fill in now? It also means getting the FBI on the case, you not being a citizen. I hate dealing with the feds."

"The FBI?" Garbaldi's mind sought to grasp an elusive memory. Then it came to him. "I want to talk to Thomas Meecham. He's in Houston."

It was Kurt's turn to chuckle. "Meecham? Not anymore. He is a bigshot in Washington these days. Why him and not the local office?"

Garbaldi gazed at the police officer and said nothing. Was the papyrus worth two lives? With Carlo now dead, he answered his question. Whoever sent the killers after him did not get their prize. What had at first been only a fact-finding exercise and talk of a joint paper now a personal mission.

It was not revenge, exactly.

Father, help me in this, my hour of need…

Chapter Four

The phone rang, loud in the small closet-size office, interrupting Tom's concentration. He quickly finished typing the sentence into the computer before groping for the receiver.

"Meecham!" he snapped, scanning the last paragraph he had written.

"It's Bruce Wellard, Tom. Got a minute to see me?"

"What's up, boss? I'm knee deep in the coordination report you wanted—"

"And I'm hip deep," said the Assistant Director, Counterterrorism Division. "It won't take a minute."

Tom knew if he didn't see Wellard now, he would have to see him later, and it would definitely take more than a minute. It always did. Working on the principle of getting the pain over with as soon as possible, he sighed and gave in to the inevitable.

"Be right there," he said and hung up.

Christ!

Ever since he moved to Washington, it had been one frigging firefight after another. As Supervising Special Agent heading the Strategic Assessment and Analysis Unit in the Counterterrorism Analysis section, he had to get up to speed with his job description, understand the workings of the Analytical Branch, and get to know his teams and assignments. He knew the job description would always be different from the actual work Wellard expected him to do. Things were especially tense, since he also marked time until the current Supervising SA running the section moved out so he could take over. Then there was the operational and political setup of Wellard's department and his own position within it.

Uncovering the Mossad black ops that sabotaged the Valero Texas City Refinery complex in Galveston two months ago, which almost caused the United States to launch a retaliatory strike against Iran, had generated a lot of positive publicity for him. In the end, Israel got roasted. When he and Mark Price were given the Medal of Freedom by President Walters himself for their work, his career momentarily went into high orbit. In Washington, FBI Director Patrick Marshal himself pinned the Meritorious Achievement ribbon on him. It also got him a plum promotion and a transfer to FBI headquarters, all good things, but he was still merely a cog in a vast bureaucratic machine, albeit a larger one, and he needed to work the system. Career management never stopped, and being nice to his superior and tolerant of his idiosyncratic way of doing things was one of the techniques.

But there were days when he longed to be back in Houston, if only a little.

DC left him bewildered. A government city, bureaucracy ruled and he had to learn those rules. Finding a suitable place to live turned out to be less dramatic than he expected; the Bureau's insider network provided a helping hand, much to his vast relief. The large two-bedroom apartment in Petworth, northwest of the Capitol, close to shopping and amenities, and more importantly, almost downtown. When he hit Georgia Avenue, it was pretty much a straight run to the Bureau. He wanted something in Georgetown, everybody did, but rents there were unreal, and Petworth was okay. He only groaned at the weekly rental instead of screaming. The nice part of his promotion, he secured a slot in the underground parking lot of the Hoover Building, a prize without price.

One pleasant benefit living in Washington, he could see Nancy. They dated twice, experiences very enjoyable for both of them, but Tom could see that apart from being friends, it wasn't going to go anywhere. She was an Air Force career woman and he an FBI career man. After the gloss of hero worship wore off, physical attraction aside, there wasn't enough connectivity on which to build a meaningful relationship. Anyway, she was still just a kid and he did not relish the idea of Mark Price coming after him if he took advantage of Nancy's innocence. He knew that sooner or later some flyboy would zoom her off her feet in an F-35 and that would be it. Until then the possibilities were still open.

More importantly, after having met Marshal, he got to know Melissa. If he wasn't careful, she could turn out to be a problem, but one he wouldn't mind having.

The FBI Director's executive assistant was a leggy blond, straight hair spilling down her back, serious, but with a mischievous streak, which he found out the hard way. He dated her a couple of times. Unlike Nancy, it hadn't been a case of hero worship. She had seen macho agents strut their stuff before and genuinely seemed to like him. The first time out, they talked about nothing in particular, laughed a lot and she drank too much. He bundled the giggling girl into his car, took her home and left her on the living room sofa with a blanket over her. The next day, wearing a bright glint in her deep green eyes and a lopsided smile, she came to see him and apologized for her behavior. To show her he didn't mind, they agreed on another date. There hadn't been an opportunity for a third, but neither kept banker's hours, and that made things awkward. They compromised by having occasional lunches together. He felt a connection between them, one he wanted to strengthen.

What did surprise him, Malena called to tell him she'd been transferred to the company's New York office. Thrilled to hear about his work, she congratulated him on his promotion. In a gesture of magnanimity, she even added that should he ever decide to become serious and make a commitment, she would be happy to pick up where they left off in Houston. Poor Malena. Life had to be on her terms or not at all. Did she expect him to drop his Washington job and ask for a transfer to the New York office where she could boss him? Right—end of a promising career.

Goodbye, Malena. It's been fun while it lasted. Still, every time he thought of her eye-popping body, his hormones sizzled. As he painfully learned, it took more than sex to make a relationship work.

Outside his office was a bullpen environment; each cubicle occupied, or supposed to be, by agents and special agents handling cases. Some of them were his teams. Along the wall were small offices for supervising agents. His did not have a window. He wasn't senior enough yet to rate one. Lined against the opposite wall were larger offices—with windows. As an assistant director, Wellard rated one. Tom didn't hold it against him. His boss had worked hard to get to his position and rightly enjoyed the few superficial privileges. Still, it made for an interesting coffee break topic, discussing each other's respective hold on the oily totem pole and who was next in line for a windowed office.

Seeing Tom walk by, Greenfield blew his nose and immediately stood up, freckles shining and carroty hair in usual disarray. "That counterintelligence analysis thing you wanted me to do—"

"Handle it," Tom snapped. "I've got to see the boss."

There was always one in any group, plodder and a grinder, happy when working to a plan, but couldn't think outside the box. According to his record, Greenfield was a terrific detective, but not a strategic or tactical analyst. In his current posting, that wasn't good. Tom wanted to move him out, but had not yet figured out how without hurting the man's career. In the meantime, he tried to give him lame assignments and suspected that Greenfield knew it.

Mentally shelving the problem, he walked quickly along the five-foot wide lighter carpet that separated offices from the bullpens until he got to the center of the floor and turned right into another carpeted corridor. Several agents, male and female, looked up as he walked by before their heads sank to resume whatever they were working on. A background of constant chatter permeated the floor: phones going off, people walking about or standing in groups of two or three, talking cases or simply gossiping.

He strode past Marsha's open office and nodded to Wellard's personal assistant and the floor gofer. Anything administrative that needed doing, people turned to her.

Tom reached Wellard's office, paused and knocked on the oak-veneered ceiling-high door.

"Come in," Wellard's muffled, heavy voice answered.

Tom stepped in and pushed the door shut with the palm of his hand. Facing Pennsylvania Avenue, the office not that different from his, except for being larger. Three floors up, he could not hear the morning traffic along Washington's major thoroughfare. Soundproof anti-surveillance glass panels made sure of that.

Wellard had his wide desk right in front of two small prison-like windows. The light gray walls on either side held open shelves filled with case files, law manuals and periodicals. Sitting down, dressed in a dark blue pinstriped suit, not a predisposing man, and easily mistaken for a bank or finance executive. He didn't wear glasses, but employed a disconcerting habit of squinting at an object or person of his attention that was unnerving. Tom had gotten inured to it and Wellard no longer used the ploy to intimidate him. Tom had won his promotion on merit and refused to crawl up Wellard's ass in gratitude, or anyone else's, for that matter. Once his boss realized that, their relationship stabilized and even became friendly within the bounds of their respective positions.

A New Yorker, he knew that Wellard held a stint as unit chief within the International Terrorism Operations Section I, earning the National Intelligence Meritorious Unit Citation for his efforts. In 2005, he was appointed assistant special agent in charge of the Washington Field Office, where he received the Attorney General's Distinguished Service Award for his work. In 2007, he served as assistant section chief of ITOS I. In 2009, Wellard became a member of the Senior Executive Service, and after a brief period as deputy director for law enforcement at the Central Intelligence Agency, received his appointment as Assistant Director Counterterrorism Division. The man was nobody's dummy.

"Thanks for coming, Tom," Wellard said gravely and extended a hand toward the right of two visitor chairs. He brushed back faded hair above his left ear, purely an unconscious gesture, and cleared his throat.

His boss actually looked uncomfortable, Tom thought as he sat down. Had he committed some unknown sin and was about to be dressed down?

Wellard locked his fingers above the wide desk and leaned forward. "Damnable nuisance, and I hate to pull you from your current job, which you're doing just fine, by the way, but the circumstances are somewhat unusual."

"What do you mean, pull me off my job?" Tom demanded with a touch of snap.

"It's all in the file," Wellard said and tapped a blue folder on his desk, "but I'll summarize it for you. Yesterday afternoon, two men entered a house in Cambridge—"

"Is that Cambridge, Massachusetts?" Tom wanted to know, looking incredulous.

"That's right, but if you will let me finish? Good. These men entered the house and killed one of the occupants. The second occupant managed to elude them by fleeing over a neighbor's fence. Then, and this is the interesting part, for reasons unknown, one of the gunmen kills his associate and leaves the scene. No one saw or heard anything."

"Figures. A falling out between friends?"

"Perhaps. The second occupant alerts the BPD who come running and discover the bodies. It turns out the second occupant is a Catholic priest who came from the Vatican to visit his now deceased friend. You now know why the FBI is involved. As to why you're involved, it's because Father Paulini Garbaldi refuses to talk to anyone about the case except you. The BPD has bodies everywhere, an uncooperative would-be victim stonewalling the local FBI office, nobody's got any answers, at least those that matter, and we've got a killer on the loose. The preliminary forensics report tells us what happened and how, but not the why. From Garbaldi's description, we got an identity drawing of the second shooter, but it's far from conclusive. You can gauge the level of frustration from everybody concerned."

"And I am to talk to this priest and unravel the whole thing, right?" Tom deadpanned, knowing what was coming, hoping it wouldn't.

"Garbaldi probably read about you in the papers and feels he can trust you. It must be something damn important, from his perspective at least, to insist on talking only to you. Whatever. Get yourself to Boston, make him spill his guts, hand him over to Garry Strand for follow-up action, and you should be back here in time for dinner. Marsha is getting your e-ticket now."

"I am to leave in the morning, then?"

"As soon as Marsha walks in, you're on your way."

"Christ! You want me to drop everything and do this today? What's the rush?"

"The rush, Tom, is that we have a foreign national who is involved in a double homicide. Not only that, he's an important Vatican researcher. If the Holy See starts asking questions, I want to be in a position to give them some answers. Good enough for you?"

Tom spread his hands in surrender. "Hey, boss, only asking."

"Humph! You're a pain, did you know that?" Wellard announced flatly and pushed the blue folder across the desk. "Everything we know so far is in there."

Tom still thought it a bunch of nonsense, but he knew how to go with the flow. Anyway, it would give him a break from that damned report of his. He picked up the file and briefly scanned through the pages. There weren't many of them.

"If I need to stay overnight?"

"You have an expense account. Use it," Wellard said simply.

With the easy part over, Tom stood up, not liking any of it. "Marsha can find me in my office. I've got some reading to do."

* * *

Shouldering his carry-on filled with toiletries, spare shirts, a suit, socks and underwear, should this turn out to be a longer stay than Wellard intimated, getting out of the General Edward Lawrence Logan airport domestic terminal relatively quick. A nervous young agent met him at the arrivals gate and drove him to the Boston FBI headquarters, not saying much along the way, clearly overawed by Tom's presence. Obviously, his reputation had preceded him, probably exaggerated by creative media coverage. The public liked its heroes and Tom didn't mind the exposure, considering himself levelheaded enough not to let it distort his sense of reality. Should that happen, he was certain Wellard would not hesitate to straighten him out, and probably relish doing it.

Almost two o'clock by the time they reached the FBI's downtown office, a huge nine-story curved building at One Center Plaza, with its imposing rectangular entrance and the stark, colorless Government Center Plaza across the street. Tom had never been to Boston before and felt mildly intimidated. Also a touch unreal spending the day in two cities. His nervous minder took him to Strand's sixth floor office without attracting more than the usual quota of curious stares.

Behind a standard issue executive desk cluttered with papers, computer screen and keyboard, wires trailing through a hole in the left corner, Garry Strand, Special Agent in Charge for the Boston Division, stood up to his imposing six foot three inches.

"Mr. Meecham, sir," Tom's minder announced diffidently.

"That will be all, Agent Clark," Strand said, his voice deep and crisp, used to command and instant obedience.

Clark nodded and softly closed the door behind him.

Strand extended a hand toward a visitor chair and sat down. "Make yourself comfortable, Mr. Meecham, and welcome to Boston."

Strand looked and acted like a busy executive giving a subordinate a generous piece of his valuable time. His dark brown hair cut short, frost colored the sides. Heavyset without going to seed, Tom figured the man must have been a linebacker or something in his younger days. That may have suggested someone used to physical action, but Tom wasn't fooled. Strand's clear hazel eyes, sunk deep into their sockets beneath neatly trimmed eyebrows, shone with intelligence.

Another New Yorker, but Tom didn't hold that against him. After earning a bachelor's from Fordham University and a master's in psychology from the New School of Social Research, Strand joined the FBI and was assigned to the New York Division where he handled terrorism investigations and intelligence gathering. In 2004, he received a posting to the Washington Counterintelligence Division, and in 2008 did a stint as an inspector in the Inspection Division before being appointed as Boston SAC last year. Married with two daughters, from what Tom read, not a man who lets grass grow under his feet.

"Thank you, sir. And it's just Tom." He made himself comfortable and crossed his legs. A heavy glazed glass panel served as an entire wall, giving him an excellent view of Boston's skyline.

Strand folded his hands over the desk and peered curiously at his visitor. "It's most unusual having you down here...Tom," he said, hinting subtly that he did not appreciate Washington's interference in what he rightly considered to be a Boston case.

Tom took it in stride without flinching. "I couldn't agree with you more, and I don't intend throwing my weight around. As far as I'm concerned, it's Agent Johnston's case and he's welcome to it. It wasn't my idea to be here. I have more than enough on my plate as it is."

Strand smiled and the atmosphere suddenly became friendlier. "I dare say you have. I understand you're heading the Counterterrorism Analysis section?"

"Not yet. I'm waiting for the wheels to turn."

The Boston office chief grinned, unexpectedly looking young. "Well, now that you're here, perhaps those wheels can start turning again. While you're here, come and see me if you get stuck. Clark will take you to see Father Garbaldi," Strand said briskly and stood up, the introduction over.

Tom pried himself out of the comfortable chair. "I would like to talk to Agent Johnston, if I could, before I see Garbaldi."

"That won't be necessary. Once you finish your interview, you can make your report to me."

"Very well, sir," Tom said mechanically and walked to the door.

He opened it and stepped through, giving Strand a backward glance, but the Boston chief was already preoccupied with paperwork. His presence might be resented, but Tom didn't hold a grudge. An understandable reaction to a stranger messing on their turf.

Sitting in a little bullpen cubicle, Clark scrambled to his feet when Tom emerged. "You want to see Father Garbaldi now, sir? This way, please," he invited and extended a hand down the carpeted corridor.

Tom followed the youngster, ignoring the people and sounds of a busy FBI field office. Strand seemed to run a tight shop, and that was all right with him. He felt no desire to linger here longer than necessary. He had plans for the weekend and Melissa figured prominently in them. Clark ushered him into a cheerless room with bare gray walls, and a dark-suited man already seated, looking tired and wary, probably worrying what would happen to him.

When the door closed behind him, Tom gave the young priest a searching look, then reached into his jacket pocket and pulled out a black leather wallet. He flipped it open and showed Garbaldi his FBI badge.

"My identification, Father. I'm Thomas Meecham. I understand you want to talk to me."

Garbaldi glanced at the ID, then peered closely at Tom. "You look like the newspaper picture, but I must be sure. The FBI could have substituted a plant."

Tom grinned. "Why would we bother? Trust me. I'm me. They're looking after you?"

Looking somewhat relieved, Garbaldi nodded. "Thank you, yes. I have a very comfortable room at the nearby Omni Parker House Hotel, but I still feel like a prisoner. They even returned my suitcase and personal effects, for which I am grateful, but I was getting nervous waiting for your bureaucratic machinery to turn, not knowing what's going on. All that someone called Johnston would say, you were on your way."

"It can be like that."

"Forgive my suspicion, Mr. Meecham, but is this room monitored?"

Tom blinked, surprised by the question and Garbaldi's fluent English. "You've seen too many TV shows, Father. There is no two-way mirror here."

"I need to know. It's important."

"Okay, let me check." Tom stood up and opened the door. His nervous young agent stood guard outside. Tom got directly to the point. "Is the room wired?"

"All interviews are recorded, sir," Clark replied stiffly. "It's standard procedure."

Tom said nothing, went back inside and jerked his head. "Come with me, Father."

Garbaldi got up and followed him out. The youngster blocking their way clearly looked uncomfortable.

"Sir, I cannot allow this person to leave. Orders from Mr. Strand."

Tom did not care if the FBI Director Marshal himself stood there. "I'm taking charge, Mister. You can either shoot me or get out of my way."

He could see that Clark was caught in a bind, unsure of his position. He had his orders, but Tom would brook no interference. Reluctantly, Clark stepped aside, probably deciding to pass the problem up the chain and let the higher-ups sort it out.

Tom pushed past him, making sure Garbaldi followed. No one stopped him as they walked out of the building. On the broad sidewalk outside, pedestrian and traffic noises along Cambridge Street a shield of anonymity. Tom searched the boulevard both ways. Finding what he wanted, he turned to his charge.

"Care for a coffee?"

"As long as it's not Starbucks," Garbaldi said looking past the bleak Government Center Plaza at the crowded coffee shop down the street and Tom laughed.

"Agreed. Let's go. While we're at it, start talking. I doubt that anyone has a directional mike trained our way."

Garbaldi smiled wanly. "I came across an old papyrus tractate that states Jesus was an apostle of John the Baptist."

Tom gaped at him. "Christ!"

"Something like that. What I had was explosive. Released, it could do a lot of damage to the Church. Before deciding what to do, I needed to validate the papyrus—"

"And Professor Carlo Noris arranged for that. Right?"

"You're quick. We dated the papyrus and text at Harvard's nuclear physics lab. Both date to around 69 CE and I knew then that we had a genuine document on our hands. My superiors found out what I had and must have gotten The Entity involved—"

"The who?"

"The Entity is the Vatican's intelligence service."

"You mean the Vatican runs a spy network?"

"You didn't know? It's been doing it since the sixteenth century."

"You've got to be shitting me."

Garbaldi grinned. "The information is on the Internet, a bit of it. Anyway, before coming here, I emailed Carlo a copy of the papyrus. That was how they found out about it. I'm assuming The Entity sent the assassins after us, presumably to recover the papyrus, and it's the likeliest explanation. The men I saw didn't look like ordinary burglars. As you know, they succeeded with Carlo, but I doubt they recovered the papyrus."

"How can you be sure?"

"You must know what happened at the house, Mr. Meecham. They tried to make Carlo talk. When he wouldn't, they killed him," Garbaldi said harshly.

"Yeah, I read the forensics report. Where is this papyrus?" Garbaldi hesitated and Tom sighed. "You don't trust me?"

"I just have to be careful. Should something happen to me, still a distinct possibility, the knowledge of the tractate and its contents could be lost forever, except to those who sent the killers after me. I cannot permit that."

"What do I need to do to satisfy you?"

Slowly, Garbaldi reached into his jacket pocket and held out a blue USB memory stick. "Everything Carlo and I were working on. The original is hidden inside the fireplace."

Tom admired the simple audacity of the idea, not resenting Garbaldi's caution. Who would dream of looking there, especially in the time available to them? Moreover, who would light a fire in July? He reached for the still warm two-inch-long device and slipped it into his pocket.

"I like it. As for the rest, let me guess. Whoever killed Professor Noris could still be after you, right?"

"I'm afraid so. It appears the Church will stop at nothing to prevent revelation of the tractate, which is what Carlo and I planned to do. My superiors don't know that and are obviously preempting. The Entity was partially successful this time, but I'm certain they will keep hunting me until I'm dead. Now that I told you—"

"I could also be a target. Christ! That's a comforting thought. What's the big deal? I don't know my early Christian history that well, but from what I do know, there were lots of different versions of New Testament gospels floating around before they settled on the four we know now. Why would your papyrus cause such a stir?"

"Don't you see? The Church is founded on the premise that Jesus is the one and only Messiah, born a god of the Virgin Mary for the remission of man's sins. The fact that in 325, Emperor Constantine created him a god for political reasons is neither here nor there. For the multitude, Jesus is part of a trinity in a single indivisible god."

"I never felt comfortable with the trinity idea," Tom remarked dryly. "Three unique entities, but still one god? It smacks too much of polytheism."

"One of the mysteries of faith, Mr. Meecham."

Tom stopped in his tracks and stared. "Or an invention of priests."

His sudden stop caused a teenager to bump into him. "Watch it, pops!" the longhaired kid snarled as he hurried by, trousers three sizes too big hanging down his butt.

Tom let him live. His objective was down Tremont Street and he steered Garbaldi over the pedestrian crossing toward it. On the corner of Beacon Street, Gloria Jean's Café was clean, comfortable, and the aroma of freshly roasted coffee smelled wonderful. He found an empty booth tucked into a corner. Midafternoon, the place wasn't overly crowded, but there were enough customers so their conversation would not stand out. Subdued traffic noises coming through tall plate glass windows helped give them anonymity.

A young waitress dressed in a green blouse and skirt, chewing gum, hair tied into a ponytail, arrived with an order pad, pencil hovering.

"Yes?"

"Try the Brazilian special blend," Tom offered. "It has a rich full body and an enticing aroma."

"I know," Garbaldi agreed. "I use the same stuff at home."

"Great!" Pleased to be sharing a cup with another connoisseur, Tom turned to the patiently waiting girl. "Two Brazilian specials with cream on the side. If you make it too strong, I'll nail it to the wall."

"Got it," she said, scribbling in her pad. "If you can get a nail through it," she added and walked off, carriage swaying with a boneless gait only women could do.

Tom frowned, turned to Garbaldi, and shook his head. "I still can't believe the Vatican is running a spy network. I'll be damned. Now I've heard everything. To coin a phrase, is nothing sacred? Never mind. You still haven't told me why the Entity is after you."

"It's simple. The papyrus not only tells us that Jesus was John the Baptist's disciple, but that John is the anointed one."

"The anointed one?"

"The Messiah, Christ in Greek."

"I thought Jesus was the Messiah."

"He is, but only one of two. According to the papyrus, John is the spiritual one while Jesus is the warrior, a worldly king who would liberate Israel from Roman rule and unite the ten tribes."

"I thought there were twelve."

"A matter of Old Testament lore lifted from Egyptian mythology. You can use either number."

"Hmm. So, if your papyrus claims that Jesus was John's apostle and a second Messiah and became public knowledge, the whole foundation of Jesus as God would be overthrown. Right?"

"As would the New Testament foundation for the Church."

"Christ!"

"I think you get the idea," Garbaldi said dryly.

The waitress came bearing two large steaming cups on a tray. She placed one before each of them and left a little tin cup of cream on the table.

"Enjoy," she added mechanically and wandered off.

Tom mixed his with sugar and a dash of cream and took a sip. The flavor defused through his mouth and he swallowed slowly, appreciating the rich coffee.

Garbaldi made his the same way. For a moment, both lost themselves in the simple pleasure of drinking an excellent brew.

"I like Gloria's," Tom mused. "It's a touch more expensive than the others, but they know how to get a customer back. Starbucks used to be like this, but now their coffees are too strong and bitter. They've turned themselves into a coffee McDonald's. It sucks."

Garbaldi smiled and took another sip. "Mr. Meecham, can you see now why The Entity is willing to murder to stop the papyrus becoming public?"

"Hold on! I accept that the Vatican might be severely embarrassed, but a motive for murder? You're talking about sanctioned killing by the Church."

"My friend Carlo is dead," Garbaldi reminded him.

"You're only supposing the Entity is behind the murders. We don't have any evidence. Still, I'll grant you a *prima facie* motive. If I do that, I would also need to accept the Entity has hitmen on its payroll and has sent two of them after you. That's tough to swallow, you know. We still don't know why one of the shooters is dead."

"Look at it from the Church's perspective, Mr. Meecham. They don't know for certain that I have the tractate or that I intend to publish, but they figure they can't take that chance, which means silencing me and anyone else who knows of its existence. The dead assassin was probably eliminated for the same reason."

Tom raised an eyebrow. "That's pretty smart thinking, Father. If your conjecture is correct, this is some coldblooded work by your Entity. It's certainly not the psalm-singing Church I know. There could be another explanation more sinister for both of us. The dead shooter may not have been the target at all. He might not have known anything about this business, and was there to eliminate the one who did. Except the plan didn't work out."

"If that's the case, the second shooter, to use your phrase, is the dangerous one and could still be gunning for me."

"For both of us, from what you told me," Tom added bleakly.

"I'm afraid so," Garbaldi agreed and sipped his coffee, clearly enjoying it.

"Well, don't wait for me to thank you," Tom growled, peering at the priest over the rim of his cup. "Tell me. Why in hell did you pick me? Any FBI agent would have helped you."

"Perhaps, but I knew for a certainty that you would."

"You saw my name in the papers, right? That was your selection criteria? Most of the stuff they printed about me is crap anyway. The real details are classified and are likely to remain so for a long time to come."

"I am a pretty good judge of character, Mr. Meecham," Garbaldi said with a smile and Tom snorted.

"Christ! Have you got me wrong! And by the way, call me Tom, seeing how we're going to be joined at the hip for a while. I was supposed to wrap this up today, hand you over to the local office and be on my way to Washington, blissfully ignorant of your papyrus and your Entity, free to enjoy my weekend."

"Are you going to do that, Tom? Walk away? And you can call me Paulini."

"I'd love to get my ass out of here, but I won't pass the buck. From what you tell me, it might be too late anyway. Wellard is going to be pissed when I tell him, though."

"Wellard?"

"My boss. Well, I'm in Boston and he's in Washington. I won't be able to hear him rage and scream from here."

"Could this be damaging to your career?"

"Paulini, just being alive is damaging. If we can find the second shooter, identify the dead one, establish a link to The Entity and keep both of us alive while doing it, I'd say we'd be ahead. Wellard can't complain if I hand him an open-and-shut case. The first thing we need to do, of course, is recover that papyrus of yours."

"Agreed. This is such an obvious move—"

"Our shooter could be waiting for us to do just that, right? The thought had occurred to me, you know."

"You could send someone to recover it for us," Garbaldi offered and Tom shook his head.

"No good. Anyone I send won't know what he's doing and won't be as careful while doing it. He'll simply be an easy target and our shooter would have your tractate handed to him on a plate. I'll do it myself."

"I'm sorry, Tom. I cannot let you do that," Garbaldi said firmly, brooking no dissent.

"If you think I'll risk—"

"I'm coming along."

Tom looked at him for a moment and nodded. "Okay. We'll do it together, even though it's against my better judgment. You do have an interest in this after all, but I hate having you expose yourself like this. Let's finish our coffee and I'll get us a car, unless you want to do it tomorrow?"

"The sooner I have the tractate safe in my hands, the happier I will feel."

"Good. Once the thing is locked in the evidence room—"

"Tom, I haven't had a friend killed just to hand it over to The Entity."

"What are you talking about? Are you saying The Entity can suborn the FBI and compromise evidence?"

"All I'm saying, the operation mounted against me was professional. We don't know who or what resources they have at their disposal."

Tom finished his coffee and placed his cup down with a click, not liking what Garbaldi implied. Could the Entity get at the papyrus in the evidence room? A chilling thought that hinted at a vast organization and supporting network.

"Your paranoia is starting to bother me, you know."

"That's what I told Carlo."

Tom thought hard for a moment. "What do you propose?"

"We retrieve the papyrus and take it to Professor Vincent Renauld at Harvard's Center for Middle Eastern Studies. I met him two days ago. He is director of the department's Steering Committee."

"Carlo's boss?"

"Right. Carlo and I were going to write a paper and Harvard would publish it. If we give the papyrus and test data to Dr. Renauld for safekeeping, whoever is after it will find it somewhat difficult to pry it loose from his hands."

"How will giving the papyrus to Harvard make it safe? Our shooter will see this as an obvious move and follow you...us, I mean. It will simply shift attention to Renauld, making him a target as well."

"It doesn't matter. Harvard has very secure vaults. Besides, Renauld isn't working alone. His deputy and the university president know of our talk, Regardless of what happens to me, and even if I don't write the paper, I'm certain Renauld will. Either way, knowledge of the tractate's contents will have become public, effectively nullifying any attempt by The Entity to suppress it. I'll make sure of that. Our shooter will no longer have a reason to pursue me."

"You hope."

"Unless the shooter is prepared to kill off half the Harvard hierarchy, we should be okay."

Tom pulled at his chin. "Mmm. I don't know. How will the shooter know…ah, you'll inform The Entity," he finished, admiring the simplicity and effectiveness of the plan. This Garbaldi guy really was clever.

"I don't know who in the Vatican runs it, but I'll do the next best thing. I'll tell the Archivist."

Tom raised an eyebrow.

"Head of the Vatican Secret Archives," Garbaldi clarified.

"Where all those ancient and embarrassing documents are stored?"

"The same."

"What if Professor Renauld doesn't want to get involved? He must know of Dr. Noris' death and may be wary."

"He is an academic first and something like this comes only once in a lifetime. He will publish. If he won't, I'm sure the Roma Tre University will."

"Your *alma mater*, eh? Okay, Paulini, let's get it done. You want to call Renauld?"

"Let's recover the tractate first. Who knows, someone might have gotten cold and built himself a fire."

Tom blinked and laughed. "And I thought all priests were tight lipped, gospel spouting, self-righteous tight asses."

"Not all, Tom. Not all."

"There is one thing I don't understand—"

"Why I, a priest, am doing this? You thought I would be the first one to bury the thing as soon as I saw it?"

"Something like that. You attended years of seminary training to become a priest. You must have believed in your calling. Then you went to do graduate work in anthropology and published two books and some nine papers in prestigious international journals. I've done my homework on you. Your entire academic output questions the Church and its foundation. It seems odd, that's all."

"My academic pursuits don't quite question the allegorical interpretation of the gospels. It questions the Church's assertion that they're historical fact and every word inspired by God, which we all know they were not. The numerous inconsistencies, errors and contradictions between and within the gospels prove that. If you want actual proof, you only have to look at two versions of the nativity, genealogy and crucifixion stories. Sadly, some of the more extreme elements within the faith indeed take the Bible as the literal word of God, inconsistencies and all. Unfortunately, biblical inerrancy has also been the cause for many of our past wars. Look at what the Church did to the South American civilizations in the name of God.

"Forgive me, I'm preaching again. To answer your question, Tom, in my research, I am attempting to uncover the facts behind all Middle Eastern religions: Egyptian, Sumerian, Syrian, and Babylonian, and to define how they contributed to development of Jewish monotheism and the subsequent writing of the Torah, and the Old Testament in general, the Septuagint, free from Hexapla prejudice."

Tom looked his question. "Septuagint and Hexapla? You've lost me."

Garbaldi grinned at Tom's confusion. "Sorry, I sometimes get carried away. The Septuagint is a Greek translation of the Hebrew Bible and a baseline for tracking subsequent alterations. Hexapla refers to variations in the Old Testament as a result of incorrect translation, corrections and additions. Taking all that into account, I want to establish the extent to which Eastern religions influenced the gospel writers and philosophies the Bible attributes to Jesus."

"But scholars and theologians have done that for centuries."

"Not quite. They all relied on old manuscripts and existing published material for source information. When the source data itself is invalid, so are the interpretations and conclusions based on it. What I am doing is using archeological and anthropological evidence as baselines to validate old material and come up with hypotheses founded on verifiable facts uncontaminated by previous interpretation."

"You've given yourself a chore, all right. Aren't you rattling old skeletons? Your work must have brought you into conflict with existing Church dogma and authority."

"It certainly has and I've been disciplined twice by the Congregation for the Doctrine of the Faith for my writings."

"The Congregation—"

"The Inquisition, Tom."

"What? I thought they were disbanded in the nineteenth century."

"No, they're still very much alive and are probably behind this witch hunt against me."

"Christ! With friends like that…You like to live on the edge, don't you?"

"Believe me, Tom, it has caused me to question my calling more than once. With my discovery of the papyrus and what the Church is apparently prepared to do to suppress it, I can no longer, in all conscience, support its authority."

"I don't envy you the dilemma. You must realize The Entity is not the whole Church. I'm not a believer exactly, although raised a Catholic, the Church has many fine men and women who have done and continue to do truly wonderful humanitarian work. You cannot tar them all with the same wire brush."

"And I'm not. Publishing the tractate should not destroy the Church, it cannot. The basis for its existence is far too compelling and powerful. It will mean some agonizing reappraisal and acknowledgment of a history that's more factual. Fact shouldn't be swept aside simply because it happens to contradict contrived truth."

Tom chuckled. "We do that all the time. Besides, many won't believe what you have is fact. You'll be up against hundreds of millions who accept without question whatever the Church tells them. You'll probably end up being mobbed for your trouble."

"I know, but the academics will question. The media will question. Ordinary people will question. Not all, but the educated ones will. The Church will have to deal with those questions sometime. Acknowledgment of new archeological evidence might be slow, and change even slower, but fact cannot be denied or suppressed forever. It took the Church four hundred years to recant Galileo's heresy that Earth was not the center of the universe and it might take as long to accept the fact of my tractate, but in the end it must. If it cannot, the desertion of the faithful will continue to accelerate as the Church becomes even more marginalized and irrelevant. Why do you think seminaries are closing and only in Third World countries does the Church continue to thrive?"

"Because in those countries the population is poor and ignorant," Tom said promptly. "Even I know that one."

"Of course. Unquestioning acceptance and obedience can only be obtained from the ignorant. Education and science is an anathema to any religion."

"As your own education so vividly demonstrates."

Garbaldi gave a weary sigh. "Well said. The realization has caused me much soul searching."

Tom sighed and shook his head. "I must say, Paulini, I never thought I would hear a priest say what you just did. Do others feel the same way?"

"Some do, but the Vatican Curia is run by powerful and conservative men who would love to turn back the clock to the Dark Ages. The Church also represents spiritual and temporal power. A lot of power."

"And apparently worth killing for. You don't rock the boat if it means losing that power, right?"

Garbaldi shrugged and his eyes flickered at the order counter. "Our young waitress is giving us the eye—order another or get out."

"Yeah, I've noticed," Tom said and stood up. "All right, let's get this thing done, and while we're walking, tell me how you found the papyrus."

At the FBI office, he requested a car and driver, and then made a call to Wellard. It wasn't pretty.

"It's a Boston problem, Meecham. Let them handle it. You've got the information out of Garbaldi, and that's all I care. Hand it over to Strand and get back to your real work. This isn't your case."

It was always bad when Wellard called him by his surname, but in this instance, Tom was sure of his ground.

"You made it my case, boss, when you sent me here. I cannot simply walk away now. The information supplied by Father Garbaldi is too controversial."

"For Crissakes! What can be so damn important?"

"I cannot tell you, not now. Give me the weekend to sort it out."

"You're one of my supervisory agents, Tom, not an ordinary field hand. I need you here."

"Sir, I am a federal law officer investigating a crime that involves foreign nationals. Isn't that my job?"

There was silence at the other end, followed by a growl of frustration. "A barracks lawyer now, eh? Okay, Tom, you win. You have your two days, but I'm warning you. If your ass is not in my office on Monday morning with an explanation, don't bother showing up!" Wellard snarled and hung up.

Tom stared at the receiver and then gently put it down. "Well, that could have been worse on so many levels."

In the corridor, Garbaldi saw Meecham's glum expression and grabbed his arm. "Is everything all right? You don't look happy."

Tom smiled wanly and shrugged. "Being happy isn't part of my job description. Don't worry about it, Paulini. It's nothing I can't handle. Right, let's get on with it."

The drive to Noris' place uneventful and spent quietly. Neither could talk about the case, not with a driver present. When the black sedan pulled up to the curb behind Noris' car, nothing indicated the house was a crime scene, and there were none of the yellow strips cordoning off the front door so beloved by TV serials.

Tom got out of the car and automatically scanned the street both ways. Apart from parked cars, everything looked clear, but that didn't mean much. If a gunman sat hiding out there, he would not be standing beside a mailbox advertising himself. Tom motioned to Garbaldi to come out, keeping him in front of him. If someone did shoot, he would have to get Tom first, something he did not particularly relish. The small of his back tingled as he anticipated a bullet in his spine. He should not have brought Paulini here.

Garbaldi dug out a spare key, quickly opened the front door, and stepped into the gloomy foyer. He reached for the light switches on the wall and flipped them on, then paused.

"Memories?" Tom queried.

"To think that only yesterday, Carlo and I were talking here, laughing, reminiscing and planning to turn the world on its head." He walked into the living room and made his way to the fireplace.

Following him, Tom looked around. The floor had been cleaned, and nothing suggested blood and shooting, except for the bullet holes in the floorboards and kitchen doorframe. Garbaldi pulled the fireplace grill to one side, knelt on the gray stone slab, and reached up. When he stood, he held a folder wrapped in plastic. After shaking off residual soot, he frowned and held out the folder.

Tom gazed at the innocent thing and wondered how an old piece of papyrus and some faded words could cause so much turmoil. Yet the Declaration of Independence had done much the same thing, he reminded himself, so why not this?

"Anything else?"

"Computer files—"

"Forget it, they're gone. The hard drive has two holes through it."

"Well, it saves me wiping it."

"Any other copies anywhere?"

"No, that's it. Everything else is on the USB stick."

"Okay. Let's go to the Omni Parker House Hotel and get sorted out. I plan on staying there myself. This evening, we'll work out our next move. You have Renauld's contact information?"

"I have his business card." Garbaldi dug into his pocket and held out the card.

Tom took it and nodded. "Excellent. In that case, let's get out of here. It's been a long day and I'm anxious to see the end of it."

He opened the door, looked quickly up and down the street and nodded to Garbaldi. "Stay behind me," he ordered firmly, his eyes still checking the street.

His senses were at full alert and the hairs on the back of his neck bristled. Something wasn't right, but he couldn't quite put his finger on it; different, like a chess piece that should not be there. Then he spotted a dark blue sedan across the street two houses up. Was the side window down?

He turned to shout a warning when he heard a wet *plop*, immediately followed by another, and knew it was too late. Garbaldi had already fallen against the partially closed door. Two red smudges shone between his shoulder blades. Tom reacted instantly. He lunged, driving Garbaldi through the doorway. A shot seared the air beside his right ear and something plucked at his right shoulder. On the floor, breathing heavily, with Garbaldi inert beneath him, he heard a car accelerate away.

He picked himself up and ran to the FBI sedan standing silent against the curb. Hadn't the fool seen or heard anything? The driver merely sat there like a log. Tom bent down beside the open side window and peered in. The driver's eyes were glazed and the skin already had the waxy pallor of death about it. He pulled at the door, leaned in for a closer look and grimaced. The shot got the driver below the left temple, the bullet exiting at the back of the head, smearing blood and brains over the seat. He couldn't be certain, but it appeared like the shooter simply walked up, probably pretending to ask him something, and when the driver slid down the window, shot him; simple, neat, and left no fuss— except for the mess. Well, no use sending the car after their boy now.

Garbaldi!

He left the car door open and rushed into the house. He could see very little blood on Garbaldi's back, which was bad. That meant a heart shot. Gently as he could, he turned him over. Garbaldi groped with his hand and clutched Tom's arm, trying to say something, but it was too much. The eyes still had light in them, but it faded even as Tom cradled him in his arms.

"Christ!" he muttered softly, holding the warm body, his thoughts dark.

* * *

"You fool!" Belconi thundered over the secure encrypted line. "You not only bungled the job, but you now have the FBI involved. Who's next? The CIA?"

Peroni listened dispassionately, his mind detached from the cardinal's emotional tirade until Belconi ran out of invectives.

"Your Eminence, a reality check, if I may. For reasons that I understand, you ordered Swens to remove me, supposedly after I eliminated Garbaldi and Noris. Unfortunately for you, he got impatient. However, Garbaldi and Noris *are* now eliminated. Accordingly, my contract has been fulfilled and I expect the balance of both transactions paid forthwith, including the bonus for destruction of computer records."

"But you haven't recovered the papyrus, the most important part of your mission!"

"I stated that recovery might be difficult."

"That's why the bonus. If you think I will pay you after the mess—"

"Created by Swens," Peroni added coldly. "I entered into the contract in good faith, which you chose to break, and the rules have now changed. I need to advise you, Your Eminence, should something terminal happen to me, there is a tape of the conversation we had in your office." He didn't have to elaborate. Belconi was a smart man and able to connect the dots.

"You wouldn't dare!"

Peroni said nothing, leaving Belconi to decide whether to test a likely bluff, which might not be the most desirable outcome for him should the cardinal succeed, always a possibility. The Entity had a long reach, but success would be bought dearly and he did not think that Belconi wanted to go down that path. After a moment, he heard a heavy sigh.

"We'll discuss that tape when appropriate. Right now, you have a job to finish and I cannot afford to waste any more time. Balance of both transactions will be paid in full, including one bonus. You're still to recover or destroy the papyrus as a matter of priority to earn the second bonus."

Peroni noted that Belconi did not bother with further histrionics or denials. There really was no point in doing so. Both were professionals and knew how to play the game, but that did not mean the cardinal would forget the threat hanging over him.

"Given the changed conditions, Your Eminence, the cost of recovery has doubled."

"I won't be subject to extortion. You presume too much on yourself, my *son*! Trifle with me and you'll have more than hellfire to contend with. Do we understand each other?"

"In that case, my work here is done. I'll be returning—"

"Wait, wait!" Belconi cried out.

Peroni could hear the grinding of teeth and smiled, knowing exactly what the old cardinal was thinking. Probably damning Swens, hoping the man already roasted in the pit. Belconi could offload the case to somebody else, but that would mean having to bring another person into his confidence, if only partially. Too many people were involved already and Peroni figured he didn't want to pursue that option. Besides, by the time Belconi had things settled, the tractate might very well be released. No, the bastard would cave in.

"Agreed. One hundred thousand for recovery of the papyrus," Belconi grated.

"Half payable immediately," Peroni added.

After some more heavy breathing, "Agreed. There is a matter of the FBI agent Garbaldi contacted. It's probable he now knows the full circumstances surrounding the tractate."

Peroni said nothing and waited. It was an obvious conclusion.

"He needs to be eliminated."

"Your Eminence, I am prepared to undertake the contract. However, we both realize that containment is now no longer a certainty. The FBI agent will undoubtedly make a routine report of the incident as part of normal procedure, if he hasn't done so already, and existence of the papyrus will inevitably become public knowledge."

"I know all that!" Belconi snapped. "That's why this must be done quickly. If Garbaldi made arrangements to publish, those efforts will be thwarted. That's not your concern. Eliminate the FBI agent. Before you bring it up, in recognition of the degree of difficulty associated with this contract, the usual fee will also be doubled. Balance of the half payment will be made immediately."

"Acceptable," Peroni said and the connection broke.

He detached the microphone coupling from the BlackBerry and switched off the pocket wire recorder. Belconi had shown himself ruthless, but he already knew that. Mentioning the recording, Peroni simply wanted to forestall any more foolishness.

He was careless with the FBI agent at the door. Instead of taking him out as the primary target, being far more dangerous of the two, the FBI man reacted with lightning speed when Garbaldi was hit, and his shots missed. He had broken a basic tenet of tradecraft: when planning, think strategy; when in the field, think tactics. An amateur ploy and he deserved what that got him. His target would now be doubly alert and getting him more difficult. As he knew, there was simply no way to cover himself completely if someone was determined to take him out and risk death to do it. He never contemplated going that far. There were just too many ways to deal out death, close or from afar, and Peroni knew most of them.

The one thing both predictable and inevitable was Garbaldi returning to the Noris house to retrieve the papyrus. He might have the thing stored at Harvard, but Peroni always considered that a low probability option. What Garbaldi should have done, of course, was have someone get it for him. Once paranoia sets in, it's hard to trust, and he probably didn't want to endanger anybody else. Noble, but foolish. What Peroni did not expect was the FBI also screwing up. They should not have allowed Garbaldi to expose himself like that. Would the FBI agent now publish the papyrus? It all depended on what Garbaldi revealed. Stay focused, he told himself sternly. Find the FBI agent and the papyrus. Nothing else mattered. It wasn't his concern what the FBI would or would not do with the thing. For the briefest moment, he toyed with the idea of asking Belconi to pay for the tractate; a retirement fund, so to speak, but immediately rejected the idea. It is not how Peroni did business, and besides, it was a sucker move. He might need Belconi again and did not underestimate The Entity's reach. Play it straight, he told himself, and everyone could look forward to a satisfactory retirement. Retiring in a pine box would not be a desirable outcome. Unfortunately, bitter experience had taught him that there was no such thing as playing fair. Eat your opponent's heart out before he ate yours. That's how things were done, as Belconi demonstrated with the Swens gambit. Of course, these days, identifying your enemy was sometimes troublesome, especially in his line of work. That is also what made the hunt exciting.

* * *

In his temporary One Center Plaza office, Tom rubbed his eyes and sighed.

"With Garbaldi down and one of our own men taken out, Strand has asked me to stay over the weekend to help Johnston with some details. The forensics team is going over everything, but I doubt they'll find anything, either at the house or across the street where the shooter parked the car. We're dealing with a professional here.

"Lieutenant Stanly Marsh, who's running this from the BPD side, will forward his findings on the dead shooter and his car to Johnston, who will have our forensics team sift through it all and we'll see what's left at the bottom. I also asked him to start an ID search on all Italian arrivals at Logan, New York, and Washington over the last ninety-six hours, including security tapes from local hotels. We might get lucky, but I doubt it. Even if we do tag a face, without prints, we have nothing to connect it with the crime scene. We need that link, but even without it, at least we'd be able to put the suspect under surveillance—if we can find him. My bet is still on the dead shooter. Only he actually met our man."

Tom could say a whole lot more, then decided against it. His boss was interested in the salient bones of the matter, not a shoulder crying session. At least Wellard had not interrupted, listening patiently, probably reserving his blast for the end.

"From what you told me, it sounds like the shooter came in at Logan," Wellard remarked at length.

"It's the likeliest possibility, yes," Tom agreed. "I'm just the cautious type and want to cover all my bases."

There was a moment of silence before Wellard spoke again. "The papyrus thing, you have it?"

"I do. Before you state the obvious, boss, I know that it's evidence material to the case, but for the time being, I'm holding onto it. Please don't order me to hand it in. I'd feel real bad about that and you would only get upset when I refuse."

"You must have a good reason for keeping it."

"I don't trust the security of the evidence room. If the thing disappears, we'd really have nothing."

"I think you're bullshitting me, Meecham, and you're up to something. You better make sure the thing doesn't disappear, that's all I have to say."

"Thanks, boss. I knew you'd understand."

"Humph! Just don't get both our asses in a sling over the damned thing. If something were to happen to you…"

"I'm touched by your concern, but don't worry. The papyrus will be safe. I'll make sure of that. *Should* something unforeseen happen, you will have my full report, including an image of the text and location of the real thing, stored in my personal case database."

"What the hell is so goddamn earth shattering about that tractate anyway? I'm getting a strong impression that we're not dealing with ordinary murders here."

"You got that right. According to Father Garbaldi, the papyrus states that Jesus was John the Baptist's disciple and he is but one of two Messiahs that's been prophesized. If true, this undermines the Church's entire dogma. I don't have proof, not yet, but the Vatican's secret service, The Entity, may have sent assassins to kill Father Garbaldi and Professor Noris to keep it from surfacing. It's all circumstantial, but the pattern is suggestive."

"God!" Wellard exclaimed and then cleared his throat. "You serious? The Entity was disbanded when Pope Benedict XVI took office."

"Yep. I was told the same thing, except that it's not true."

"But…if this papyrus is so damn important—"

"They could now be after me, I know. As a matter of fact, they already are. This time, though, the shooter missed."

"Are Strand and Johnston in the loop?"

"I've briefed both of them."

"I don't like this, Tom. You've done your job and more. Much more. Hand this over to Strand and let him handle it. He is the Boston Division chief and this is a Boston case. I don't want you a target over some two-thousand-year-old piece of papyrus, no matter how revolutionary. You have a job here."

"Boss, I told him I'd stick through the weekend. There are loose ends I need to tie up with Johnston."

"For Crissakes, Meecham. You're not to go off on some personal crusade here because of Garbaldi. You got that? This is a federal crime case, nothing more. If I hear one whisper that you're doing something else, your ass is mine. Do we understand each other?"

"You're making it quite clear, boss," Tom said crisply. At least with Wellard, you wouldn't die wondering.

"Glad to hear it. Anything else?"

"I'll keep you updated as things develop."

"A pain. That's what you are, Meecham. A damned pain," Wellard growled and hung up.

Tom smiled as he replaced the receiver and pressed the yellow scramble button. Wellard was okay. A bit of a pain himself sometimes, but Tom could live with that. His boss did not micro manage, trusting him to know what he was doing. By now, he should. He appreciated that level of latitude.

If he could not exercise the authority of his position now, he deserved to be back in Houston.

He reached for the mug beside the keyboard and sipped. Gone cool a while back, he didn't feel like getting up to make himself a fresh one. Although Wellard may be half-serious about him taking on a personal crusade, Tom knew exactly what he needed to do. Foremost, he was a federal officer, and getting to the bottom of the case his first priority. He would be in dereliction of duty if he contemplated anything else. If Johnston broke the case, Tom did not mind sharing the kudos. He was not being altogether altruistic either. With the technical aspects of the investigation run by somebody else, it freed him to pursue a piece of unfinished business. It was *sort of* related to the case should Wellard get nosy, albeit a thin alibi to stake his career on. He was *not* undertaking a crusade, exactly.

He'd been careless with Garbaldi and should have never allowed him to return to the house. He *knew* the second shooter would have anticipated the move and could be waiting. After all, he needed to recover the papyrus sometime. Tom had violated basic procedures by being predictable, not that he could have avoided it this time. On the other hand, had he asked Strand to send someone else, the man could very well be dead right now and the tractate gone. The same thing may have happened had he gone after the thing alone. Even if somebody did recover the tractate without incident, it would now be in the evidence room and likely out of his reach.

He was only making excuses and knew it. He should have brought in a squad of men and properly sanitized the area before bringing Garbaldi in. Garbaldi's paranoia had gotten to him. Perhaps it was an unconscious desire to not put anyone else in harm's way; forgetting it was an FBI agent's duty to place himself in the line of fire should the job demand it. Then again, was he anxious to wrap this up and get back to Washington? Whatever, it had been a costly mistake.

There was no getting around it. He messed up, and because of it, Garbaldi lay dead. The least he could do now was atone a little for his error, but what he contemplated could put him on dangerously thin ice. Glancing at the neat furrow in the right shoulder pad of his jacket left by the bullet, he shook his head, figuring he'd been lucky. Staring at it, he wondered if the jacket could be repaired.

He took Professor Renauld's business card out of his pocket, tapped it against the desk and put it down. He then opened the blue folder Wellard gave him and stared at the plastic-covered papyrus. More misery inflicted in God's name, would it ever end? He closed the file with a snap, picked up the phone and dialed Strand's secretary.

"Mr. Meecham, is there anything I can do for you?"

Tom grinned. Was that an invitation or what! Sylvana was a strikingly pretty woman, and probably had a beefy boyfriend who would not be amused by Tom's amorous, lust filled more likely, advances. Never mind, it was only a harmless diversion. What the hell was she doing in the office at this late hour?

"I need you to track down an address for me, please. A Professor Vincent Renauld, Director of Harvard's Committee for the Center for Middle Eastern Studies. I've got his home number." He read it to her from the card.

"It will take a moment, sir," she replied and hung up.

Tom glanced at the phone's rectangular gray LCD: 6:13 p.m. With the semester over, there was a good chance the old boy would be home now, unless he had taken off somewhere for the evening.

Two minutes later, Sylvana rang back and gave him the details. He thanked her and dialed. After three rings, someone picked up.

"Hello?"

A woman's voice, wife or daughter? It didn't have the high pitch he would normally associate with a young woman or teenager.

"Mrs. Renauld?"

"That's right. Who is this?"

"My name is Tom Meecham, FBI Special Agent. May I speak with Professor Renauld, please, if he is available?"

"Just a moment. I'll get him for you."

Tom didn't have to wait long, probably long enough for Renauld to deny to his wife any knowledge why the FBI wanted to talk to him.

"This is Dr. Renauld, Mr. Meecham," a man answered politely in a hard voice, deep but not resonant. Tom pictured a silver-haired distinguished gentleman in his fifties, accomplished and sure of himself. "What can I do for you?"

"I understand that two days ago you met Dr. Paulini Garbaldi, Professor."

"Father Garbaldi? He was my guest at the faculty. A most accomplished scholar and a fine thinker. I wouldn't mind having him on the team. What about it?"

"I regret to inform you, sir, he was killed today by an unknown assailant."

"What! Why, how terrible. I cannot believe it. He and I were discussing…of no importance now, I guess. How am I involved?"

"Because you met him and talked to him."

"I don't understand."

"Professor, Father Garbaldi and I spoke at length about the purpose of his visit to see Dr. Noris—"

"Noris, what a tragedy. I was shocked when I saw the news clip. So senseless. I lost a friend and an astute intellectual. He had a bright future at Harvard. We were going to offer him tenure in January. Are you saying there is a connection?"

Another smart man, Tom figured. "There certainly is and you know it. Professor, I have the object Father Garbaldi brought to the United States."

Silence, then Renauld cleared his throat. "I will not pretend to not know what you're talking about, Mr. Meecham. What do you have in mind?"

"I need to see you. Tomorrow morning, ten o'clock, your office. It's a Saturday, I know, but…"

"No need to explain, Mr. Meecham. You will bring *it*?"

"Yes. I need to have it secured. I also need you to announce that Harvard will publish."

"You want to give the papyrus to Harvard? I don't know much about FBI procedure, but won't your action get you into trouble with your superiors?"

"Probably, but I'm prepared to face that and I want to finish what Garbaldi started."

"If I get involved, will I be in any danger?"

Clever man, all right, Tom thought, one who certainly understood the implication of the offer and his part in it. "I don't see how. Once you go public, any potential risk will be removed."

"Given what's happened to Noris, I wish I could believe that. Tell me. Why are you doing this, Mr. Meecham? You couldn't possibly have any interest in having the tractate published, although you must know its import."

"Let's just say I want to atone for a sin, Professor."

"I see. Very well. Ten o'clock, but I make no promises," Renauld said briskly and hung up.

Holding the receiver, dial tone humming, Tom bit his lip. Renauld didn't have to make any promises. For a chance to lay his hands on a controversial piece of history, the man was hooked, like Garbaldi said he would be. He dialed Sylvana again, but Strand himself answered.

"Don't you ever go home?" Strand complained without malice. Both were burning the long candle today, if for different reasons.

"In a while, sir. Before I get out of here, I have a request."

"You're holding vital evidence related to four murders and you want a favor? You've got balls, Meecham, but I admire your style. What is it?"

"To possibly prevent a fifth murder, I would very much appreciate if you could put a detail on Professor Renauld's residence, 34 Quincy Street, Somerville. Somebody should also be with him inside. He is intimately connected with my case and I'd hate for something bad to happen to him."

"Shit, Meecham! Is everyone you talk to on The Entity's hit list?"

"I don't want to repeat a mistake I made with Father Garbaldi," Tom said stiffly, feeling the loss more than he thought he would.

"All right, you've got the men. You want them in place now?"

"That would be good. The Professor and I are due to meet at Harvard tomorrow at ten to go over his discussions with Father Garbaldi. The detail should follow him there and one man with him in his car. Also, please alert Harvard University to watch out for anyone who doesn't belong there. Especially at the Center for Middle Eastern Studies."

"That's a pretty big request. You're serious, aren't you?"

"If I'm right, The Entity has murdered four people over that papyrus. I don't want to add to that list."

"If you simply want to interview Renauld, haul him in. Why the meeting at Harvard? You're up to something, Meecham."

"Believe me, you don't want to know."

"Call it a day, Tom," Strand advised and hung up.

Good advice and Tom had every intention of following it. To think that this morning, his only worry was getting that damned coordination report done. It still seemed so surreal.

Welcome to Wonderland, Alice.

After opening Internet Explorer, he did a quick search, found what he wanted, jotted down the email addresses, and opened Outlook. It took a few minutes to compose and edit his message. He attached the image of the tractate from Garbaldi's USB stick and clicked Send.

It should either stop the nonsense or it would be business as usual tomorrow. He was not prepared to lay down a fiver either way. After cracking his knuckles, he quickly scrolled through the FBI's internal email address list and clicked on a name. The message was brief, but the idea was to send the image of the tractate, not write a novel. After sending it, he reached for the phone. Four rings later a gruff voice answered.

"Doctor Peters."

"Hi, doc. It's Tom Meecham. I hoped to catch you."

"Just about ready to get out of here," Brian Peters retorted firmly, giving a broad hint that whatever it was, he didn't want to be bothered. "In case you wanted something, I am officially no longer in the building."

"Wish I could say the same thing," Tom told him and grinned.

After securing evidence that nailed Mossad for the sabotage of the Valero refinery, Charles Beltrain, the Special Agent in Charge of the Houston Division, finally signed off on Peters' transfer to Washington, but not before some arm twisting from

Stefan Vučak

Tom. He could even sympathize with Beltrain's position. The Houston office would be losing its most experienced forensic specialist, but Peters more than deserved the promotion.

"Why the call, Tom? It's Friday night and I want to get out of here."

"A hot date with one Dr. Patricia Riley?"

"She's my boss and it would be unseemly—"

"Yeah, I thought so. You go for it, doc."

"Look, you didn't call me to discuss my love life. What do you want?"

"I'm afraid this is going to ruin your plans for the night."

After a few seconds of silence, Tom heard a soft sigh of resignation. "I knew I should have left the phone off the hook. Come down to the lab and tell me about it."

"I can't, Brian. I'm calling from Boston."

"Boston? What the hell are you doing there? Okay, I won't pry. Talk to me while I'm still in a good mood, which is fast evaporating, by the way."

"I wouldn't have called if it wasn't important."

"I know. That's why I haven't hung up on you, yet. Now, are you going to tell me what you want or do I hang up?"

"Okay. I sent you an image of a first century papyrus. What I need is a reasonable fake that will pass a casual visual inspection. I also need you to dope it with something that'll stick to the handler's fingers for a few days which we can detect under UV light."

"And you need this by…"

"Courier it to me by morning, care of Garry Strand."

"Morning? You're kidding, right?"

"I'm sorry as hell to do this to you, but—"

"I know, it's important. You already said that, but do you have any idea of the work involved? Most of my people are already gone."

"Can you do it?"

166

"I'm sure I'll be able to dig up a papyrus sheet from somewhere and make it look like your image. As for the text, that's easy enough. We'll coat the sheet with a photographic emulsion and simply copy the image to it. Making it look authentic with iron-gall burns will be a bit trickier, but you said it only needs to pass casual inspection, right?"

"That's it."

"Then that should do it. Embedding a tracer that won't wash off will be tricky. Still, there are lots of chemicals and minerals that fluoresce and there are ways to make them stick. Leave it to me, I'll think of something, but your name isn't going to be very popular down here, you know."

"I'll make it up to you. I mean it."

"Forget it. I was going to have a pizza brought in anyway. Now I can have it here."

Peters hung up and Tom replaced the receiver, feeling like a heel for ruining his evening. He logged into the FBI database, opened his case file and created a new directory. After summarizing the salient points of the day, conclusions and intentions, he read over the text and made some corrections. What he planned to do could indeed get him into trouble with Wellard like Renauld said, but he couldn't wash his hands of the thing now for the sake of simple expediency. He had to live with his conscience. After checking the entries, he frowned and deleted the line about creating a fake papyrus and location of the real thing. He could not explain why he did that. Just a hunch. Satisfied, he logged out.

Staring at the screen, he absently picked up his mug. After glancing at it, he put the empty cup down. Part of his conversation with Garbaldi kept going around in his mind. He sighed, went to Internet Explorer again, and started searching for information about the prophesy of two messiahs. Like he told Garbaldi, he was raised a Catholic, but he had long since abandoned a Church that had little relevance for him. The one thing he never understood, why did the Church continue to amass material wealth when millions starved around the world? If the Church practiced what it preached, it would not have to worry about losing its flock. Unfortunately, the shepherd seemed to have stepped out for a beer and left the sheep to the wolves. Like other multinationals, the Church saw no profit in charity. Be that as it may, the idea that the Bible spoke of two messiahs fascinated him and he wanted to find out more.

Google spewed out page after page of references and he was staggered at the wealth of available material. Ignoring writings from fringe nut groups and evangelical extremists grinding their own wheel, there was still an abundance of respected scholarly articles that pointed at existence of two messiahs. They could not be all nuts. He clicked on one that looked promising and began to read.

It appeared that as far back as the sixth century BCE, Jews exiled in Babylon wrote about an Anointed One who would liberate them. Several of their prophecies were fulfilled when the Persian king Cyrus the Great allowed them to return to Israel. That might have been more to do with local politics than religious fulfillment. In the second century BCE, the Jews were again under occupation and the old prophecies were dusted off. Some were looking to a military leader who would free them from the oppressor and establish an independent Jewish kingdom, while the writers of the *Psalms of Solomon* stated that the messiah was a teacher who would restore Israel under Mosaic law. Take your pick.

The turbulent and confused history of the early Jews made for heavy reading. His interest lifted when he dug into references from the Dead Sea Scrolls. Reading about the Essenes who lived in Qumran with supporters of the traditional Zadokite priestly family who rebelled against the Hasmonean priest/kings even more convoluted. According to the article, the *Damascus Document* and the *Messianic Rule* texts clearly stated that the Qumranites expected the coming of two messiahs. There did not seem to be any doubt to the author of the *Testaments of the Twelve Patriarchs*.

> *My children, be obedient to Levi and to Judah. Do not exalt yourselves above these two tribes because from them will arise the Savior from God. For the Lord will raise up from Levi someone as a high priest and from Judah someone as king. He will save all the gentiles and the tribe of Israel.*
> [Testament of Simeon 7.1-2]
> *To Judah, God has given the kingship, and to Levi, the priesthood. And He has subjected the kingship to the priesthood. To me He gave earthly matters and to Levi heavenly matters. As heaven is superior to the earth, so is God's priesthood superior to the kingdom on earth.*
> [Testament of Judah 21.2-4a]

That one set Tom thinking, but the most intriguing text he found supporting the idea of two messiahs came from the *Messianic Rule* 1Q28a document, called the *Rule of the Congregation*.

> *This is the sitting of the men of renown called to the assembly for the council of the community when God will have begotten the Messiah among them. The Priest shall enter at the head of all the congregation of Israel, then are all the chiefs of the sons of Aaron, the priests, called to the assembly, men of renown. And they shall sit before him, each according to his rank.*
> *Afterward, the Messiah of Israel shall enter. The chiefs of the tribes of Israel shall sit before him, each according to his rank, according to their position in the camps and during their marches; then all the heads of family of the congregation, together with the wise men of the congregation, shall sit before them, each according to his rank.*
> *And when they gather for the community table, or to drink wine, and arrange the community table and mix the wine to drink, let no man stretch out his hand over the first fruits of bread and wine before the*

Priest. For it is he who shall bless the first fruits of bread and wine, and shall first stretch out his hand over the bread. And afterward, the Messiah of Israel shall stretch out his hands over the bread. And afterward, all the congregation of the community shall bless, each according to his rank.

There were other articles about the Dead Sea Scrolls, most of them citing the same references. Tom then turned to the Old Testament and hit a brick wall. Much of the material written by the extremist fringe who produced convoluted conclusions that made little sense. There were several verses that hinted at two messiahs he could interpret for himself. Zechariah being the main one. In chapter 9:9-10, he prophesizes a meek king:

Rejoice greatly, O daughter of Zion! Shout in triumph, O daughter of Jerusalem! Behold, your king is coming to you; He is just and endowed with salvation.
Humble, and mounted on a donkey, even on a colt, the foal of a donkey. And He will speak peace to the nations; And His dominion will be from sea to sea,
And from the River to the ends of the earth.

But in 14:2-4 he foretells of a warrior:

And in that day living waters will flow out of Jerusalem, half of them toward the eastern sea and the other half toward the western sea; it will be in summer as well as in winter. And the Lord will be king over all the earth; in that day the Lord will be the only one, and His name the only one.

Some articles, including the Catholic Encyclopedia, suggested that this merely prophesized the coming of a single messiah on two different occasions, but Tom found that reasoning hard to swallow. He figured it was a fig leaf the Church held up to cover its embarrassment for failing to 'correct' Zechariah. There were also references from the New Testament, but they required some agile mental gymnastics to accept.

After logging off, Tom sat there, deep in thought.

As an adult, he had never given much thought to God, faith or the Church. Even as a kid, his parents did not push him very hard to attend Mass or Sunday school. When he became a teenager, they gave up completely. When he did think of the Church, it was in pretty derogatory terms. Since grade school, his image of the Church was one of fat priests driving posh cars and living in fancy houses, obsessed with money collection and preaching dull sermons that made little sense. When he thought of Rome or the pope, he saw pomp and ceremony and unbelievable opulence. It all seemed far removed from what he thought the Church should be doing, helping the poor and the destitute. After all, wasn't that what Jesus and his disciples were about? Notwithstanding the good work of many, the rule seemed to be, do as I say, not as I do.

As for believing in the Bible, what was there to believe? It held the one and only truth, and that was that. The tenets were an unstated part of his life and he more or less obeyed the commandments. Just because he had not been to Mass in years, he didn't believe being cast into an everlasting hell for it because it pissed off the local priest. A pretty grim idea anyway; condemned to an eternity of punishment for something so trivial. Out of proportion, and if God existed, he did not accept that He would demand such retribution.

Despite all its faults and scandals, he kind of accepted the Church and had a live and let live truce with it. After all, the priests and cardinals were merely men, subject to all the temptations and failings of men everywhere. To have someone like Garbaldi, a priest himself, rub his nose in the raw facts was unsettling to say the least.

Christ!

171

Were all religions merely charades, inventions of priests to maintain themselves in a life of ease, peddling salvation to the poor and ignorant because that is all they had to cling to in an otherwise miserable existence? It seemed a great job if you could stomach it.

The Vatican maintained a spy service and used hit squads…

Tom sighed and shook his head. Perhaps sometimes it was better not to know. Knowledge simply got in the way of believing. If a priest like Garbaldi could stop believing, there wasn't much point to it, was there?

After a moment, he picked up the wrapped papyrus, got up and switched off the lights. Outside, the sun hung low over the skyscrapers, painting the wispy streamers of clouds orange and gold. Being a Friday, pedestrians crowded the sidewalks and noisy cars filled the street, but he felt isolated from the people around him, alone. A cool breeze ruffled his hair and he gave an involuntary shiver. He turned right and began walking down Tremont Street toward the hotel, his footsteps lost among a multitude of others.

Chapter Five

Wellard signed off the last memo and put it in his Out tray, then leaned against the seat and stretched his arms. The joints popped and he stifled a yawn. Still dusk outside, but Washington already blazed with light, and Pennsylvania Avenue swarmed as always with mostly government workers and Beltway bandits threading their way out of town. He should be getting out of here himself. By the time he got home, it would be late, but Caroline would understand and have his dinner ready as always. Anyway, Georgetown was not all that far. With Brad at Stanford and Nancy at Harvard, both doing graduate work, he did not have to worry about having offspring underfoot. Why Brad wanted to go to California for his studies, and Stanford of all places, was beyond him. Freedom to spread his wings? Both promised to visit during the summer break, but he knew how that worked. They had their own lives now and were no longer bound to their parent's apron strings. Still, it would be nice if at least one of them came home occasionally. It didn't matter. He and Caroline had adjusted to the fact that their children were no longer teenagers. It gave them time to enjoy life more, talk, be together and rekindle something that had been only smoldering for far too long.

He should be looking forward to the weekend, but hands locked behind his head, he felt deeply disturbed. Meecham's call had shocked him and he spent his day in moody silence. If the papyrus thing was genuine as Tom said, and he had no doubts, his superiors should be warned. They may even be able to help The Entity recover it. Should he interfere in what may already be under control? By getting involved, he would be committing a grave breach of FBI security, but he had a clear duty. He answered to a higher authority than the FBI.

Making a decision, he pulled the keyboard toward him and faced the 48cm LED flat screen. With his access privileges it took only moments to gain entry to Meecham's case database. He hesitated when he came to the Vatican directory and double-clicked the entry. A single Word file, a JPG graphics image, and a copy of an email. He opened the file and began to read. When he came to the translation, his face drained and his heart hammered. There was also an embedded image of the tractate, which he skipped, the Sahidic text having no meaning for him. Everything there as he feared, and much worse. This was explosive material that threatened the very foundation of the Church itself. Sitting back, he thanked the Lord for giving him strength to intervene.

He scanned Tom's summary and conclusions, and an outline of leads he was following. The report clearly a work in progress, to be updated as events unfolded. Tom's declaration to hand the papyrus to Professor Renauld for secure storage was a major concern. It seemed the meddlesome young fool intended to finish what Garbaldi started, after he told him not to get involved. He read the email entry and his blood boiled. Seemingly innocent, it appeared that Tom was being deliberately provocative.

No longer a question of loyalty to the FBI, it touched directly on everything he believed in. For anyone to dare dispute that the Lord Jesus Christ was not the Messiah or God incarnate in a holy trinity was a blasphemer and a heretic, deserving of the Lord's wrath. The papyrus Father Garbaldi unearthed might be a valuable historical curiosity, but its revelation would only aid Satan and his followers. That Meecham could be swept up in such a monstrous conspiracy was lamentable, but the man should have known better. After all, he was supposed to be Catholic.

Wellard closed the file, sat back deep in thought, intensely unsettled. He wiped his palms against the trousers and swallowed hard. He must stop Meecham handing over the papyrus as a matter of priority. That was clear. He resisted the impulse to call Strand and have Tom arrested and the document confiscated. On what charge would he hold him? Withholding evidence? He dismissed that one out of hand. No, he had a better way. He would report this and let Authority deal with it, knowing that by doing so, he was potentially implicating himself. The thought hardly bothered him. One scarified career in the greater scheme of doing God's work meant nothing. He firmly believed in the creed of his order's founder: 'Sanctify your work. Sanctify yourself in your work. Sanctify others through your work.'

He liked to think that he had obeyed the creed faithfully.

Logging onto his personal email website, he quickly composed a brief message and attached Meecham's Word file. Staring at the text, he hesitated before clicked the Send icon. His action might possibly cause some harm to Tom and Renauld, something that rested heavily on his conscience. As one of Lord's soldiers, it was his duty to protect the Church at all costs. Wearing a heavy frown, he clicked the icon.

Somehow, that did not lighten the load pressing on his shoulders. The Entity had already killed to recover the tractate and he feared it might do so again with the information he had now provided.

"I'm sorry, Tom," he mumbled, swiveled his chair and looked out at Washington's jagged skyline, wondering what he had set into motion. It wasn't always easy doing the right thing. What he did now, was it right? Despite having done his duty, he struggled to find an acceptable answer.

* * *

In New York, the imposing seventeen-story building located at the corner of Lexington Avenue and 34th Street mostly dark. Only a window here and there showed a light. On the sixth floor,

Father Kelvin saw a flashing icon indicating an incoming email from one of their special sources and opened the message. He handled exceptional traffic, and got perhaps one or two a week. The quality of the source demanded that such messages be processed at once. When off duty, others stood watch.

He read the brief memo from Wellard and sat straighter in his chair. After checking the attachment, he shuddered in alarm.

"Oh, my God. Oh, my God." That such a thing could befall the Church…

He immediately picked up his phone and dialed a direct line.

"Kelvin, it's seven o'clock! Only you would have the temerity to call me at this ungodly hour," answered His Excellency, Anthony Rodriguez, fourth Prelate of Opus Dei, the 'Work of God'.

"Sorry, Anthony, but this cannot wait." Kelvin not sorry at all for interrupting Rodriguez in his private chambers. God's work did not keep banker's hours. "Can you come down?"

"Now? I'm about to retire. Can't it wait?"

"It's got to be now, I'm afraid."

"Very well, but you better not be wasting my time, that's all I can say."

"I'll do ten extra Hail Mary's if you think I've wasted your time."

"You'll do a hell of a lot more than ten," Rodriguez warned, then laughed. "Okay, I'll see you in a minute."

It was actually twenty minutes by the time Rodriguez took care of a few personal needs, downed another glass of excellent sacramental merlot, and pulled on a deep red corduroy evening jacket. Rank did have its little privileges and he enjoyed them all. A devout and willing tool for God, but that didn't mean he had to be a suffering one. Flagellation was for the Supernumeraries and he far too worldly to be swayed by his organization's propaganda.

After the untimely death of Monsignor Javier Echevarria through prostate cancer—being a Prelate of Opus Dei did not guarantee longevity—Rodrigues had succeeding to the post. He spent most of his time commuting between the Rome headquarters and New York. He didn't mind, not when done in first class. Being the pontiff's personal prelature, Opus Dei came in for its share of jealous criticism from the Curia, and in his opinion, most of it grossly unwarranted. His organization exerted considerable influence over the Church, and rightly so. As for its alleged secretiveness, elitism, and right-wing fascist leanings, these were nothing more than misrepresentations by a biased media.

Certainly, Numeraries were sometimes required to submit their incoming and outgoing mail to their superiors for scrutiny, and members were forbidden to read certain inflammatory books. It was for their own good and maintained purity of purpose. When a Numerary's association with a non-member, or even his own family, threatened to undermine Opus Dei doctrine, what was wrong with the Numerary severing all ties with the godless if failure to do so placed his soul in jeopardy? Rodriquez saw nothing evil in taking the fight against communism to countries where the sons of Lucifer lived. If that was fascism, so be it. He firmly believed in Josemaria Escriva's teachings as outlined in his book *The Way* and saw no reason to deviate from it. That, in 2002, Pope John Paul II canonized Escriva only fitting. Everything else was the failing of detractors to see God's work actually being done in these turbulent times. Especially now, a firm hand was needed to guide the wavering.

The elevator took him down from his penthouse apartment to the sixth floor, the doors sounding unnaturally loud as they closed behind him, and a deserted corridor. He quickly walked into Kelvin's spacious, but modest, office without knocking, his footsteps echoing on the parquet floor. Two large windows opened to 34th Street, at the moment closed off by heavy beige drapes. A small imitation crystal chandelier flooded the room with bright light.

Kelvin looked up from his screen and motioned Rodriguez to come over. "Pull up a chair. You will have to read this for yourself."

"What is it?" Rodriguez demanded impatiently as he snagged a chair, dragged it over and sank his corpulent body into it.

"An email from one of our Associates, Wellard. He is an Assistant Director—"

"I know him, a dutiful disciple. What does the FBI have that could be of interest to us?"

"It's not actually for us," Kelvin said and pointed at the Word document, a faint smile creasing his mouth.

"What are you smirking about?" Rodriguez demanded.

"Oh, nothing."

"Hah!" Rodriguez bent and stared at the screen. When he finished, he swallowed, tasting bile. "This is monstrous, an abomination that must be scoured clean from the minds of men forever. It's scurrilous untruth, something I would expect from the Coptic heretics."

"Did you see the dating data?" Kelvin prompted. "The papyrus wasn't written by the Coptic separatists. It's a fragment of an earlier gospel, possibly part of the Q source itself."

"Blasphemy! It cannot be true!"

"True or not, I suggest that Cardinal Belconi be advised. With Wellard's input alerting us to Agent Meecham's every move, His Eminence should be able to contain this easily."

"I'm not so sure that it can be contained, not now, but you're right," Rodriguez mumbled absently, thinking furiously.

Alerting Belconi clearly the correct thing to do, but what if Opus Dei finished the job instead? Belconi would owe him a huge favor and it was always useful having The Entity obliged to him. After a moment, he thought better of it. However attractive the idea, he had to reject it. He had at his command members whose skills spanned the entire range of professions: military, law enforcement and intelligence; resources available across the entire globe. They were not assassins, exactly. It was true that Opus Dei had local affiliates such as the Knights of Malta and the Jesuits, who could be called upon to carry out an unpleasant piece of God's work from time to time, but getting things moving would take planning, coordination and secure communication. All that would take time, something he probably did not have. While the FBI agent had the papyrus, it was imperative that it be recovered as quickly as possible before the damned thing became public. In that, Wellard quite rightly passed this on. No, better let Belconi know and be an appreciated partner rather than risk the Vatican's wrath later should things melt down, the pontiff's protective hand notwithstanding. Besides, Belconi already had an operative active on the job to clean up the mess, with all the control and communication mechanisms in place. It was not wise to cross The Entity, definitely not.

He glanced at his watch. Seven-thirty here meant past midnight in Rome. If his evening was ruined, he didn't see any reason not to ruin Belconi's.

"Put a secure call through to his direct line. If he's out, try the private number. I doubt His Eminence will mind being disturbed for this."

Kelvin grinned, got up and stepped to his desk. It took only a moment to establish a connection. Still grinning, he handed the phone to Rodriguez.

"Your Eminence, my apologies for waking you... You're already awake... Bishop Anthony Rodriguez. I have some information that should help you track down a certain piece of papyrus. Interested?" He listened and nodded, "Good. By a fortuitous set of events, I am in a unique position to assist you with this delicate matter."

* * *

The gauzy curtains barely stirred in the light breeze and the city quiet. Cardinal Avero Belconi grunted, turned in his bed and rubbed his sagging stomach. He had dozed off a couple of times, but could not sink into deep sleep. A late dinner of sizzling bratwurst sausages, browned until they were almost burned, finely baked potato wedges spiced just right, and crisp coleslaw tossed in a tangy dressing with a side order of Polish sweet-and-sour pickles, had put him in a mellow mood. A snifter of fine Otard cognac topped off a splendid evening and he retired feeling pleased with himself and the sinful world at large.

He tried to forget the irritating conversation with Peroni earlier in the day, but it kept churning in his head, keeping him awake. The man was a heathen predator, but also one of the few independent professionals he trusted to do a job properly, unlike Swens. The idiot tried to remove Peroni before they took care of Garbaldi and got shot instead. To compound Belconi's misery, Peroni apparently made a recording of their deal. How the godless man managed to get a recorder through Vatican's security defied reason, and something to be studiously investigated. At least Peroni held no grudge. Nevertheless, he didn't want to make the same mistake again and have the man turn on *him*. He shuddered at the thought, likewise having to explain his action to the pontiff should Peroni's recording ever surface. Once he resolved the current situation, something permanent would have to be done about Peroni and his recording. It would be an intolerable state of affairs to have that hanging over him.

Beside him, the phone rang and he jerked involuntarily, startled by the loud noise. He muttered a few unholy words, flipped on the reading lamp, blinked at the sudden harsh light, and groped for the receiver.

"Cardinal Belconi," he growled, his mood definitely not charitable.

"It's Renaro."

"Damn it man! You know what time it is?"

"It's late, I know. But never mind that. What in sweet heaven is going on in Boston, Avero? I thought you would dispose of the Garbaldi matter quickly and quietly. Instead, you've lost control completely!"

Belconi blinked, his thoughts totally disorganized. "What the hell are you talking about?"

"I forwarded you an email addressed to Albani with a CC to me. You should read it. Clean this up before we all get splattered," Marati said heavily and hung up.

Frowning, Belconi wondered what could be so earth-shatteringly important to warrant waking him at this ungodly hour. What in heaven was Marati doing prowling about so late? Damn him anyway. Grunting, he swung his thick legs out and slid them into a pair of cold slippers. Feeling grumpy, he wrapped on a silk robe, padded to his study, and switched on the computer. He quickly logged on and opened his email Inbox. There were twenty-two messages waiting for his attention. Marati's second on the list and he double-clicked it. Addressed to Albani, all right. He noted the FBI logo on the header and tensed.

Your Eminence,

My name is Thomas Meecham, Supervising Special Agent attached to the FBI Counterterrorism Division, Washington.
I regret having to inform you of the death today of Father Paulini Garbaldi at the hand of an unknown assailant. Before he died, he made me aware of a Coptic papyrus and his intention to publish the text.
You have my assurance that the FBI will prosecute this case until all persons responsible for his death are apprehended. In accordance with Father Garbaldi's wishes, I want to advise you that I will hand over the tractate to Harvard's Center for Middle Eastern Studies for storage and disposition as they see fit.

I remain sincerely,

Tom Meecham

Belconi read the message again and clicked on the attachment, knowing full well what it contained. He stared at the damning text and sat back in his chair, his night thoroughly ruined.

Had the FBI agent confided in somebody else? The tone of the email suggested not, but he had most likely made a routine report to his superior. That made things more complicated, but the situation may yet be retrievable. Meecham had the papyrus, but did not hand it to Harvard yet, a key point. Peroni could conceivably still finish the job satisfactorily, if he managed to find Meecham in time. That could be problematic, but Peroni was resourceful, not overly concerned about somebody else being aware of the papyrus. An inconvenience, but without the tractate itself, the FBI would be left holding secondhand information, provided Peroni managed to recover the thing. Staring at the email, he reflected that Albani would need to be told how to respond to Meecham and how to keep his own mouth shut if he knew what was good for him. He understood now why Marati was jittery.

His desk phone rang again and he picked up. He might as well be in his office!

"Your Eminence, my apologies for waking you—"

"No matter, I'm already up."

"You're already awake?"

"Who is this?"

"Bishop Anthony Rodriguez. I have some information that should help you track down a certain piece of papyrus. Interested?"

Belconi willed himself to stay calm despite a slight flutter in his chest. How in sweet heaven had Opus Dei stumbled onto this? The whole thing had gotten out of hand. Perhaps Meecham had it right and it was time to prepare for the onslaught that publication of the tractate would unleash. Still, the papyrus was not published and he had options. No need to think of giving up just yet.

"I am interested."

"Good. By a fortuitous set of events, I am in a unique position to assist you with this delicate matter."

"Please tell me what you have in mind, Your Excellency."

* * *

Peroni disconnected the call from Belconi and shook his head with bemused wonder. Opus Dei...of all people to be involved with! He would rather hassle with the devil. Thinking about it, he figured he probably already was. At least he understood this particular demon. Opus Dei, on the other hand, grim news, and he had no desire to fall into their clutches. The one anonymous job he did for their Rome office a while back made him wary. Behind their façade of charitable works, honorable in itself, lay a sinister organization whose purpose was to influence Vatican policy to further its own control of the Sacred College, which ultimately elected the pope. Like the Jesuits, Opus Dei wanted the pope to be not only the world's spiritual leader, but a temporal one as well, with one or both of them at his side pulling the strings.

Perhaps he attributed too much influence to them, but he was certain of one thing. Under no circumstances did he want them to know his identity. When Belconi suggested that Father Kelvin contact him directly with updates on Meecham's movements and plans, he shuddered at the thought. He operated alone, his name known only to Belconi, and he wanted it to remain that way. His one entanglement with Swens merely reinforced that policy. On the other hand, given the five-hour time difference between Boston and Rome, having a three-cornered communication link hardly practical. Events were too fluid and he could not afford to wait for day-old information from Belconi.

After some wrangling, the compromise he suggested readily accepted by everyone. Kelvin had created a random Gmail account that would serve as Peroni's information pipeline. A simple matter to link the BlackBerry to the email account. He already used it to download Meecham's report.

Because of it, he now found himself in a quandary. Belconi insisted that Renauld had to be eliminated as a warning to other institutions who might contemplate publishing the papyrus. Knowing that both his targets would be together at a set time presented an ideal scenario to take them out—too ideal. Meecham made a tactical mistake with Garbaldi, one he was not likely to repeat. The FBI and university security would be watching. If he were Meecham, he would have the Renauld residence under surveillance as well, but also a far softer target. Tactically, as far as he was concerned, eliminating Renauld, apart from its psychological impact, the gains were nil. Well, not quite. It would net him another hundred thousand. The thought made him smile. If he survived to walk out of this with his skin intact, he could afford to retire, or at least semi-retire. His accustomed lifestyle demanded considerable financial support. Renauld was merely a diversion. He still needed to remove Meecham and recover the papyrus, his primary mission. The FBI agent was highly trained and would now be extra wary. He could not hope to have Peroni's skills, but Meecham had lots more resources available at his disposal.

Keep the situation simple and reduce as many variables as possible, an old lesson from Peroni's training and one he followed diligently. Very well. He would take out Renauld and isolate Meecham. With Kelvin's source providing movement updates, a situation would present itself where the FBI agent would be vulnerable. All Peroni needed to do was exercise patience and bide his time. Of course, he could not afford limitless patience. However unlikely, over time the FBI machine would assemble sufficient pieces to profile him and set up an entrapment gambit.

His assignment compelled him to pursue his target and the FBI would play on that assumption. He did not intend falling for such an obvious, but unavoidable tactic. He would give himself two more days to finish this. Once he crossed that safety margin threshold, he was done, a rule he never violated. Belconi could rant and rave, but Peroni had no desire to become a martyr for a cause he didn't believe in. This was business. The papyrus and its contents were strictly Belconi's problem. Let Opus Dei finish the job for him if he wanted.

Peroni liked the one about reaping what you sow. It brought another smile to his face.

He glanced at his black Rado wristwatch: 10:20 p.m. Late, but he needed to check out the neighborhood around Renauld's house and establish an effective extraction route. He did not want to shoot another FBI agent like he did at the Noris residence simply to ensure his getaway. He did not charge Belconi for that one, being an operational necessity.

The Sheraton Commander Hotel basement parking lot had adequate lighting, and held a sprinkling of cars, but otherwise deserted. He was exposing himself and his movements to surveillance cameras, something he could not really avoid. Besides, by the time the FBI got around to processing them, which they would certainly do, he should be long out of the country and beyond their reach. Making his way through the parking lot, the place smelled of oil, rubber and gasoline. He unlocked his Honda and climbed in. The motor started at the first press of the ignition button.

He had studied the Boston street directory and knew roughly how to get to Quincy Street in Somerville, but the car's GPS locator screen helped take the worry out of finding the way. It wasn't a long drive from the Sheraton anyway. Working at Harvard, Renauld clearly preferred being close to Cambridge, something that Peroni appreciated.

He parked the car on Summer Street, a block from Renauld's address and looked at the GPS map more closely. A narrow walking lane cut across Church, Quincy and School Streets, and ran beside the Renauld house. This could turn out to be easier than he figured. Getting out of the car, he did a quick visual around to fix the neighborhood in his mind. In the dark the markers always looked different than they did during the day, but his training allowed for that. Being a major artery, traffic still flowed in both directions along Summer, making soft whispers as they went. With quick strides, he walked down Church Street toward the lane between the houses. When he reached it, he turned right and slowly made his way along the dimly lit sidewalk, bordered by brick walls and two-meter-high steel or wooden fences. Every now and then, he saw a small gate, presumably to allow access to the backyard.

At the end of the lane, he paused and looked up and down Quincy Street. Cars were parked everywhere, garage space an impossibility with the narrow house lots here. Across the street at the Renauld house, a light shone from the top story window. Clearly, someone was home. A dark sedan stood parked in front of the house. Peroni bit his lip and sighed. Nowhere he could hide and keep the house under observation until Renauld emerged, and the lane was completely exposed. Moreover, it was obvious. Even if he managed to nail Renauld, he would find it difficult to run down the lane to Church Street and drive off without being spotted by the FBI stakeout he felt certain lurked here somewhere.

He retraced his steps and walked toward Somerville Avenue. When he got there, he paused, judging distances, figuring roughly two hundred meters to the lane. The street was brightly lit and a steady stream of cars kept it from being a lonely place. He could wait in his car and keep an eye on the house until the good doctor came out. A single rifle shot and that would be it—if he managed to get off a shot and if he had a rifle. However, he had another more serious consideration. Sitting there on a busy street in broad daylight, he would stand out like a sore boil. Anybody watching would spot him and the awkward questions would start. Not good.

Having eliminated two possibilities, he contemplated another. Making up his mind, he turned right, walked two blocks to School Street, and turned right again. When he reached the path, he turned right. The same pattern of wall, fence, and gates. When he neared Quincy Street, he stopped and grinned. The Renauld residence had a gate. He grasped the cold metal handle and pushed down. A click and the small gate opened inward a fraction without a squeak. Obviously, people were trusting here. Satisfied, he closed the gate and wiped the handle.

He walked back to his car and got in. Without hesitating, he opened the glove box and took out the silenced semi-automatic. Chambering a round, he slid the weapon into his waistband, wondering mildly whatever happened to Swens' surveillance team and the tree camera. He relaxed, emptied his mind and waited. After a time some inner clock gave a tick and he opened his eyes. He did not intend doing the job now, but all the factors were favorable and he didn't believe in wasting an opportunity. Pulling on his gloves, he got out of the car.

Going through the back gate at Renauld's place, he stepped on soft soil beside a brick lane. Looking down, he patted down the footprint and wiped his shoes against the moist grass. Getting into the house was easy, the rear door unlocked. A dim safety light lit the kitchen and he walked through a side door into a narrow corridor. He paused, listening for any sound that did not belong. An FBI agent could be on guard, but he sensed he was alone. One of those instinctive things. He just knew. Near the front entrance, stairs led to the upper level. He tested the first step, but the carpeted treads muffled any sound. At the top, he stopped and waited. A body shifted, followed by a muffled cough. Peroni tiptoed to the bedroom door and slowly opened it, anticipating a squeal, but it moved without sound.

A single front window opened to the street, a curtain diffusing the outside light. A queen-sized bed stood tucked tight against the right front corner. Renauld lay on the left near the window, his right arm flung out. His wife lay curled facing the wall. Peroni pulled out the handgun, flipped off the safety and straightened his right arm. He aimed and pulled the trigger. The soft *thuft* seemed unnaturally loud in the thick silence, but Renauld's wife didn't even stir. Renauld, of course, certainly did not.

Peroni carefully closed the bedroom door behind him and walked down the stairs. Once out in the lane, he allowed himself to relax fractionally. It wouldn't do to be careless now. At the end of the lane, he turned left, pleased at having done a clean hit. The FBI surveillance boys would have some tricky questions to answer in the morning, but hardly his concern.

With everybody now accounted for, time to check out of the Sheraton and move downtown closer to the FBI headquarters. After all, that's where he would find Meecham. That could wait until morning.

* * *

Hands clasped behind his back, staring at nothing in particular, Cardinal Albani fought to still the disquieting demons that warred with his soul. Morning sunshine cast dark, slanting shadows across the papal gardens. On his left, he could make out the Fountain of the Sacrament, sending a silver stream of rainbow water toward a cloud-streaked sky, only to fall back in a shower of glittering pearls. Caretakers tended rows of colorful flowerbeds along cobbled paths, pulling up weeds and plucking at withered petals. After giving so much pleasure and joy, they were now to be discarded, forgotten, to rot on a compost heap.

It should have turned out to be simply another day among many. He mourned the senseless loss of Father Reoni, a gentle soul and a dedicated scientist, wondering why God allowed such things. Reoni's death had seriously disrupted work at the Conservation Laboratory, placing him in a bind for a suitable replacement, but Giacomo was already on that. He knew his thoughts bordered on the sacrilegious, implying criticism of the Divinity, but he couldn't help himself. If it had not been God's will, man's wickedness must have perpetrated the deed. A new kind of thinking for him, which he would not have entertained if not for that disturbing FBI email.

When he came in this morning, Sister Angela stood up, her face tragic, eyes glistening.

"Your Eminence…"

Immediately concerned, he hurried to her desk. "What is it? What happened?"

"It's…it's Father Garbaldi, Your Eminence. He's dead."

He paled and his mouth went dry as awful scenarios flashed through his head. "Dead? How?"

"I was sorting your general emails as I usually do every morning, when I came across this." She picked up a printout from her desk and held it out. "It's from the FBI in Washington."

"Washington?" What possible interest could the FBI have in Garbaldi? The man was here, on a sabbatical writing his book. Wasn't he?

Confused, he took the page and quickly scanned the brief message. A chill ran down his back and he inhaled sharply. Garbaldi was not home, but in America, and talking to Harvard! Surely, the young fool did not intend…he hardly dared contemplate the awful possibility. When he last talked to Marati, it seemed ages ago now, they were discussing possibilities, options. Bad enough having to deal with Garbaldi, but the FBI! Stunned, he slowly opened the heavy door to his office and walked in.

"Your Eminence?"

His head jerked up and he glanced at Angela. "It's all right, Sister. Leave it with me," he whispered and closed the door after him.

Without thinking, he made his way to the window and the inviting light outside, for he badly needed light and guidance. Standing there, numb, he looked at the printout again, noticing the CC address. Why would the FBI forward a copy of the email to Marati? He should have felt surprise, something, but he only felt cold acceptance as he recalled the grim hardness on his mentor's face that fateful day. Did the FBI believe this was not a simple murder? Marati wouldn't…he struggled to form the monstrous thought. No, his friend would never stoop to something like that. As Prefect for the Congregation for the Doctrine of the Faith, Marati was the Church's protector! It was outrageous to contemplate he could somehow be involved in Garbaldi's death. Outrageous or not, the thought kept teasing him.

Part of him cried to leave it alone. It wasn't his responsibility. But weren't they all responsible?

Gazing at the fountain, badly shaken, Albani allowed the paper to slip between his nerveless fingers. His comfortable, predictable world had tumbled into something dark and sinister, which he didn't recognize. If death ruled in this world, did he want to be part of it? With a stab of conscience, he realized he was already a part and, however inadvertently, may have contributed to Garbaldi's death. After a long moment, he took a deep breath and sat at his desk. A coward dies every day, but a righteous person can only die once, unpalatable as that might be. He picked up his phone and dialed a direct number.

"Cardinal Marati," a gruff voice answered, cold and impatient.

Albani hesitated, wondering if he knew the man at the end of the line. He could still walk away, but if he took that next step, there would be no going back for anyone.

"It's Gulio."

After a moment of poignant silence, Marati sighed. "Not an unexpected call, my friend."

"I dare say. You saw the email?"

"I saw it."

"Just tell me you had nothing to do with it, Renaro."

"You know I cannot tell you that."

"And Reoni?"

"If you got this far, you should be able to figure out the rest."

Albani did and his mouth tightened, anger welling from deep within his soul. At least Marati had not bothered with histrionic denials.

"You went to that butcher Belconi, didn't you? Why, for God's sake? We were supposed to talk to Garbaldi, nothing more!"

"He only had to see Giacomo as he was supposed to and he would still be sifting moldy manuscripts in your Archives dungeon. But no, he went off on some personal crusade—"

"You can't be certain he intended to publish the papyrus."

"The FBI had no doubts, and that FBI agent certainly didn't."

Utterly weary, Albani pulled out his chair and sat down. "Is this what the Church does now? Is this what it takes to protect the faith? How far do we go?"

"We do what is necessary. Once you get over your moral outrage, Gulio, remember this. Your hands are not exactly clean either. Instead of handling the matter yourself like you should have, to salve your conscience, you came running to me. Your blustering indignation now has a hypocritical ring to it, my friend. We faced a situation and we dealt with it!"

"Not like this! We can never justify this."

"The alternative being to do nothing, is that it? Don't pretend you don't know what The Entity's mission is all about. Get back to that FBI agent. Tell him you're appalled to hear of

191

Garbaldi's death and deny any involvement by the Vatican's security services. I would also suggest that you demand immediate return of the papyrus," Marati grated harshly and cut contact.

Albani stared at the receiver and chuckled, his friend's words a bitter fruit in his mouth. No matter which way he looked at it, playing the Pontius Pilate would do little to ease the ache in his soul or the burden of his guilt.

Would he be the next petal? Would Giacomo? He had no ready answer.

Marati was wrong about one thing. They faced a situation, all right, but it had not been dealt with. Okay, he may have failed the first time, but he would deal with it now. Expression grim, he picked up the phone and pressed a glowing button.

"Yes, Your Eminence?"

"Sister, please call Father Tomboli. I need to see the Holy Father."

* * *

"Christ! Somebody was supposed to be in the house with him!" Tom raged, hands planted on Strand's polished desk. Utterly frustrated, he wanted to jump over the desk and slug the Boston chief.

Clearly uncomfortable, Strand nevertheless did not avert his gaze. "I didn't want to unduly alarm him or his wife with what was a remote possibility at best."

"Remote possibility? I *told* you he was a likely target!" Tom pulled back, looking disgusted. "Well, you won't have to worry about alarming him now. He's dead. I can only imagine his wife's reaction when she woke to find her husband's bloody body."

"Okay, Meecham, I messed up and you can make out your report accordingly," Strand snapped. "I apologize, not that it's any consolation."

"It isn't," Tom growled, dragged out a chair and sat down.

He could make life difficult for the Boston chief, certain that Strand knew it. It would be a Pyrrhic victory. Renauld was dead and nothing would bring him back. Besides, he needed Strand's cooperation far more than Strand needed his. There remained the necessary technical legwork by Johnston. Galloping around in moral outrage wasn't going to help anybody.

"Forget it. It was a judgment call. We're dealing with a highly skilled professional here and we've given him enough freebies."

"Thanks, Tom, and I'm sorry," Strand said softly. "I still can't believe it. The son of a bitch just walked in. Incredible."

"We both made a mistake. Do we have anything more from the forensics team? I mean the Noris residence and the car out front."

"Let's get an update," Strand said formally and touched a button on his phone.

"Yes, sir?" Sylvana answered politely.

"Have Agent Johnston come to my office if he is in."

"Yes, sir."

A lanky, taciturn, middle-aged man, Johnston wore his dark gray pinstripe like a sack. His bald head shone under the lights, but his eyes were alive as he seated himself. According to Strand, the morose man had joined the Bureau late in life, transferring after a career in the LAPD, and had turned out to be an excellent agent. Johnston glanced at Tom and gave a brief nod. If he resented doing the grunt work on the case, he didn't show it.

"We got nothing inside the house," he said in a deep, slow voice, face expressionless. "Not a single print. The recovered bullets and casings were all 9 millimeter and the grooves left by the barrel rifling suggests identical handguns, Hi-Point C-9s. If we're lucky, we may get a print off a shell casing, but I wouldn't bet on it. We found a grocery receipt in the dead shooter's pocket from Alhoda Market, which is just around the corner from the Noris residence. The store surveillance tapes are being looked at.

"It's a start, but I'm holding out my hopes with the stolen Astra. We lifted a bunch of prints on which we ran checks. A set matches our dead shooter, one Martin Swens. The others belong to the car's owner and a woman, probably his wife. The bag in the trunk suggests that Swens most likely supplied the hardware. That would make sense if the second shooter flew in and didn't want to risk smuggling in a weapon. The prints recovered off the weapon from the Noris house belong to Swens."

"What's the story on the guy?" Tom asked, his mind working the information.

"We're still running that down, but it's murky. He's a nasty character, former SEAL and general badass. We had him investigated a number of times on suspicion of murder, but nothing ever stuck. Doesn't have a job, but checking his apartment, he seems to live well enough. We don't know where he gets the money to support himself—yet. I'm arranging for a court order to look at his bank records. We seized his computer and are sifting through it. An initial run through the directories revealed files on the Society of Jesus."

Tom and Strand exchanged glances. "The Jesuits?"

"Provides another link with Garbaldi's Entity," Johnston said with a tight grin. "We're also running the usual checks on his phone and cellphone records. We haven't recovered his cellphone, and it's possible the second shooter took it. Why he would do that is anybody's guess."

"He might have wanted to download the SIM card and the phone's memory chip," Tom mused. "Or simply to remove a trail. Anything from airport surveillance tapes?"

"Give me a break! It's only been a day. If Swens met the second shooter at Logan International, we'll nail him. I'll give you an update when I've got something more."

"Find out Swens' cellphone number," Tom told him. "He's probably got bills lying around. Then call the NSA and get them to provide us with transcripts of all calls he made over the last five days."

"Can do."

"I don't suppose you have anything on the Renauld hit?" Tom added hopefully and Johnston shook his head.

"Wish we had the guy working for us. That was slick work. Our boys never saw a thing."

Tom snorted. "That's obvious."

"The only thing he left is a partial shoeprint beside the side gate. There were also soil smears on the kitchen tiles. Forensics took a cast, but it's just another loose end. What we know of our man, he'll probably ditch the shoes. I would."

Tom smiled. "Yeah, me too. Okay, thanks."

Johnston stood up, nodded to Strand and walked out.

"Good man," Strand said, "although a constipated cold piece of fish. Swens mixed up with the Jesuits?"

"Makes you wonder how far this Entity can reach," Tom added. "Too bad about Renauld. I don't suppose Johnston is going to be thanking me anytime soon for the extra work."

"As long as he gets the job done," Strand said indifferently and Tom shrugged, his expression thoughtful.

"I've been wondering how the shooter knew about Professor Renauld. Apart from you and me, nobody knew of our proposed meeting. Nobody! So, where did our boy get his information?"

"I wondered that myself," Strand said softly, his eyes hard. "You're maintaining a case file?"

"Of course," Tom started, then his shoulders sagged as the realization sank in. "It's Wellard."

Strand stared. "The Assistant Director? You're crazy!"

"Perhaps, but unless our shooter is able to hack into my case database, not beyond the realm of possibility, and something I'll check, I'll stick with the simplest explanation."

"You know what you're saying?"

"I'm not saying anything. All I have is a likely suspect, and without corroborating evidence, that's all he is."

"But Wellard? I can't believe it."

Tom did not want to believe it either. Nevertheless, only Wellard knew all the details. He must have accessed the case file and read his report. If he followed that thought one step farther to its logical conclusion, it meant that somehow Wellard had contact with The Entity. An FBI Assistant Director a Vatican spy? It seemed incredible and Tom reeled at the implication. It appeared that Wellard had knowingly participated in the planning of Renauld's death and possibly his. What if he was charging up a wrong tree and the shooter had somehow cracked his file after all?

There was, of course, another possibility.

Christ! He was getting paranoid and letting his imagination run away from him. He *had* to trust Strand.

"We need to find out. I'll update my case report saying that Johnston and I will be at Swens' apartment early this afternoon looking at evidence that links Swens to the shooter. I'll provide an address like the good diligent agent that I am."

"But we don't have such evidence," Strand protested.

"Sure, but Wellard doesn't know that and neither does the shooter."

Strand frowned and shook his head. "Even if Wellard is the leak, it's too contrived. The shooter will smell a trap."

"Which it will be. You will put two men in the apartment in case our boy tries to get in ahead of me. Since we don't know what he looks like, not for certain, it's no use saturating the area. We'll wait for him to show his hand."

"Great! And the minute you appear, you'll be making yourself a perfect target for a long range shot."

Tom shrugged. "There is that, of course."

"I don't like it. If we only have a marginal chance of apprehending him, what's the objective? Apart from getting you shot," Strand added dryly.

"The objective is to prove if Wellard is our leak," Tom said patiently.

"And how will this move prove that? Watch him while he reads your file?"

Tom beamed at Strand's evident frustration. "Not exactly, but close. To do that, I'll need to call someone. Sorry, but I cannot tell you more."

"You don't have to. I can read between the lines. You'll have the CIA or the NSA monitor his communications, right?"

Tom was impressed at how quickly Strand got there. But then, the man was Boston's office chief and you don't get to hold such a position by being thick.

"Something like that. I have another twist. It will look perfectly natural and expected if you called Wellard to let him know how I'm doing. It's Saturday, but he's usually in, at least until lunchtime. While you're at it, you can casually drop that I'm staying at the Omni Parker House Hotel. He'll probably howl at the profligate use of FBI funds to enjoy myself, but it's a convenient five minute walk from here."

"That's smart thinking, Tom. I like it. I wouldn't mind staying at the Omni Parker myself," Strand commented bleakly, but his eyes twinkled. "If Wellard is the leak, he'll let our shooter know where you are and you'll expect him to come calling?"

"I don't know how to make it any easier for him."

"You don't intend to walk into your room just like that, do you?"

Tom smirked. "I'm good, but I'm not foolish. Plant a button camera in my room and have your men watch any comings and goings. If our boy shows up to wait for me, your guys can grab him. If he tries to pull the Renauld gag, someone can babysit me while I sleep. Of course, he might not try to hit me tonight, and that means a watch on me for the duration."

"If he does show up, we'll have our mug shot and we won't have to worry about airport surveillance tapes," Strand mused, then sighed. "I'm not comfortable with you holding the papyrus. I think you're up to something. Are you?"

"My objective is to tie up all the loose ends before I'm out of here."

Strand snorted. "A nice evade and I think you *are* up to something. What's more, I think I know what that is, but I won't press you. Whatever it is, don't let it trash your career. You're good and it would be a shame to toss it away because of misguided loyalties."

"I'll try not to do anything that drastic."

"Good." Strand chewed his lower lip, then reached into one of his desk drawers and pulled out a thick A3-size brown envelope. "This came for you from Washington."

Tom beamed and took the proffered package. Peters had come through for him. But then, he never doubted he wouldn't. The poor guy and his team had obviously worked on it all night. He reminded himself to do something nice for the forensic expert once he got back to DC.

"Just what I've been waiting for, thanks."

"Can you tell me what that is, or shouldn't I ask?"

"No reason for you not to know. It's a fake copy of the papyrus which I intend leaving in my hotel safe. I made an entry in my case file saying that's where I hid the thing."

"And you think that Wellard will tip off the shooter. Bait?"

"That's it. As soon as I check it, I'll go over there and plant it."

"And the real thing?"

"It's somewhere safe."

Strand looked at him, the unspoken question obvious, but Tom was not about to be swayed by threats or hollow platitudes.

Strand pointed at the package. "You know, if our shooter shows up at your hotel, it might be better if we let him go. He'll probably be armed and someone could get hurt if we try to take him. Once he has your fake papyrus, he may decide that his job is done. With a mug shot, we can alert the airports and grab him when he tries to leave. I doubt he'll do something silly like carrying a handgun past airport security."

"You're forgetting that I'm still a target," Tom reminded him.

"No, I haven't forgotten. With the papyrus in his hands, what's the point of going after you? Even if you talked, without the original, who would believe you? You may have an electronic copy, but that will hardly cut it."

Tom stared hard at Strand, his thoughts in turmoil. What the Boston chief said sounded logical and made a lot of sense, but would that necessarily carry any weight with the shooter? It all depended on his orders and Tom had already surmised that The Entity was not acting rationally. Still, the shooter *might* decide to cut his losses and let it go after he had the tractate, in which case Tom would be screwed. A mug shot did not constitute sufficient evidence to secure a conviction, and he was a still long way from obtaining anything solid.

"I'm not convinced the shooter will stop if he gets the papyrus, but it's possible. You could be right about someone getting hurt, even though we'd be running the risk of losing him. Okay, let's get a camera in place and we'll leave it at that for now. I'll be upset if he manages to shoot me."

"Look, Tom. I know you want to get your hands on the guy and personally wring his neck, but I don't want an innocent bystander getting hurt unnecessarily if there is a better way to get him. We're talking about an ancient scroll, regardless how valuable. It's not worth a life."

"It already cost five lives, Garry," Tom said bleakly.

"Let's not add to the count."

"Okay, you win. As long as we do get him, that's what counts."

"You realize, of course, even if we do apprehend him, we don't have anything solid to hold him on. Not for long anyway."

"Tell me about it."

Strand grinned. "Frustrating, isn't it? Give me half an hour and I'll have two of my techies go with you."

"Thanks, but I've got a few chores to attend to first. Send them out whenever they're ready." Tom reached into his pocket and slid his room keycard across the desk. "They'll need this. I'll get another from Reception."

"You'll be taking the usual precautions?"

"I've been given one of your special lightweight vests." Tom hoped it would be enough. He'd be out of luck if the shooter went for a headshot.

In his temporary office, holding it between his hands, he nursed a mug of fresh coffee. A tendril of steam slowly rose from it, only to dissipate into nothing. After a moment, he turned and glanced at the fake papyrus. To his untrained eye, the thing looked genuine enough and he hoped it would look genuine to the shooter. Why wouldn't he believe the thing wasn't real?

Things may be moving, but like Strand said, he still had very little to go on. Johnston might still come up with something concrete, but he doubted it. The shooter far too proficient to leave behind anything obvious. Even the best of them can make a mistake. He had. He hoped forensics would find something on Swens, his car, or the link with the Jesuits, tenuous as that was. Keeping a tab on his hotel room a prudent precaution, but something the shooter would anticipate. He seems to have anticipated everything else. Still, it was worth a try. Tom needed a photo ID from one of the surveillance tapes before the case could move on. He needed a face. It did not help his cool at all knowing the shooter was probably aware of this.

Swens…the man just didn't fit the profile. Why would the shooter involve himself with a local gun when his movement pattern suggested he preferred to work alone? A falling out between pals as the BPD report hinted? Or The Entity wanting to clean up after Noris and Garbaldi were eliminated, and things didn't work out as planned? Like Johnston said, the shooter needed a weapon and could not risk carrying one through Customs, which meant that either the shooter or The Entity had an arrangement with Swens. Could Swens be a Jesuit hitman? It would explain a lot. By now the shooter must know he'd been set up. Why continue by going after Renauld?

Tom chewed that over and didn't like the taste at all. The man was a professional, and The Entity still wanted to recover the papyrus and silence anyone who knew of it. The attempted hit on him impersonal, part of the price for doing business. Tom tried to picture such a man and a shiver ran down his spine. Short of being killed, that kind of man would never stop, never give up. He would keep going until he completed his mission.

Or would he?

The shooter had to know that time was against him. Sooner or later, one of Tom's snares would catch up with him. Which was more important to The Entity? Removing all and sundry, or recovering the papyrus? If it were up to him, probably both, which meant the shooter would need to confront him and extract the papyrus before killing him. Was that necessarily true? The shooter killed Garbaldi with a double tap and tried the same with him without having recovered the tractate. With Tom dead, Omni Parker security would hand the papyrus to the FBI and the whole messy business would start all over again, maybe.

So, he was a target regardless of whether the papyrus was recovered or not. Dead men and tales, eh? The Vatican appeared prepared to risk posthumous exposure in order to eliminate a chain of corroborative witnesses. Stupid and did nothing to remove the source of the problem, namely, recovery of the papyrus. As long as it existed, it constituted the main threat, not the people who knew of it. Remove the papyrus and you removed the threat. The Entity's reaction could be classified as obsessive, even fanatical, rather than reasoned, which he already suspected. He wondered how many people in the Vatican Curia actually knew what was going on. Events to date suggested a covert cover-up operation to clean things up before the whole thing blew up in everybody's face. Perhaps he dealt with two men only: the shooter and someone in The Entity…and Wellard.

Even if his suppositions were correct, it did nothing to reduce the gravity of his position. It only took one bullet. He knew how to defuse the entire situation, of course. Simply hand the papyrus and the dating data to Harvard, or better still, *The Boston Globe*, then sit back and watch the ensuing fireworks. The latter an option of last resort. It would certainly get the shooter off him, but it would also allow him to get away clean after committing five murders. No, Tom wanted this man to pay in full, and any other involved party brought to justice. On the other hand, if he published the papyrus, the pressure would be off and Johnston could then methodically run down every tenuous lead until the case was solved. The United States had an extradition treaty with Italy, but would they hand over the shooter if the Vatican demurred? Besides, he had no way of knowing whether the shooter would stay in Italy, preferring to fade out of sight for a while until things cooled down.

Tom chewed his lower lip. Handing the case to Johnston would also mean that he would have to return to Washington, making it Strand's case, not his. A touch of hubris? Perhaps a tad, but he firmly believed in finishing what Garbaldi had given his life to see happen. He shook his head with bemused wonder. The last thing he expected was to be a cross bearer for someone else's cause.

Christ!

He was not the stuff of martyrs.

Staring at the FBI logo on the computer screen, he reached an unpalatable realization. Despite what he told Wellard, he had allowed himself to become emotionally involved in the case, forgetting he was foremost a federal law officer, personal considerations notwithstanding. Reaching a decision, he grimaced at the unfairness of it all and nodded.

Logging on, he checked his emails, not surprised to see one from Cardinal Albani, with a CC to Wellard. Nothing from Cardinal Marati, also expected. Having Wellard involved tricky on many levels. If Wellard was the leak, the email would not be news. If not, it only identified another possible target for the shooter. He did not regret sending his email, a tactical ploy, but he definitively did not want the FBI hierarchy involved just yet. If the Vatican wanted to make this a diplomatic matter, he could find himself in some uncomfortably warm water. Well, he would face that when and if.

He quickly read the email without expecting a confession. The cardinal was naturally shocked at the death of one of his researchers and taken aback by any insinuation that the Vatican could in some way be involved. He expected a formal apology from Tom and direct return of the papyrus.

The thing is, Tom had not made any such insinuation. Was Cardinal Albani talking or somebody else feeding him the lines? No way to tell, but he felt certain his hidden message was heard. Even if heard, after disposing of Renauld, he doubted The Entity would stop now. The thought didn't cheer him up at all. He ignored the demand for the papyrus as hollow bluster.

Putting the email out of his mind, he took two long pulls of the now tepid coffee and opened his case file. Under a dated entry, he provided an update on Professor Renauld's death and his suspicion that the shooter, either alone or with expert help, had gained access to the FBI database, compromising Renauld. To mitigate the risk, he would now limit the intelligence content of future entries to bullet points. He summarized Johnston's investigative efforts, concluding with his intention to visit Swens' apartment; routine and something that Wellard would expect.

He checked the entries and nodded; brief and to the point, without excess wordage or injected emotion. Reading the entry about the papyrus location, despite smelling a possible trap, the shooter might risk capture to go after it, which would complete his mission. Wearing a wry smile, he closed the file and reached for the phone. He started punching numbers when his cellular rang. Dragging the thing out of his pocket, he flipped open the lid, read the call line identifier, and groaned. The call had to come sooner or later; he simply preferred that it be later.

"Meecham," he said with resignation, knowing what was coming.

"Are you trying to cause a diplomatic incident?" Wellard roared without wasting time on polite preliminaries.

Tom winced. "I guess you saw the email."

"Damn right I did! Why in hell did you want to do something stupid like sending the Vatican that email?"

"To provoke a reaction."

"Hah! You certainly got that."

"I don't know why you're upset, boss. Nothing in my email to Cardinal Albani could possibly be construed as suggesting that the Vatican is in any way involved."

"That's beside the point. The mere fact that he thinks you're making an accusation is enough. What did I tell you about launching a personal crusade, eh? You're about a hair's width from suspension. The only thing saving you from disciplinary action is that I can't reach through the phone to strangle you. Tell me what's going on, Meecham, and make it good. If I sense that you're snowing me, you're toast. Do you read me?"

From the decibel level, Tom read him loud and clear. If Wellard had already read his file, it was a masterful performance of ignorance. It also explained why he asked for case details. He had nothing to fear from The Entity, maybe.

"Boss, with Professor Renauld on a slab, I now have five bodies—"

"Renauld? Who's he?"

Tom suppressed a smile. Like the bastard didn't know. "Vincent Renauld was Director of Harvard's Committee for the Center for Middle Eastern Studies. The shooter got to him last night. That tells me he is anxious to get his hands on the papyrus and eliminate anyone who knows about it. I've got a couple of scenarios to entrap him and we'll see what happens later today. Either way, Johnston has the technical side of the investigation in hand. There is no need for you to get involved."

"Not get involved? I *am* involved! Lucky for both of us that Cardinal Albani did not CC his email to the FBI Director, or you would be on the receiving end of an entirely different conversation. That doesn't get you off the hook. What's this shit about handing the papyrus to Harvard? You want to be indicted for obstruction? I told you before, and this time it's an order. Give the thing to Strand and get back here. He speaks highly of you, I just talked to him, but it's his case. Let him handle it."

"I cannot hand over the papyrus to him and you know it. As long as I hold it, I'm the only target, which doesn't exactly enhance my cool. I don't want our shooter adding Strand or Johnston to his box score. Or you."

"For Crissakes, Meecham! The shooter doesn't know who's got the damned thing. He can't go around killing off half the FBI on the off chance somebody knows about it."

"Boss, do we want to take that chance?"

"According to your theory, handing it to Harvard will simply make them the target."

"No it won't, not if The Entity knows they have it. That's been part of the problem, keeping the thing secret. Once Harvard has the papyrus, they announce their intention to publish and

The Entity will have the ground cut from under their feet. Our shooter will be out of a job."

"You hope! After this latest murder, you think that Harvard will touch it?"

"The mistake I made with Renauld is keeping it confidential. That won't be the case this time. As for handing over evidence, once we get our shooter before a jury, I'll make sure that Harvard makes the papyrus available. It will be one of my conditions."

"And the mistake I made was to get *you* involved. We could always return it to the Vatican, you know. After all, it is their property."

"And give up the only solid piece of evidence that may link them to five murders? They'd be in a position to deny everything. Anyway, it's not their property really. It belongs to the Coptic Orthodox Patriarchate of Alexandria."

"You're splitting hairs and you know it. You're allowing personal considerations to cloud your professional judgment. I expected better from you."

Tom pursed his lips. That one stung because it was partially true. "I'm sorry you feel that way, sir. After getting Father Garbaldi killed, I won't deny that I have a personal interest, but that has not in any way clouded my professional judgment."

"Look, Tom. I didn't mean what I said, but I've had enough crap, okay? Let me spell it out for you one last time. This is a Boston case. The papyrus is material evidence to that case. Hand it to Strand and let Johnston worry about catching the shooter. It's his job! If necessary, we'll get the Italian police to work with us. Once we wrap things up, the FBI will decide what to do with the papyrus. Trying to finish what Garbaldi started is not your responsibility. Do I make myself clear? I better see your ass here on Monday or you're suspended. Are we on the same page, Agent Meecham?"

"Boss—"

"I haven't heard a 'yes' yet."

Tom sighed and his shoulders sagged. "Yes, sir."

"That's better. And Meecham, the FBI doesn't pay people to stay at a place like the Omni Parker House Hotel. You're burning taxpayer money. Find something less expensive."

Tom hung up, pocketed the cellphone and exhaled. He was totally screwed. Worse still, Wellard had to know he wouldn't drop this, not now. Did Wellard try to protect him by getting him out of Boston? Perhaps, but handing the case to Strand would not deter the shooter at all. Tom simply knew too much. He needed to make the existence of the tractate public and defuse the shooter. The downside of that option, of course, his man would probably leave the country, making the job of catching him that much more difficult. It should end the killings, and wasn't that the priority? Stacking up more bodies just wasn't worth it, regardless of any merit, if that was the right word, to having the papyrus published. Like Wellard said, they could always go after the shooter in Italy. Officially, still his case until Monday. That gave him a better part of two days before he faced probable suspension. He reached for the phone and jabbed numbers for a direct line. It took two rings before a familiar voice answered.

"Mark Price."

With everything melting down around him, it was nice to know he had one person he could trust implicitly. Wearing a broad grin, Tom allowed himself to relax.

"It's Meecham, Mark."

"Well, crap! About time you called, even if it's a weekend. With your new exalted position, I figured little guys like me were now beneath your notice."

Tom laughed with genuine pleasure. Director of the National Operations Center, the action part of the Department of Homeland Security's Office of Operations Coordination, he would hardly call Mark a little guy. After the Valero refinery incident, in addition to his normal duties, Mark was now President Walters' informal advisor on formulating a framework for dismantling or drastically streamlining the burgeoning DHS bureaucracy.

On their way to Israel, Tom made a passing remark that most DHS functions were already the responsibility of the FBI. Give them direct access to the intelligence agencies information, authority to coordinate during a domestic crisis, and DHS could disappear. Mark shrugged it off as a fanciful idea, but later confided that he made the same point to the President. Riding on a wave of domestic and international acclaim for showing restraint by not bombing Iran when all evidence pointed to them, Walters now had what amounted to a blank check for his legislative agenda. Public opinion guaranteed that Congress would not stand in his way, not too much anyway. Some things just didn't end, and partisan party posturing was one of them, regardless of any national interest, even if that posturing came from your own party. Still, it looked like DHS and other superfluous government bureaucracies had lots of reasons to be justifiably nervous. Tom would not be at all sorry should they go.

"Christ, Mark, it's only been a week since we had that drink."

"That long? I thought it's been a month."

"Asshole. Any new disasters to worry about?"

"Israel is still in turmoil as expected, but at least the Sayar government is following through on its promise to remove settlers from the West Bank and Gaza, most of them anyway. East Jerusalem might be a problem for him, as he cannot very well clean out every apartment building already there. It simply isn't practical. The move has left Hamas nonplussed, having nothing to agitate about, but from what we can tell, the Palestinians on the street have embraced the initiative."

"And the Israeli on the street?"

"You've read the papers. The religious extremists and the far right are continuing to march in protest, but the government seems to have secured popular support for now. If Prime Minister Sayar has internal problems with the Defense Force hierarchy, he isn't telling. So far, we haven't heard anything."

"I wish him luck," Tom murmured.

"Yeah. He'll need it."

"You're close to President Walters these days. What's he doing about that underground nuclear test by Iran? Israel is not at all happy."

"I don't think that Israel not being happy rates all that high with the President right now, but I know what you mean. Keep the dialogue going with President Hamadee Al Zerkhani and calm everybody's nerves, I guess."

"I suppose. Anything else happening?"

"Pretty quiet at the moment, but you know how it is. It can come right out of the blue."

"No kidding. I've just been struck in the ass by one of those bolts."

"Oh? That's why the call?"

"Afraid so. Wish it were otherwise. Are you secure?"

"Shoot."

"I need a favor. I could do this myself, but it would leave a trail, something I cannot afford right now."

"You want somebody sanded? Wrong department, my boy."

"You're close. I need you to request a tasking order with the NSA and ask them to pull all communication records, including emails, made by Assistant Director Wellard—"

"Your boss?"

"—and Garry Strand, in charge of the FBI Boston Division."

"Well, crap! Anyone else you've taken a dislike to lately?"

"The list is lengthy, but that's it for now. I need everything from 1800 yesterday."

"Any particular reason to snoop on them or shouldn't I ask?"

"I can't tell you much, Mark. Not now. If a certain party found out, I could be placing your life in danger."

"And this certain party is after you now?"

"You go it, and I suspect with Wellard or Strand's help. My bet is on Wellard."

"With a friend like that…But if you suspect him, you've taken steps to prove it?"

"Definitely."

"Ah, the light shines. NSA records will constitute legal evidence."

"That's it."

"I can see now why you don't want to do this yourself. Okay, consider it done."

"I don't know what I'm looking for, Mark, but I'll know when I see it. You have my word that all records outside my immediate interest will be destroyed once I have what I need and I'll let you know when to stop the taps."

"Good enough. Are you sure you can't tell me what's going on? I have resources and connections at my disposal that could come in handy."

"Thanks, Mark, I appreciate that. Let me play out a couple of scenarios first. The situation might resolve itself by then. If not, you'll be hearing from me."

"Be careful out there, Tom."

"Count on it. And for God's sake, make sure those NSA clowns keep their mouth shut or my ass is grass."

"I'll call you as soon as the stuff comes through."

"One more thing. I've been on the Internet, but there isn't much there. What I need is a briefing paper on The Entity."

"The Entity? Phew. You're talking about some nasty operators there. I've worked with them and they're bad news. No sense of humor. Are they the certain party—"

"That's what I need to prove."

Mark chuckled. "You got the good guys and the bad guys after you. I'd start thinking about settling my affairs. Are you sure you don't want my help?"

"Let's see what happens with those scenarios first, okay?"

"I'll be in touch," Mark said and disconnected.

Tom hung up and smiled. Settle his affairs? Not likely. He might be chasing his tail, but one way or another, it should nail Wellard. He did not believe that Strand had sold him out, but he was the cautious type. His boss must know that he is a suspect, even if Tom hadn't said so outright in his report. The fact that he hadn't would be enough to put Wellard on guard. Given that suspicion hanging over him, would he continue being a conduit to his affiliates? So far, what he had done, or might have done, was strictly speaking not illegal. He had simply reported the contents of Tom's case file, a disciplinary matter at worst. Although he may have suspected it, he couldn't have known that his action would result in Renauld's death. Should events progress as anticipated, it would definitely make him an accessory before the fact and Tom would be gunning for him, son of a bitch. Just to make sure…

He picked up the phone and dialed Simon at the FBI's Cyber Division. If the shooter *had* cracked his database, there might be a trail and Wellard would be off the hook, with a huge apology due from Tom.

After making himself a fresh cup of coffee, he requested Sylvana to track down Professor Sidris Norginson for him. He didn't know what Strand's secretary was doing in the office on a Saturday morning, but glad she was there. Glancing at his watch, only nine-twenty, but it felt like he had already put in a full day.

The phone rang and he picked up.

"Mr. Meecham, Professor Norginson is on the line, sir."

"Where is she calling from?"

"I've got her on her cellular. She is actually at the university."

"Thanks, Sylvana. Please put her through…Professor Norginson?"

"That's right, and call me Doctor. I'm curious what the FBI wants with me, Mr. Meecham."

Her voice polite, but cool, Tom stifled a sigh—another one of those strong driven women. Then again, as the university president, she could afford to be cool and still expect deference. He figured that most of the time, she doubtless got it.

"I apologize for any inconvenience, Doctor, but the circumstances are somewhat unusual, as is my request."

"Your request? I assume this is an official FBI matter and not a personal inquiry?"

Tom beamed, wishing he could see her face. An able executive, eminently qualified, tough enough to thrive in a male-dominated environment, she was not likely to suffer fools gladly. Holder of two PhDs, author of five books, past Professor of Social Sciences at Harvard, Professor of International Relations at Georgetown University, and a slew of honors behind her, she would be one formidable lady. He had checked up on her.

"Strictly official, Doctor."

"Very well. What is this unusual circumstance you're referring to?"

"You're aware of the death of Professor Carlo Noris?"

"Ah, Dr. Noris…Before you continue, Mr. Meecham, I also know what happened to Father Garbaldi—"

"I regret being the bearer of bad news, Doctor, but you can now add Professor Renauld to the list."

"Renauld? My God. When did it happen?"

"Last night."

"This is awful. I spoke to him on Thursday. He sent me an email outlining his discussion with Father Garbaldi regarding publication of a certain tractate. He seemed very excited about it. As Director of the Center's Steering Committee, he exercised a lot of autonomy, but he could not make a decision on something like this on his own. I had to know. If you were about to tell me that this tractate is the linking factor to the three deaths, don't bother. It's obvious, but I still can't believe that Vince is gone."

Tom admired Norginson's forthrightness and smarts. "I'm sorry that things have turned out like this, but I am relieved that you understand. It makes my job easier, and you should then know what I'm going to request."

"Tell me anyway."

"I want to hand over the papyrus to you on the condition that Harvard announces it will exhibit and publish the text."

"You did say, hand over, not sell?"

"I am a federal law officer, Doctor. This isn't a private transaction for personal gain."

"Forgive me, Mr. Meecham. We get offers from time to time…Anyway, the person you want to talk to now is Professor Tyrone Ryker. He is the associate director and will most likely be running the Center for Middle Eastern Studies until a new director can be appointed. I understand what you're getting at. By announcing we have the papyrus, you're hoping it'll stop whoever is trying to recover it and presumably end further killings. The Vatican must be desperate."

"It's the best way I know how to defuse the situation."

Norginson laughed, a rich, clear sound of a mature woman in her prime who knew power and wielded it with skill. "By breaking FBI regulations and leaving Harvard open to possible legal action if we accept evidence material to your case?"

"Dr. Norginson, your lawyers can confirm this, but accepting the papyrus will not in any way leave Harvard open to legal proceedings by the government."

"Perhaps, but we're not dealing with a lost purse here, Mr. Meecham, and we both know it. This could have far reaching international repercussions. Never mind. We're getting ahead of ourselves. Are there any other potential claimants? I don't want Harvard involved in a legal wrangle over ownership."

"Father Garbaldi found the papyrus hidden in a codex given to the Vatican by the Coptic Orthodox Patriarchate of Alexandria. From what I understand, they were not aware of its existence. The Vatican has already claimed ownership and demanded its return."

"Not surprising."

"Technically, Doctor, the papyrus belongs to me." From the silence at the other end, Tom could visualize Norginson's startled expression.

"Finders keepers, eh? A novel interpretation that may have some validity. I will have my lawyers get back to me on that, but you have me intrigued enough to look at what you've got. Even though Vince assured me of its authenticity, I need to see a copy of the papyrus and dating data before making any decision."

"Of course, I understand and I appreciate your interest."

"Poor Vince. I still can't believe he's gone."

"A regrettable loss all around. If you can let me have your email address, I'll send you the information right away. You're aware, Doctor, despite what I said, if you go through with it, I could be placing you and some of your colleagues in danger. Not only from the Vatican's intelligence service, but religious extremists everywhere once you publish. I will understand fully if you don't wish to get involved."

"Thanks for the warning, but that's not exactly news and I'm not being entirely altruistic either. Your exhibit could make Harvard a pilgrimage site for every theologian around the world. That's worth taking a risk or two, and we can take steps to safeguard ourselves. If we both live through this, I'll create an endowed chair in your name, Mr. Meecham."

Tom sat up, momentarily surprised by the idea. "That won't be necessary, Doctor. Having the thing published will be fame enough."

"There is more to this than meets the eye and I look forward to hearing your version. Let me make a few calls. If Harvard decides to accept your proposal, I'll want the original when we meet."

"That's understood."

"How much time do I have?"

"The offer is open until three p.m. today."

"Or you will take it to *The Boston Globe*? You must be desperate yourself, Mr. Meecham."

Tom did not bother answering that.

Chapter Six

Refreshed, Peroni stepped out of the shower, grabbed a terry-cloth towel off the rail and rubbed himself down. After running a comb through his hair, he quickly climbed into his spare navy blue trousers and new loafers, having dumped the old shoes, reminding himself that he needed to get another pair of slacks and casual blazer. Although he showered before checking out of the Sheraton, rather late after having slept in a bit, the hassle of wiping down and returning his rental car and the hot cab ride downtown had taken the gloss off his morning. The bedroom electronic clock display read 10:50 a.m. Leaving off the tie, he pulled on his jacket and moved to the wide window.

From the Ames Hotel fifth floor, Boston's jagged skyline looked like any other collection of city skyscrapers. Below him, Court Street curved gently westward toward the colorless Government Center Plaza to merge with Cambridge Street. Traffic streamed in unbroken lines going both ways, punctuated by an occasional horn and police siren. Opposite the plaza stood the imposing nine-story One Center Plaza, housing the local FBI offices. Across the harbor, aircraft were coming in over Apple Island, or climbing out through the smog.

The BlackBerry on the bedside cabinet trilled and a melodious voice announced: "You have mail. You have mail."

He walked to the made bed, touched the flashing email icon and waited for the message to display. He read Kelvin's bullet-point summary and disconnected. It appeared the FBI source was still active, and ordered him to be on the job through the weekend. Peroni had no qualms about that. If he had to work on a weekend for his dollar, he saw no reason why somebody else shouldn't either. How reliable was the information from their source? That Meecham would want to check out Swens' apartment predictable, and the possibility of a trap. He understood why Meecham might want to go there, but he must also know he was exposing himself unnecessarily. Then again, he was an FBI agent doing his job. Peroni had done his homework and studied Meecham's profile, at least the material available in the public domain. It merely confirmed his opinion that he faced a very capable operative and he had no intention of underestimating his adversary, not that he naturally would.

Second-guessing Meecham's motive got him nowhere. Even if he were inclined to act on Kelvin's information, there was simply not enough time to case the location, the building or the apartment itself. As for Meecham's hotel, that was something else entirely, with plenty of time to sniff out the place for a trap. If clean, he would have his quarry. The tantalizing thing that made his eyes sparkle, he actually had a real opportunity to retrieve the papyrus. Simplicity itself. No one would suspect that Meecham had the balls to place a priceless artifact in something ordinary like a hotel room safe, and also demonstrated how Meecham thought. The one single item in Kelvin's report he totally believed and could reliably act on.

But first, he had to get into Meecham's room.

Hot sunshine streamed down from a murky sky and Peroni squinted as he stepped out of the lobby onto a busy sidewalk. Being downtown, the street crowded with pedestrians and noisy traffic. He adjusted his jacket, already feeling uncomfortable beneath its weight and incipient warmth. Carrying a handgun tucked against his left side, his choices were limited. It wouldn't do to display a weapon openly. Ignoring the cars whispering along Court Street and hurrying pedestrians wearing vacant, self-absorbed looks, he turned right and started walking purposefully toward the Tremont Street intersection. With the sun almost directly overhead, the tall buildings around him provided little shade. Anyway, he had endured worse summers in Rome's sticky cauldron.

At the Y intersection, he waited stoically with others for the lights to change and then crossed over, making his way down Tremont. Opposite him stood the curved One Center Plaza building. He barely glanced at it, having nothing to fear from the FBI. Those people were clueless and he wanted to keep them that way. If he managed to recover the papyrus, they would remain so. Heavy traffic streamed both ways down the broad street. Naturally, not wanting to wait at the proper pedestrian crosswalk, enterprising individuals chanced their luck by crossing along the wide street when vehicles, exhausts rumbling, were forced to wait patiently for the lights to change. It took him less than two minutes to reach the small vacant lot of the King's Chapel. Three tall maples provided welcome greenery in an otherwise stark landscape of tar and concrete. Reaching the corner of School Street, he paused and stared at the old Omni Parker House Hotel façade on the other side. The ornate molding looked a little out of place among the modern utilitarian architecture around it. He waited for the green light and strode across with other pedestrians.

A doorman stood patiently beside the entrance, lightly tapping white-gloved fingers against his left thigh. Gazing at him, Peroni figured the heavy orange uniform had to be somewhat comfortable. An elderly executive type emerged out of the hotel with a young thing hanging on his arm. He frowned at the pale sky and they both sauntered off. The doorman gave them a brief salute, which nobody noticed. Smiling ruefully, Peroni glanced at the tall bronze-tinted plate glass of Parker's Restaurant and almost missed Meecham coming through the entrance. He could hardly forget the FBI agent: tall, powerfully built, dressed in an almost black pinstripe suit, clear featured, determined. There could be any number of reasons why Meecham was at the hotel, but he didn't care. Chance had favored him with an unprecedented opportunity to take out the agent. Thinking quickly, he paused until Meecham moved past him and then fell into step behind him as the agent walked toward the intersection.

Waiting for the signal to turn green, surrounded by people also waiting patiently, he reached inside his jacket, eased out the Hi-Point, keeping it hidden, and flicked off the safety. The city noises seemed suddenly unnaturally loud as his senses sharpened and his situational awareness expanded. Next to him, two teenage girls were chattering nonsense. The red and purple stripes in their long black hair flashed in the bright sunshine. Behind him, he could clearly hear a businessman talking into his cellphone, a meeting that had to be rescheduled. Two cars put on a burst of speed to beat the yellow light and the whole gaggle started to cross Tremont without waiting for the green Walk sign.

Peroni saw Meecham stiffen, sensing something wrong. The man was good and he had to do this quickly. When the oncoming group started to merge and jostle, he lifted his semi-automatic, making a slight bulge in the jacket. The faint *thuft* of muffled shots he sent into Meecham's lower back were hardly noticeable. The FBI agent stumbled from the force of the shots, flung out his arms and sprawled in a heap to the annoyed mutterings and cries of alarm from the milling pedestrians. Peroni sidestepped the crumpled body and hurried to the opposite sidewalk.

Following the example of others on both sides of the street, he stopped and turned, another concerned citizen wanting to see what was going on. Two men in dark suits were bent over Meecham's body while a young woman dressed in gray trousers and jacket stood next to them with arms raised to stop the cars when the lights changed. The two men quickly dragged Meecham to the sidewalk and the woman hurried after them, arms still raised. With the road clear, cars wasted no time roaring across. Kneeling next to the prone body, one of the men pulled out his cellphone and punched in numbers. After a short pause, he began to talk rapidly, presumably calling for an ambulance or the police. Perhaps both. Peroni did not want to linger and began walking south down Tremont. Other hangers-on on both sides apparently got the same idea and the gathered crowds quickly melted, not wishing to be involved. Even if someone heard the shots, the powerful urge not to get entangled in something messy worked in his favor. Apart from a sprawled body, nobody really saw anything.

With the FBI agent eliminated, he could not have survived those shots, nothing stood in his way from recovering the papyrus and successfully finishing his mission. That it should end so fortuitously, he considered a bonus, one he never questioned. He had seized an opportunity and random factors had rewarded his bold move. Waiting for a better moment that might never come was a policy of the timid and the uncertain. As a professional, he had learned well the difference between decisive action and calculated prudence.

Walking casually with the flowing pedestrians, he nevertheless felt the prickle of sweat behind his neck and under his arms from the adrenalin rush.

With a large hole and burn marks in his coat, he needed to get rid of the thing before someone noticed them. Without turning or looking at anyone, he casually removed the jacket and folded it across his left arm, the drawn gun held firmly in the fold. Given the hot day, no one paid him any attention. He crossed Tremont and made his way down the narrow Bosworth Street, more an alley than a street. At Province Street, he turned left and headed up toward Court Street. Behind him, he could hear the mournful wail of an ambulance.

In his hotel room, he dumped the jacket into the bathtub. Leaning over the tub, he opened the hot water tap, then spilled teabags and coffee packets from the kitchenette into the tub. For good measure, he poured in spare shampoo and conditioner bottles into the brown colored soup. After a few hours of soaking, he doubted that any forensic test was likely to lift usable DNA off the jacket, even if found after he left it in some dumpster. He would prefer burning the thing, but that would only attract unwelcome attention. Satisfied, he thoroughly washed his hands. Feeling more settled, he dressed in a spare shirt and changed into a fresh suit. He took Swens' cellphone, having already disposed of the SIM card, but not before discovering some interesting numbers, one of them being Belconi's. Removing the miniature tape cassette, he pocketed the plastic recorder and gloves carefully wrapped in tissue. Although he wiped them last night, it was possible that traces of powder residue still remained on the leather. Taking a coat hanger from the clothes cabinet, he hung up his trousers and two soiled shirts. Outside the room, he tagged a 'Do not disturb' sign on the door and walked toward a bank of two elevators.

At the reception desk, a middle-aged attendant looked up from his paperwork, face expressionless.

"Yes, sir?"

Peroni held up the clothes hanger. "I would like these laundered and back in two hours."

"I'm sorry, sir, but laundry pickup closes at eleven a.m."

Peroni placed the clothing on the counter and dragged out his wallet. A fifty-dollar bill appeared beside the clothing.

"Perhaps you could open it again…as a personal favor?"

His expression still severe, the attendant glanced at the bill. "I'll see what can be done."

Peroni nodded and walked out. It was the same everywhere; petty officious pipsqueaks reciting rules with evil relish rather than being helpful, which they were supposed to be. When they *were* asked for help, they hemmed and hawed as though an improper suggestion was being made. Money did grease the axle on which the world turned.

A brisk walk later, he stepped into the Omni Parker lobby and took in the scene with one sweeping look, noting the dark entrance to the restrooms and the green Exit sign above it. He might be under hotel surveillance, but there was no avoiding that and he did not plan to linger long. The place was almost deserted. An elderly spinster sat in a leather chair beside a plate glass window that faced the street, head buried in a newspaper. Through the open doorway on his right, judging by sounds of animated conversation and clinking of cutlery, Parker's Restaurant was full. Two young business types sat on round stools, propping up the bar. Tall glasses of rich beer stood half empty before them. Eyeing the beer, Peroni licked his lips. Right then, one would go down real nice.

He stepped to the check-in desk and flashed the pretty attendant a warm smile. She smiled in turn and with a feminine gesture, pulled back a lock of long blond hair behind her right ear.

"Yes, sir?"

"I'm Paul Markam, FBI," Peroni said in a stage whisper and reached for his wallet, supposedly to show his ID. "Can you give me Tom Meecham's room number, please?"

"My, you people are busy today. Two of your colleagues are already up there. Room 304."

Peroni frowned. He was not sure what the FBI agents were doing in Meecham's room, but not hard to guess. Probably installing surveillance equipment, which meant Meecham had anticipated his move to retrieve the papyrus and meant to trap him. No matter. It wouldn't do him any good.

"Hmm. I thought they'd be done by now. Never mind. Thank you, Miss…"

"Gladia," the receptionist replied in a husky voice, letting her eyes wander over his trim form.

"Thank you again." Peroni flashed her another smile and turned toward the elevators.

"Hey! You'll need a passkey."

He glanced at her and took the proffered plastic card. Although he had an adequate method to defeat today's electronic hotel locks and didn't need a card, it did make things easier.

"I'm not supposed to hand those out, you know," Gladia confided with a conspiratorial wink. "They can open any door, but since you're FBI, it's all right. You'll bring it back?"

"As soon as I'm done," he assured her, slipping the card into his pocket.

"Say, what's going on? You're not expecting a terrorist attack or something, are you?"

"Surveillance. I can't tell you any more than that. Sorry."

She beamed at him. "I understand. Good luck."

When the elevator doors slid into the wall on the third floor, two dark-suited men were waiting to get in. The taller of the two spoke hurriedly into his cellphone. Neither gave Peroni a glance as he stepped out. They immediately got in and the doors closed after them with a soft click.

Beside an open room down the corridor ahead of him stood a janitor trolley piled with spare towels, cleaning materials, soap and shampoo bottles. He checked which way the room numbers went, walked quickly past the trolley, helping himself to a white towel. Soft singing came from the room, accompanied by sounds of a vacuum cleaner going. Farther down, he stopped before room 304 and knocked. This is where he was vulnerable. He pulled out the gun and took a slow breath.

"Hotel security!" he shouted, not too loudly, listening for any movement inside.

Satisfied the room was empty, he inserted the keycard. The red light above the door handle turned green and the lock clicked. He opened the door a fraction and wrapped the towel around his head, leaving only a slit for his eyes. Pushing the door fully open, he stepped in and crouched, searching the gloomy room, gun arm held out straight.

He pushed the Hi-Point into his trousers and closed the door. Without turning on the lights, he walked quickly to the clothes cabinet, slid back the panels and gazed hungrily at the room safe. If this was a trap, Meecham would want to make it easy for him to crack the combination. It was possible the papyrus might not be in there at all, the purpose being to identify him. Trap or not, he had to check. Glancing at his watch, he needed to hurry in case the receptionist blabbed and the real FBI agents showed up. Even though he was armed, he did not relish the idea of a shootout in a confined space, not when there was an excellent chance of him getting shot. That just wasn't in his game plan.

Most hotel safes had only a four-digit code, but with ten numbers, that still made for a lot of possible combinations—far too many to try cracking the long-winded way. Training taught him that people using hotel safes rarely made up clever number sequences, preferring something simple. After all, one did not want to risk forgetting the code when money, passport or other valuables were inside.

He first tried the basic 1,2,3,4 sequence—always a favorite—then the 4,5,6,7 and the 7,8,9,0 sequence. The lock remained closed. So, not so simple after all. He then went down the 1,4,7,0 and other sequences before going across again. The lock clicked on 4,5,6,1 and Peroni smirked.

Meecham, your mind works like a steel trap.

He slowly opened the heavy metal door and peered inside. Rolled in a cylinder lay a piece of black cloth sealed in a clear plastic bag. So, his suppositions were correct. The tractate was not fragile and didn't require special handling. That simplified things enormously. He retrieved the roll, opened the bag, and reached for the cylinder inside. Fingering the soft cloth, he realized it was felt. Looking behind him, he stepped to the small desk and unrolled the cloth to faint sounds of crackling. Sandwiched inside was the papyrus. Staring at the Coptic text, he absently ran his right thumb across the top of the tractate, then quickly wrapped the precious thing, sealed it in the bag, and slipped the roll into his left jacket pocket. Satisfied with a job well done, and relieved it was over, he closed the safe and reset the combination. After wiping everything he had touched, he walked out.

Outside the room, he unwrapped the towel, hurried to the janitor trolley and placed the crumpled towel among other used laundry. He dug out the keycard, wiped it down and dropped it into the small tray of shampoo bottles and soap bars. Hesitating, he picked up a small facecloth and wrapped it around his left hand. Muffled singing came from the open room, the vacuum cleaner silent. Without a backward glance, he walked quickly toward the emergency stairs door and stepped into the cold stairwell. The door closed behind him with a hollow clang. Clinging to the handrail with his left hand, he took the stairs down two at a time.

On the ground floor, Peroni paused and took two deep breaths to steady himself. Feeling the chill in the stairwell, he opened the exit. A wave of noise and stifling heat rolled over him as he stepped into the alleyway beside the hotel. He blinked at the prickly humidity, knowing it was not that hot. It only seemed that way after the coolness of the stairwell. Momentarily uncertain which way the alley went, he turned left toward School Street. Reaching the hotel entrance, he hailed a waiting cab. The doorman rushed to open the door for him, but Peroni froze him with a glance. He climbed into the rear seat and slammed the door shut.

"Where too, buddy?" the driver growled, a toothpick hanging from the left side of his mouth.

"Emergency Room, Massachusetts General," Peroni snapped, letting himself sag against the upholstery.

"You got it."

The cab's heavy engine rumbled as the long car pulled into the street.

"Hot day," the cabby commented amiably and shifted the toothpick to the other side of his mouth.

Peroni saw him glance at him. The driver was about to say something, changed his mind and shrugged. Peroni didn't feel like chatting and looked at the passing scenery.

At the next intersection, the cab turned right, then right again onto Tremont. As they passed One Center Plaza, Peroni allowed himself a small smile at the thought of FBI cursing when they saw him walking into Meecham's room wrapped in a towel. Planting a camera had been a good idea, but what they should have done was have men waiting for him, unless they wanted to let him get away? Possible, but unlikely. What reason would they have for doing that? Prevent a shootout that might get a luckless guest hurt? Probably lack of evidence to hold him. None of it mattered. They were not there and he had gotten away clean, mission completed. After this, though, he would stick to Europe for a while. With different languages, customs and laws, that theater was far more manageable.

The sprawling Massachusetts General Hospital was a miniature town in its own right, with buildings stretching all the way to the bay. The cab pulled off Cambridge and rolled toward a six-story block. Getting a spot in the queue of cars, vans and motorbikes, the cab slid to a stop and the driver turned.

"That'll be eleven-fifty."

Peroni handed him a ten and a fiver and got out.

"You have a nice day too," the cabbie muttered, shifted his toothpick and got the car into gear.

At the broad glassed entrance, people were going in or coming out in a never-ending stream. The place looked like an airport arrivals terminal. Peroni walked slowly to a large rectangular slab near the entrance showing a multi-colored map of the campus. After a moment, he started briskly toward a McDonald's at the left end of the building. Looking at the fast food outlet, it seemed somewhat incongruous having a junk food factory at a hospital, he shrugged. Some things were beyond understanding. Rounding the corner, he walked briskly around customers going in or people leaving and turned a corner again to what was now the rear of the building. Here, small trucks and vans stood parked, taking away or bringing stuff this part of the hospital complex used. Three dumpsters stood lined up against a drab gray concrete wall. He stopped beside the center one that had its lid partially open. With a quick glance around, he pulled out the handgun, unscrewed the silencer and wiped the thing with the facecloth. With a flick of his arm, he tossed the little cylinder into the dumpster. The spare clip got the same treatment, as did the clip from the gun and the recorder. Wiping down the Hi-Point, his mouth twitched as he flung the thing into the dark maw, wrapped in the facecloth. It had been a good weapon to him. Walking past McDonald's, he dumped his gloves and Swens' cellphone into a trashcan.

At the hospital entrance, he flagged a cab and slid into the back seat. For the first time, he permitted himself to loosen up completely. He still had to get out of the country, but he did not foresee any difficulties there. Even if apprehended, the FBI simply had nothing to hold him on. The engine burbled as the cab pulled away from the curb.

No doorman waited for him at the Ames Hotel, but Peroni didn't mind. Jacket draped over his left arm, he ambled through the entrance into the almost cold lobby and headed for the elevators. His room warm and stuffy when he got in, the power supply activated by inserting his keycard into a slot next to the door. He got the air-conditioning going and threw the jacket on the bed. Checking the clothes closet, he took out a plastic laundry bag and walked into the bathroom. The jacket in the tub all splotchy with brown stains. The air smelled of coffee and shampoo. Rolling up his sleeves, he massaged the jacket, rubbing down the collar and the armpits. Satisfied, he squeezed the jacket and popped it into the laundry bag. After retrieving the teabags and dumping them into the wastebasket, he drained the tub and carefully wiped it down.

Holding the laundry and trash bags in his left hand, he removed the keycard from the power slot and stepped into the corridor. The emergency exit stairs took him to the ground floor. Outside, he jammed open the door and beamed at a row of dumpsters lined neatly against the back of the hotel. No one saw him get rid of the bags.

A cool shower lifted his spirits. Dressed in a white terry towel robe, he mixed himself a whiskey and dry and padded toward the bed. Taking a sip, he picked up the phone and asked to be connected with an airline booking office. A breezy girl airily confirmed that there were business class seats still available for tonight's flight to Rome. Delta Air Lines departs at seven p.m. and stops at Amsterdam with a one-and-a-half hour layover. However, Alitalia had a direct eight hour flight, but it leaves at five forty-five p.m. Would that do? Staring at his watch, Peroni thought it over. Now one-forty, although it seemed much later, plenty of time for him to have lunch, pick up his laundry and be on his way and he saw no reason to linger. He confirmed the Alitalia flight and told the girl he would pick up the e-ticket at the airport.

Sprawled against the cushions, he took out his BlackBerry and checked that the voice encryption software was running. He typed in his ten-digit PIN and made a connection to a special number. Still early afternoon here, so the five-hour time difference should not be too much of an inconvenience for the cardinal.

"Cardinal Belconi," the heavy voice answered and Peroni felt a chill run down his spine.

The ungodly man was a repulsive people user and he wondered how a red hat could hide all those sins. How did the Church? Still, this was business and of no concern to him how the cardinal reconciled his conscience with God.

"Peroni, Your Eminence."

"Ah, I hope you have some good news for me, my son."

"Meecham has been eliminated and I have the papyrus."

"Excellent! Very good work. You have confirmation of Meecham's death?"

"No, only a high level of probability."

Belconi sighed. "Payment can only be made on confirmation."

"That's understood. I'm only reporting conclusion of my mission and advising that I'll be in Rome tomorrow morning."

"And the papyrus?"

"I'm making arrangements for its extraction out of the country."

"You're not bringing it back with you?"

"That would be most unwise, Your Eminence."

"Mmm. I suppose so. Can you guarantee delivery?"

"That isn't possible. I can only give you a high level of probability."

"It's always probabilities with you, Peroni," Belconi growled irritably, "and I don't like the risk you're taking with it. I don't want to lose the thing now, not after all the steps I've taken to recover it."

"The risk would be greater if I were caught with it. There is still a possibility that I might be apprehended, however remote. That's something neither of us wants to see happen, Your Eminence."

"Very well. When can I expect delivery?"

"Probably Monday, but I'll be in touch."

"When I have the papyrus, you will have the bonus payment."

"Satisfactory."

Peroni ended the call and snorted. Scum!

Dressing quickly, he tucked the papyrus bag under his left arm and stepped into the corridor, tugging the door handle to make sure the lock engaged. At Reservations, he leaned against the counter and waited to be noticed. A young attendant dressed in a black suit, looked up from his computer screen and quickly walked over.

"Yes, sir?"

Peroni slid the papyrus onto the counter. "Can you FedEx this for me?"

"Of course, sir. Just that item?"

"Yes."

The attendant bent down and dug out a white padded bag with the familiar purple and red logo. "If you would fill in the details, please."

"Do you have bubble wrap and two pieces of stiff cardboard? I don't want the contents crunched."

"Well…"

Face expressionless, Peroni held up a hundred-dollar bill. "I think that should cover everything."

"Yes, sir!" The attendant beamed and the materials magically appeared.

Peroni filled in the address details using an alternate identity, slipped in the mini cassette and pushed the sealed package across the counter.

"Rome?" The attendant raised an eyebrow. "Your party should get the thing within twenty-four hours."

"Excellent. Say, I haven't had lunch yet. Can you recommend something?"

"Houston's Restaurant has very good seafood cuisine, sir, and it's right next door, but the hotel establishment is quite acceptable."

"I'll hold you to it." Peroni fluttered another twenty and waited for it to disappear.

* * *

Meecham pushed open the heavy glass door before the door-man outside could get to it and walked into noise, pollution and sticky heat. He glanced at the hard sky and gave a long sigh. During summer, Houston's uncompromising weather not much better, and he wondered what winter would be like in Washington. Snow and ice, no doubt. The prospect did not cheer him up at all. Not that he had anything to be glum about. The fake papyrus planted, all he needed to do was have the camera installed in his room and his little snare would be primed. While locking up the papyrus, he was mildly surprised by Strand's call, telling him that the technicians would be finishing shortly; something to do with setting things up at their end. Tom hoped the setup would not take the whole damn day. He didn't want the shooter getting away with the tractate and no photo.

The doorman touched his temple with the tips of his fingers and Tom nodded to him. He turned left and started walking toward the Tremont Street pedestrian crosswalk, hoping Johnston was ready to go for their little visit to Swens' apartment. Traffic heavy along Tremont, he wrinkled his nose at the acrid smell of unburnt gasoline. Waiting for the light to change, other pedestrians crowded around him, eager to get to wherever they were going. Then again, perhaps not.

A tingle of unease ran down the back of his neck and his senses searched for the source of the warning. Someone was behind him, close, and not just another pedestrian. It was a hunter's instinct. About to turn when the walk sign illuminated and everyone started to cross, he felt danger growing, urging him to do something and do it quickly. Half way across, prepared to stop, two sharp stabs pierced his lower back and thrust him forward. He gasped at the burning fire consuming his side and flung out his arms, colliding with the man in front of him as he fell. He didn't even have the strength to cry out as ballooning pain momentarily turned everything white. His arms managed to break most of the fall, but he still landed heavily. He heard angry shouts, and then there was a moment of total silence and peace, and he wondered whether this was death.

Then the pain returned and he moaned as someone grabbed his arms and began to drag him over the asphalt. The jolting sent spears of fire through his side, and blackness. When he came to, a middle-aged businessman knelt beside him, talking into a cell-phone. An attractive woman dressed in gray slacks and jacket hovered near him. He could see concerned faces looking down at him and the gathered crowd slowly dispersed. He tried to prop himself up, but the effort seemed too much. The man next to him placed his palm on Tom's chest and held him back firmly.

"Take it easy," the man said soothingly. "I've called an ambulance. You'll be all right."

"You don't understand," Tom mumbled through the pain, trying to sit up, but the man held him down.

"It's you who doesn't understand, Mister. Judging by the holes in your jacket, you've been shot, but there's no blood, which is odd. Now, lay still until the ambulance gets here, okay?"

Slumping back, Tom figured that all in all, it was good advice. He was in no shape to go charging after his shooter, even if he knew what he looked like. Clearly, that had not been a problem for his man. The shooter had waited for him to show up and sprung his trap beautifully. His spine tingled and he had a momentary flash of horror at the thought of being paralyzed. He exhaled with relief when both his legs moved. From the pain, the shooter had hit him above the right kidney. A little farther left and the slugs might have seriously damaged his spine, flack jacket or not. As it is, he may have broken ribs, certainly a nice rainbow bruise to admire. All things considered, he'd been lucky.

A young cop showed up and things became chaotic as he took down conflicting statements, which was only natural. People were not impartial recording machines and saw everything through tinted glasses of individual perceptions, bias, prejudice, emotions and life's baggage of experience. It did not matter what they saw. Not one of them would be able to identify the shooter, and that was the downside.

When the ambulance arrived, its siren winding down, doors banged and two paramedics rushed to his side. One checked his pulse and flashed a light into his eyes while the other got out a gurney.

"You remember your name and where you are?" the medic demanded briskly.

"Look, I've been shot in the back at close range," Tom snapped, impatient with all the fussing around.

The paramedic blinked, but that did not stop his examination. When he opened Tom's shirt to attach a stethoscope, he saw the bulletproof vest and gave a sharp hiss.

"Looks like this is your lucky day," he said and motioned to his partner, "but we still need to check you out."

They loaded him onto the gurney and rolled him into the ambulance. The cop climbed aboard and the siren started its wail as the van accelerated down the street. Seeing the vest, the cop leaned over him, one hand clutching the overhead rail.

"You're a police officer?"

"FBI," Tom told him wearily, feeling like he'd been worked over with baseball bats. "My ID is in my jacket pocket."

The cop reached into the jacket and pulled out the badge folder. He studied the ID and then looked up.

"Meecham? Are you—"

"Yeah."

"Say, that was slick work you and Mr. Price did on the Israelis. What's the setup here? I've got to make out a report."

"Report what you saw and did. Call Lieutenant Stanly Marsh if you want. I cannot tell you anything more."

"Marsh, eh?" The young cop frowned, clearly unhappy with Tom's brief response, but there was nothing he could do about it. "Okay, it's your case."

Tom winced as he twisted to dig out his cellphone. He flipped open the lid, scrolled down the address list and pressed Dial.

"Strand."

"It's Tom. I've been shot and they're taking me to a hospital to get checked out. It looks like our shooter waited for me."

"Are you okay?" There was no mistaking genuine concern in Strand's voice.

"Maybe a busted rib or two, but I can't tell until they do the x-rays. You better let Johnston know I won't be doing any visiting today, but that should not stop him from going there."

"Anything else?"

"Yeah. Start monitoring my room."

"Shit, Meecham! What if your shooter recovered the fake papyrus?"

"That's why I want my room monitored. We need that mug shot. Once I'm up and around, I'll check my safe. Then we'll know."

"Did you see him?"

Tom sighed. "He got me in the back. I didn't see a thing."

"Professional," Strand muttered wearily. "This doesn't look good for your boss."

"He could have tailed me from the FBI building," Tom countered judiciously.

"You're just covering Wellard's ass and you know it. Call me once you're done with the checkup."

"You got it," Tom acknowledged and hung up. He looked up and saw lively interest in the young cop's eyes, but he had little time for him.

Barreling down Cambridge Street with traffic scattering before the ambulance, it took less than five minutes to reach Massachusetts General. Tom appreciated efficiency when he saw it. The attending emergency resident took the paramedics' statement while methodically carrying out his own examination. He gave a noncommittal grunt when he saw the purple bruise left by the bullets. He was about to throw them away after extracting them from the vest when Tom intervened, citing they were evidence. The resident handed them over without a word and sent his patient to Radiology. An hour later, discharged and left with nothing more than a heavy bandage strapped around his body for his pains, and curiously the bandage did help ease his discomfort when he moved, he was in a cab returning to the Omni Parker Hotel—with bullet holes in his spare jacket and two suits ruined. He wondered if the Bureau would reimburse him.

"Only a heavy bruise," Tom told Strand from the cab's back seat. "I'll be strapped in for the next couple of days, but that won't restrict my movements."

"It could have been worse," Strand commented amiably.

"Yeah."

"When you get to your room, don't be surprised if you find the papyrus gone."

"Oh?"

"Our guy was visiting, but we didn't get a thing. You won't believe this, but he had a towel wrapped around his head."

"Christ!" Tom had to laugh at the balls of the man. "Then we really have nothing."

"Not quite. We know what the shooter wore. Johnston is at the hotel now going over security footage of the lobby. His visit to Swens' place postponed. Once we find a matching suit—"

"We'll have our mug shot. I like it."

"I thought that would brighten your otherwise gloomy day."

"I'm just about there," Tom said as the cab passed One Center Plaza. "When I'm done, I'll come and see you."

The cab turned left onto School Street and slowed as it approached the Omni Parker entrance. Tom gathered his jacket and handed the cabby his Amex card. He signed the receipt, added a tip and got out, grunting as his side protested. The doorman held the cab's door open for him, looking curiously at his scratched trousers and mussed jacket. Tom gave him a folded dollar bill and headed for the entrance. It was service he didn't want or ask for, but he got even by not giving him anything when the man hurried to open the heavy glass door to the hotel. He walked in with only a nod.

Cradling the jacket over his left arm, he walked quickly to the reception counter. The attendant lifted her head, brushed back a lock of golden hair and beamed at him.

"Ah, Mr. Meecham. Your card, sir," she gushed and held out a keycard, unfazed by his appearance.

"Thanks. I understand Mr. Johnston is with hotel security."

"Yes, sir. It's the second door on your left. I'll let them know you're coming."

Tom nodded and walked into the brightly lit corridor left of the reservations counter. There were only two doors and he made for the last one. He was about to knock when it opened. A heavyset youngster, who looked like he would be more comfortable standing guard at a strip bar, looked him up and down, not impressed with what he saw.

"Mr. Meecham?"

"That's right." Tom dug out his ID and held it up. The man opened the door wide to let him through.

The room was compact, but racks of DVD players, router boxes, servers and two computer screens mounted on a narrow bench made it appear smaller. Johnston looked up from the bench and got up.

"I was told you'd be coming over. How's the side?"

"Sore, but nothing's broken," Tom said, taking in the equipment.

"Looks like you're a bit worse for wear," Johnston said sternly, noting Tom's disheveled attire and leaned across the bench. He picked up a stack of color prints and held them out. "Our guy."

Dropping the jacket over a chair, Tom glanced at the security man. "Can we have a moment alone, please?"

The man frowned, clearly annoyed at being dismissed like this, but he obviously knew better than to interfere. He grunted and stomped out.

Not worrying about it, Tom reached for the prints and peered closely at the top photo of a man taken in the lobby. The dark blue suit smart and well-tailored, but could not hide the man's power and strength. This was someone aware and on guard at all times. Tom would not care to match himself against him. That's not what interested him.

He lifted the second photo and studied the close-up of a face. Not a clear profile, the camera's overhead position making that impossible, but it didn't matter. It was the same man. The sketch made from Paulini's description had not been far off. He spent a moment looking at the hard olive features, thick black hair and firm jaw. A tough customer, all right, and Tom had him now.

Looking at the next photo, he scowled. Taken in a darkened room, the CC camera's enhanced image showed a man with a towel around his head. Tom looked hard at Johnston.

"How does this photo connect us to the man in the lobby?"

Johnston's smile was grim. "Take a look at the next shot."

Tom slipped the photo under the stack and stared. A grainy image of a left wrist wearing a black Rado watch that partially covered a jagged scar.

"The guy in your room," Johnston said softly.

Tom quickly looked at the remaining shot—a blue-suited man also wearing a black Rado. He glanced at Johnston and tapped the photo.

"You've got nothing. Two men wearing the same type of watch."

"Not quite." Johnston indicated at the remaining photos.

Tom retrieved the last two shots. Both were close-ups of a wrist taken from different angles. He brought the two photos together. The watch, the scar, tendons and veins on the hands were all identical, good as a fingerprint.

"One's from my room?" he demanded and Johnston nodded. "Patchy, but not bad," Tom muttered approvingly.

"We'll have them computer enhanced," Johnston said, "but when Strand saw them, he immediately issued an all-airports alert in case our man tries to fly out."

"Good. Anything from the Logan tapes?"

"Not yet, but I've got something better," Johnston said smugly and reached for a large brown envelope on the bench. "Our shooter and Swens at the Alhoda Market in the stolen Saturn Astra, courtesy of our imaging lab."

"My man!" Tom grinned broadly and snatched the envelope from Johnston's hand.

He pulled out half a dozen prints and quickly scanned them—standard overhead surveillance shots of a black hatchback, driver and passenger holding up his left arm that just happened to cover his face. About to comment that this was all tentative, a black watchband caught his eye and he quickly looked at the next photo. A close-up of the same wrist, Rado, and scar. He pursed his lips and nodded.

"Now we're getting somewhere."

"Our pretty reservations clerk authenticated the shooter. He was posing as an FBI man and the timing places him just as our two techies finished with the install."

Tom had another piece of corroborative evidence and things were slowly falling into place, but they still had nothing solid to link the shooter with the murders. If the shooter had taken the fake papyrus, that would count for something. Suggestive and of little value in court, except for a charge of theft, but perhaps his man might cooperate when faced with a string of connective suppositions. So far, everything they had was circumstantial. They were yet to catch him. Recalling the hard features in the photo, Tom thought it unlikely that such a man would cave in easily. Without other evidence to hold him, he had to play the cards in hand.

He handed the photos to Johnston. "Secure the hotel tape and lock it up somewhere safe. Don't hand anything to the evidence room. If you have stuff already there, take it out."

Johnston raised an eyebrow and shrugged. "Nothing about this case is usual, so why start now?"

"With a positive ID, check the neighborhood hotels. Our man may have stayed in one of them. While you're at it, get someone to double-check the hotels around Cambridge and Somerville. I want to nail down his movement pattern. I also want men to start looking for a 9mm handgun, most likely a Hi-Point C-9 fitted with a silencer and a jacket with a bullet hole in it. Call Lieutenant Marsh for help. Our man will want to dump both before flying out, if he hasn't already."

"The stuff could be anywhere!" Johnston protested, showing dismay at the magnitude of the task.

"Yeah, but think like the shooter. With his job done, he'll want to be out of here quickly. There are only so many alleyways and dumpsters around here."

"And drains and holes and the bay," Johnston added morosely.

Tom beamed at him. "If it were easy, it wouldn't be fun, but we've got to do it."

"Even if we find the weapon and the jacket, how do we link them to the shooter?"

"Let's establish a chain of evidence first. Good work with the photos, by the way. Email me a set, will you?" Tom ordered, snagged his coat and walked out.

Waiting for the elevator, his cellphone rang and he fished the thing from his pocket.

"Meecham."

"It's Simon, Tom. I've got the data you wanted. Your boss' terminal was definitely used to access your case database last night and this morning. No one else messed with it. You want the times?"

"That's not necessary. Just email me the details. And thanks for the quick turnaround."

"Cyber Division is efficient."

Tom laughed and ended the call. He now had three big pieces of the puzzle in place, but unless Mark managed to get something from the NSA, he'd be left with a dark suspicion and nothing much else.

In his room, he opened the safe and not unexpectedly, found it empty. Staring at the black cavity, he wondered whether he was right to agree with Strand not to set up an ambush. Right or not, the shooter had taken the bait and that definitely didn't look good for his boss. Without Wellard's input, the shooter could not possibly know where Tom was staying, or where he had hidden the papyrus. That wasn't quite true. Like he told Strand, the shooter could have staked out One Center Plaza and followed Tom to the Omni Parker House, but he couldn't have known that he had the papyrus locked in the room safe. Then again, he *might* have acted on a suspicion that paid off. It was frustrating. He needed real evidence, not prepared to allow the shooter to get away clean with five murders.

Now that his man was in possession of the fake papyrus, Tom hoped he handled the thing and was now contaminated. That, of course, would only prove he stole the tractate, nothing else. Petty larceny was a far cry from murder one. Tom wanted a whole bunch more. He wanted the faceless man in The Entity who gave the orders, and presumably, who now waited for the tractate to be returned. This is where he would need some high-powered help. Someone who could get in touch with the Vatican's Secretariat of State and arrange for senior Entity officials to be UV scanned. Then what? All he would have is a man who handled the papyrus. It wouldn't be a conviction, but he wasn't ready to give up yet.

Don't worry, Paulini, we'll get them, one way or another.

His cellphone rang and he flipped open the lid. "Meecham."

"This is Dr. Norginson, Mr. Meecham. Further to our discussion, Harvard is interested in your proposition. When can we meet?"

"Are you able to come downtown, Doctor? If not, I can come to the university."

"As a matter of fact, I'm already downtown, in Mr. Strand's office, to be exact. He had some interesting things to say, not all of them complimentary to you, I might add," Norginson said with dry understatement.

Christ!

Tom could only imagine what those things were. It looked like his suspension might come early. He gave a resigned sigh and his shoulders sagged, seeing his career in ashes. Well, there was always New York and Malena. Maybe NYPD could use a slightly worn agent.

"I'll be there in ten minutes, Doctor."

"Don't despair, Mr. Meecham. Things are not as bad as you might think. I look forward to meeting you at last," she added and rang off.

Tom stared at the cellphone's LCD screen for several long seconds. Now what the hell did she mean by that?

Retrieving the original papyrus from the hotel security safe, he made his way to One Center Plaza, not looking forward to the coming confrontation. He was dragging his feet and not only because his back and ribs were sore. As he neared the imposing nine-story building, his spirits lifted. Apart from throwing him off the case, a real possibility, there was little else that Strand could do. He certainly could not compel him to hand the papyrus to the FBI. Although evidence as to motive, the tractate itself had marginal relevance in prosecuting the murders. A somewhat tenuous assumption and he suspected one that would probably not hold much weight with Strand, but Tom would let Norginson's lawyers handle that part.

He took the elevator to the sixth floor and strode briskly to Strand's office. There was little point in brooding over possibilities that would reveal themselves soon enough. A knock on the gray painted floor-to-ceiling door rewarded by a muffled, "Come in!"

Tom walked in and closed the door, his gaze on Strand, gauging his mood. The Special Agent in Charge held his eye for a moment and then shifted to his other visitor.

"Meecham, I want to introduce you to Professor Sidris Norginson, President of Harvard University, although I understand that you have already met."

"Only over the phone, sir," Tom said and turned to face a smiling woman prying herself loose from a chair.

What struck him was her youthful appearance; tall, probably around five-foot nine, slim, brown hair held up in a curl, clear complexion and large gray eyes that seemed to laugh at him. Dressed in black slacks and business jacket, she didn't look her forty-six years. She wore no lipstick and he could not detect any makeup, but it was hard to tell given the stuff women used these days.

She held out a long hand. "A pleasure, Mr. Meecham."

At least he recognized her voice, crisp and firm. Looking at the striking woman, he extended his hand and clasped hers. It was small, warm, and dry.

"I'm glad to see you, Doctor," he said earnestly and held out the wrapped papyrus—in case Strand had ideas. "The object of all our difficulties."

Norginson glanced at his boss, bit her lip and gingerly reached for the package. She stared at the precious thing and then looked up, her eyes bright.

"Thank you," she replied and Tom felt relieved. Whatever happened next, this was right, and a load rolled off his shoulders. He liked to think that Garbaldi would have approved.

Holding the papyrus against her stomach, she turned to the silent figure behind the desk. "My appreciation for your cooperation, Mr. Strand. The find will mean a lot to Harvard."

"As long as Harvard fulfills its side of the agreement, Doctor, the FBI is pleased to get rid of the thing. I can only hope it won't be as much trouble for you as it has been for us."

"If you close the case, it won't be," she replied tartly and looked at Meecham, her gaze speculative. "Harvard will publish and Professor Tyrone Ryker will make an announcement to that effect on Monday."

"I'm pleased to hear that, but if I can make a request? Please hold off on the announcement until you hear from me."

"Oh? I understood that's what you wanted."

"It is, but circumstances have changed since morning, and premature disclosure would now compromise our investigation."

"I see. Very well, I shall wait to hear from you."

"Hopefully, you won't have to wait long."

Norginson's eyes flickered to Stand. "I will leave you two to pursue your case."

"You've got transportation?" Tom asked, not comfortable with the idea of her walking around town carrying the package under her arm.

"I have university security with me. Don't worry, your tractate will be safe. And call me, Mr. Meecham. I would like to know more about the papyrus. Gentlemen…" She nodded to Strand and walked out.

When the door closed, Strand glared and waved at a chair. "Sit down, Tom," he growled and waited for Tom to make himself as comfortable. "You don't have to tell me why you gave the papyrus to Dr. Norginson. I won't delve into the personal reason, preferring to stick with the official line."

"The official line?" Tom ventured, priming himself for a blast.

"I wasn't found in a Cheerios box, Tom. Allow me a modicum of intelligence, okay? If the shooter didn't pick up the fake papyrus, giving the real one to Harvard was meant to defuse the situation, provided Norginson announced they now had the thing and were prepared to publish. Either way, it would have cut the ground from under the shooter's feet, hopefully inducing him to split. Sounds about right?"

"That was the general idea."

"But our man *did* take the fake papyrus, as you intended. You had no need then to give the real one to Norginson. Which leaves the personal reason. You can spin me a line about wanting to ensure its safety, but you'd be standing on a wobbly leg. You realize, of course, you've opened yourself to disciplinary action, but since you don't report to me, I'll leave that to Wellard."

Tom had expected an exemplary reaming out, but Strand's position confused him. "Why are you doing this, Garry? You could have stopped me, you know."

Strand shifted in his seat and cleared his throat. "By rights, I should have you suspended and cited for obstruction. That's what the book says, but I can't. This case is much more than simply five murders and we both know it. Some will consider what you did noble, but hardly professional, and I'd be one of them."

"You could be facing disciplinary action yourself, you know."

"Perhaps, but I don't think so. I'm betting that you'll nail Wellard before the FBI Director starts looking too hard at what we've both done. He'll be too busy dealing with that to notice us."

"That's presupposing I *do* nail Wellard."

"Yeah, there is always that."

Tom studied his superior. "You could have made this hard for me."

"I still can if Wellard gets off the hook," Strand snapped and peered at Meecham. "Are you satisfied that I'm not the leak?"

"I'm not," Tom said with a grin and Strand chuckled.

"I guess you have to consider everybody. How's the side?"

"I feel like I've been kicked by a horse. What now?"

"We wait for our man to surface. There isn't much else we can do."

Strand pulled open a drawer on the left side of his desk, took out several prints and pushed them across the desk. Tom stood up with barely a wince, stepped to the desk and picked up the photos. All were of Swens and the shooter, each taken at slightly different times. He knew right away what they were.

"Airport surveillance?"

"They just came from the lab. We now have a chain of corroborated movements. Our man has some challenging explaining ahead of him."

"If we get him," Tom murmured, studying the photos.

"We'll get him. You might as well get some rest. I'll call you if anything happens."

Tom placed the photos on the desk. "Thanks...I mean it."

Strand glared. "You're a pain, Meecham. Did you know that?"

"Yeah, so I've been told."

* * *

At four-fifty, Peroni collected his boarding pass from the business class check-in counter, ignoring the queue of anxious economy passengers still waiting to be processed. He wondered if all of them would make it in time. The pretty Alitalia attendant flashed him a smile that didn't touch her eyes as she slid his passport and boarding pass across the raised counter.

"Enjoy your flight, sir," she said briskly and immediately motioned to the next economy passenger in the line.

He flashed her a small smile and nodded to her, slipping the documents into his jacket's breast pocket. Incessant conversation and public speaker announcements filled the large terminal. Up and down the length of airline check-in counters, people hung onto carts piled high with suitcases, talking animatedly with family, friends or partners, waiting to inch forward, impatient to get the administrative chore done. Peroni didn't know how they did it. He had a low boredom threshold and shuddered at the thought of having to endure a session of check-in line torture.

He didn't dwell on it or expended too much sympathy. Somebody had to fly coach. Clutching his garment bag over his left shoulder and briefcase in his left hand, he made his way through wide double doors into the passport control area and more lines. This one, he had to endure. There was no business class line here.

Standing there, he toyed with the idea of visiting his parents. An atavistic impulse, but the thought of ambling among gently rolling Tuscany hills wreathed with orderly rows of vines, its green fields and cool woodlands, made him feel uncharacteristically nostalgic. He wanted to sit beneath the towering crown of the old walnut tree outside his parent's farmhouse; eat cheese with crusty warm bread and smoky *prosciutto*, and drink fine Chianti. He wanted to hear the hollow ringing of cowbells as the slow animals were driven back into the stables after a day at pasture. He wanted to smell cut hay, watch a fiery sunset and greet the winking stars. He wanted…the innocence he had lost.

When his turn came, he handed over his passport and boarding pass and waited as a stern-faced Immigration officer did his computer check. The officer raised his head, his eyes lingering on him momentarily, then asked him to press his right thumb against the sensor pad, followed by his left thumb and more waiting. Eventually the officer pushed through his documents. Peroni pocketed the paperwork and about to make for the carry-on x-ray scanner when someone coughed behind him.

"Sir, if you would turn around please."

The voice carried authority and Peroni slowly turned. A muscular policeman wearing sergeant stripes reached for his right hand and snapped on one end of stainless steel cuffs. The other already attached to his own left wrist. A chubby female officer, hand on her weapon, clearly ready for anything, dared Peroni to make a move. Her hazel eyes never left his. A smooth, clean snatch and he admired their professionalism. The passengers around him stepped back in alarm to a buzz of excited comments.

"Mr. Peroni, you're under arrest on suspicion of five counts of murder," the sergeant announced pleasantly, but his body language showed that he would not mind pounding on his prisoner at the slightest provocation. Showing no reaction, Peroni did not intend to provide one.

How he'd been made was irrelevant: airport surveillance when he met Swens, cameras in the Omni Parker House lobby or Meecham's room? It didn't matter. What did matter was how to extricate himself. Standing perfectly still, he gave a slow grin.

"This is a mistake, officer."

"Perhaps, but that's for others to sort out," the sergeant said and read him his Miranda rights. "Now, let's walk quietly and nobody will get hurt."

Peroni twitched his hand. "Lead on."

Followed by curious stares, they marched him past Immigration cubicles toward a short corridor with two doors. The sergeant opened the first and pulled Peroni into a small, white-painted room that held a plain gray Formica table flanked by two metal-legged chairs. Peroni placed his briefcase on the table and folded the garment bag over a chair. The officer unlocked the handcuff and motioned at the wall.

"Spread 'em."

The patting down quick and efficient. Satisfied, the sergeant jerked his head at an empty chair.

"Take a load off while we wait. This shouldn't take long."

Peroni pulled back a chair with a scrape and sat down. The wait presumably for the FBI to get here. Although alert, he was not tense or nervous. The feds had nothing, perhaps a charge of theft, but murder? He doubted that they could make it stick. Still, he did not want to underestimate his opposition.

"I'd like to make a call on my cellphone, if that's all right?"

The sergeant chewed his lip. "I guess."

Peroni dug out his BlackBerry and slowly looked at his captors. "In private." When the sergeant hesitated, he gave a disarming grin. "It's unlikely that I will crawl out through the air-conditioning ductwork."

The sergeant snorted, gathered his partner with a glance and they filed out. Peroni smiled when the door closed behind them and scrolled quickly through the phone list. It would be past ten p.m. in Rome and he hoped the cardinal had his cellular on, he usually did. It only took two rings.

"Belconi," the familiar voice grated.

"Peroni, Your Eminence," he said softly in case anyone listened outside. "I'm being held at Logan International airport and waiting for the FBI to show up. I'd suggest you activate whatever measures you have in place to get me out of here."

To give him credit the old man didn't hesitate. "Are you compromised?"

"I doubt it."

"Leave it with me," Belconi said heavily and hung up.

Peroni immediately initiated an application that wiped everything off the cellphone's memory chip, then took the back cover off the device and extracted the SIM card. He placed the little chip on the hard floor and stomped on it with his heel. There was a soft crunch. He picked up the mangled chip and threw it into a corner wastebasket. It would be inconvenient if Belconi tried to call him, but given the circumstances, he doubted that the cardinal would. If he needed to call, he had the necessary numbers memorized, including the one where his tape recording was stored. Losing the apps and data posed no problem. He had backup files at home and could always update the cellphone and initialize a new SIM. Satisfied, he pocketed the cellphone and leaned against the hard chair.

Some twenty minutes later, he heard angry shouting outside and the door jerked open. Two dark-suited men walked in and Peroni fought to keep his dismay from showing. One of them was Meecham. Keeping still, they waited for the sergeant to close the door. Both pulled out their IDs and flashed them before pocketing them.

"I am Supervising Special Agent Thomas Meecham, and my associate, Agent Johnston. Mr. Peroni, you were advised of the charges against you and informed of your rights. Do you understand those rights as they were read to you?"

"I understand them."

"Having those rights in mind, do you wish to talk to us now?"

Peroni shrugged. "You first."

"Okay. We're here to take you to FBI headquarters where we hope you will cooperate in assisting us with our investigation. Now, if you would stand up and empty your pockets."

Peroni stood, but made no other move, his eyes fixed on Meecham. The FBI agent looked attentive and showed no obvious signs of injury. A bulletproof vest? He underestimated him, potentially a costly mistake, annoyed at having missed out on another hundred thousand.

* * *

Mouth set, Tom studied his assailant. Now that they were actually face-to-face, Peroni didn't look like a hitman, they never did, but his alertness, obvious military bearing and physical strength said it for him. Tom was dealing with a deadly predator and had no intention of dropping his guard. Not like the two fools outside, leaving Peroni alone. Well, no way to undo the damage now.

"Your pockets," Tom prompted.

Peroni shook his head. "That constitutes illegal search, Mr. Meecham. I would need to see a warrant first showing cause."

Tom smiled, surprised at the man's legal knowledge. And of course, he was right. "Very well, we'll do it your way."

Refusing to be searched may be a petty victory, and Tom understood that Peroni wanted to maintain psychological advantage. It put the FBI on the defensive, not that it would do Peroni much good in the long run.

Tom nodded to Johnston who produced a set of cuffs.

"Turn around and place your hands behind your back," Johnston ordered.

Peroni did as he was told.

The ride downtown spent in stony silence, Tom did not expect Peroni to try any amateurish getaway gambits. It was up to the FBI to make its case.

When they reached One Center Plaza, they left the black sedan in the underground parking garage and made for the elevator. Tom didn't give his prisoner any time to look around the open floor as he marched quickly into a small interview room. An old tactic he used before: keep the prisoner disoriented, don't give him time to settle down, and harangue him until he broke. After removing Peroni's cuffs, he was shoved into a plain plastic seat.

Meecham nodded to Johnston, who immediately took off. After a moment, he returned, handed Tom a brown envelope and closed the door.

Tom sat opposite his prisoner while Johnston stood guard. To Tom, Peroni looked calm, unruffled by his surroundings; too calm for someone facing five murder raps and a charge of theft, although that one was still to be raised. He wondered about the call Peroni made and cursed the two airport security personnel for being so careless. Peroni was entitled to a call, but Tom wanted it done under controlled conditions.

Meecham reached for the envelope beside him and pulled out a stack of 6" by 9" prints. He slid the top one across the table.

"Mr. Peroni, you met one Martin Swens at Logan International airport last Thursday, July twenty-first, at two forty-six in the afternoon. Airport surveillance footage shows both of you leaving together. How did you happen to meet him?"

Peroni did not look at the photo and Tom bit his lip, knowing how thin his case was. The photo probably didn't tell Peroni anything he didn't already know; circumstantial evidence, nothing more. If Tom tried to use it, he would be laughed out of court—if the case ever came to court.

"A chance meeting," Peroni said coolly. "A friend he waited for didn't show up. As I was going his way, he offered me a lift."

"I see." Tom slid across another photo. "Both of you again, this time at the Alhoda Market, Cambridge. Care to comment?"

Peroni shrugged. "I needed to buy a few things before going to my hotel."

"We'll come back to Mr. Swens and your hotel later. Please take a look at these two shots. One was taken at the Omni Parker House Hotel lobby. The other is from my room at the same hotel. The man in the lobby is clearly you. You were also in my room where a certain item was removed from my safe. Can you explain that?"

Tom could see Peroni fighting an instinctive impulse to look at the photos.

"Are you charging me with theft, Mr. Meecham?"

"Impersonating an FBI officer is a serious matter. Hold out your left arm," Tom ordered.

Looking uncertain, Peroni complied, a slight frown creasing his face. Tom reached across the table and pulled back the sleeve, exposing a black Rado and a scar. He then pushed across two more photos.

"The same hand, Mr. Peroni. The same watch and scar. The same man at the Alhoda Market and my room…you."

Peroni's eyes flickered at the photos and he shrugged, folding back his arm. "Granted, a superficial similarity, but I'm not the only one wearing a Rado."

"Perhaps not, but you're the only one with that scar," Tom said when a knock interrupted the proceedings.

He glanced at Johnston who opened the door. Clark peered in and handed Johnston a UV scanner and a bulging white plastic bag, then reached into his jacket pocket and held out a piece of paper. Tom took it and slid it across the table.

"Our warrant, Mr. Peroni, authorizing us to search you and your possessions." He nodded to Clark who picked up the garment bag off the chair and softly closed the door.

Barely looking at the paper, Peroni started to empty his pockets. Tom picked up the BlackBerry and pried open the back cover. He stared at the empty SIM slot, replaced the cover and laid the phone on the table. Peroni's expression didn't change, but Tom fancied he could see a gleam of satisfaction. It was now clear why Peroni wanted to make his call in private. He may actually have called someone, but what he wanted was to destroy any incriminating information stored in the SIM. This was discouraging. Tom had been thwarted at every step and he wondered if he was wasting his time here. Peroni did not look like he would crack, not at all fazed at the prospect of a theft charge. On the contrary, the man looked smug.

But Tom wasn't done yet. He glanced at Johnston who reached into the plastic bag and pulled out two yellow tinted plastic glasses and a digital camera. He donned one of the glasses and handed Tom the other pair and the camera. Putting the bag on the table, Johnston held up the scanner.

"Mr. Peroni, please cover your eyes. This is a UV scanner and I need to check your shoes."

Looking contemptuous, Peroni placed his left palm over his eyes. Tom sensed the man's confidence and disdain, and longed to push Peroni's face in.

Johnston didn't bother with the shoes, quickly plying the blue beam over Peroni's hands. Even though his right hand was lightly clenched, the ball of his thumb was exposed, glowing ruby red. Tom quickly snapped two shots and exchanged satisfied looks with Johnston.

"Okay, Mr. Peroni, that will be all," Johnston said.

"Found what you needed?"

"Your shoes are clean," Tom said, allowing feigned frustration to creep into his voice, but not all that feigned either.

He might not have gotten a confession, but he certainly learned a lot about Peroni's character, confirming what he already knew. He faced a highly skilled and intelligent professional who knew how to kill in cold blood, used to dealing with police and security services. No one, no matter how confident, stranded in a foreign country, could display such derision and indifference without having a powerful backer hovering over him. Even without a backer, given the flimsy evidence against him, Tom would also display disdain. Still, his business wasn't done yet. There remained a little matter of Swens shot at the Noris residence and the identikit drawing from Garbaldi. Peroni would face some hard questioning before he walked out of here.

"There is one more thing," Johnston said as he extracted a plastic vial from the bag and pulled out a swab stick. "Open your mouth."

Peroni smiled and then complied.

Johnston took the saliva sample, sealed the swab in the vial and labeled it.

Another knock on the door and Tom looked up. Clark shoved his head in and handed Johnston the garment bag. He then glanced at Tom, who immediately stood and walked out.

"You got swabs off everything?"

"Yes, sir. Mr. Strand wants to see you right away."

Tom frowned. "Now? Okay, you go in there with Agent Johnston and get swabs off the suspect's hands, shirt and trousers. Make sure everything is correctly labeled. First, get Peroni's cellphone memory scanned. There may be something there we can use."

"Yes, sir."

Tom sighed and walked quickly toward Strand's office, wondering what was so burning urgent. He knocked on the door and walked in. Strand looked up and waved at a chair. Tom remained standing.

"I just received a call from Marshal himself, ordering me to release your prisoner."

"The FBI Director is ordering us to release him? You've got to be shitting me! We've hardly had a chance to talk to him. How the hell is the Director involved?"

"I don't like it much either, but this came from a First Secretary at the Italian Embassy. Your man has been granted diplomatic immunity. Unless we can show evidence of a capital offense, we're to release him immediately as a *persona non grata*."

"Christ! That's not playing fair."

"Tell me about it."

"Give me twenty-four hours. I need to chase up NSA and we need time for the lab to process his DNA and clothing swabs."

"Sorry, Tom. No can do. You know the procedure. Get Clark to find the next available flight to Rome and get your man on it, then come back here. I know you've had a tough day, but we need to talk."

"But we've got him! I know it!"

Strand stared at him. "I don't like it either, but can you prove it?"

On his way out, Tom didn't exactly slam the door.

He walked into the interview room, glanced at Clark and jerked his head. The young agent immediately hurried out.

"Anything on the cellphone?"

"Sorry, sir. The thing is completely wiped."

Tom ground his teeth in frustration and his shoulders slumped. This was depressing.

"Book a deportation flight for Peroni to Rome. Anything you can get. Call me on my cellphone when you have the details. Get me a car and driver right away."

"We're letting him go?"

"Afraid so," Tom growled and eased back into the room. He picked up the folded garment bag and threw it at Peroni. Johnston stared at him, not understanding.

"Let's go. Your embassy has given you diplomatic status, but your visa is cancelled and you're being deported."

As Peroni slowly stood, Tom could clearly see the man was satisfied with the proceedings. Tom turned to Johnston. "Cuff him and get his stuff."

Johnston quickly pulled out a set of cuffs from his jacket pocket and dragged Peroni's arms behind his back. After clipping on the cuffs, he pushed him toward the door.

Peroni straightened, then paused in the open doorway. "No hard feelings, Mr. Meecham. The FBI simply made a mistake."

Tom's smile was tight. "You're the one who made the mistake, Mr. Peroni, by coming to the United States. I'll be seeing you. Count on it."

The driver threaded his way slowly through the traffic along I-90 toward the Ted Williams Tunnel. Johnston sat unmoving in the front seat. Tom did not bother looking at Peroni sitting beside him in the back seat. The man wasn't going anywhere. Tom's

thoughts were dark. As a case, this one rated as the most challenging and the most frustrating. Perhaps The Entity had it right.
If you encountered an obstacle, simply remove it. Legalities only
got in the way. Maybe he could take out a contract on Peroni. He
knew one or two guys who would not mind handling the job.
That may give him momentary satisfaction and avenge Garbaldi,
but would do nothing for his conscience. He was a federal law
officer and stooping down into the gutter, resorting to techniques
of the scum he was after, would only serve to reduce him to their
level and the dividing line between them would be forever erased.

It wasn't always convenient being the good guy.

Clark called, saying he had arranged a flight with Virgin Atlantic Airlines departing at seven forty-five p.m. Tom checked his
watch: six-forty, plenty of time to catch the flight. A five-hour
layover at Heathrow, but he did not think Peroni would mind.
Even if he did, Tom didn't particularly give a shit. He'd had a
long day, his back was sore, and it looked like he would have a
long night as well. Two days of running around and precious little
to show for it.

Airport security waited for them and took charge. There was
a small hassle at the Virgin customer service desk when Peroni
demanded a business class seat, producing his Alitalia boarding
pass, but it got sorted out. At the departure gate, with Johnston
in tow, Tom waited until boarding was called and watched as airport security escorted Peroni onto the aircraft. Nobody waved
bye-bye.

Returning to the city, there was nothing much to say, and
Tom didn't feel like chatting. It had not been his greatest day and
he felt like being moody. He was also angry that the fates con-
spired to snatch his prize when he *had* his man.

He walked into Strand's office without knocking, sprawled
into a chair and gave a long sigh.

"Isn't anybody around? The floor's deserted."

Looking up from his desk, Strand frowned. "What did you expect? It's Saturday. Didn't you get the memo?"

Tom sighed. "There's got to be an easier way to do this, Garry."

"My wife's complaining that she can't recognize my face," Strand remarked in a neutral voice. "But it makes for great reunions. You married?"

"Been close once. Broke up recently. She's in New York now and I'm in DC. She also complained that I was never around."

"Anybody else on the horizon?"

Thinking of Melissa, Tom shrugged. "Perhaps, but I'm not taking anything for granted just yet."

"Don't be surprised if she snags a banker or something. At least she'll have him around to chew out. Hell of a life we've got, eh?"

"Yeah. Maybe I should go into Peroni's line of work. The pay's got to be good and he gets to pick his own hours. Everything's first class."

"Even the women," Strand added with a grin and Tom chuckled.

"Probably. And we had him! That's the rotten part. We had him. Twenty-four hours, that's all we needed."

"It sucks when you don't have evidence, and that diplomatic doge? Real cute." Strand got up, walked to the wall unit and slid back a panel. He took out a bottle of amber liquid and held it up. "Care for a belt?"

"Hell, might as well finish the day on a good note."

Strand smiled. He dragged out two tumblers and began pouring. After adding ice, he walked to his desk and held out a glass.

Tom took a sip and raised an eyebrow in appreciation. "Not bad, not bad at all. What is it?"

"Crown Royal, Canadian rye."

"Must remember it."

Strand sat down, sipped and leaned back against his seat. "What now?"

Tom shrugged. "We keep after him. At least we've proven one thing. He handled the fake papyrus."

"Oh? How do you figure?"

"The forensics team at DC doped the thing to fluoresce under UV light and Johnston got a positive scan."

Strand appeared to chew that over and then took a long pull of his whiskey. "I can see where you're going with this, but that's still a long way from getting Peroni or his handler to court."

"I know, but it's a trail. We'll have our link if NSA comes through checking Swens' calls. He and Peroni must have talked at some point. On the way from the airport, I asked Johnston to also look at records where Peroni's name was used, as we don't have his cellphone number. He trashed his SIM."

Strand laughed at Tom's evident frustration. "No fool, is he? Even if NSA identifies his handler, we'll need the Vatican's co-operation. Without their help, we'll be stuck."

"If NSA gets me those numbers, I'll have Peroni and that's all I need to get The Entity. He committed five murders for them and might be willing to talk if we offer him a deal. No matter the motive behind them, I cannot believe the Church hierarchy sanctioned it. Then again, maybe I'm just being naïve. A lot of my notions took a pretty severe beating these last two days. If Garbaldi is right about that tractate, the Vatican is in for some very rocky times, but that doesn't necessarily mean they'll be prepared to hand over one of their own. The problem is, we don't know *who* is implicated. They'll have enough on their plate dealing with the papyrus fallout without having it known that their own intelligence service undertook murder to keep the thing from becoming public."

Strand sighed and shook his head. "It's just beginning to dawn on me. That papyrus could spell revolution. The Church may be in it up to its neck, but is that worth setting the world on fire? Perhaps you were a tad hasty giving it to Norginson."

Tom looked hard at the Boston chief. "I've thought about that, a lot. I don't know what will happen when the thing is published, but I do know this. If the Church's cause is right, it cannot sanction killing. If they've been perpetrating a lie on the world for the past two thousand years, resorting to murder to keep the truth from being known simply to maintain themselves in power, that constitutes a crime. A crime committed against one of their own and four American citizens. Like it or not, I'm involved and I intend to prosecute the case until every perpetrator is apprehended, whoever and wherever they are."

"Shit, Tom, I can almost see that halo," Strand said, smiling broadly.

Tom gave a sheepish grin. "I don't like to lose."

"I can see that," Strand said slowly, looking speculatively at Tom. "Tell me. You read the text, what did it mean to you?"

Startled by the question, Tom scratched his chin, struggling to make order out of jumbled thoughts. Intellectually, he knew what the papyrus represented and the likely impact it would have, but what impact did it have on him?

"Honestly? Not much. Sure, it casts a different light on Jesus and the New Testament, but it's just another revelation in a long string of revelations. When I read that Jesus himself may be a myth, a fabrication of Christian founders, the fact that he could be John the Baptist's disciple will probably not count for much to the ordinary Joe on the street. It hasn't with me. The believers will continue to believe, and I always remained pretty much ambivalent. I can see it affecting the academics and the Vatican Curia a whole lot more. If the papyrus is the truth, the Church will have to deal with it. There will be a stir, but it will blow over." He glanced at his tumbler and took a sip. "What about you?"

Strand frowned. "My parents are Presbyterian and I guess that makes me one too. I haven't attended services in years, but

Stefan Vučak

we sent our kids to Sunday school, taught them moral values and to follow the commandments, more or less. I don't know what the papyrus means to me. I believe in God and hope there is something to this after death stuff. If not, I wouldn't have lost anything. Having killed in line of duty, I already have enough on my conscience. As far as I'm concerned, all the denominations have corrupted the faith and turned it into a business. No doubt, many will decry the existence of the papyrus and what it has to say, but I'd like to think that most wouldn't mind seeing the Church shaken up a bit. In my opinion, it's been long overdue for a spring cleaning."

Both men drank in silence to the echo of their words. Tom drained his glass, stood up and placed it on Strand's desk.

"I'm going back to my hotel and drink some more. After I've downed a few, maybe all this will start to make some sort of sense."

"Don't count on it," Strand cautioned with a broad smile. "It hasn't to me."

"I'll just enjoy getting sloshed, then."

Walking down Tremont, oblivious to traffic noises, gaudy displays and people hurrying around him, Tom gnawed at his options. There were not many of them. Actually, only one. Without the NSA data, he had a dead case. No Peroni, no Entity big boss. If he had any brains, he would quit, return to DC and his apartment and take a long spa bath. His apartment did not have a spa bath, but it was pleasant thinking about it. To hell with it. Publishing the papyrus would screw the Vatican's day and Garbaldi can rest in peace, if there is such a thing. At least he was beyond caring.

Waiting at the lights to cross over onto School Street, Tom realized that he couldn't let it go. However easy the option, he couldn't give up, but he already knew that. Feeling sorry for himself perhaps? With sore ribs and back, he could afford to indulge in a little bit of self-pity.

The hotel doorman opened the door for him and he walked into the cool lobby, making straight for the elevators. In his room, he closed the door, leaned against the warm wood and gave a long sigh. Taking off his jacket, he threw it on the bed in a crumpled heap and stepped to the bar fridge mounted into the polished wood wall unit. He pulled out a can of dry ginger ale and a plastic airplane-service bottle of Wild Turkey. Finishing the mix, he took his tumbler to a small balcony and gazed at the Boston lights. After a while, he sat down at the round writing desk and dragged the phone toward him.

"Mark Price," a cheerful voice answered and Tom winced, hating to be a nuisance.

"You okay to talk?"

"It's been a long day, but I'm all done."

"Me too. Apologies for bugging you this late, but remember that offer of help? I'm afraid I'll have to take you up on it."

"Well, crap! That didn't take long, but I'm glad you called. What's up?"

"I'm not interrupting anything, am I?"

"Just having a quiet evening on the back porch, smoking a cigar, nursing a drink and enjoying steamy Washington."

"Got a spare seat? I wouldn't mind joining you."

Mark laughed. "Come on over."

"Rain check. That party I talked about earlier? Well, he's flown, literally. Would you believe it? I actually had him, but we were forced to let him go. Insufficient evidence."

"Yeah, it can work out that way and it's a bitch when it happens. That help, it wouldn't have something to do with tailing him, would it?"

"Christ! You've got a nasty and devious mind, Mark."

"It wasn't hard to figure and I've done that kind of stuff myself, remember? Okay, what do you have in mind?"

"It will take time to get the evidence I need. Hopefully, not too much time. While that's happening, I don't want to lose him. I thought of going through regular CIA channels—"

"Shit, Tom! You don't want to do that. By the time the wheels turn, you'd be collecting your pension."

"That's what I figured. About an hour ago, we bundled my guy on a Virgin Atlantic Airways flight to Rome. It's due at Heathrow at six thirty-five in the morning. Although he has a five-hour layover, I doubt he'll hang around that long."

"You're right. I wouldn't either. I presume you want a tail on him once he gets to the da Vinci-Fiumicino, right?"

"It would be very useful to know where he lives and who he sees over the next couple of days. Mark, if our guys are spotted, it's all over. The man is a professional."

"I read you."

"I thought of getting the Italian State Police to do this, but—"

"Yeah. By the time you finish explaining, your man would have vanished."

"That's it."

"A photo or something would be handy, you know."

"I'll email everything to your personal address within twenty minutes. And Mark? I don't know how you're going to pull this off, but thanks."

"Don't mention it."

Staring at the receiver, Tom placed it in its cradle and sighed, not looking forward having to get back to the office.

Christ!

Chapter Seven

Father Tomboli emerged from the pontiff's study, saw Albani and nodded.

"You may go in, Your Eminence."

"Thank you," Albani said brusquely, annoyed that it took this long to arrange an audience.

Normally, seeing the Holy Father did not take much arranging, not for him. Heavy robes swirling around his legs, he strode past the pope's private secretary and walked through the open doorway into the study. Tomboli bowed slightly and closed the door after him.

Sitting behind a wide ornate desk littered with papers, Pope Paul VII lifted his head and smiled broadly. A large youthful man, he dominated his surroundings. Only fifty-nine, hair still black with a hint of gray at the temples, Marino Francesco Pagiano, former Archbishop of Milan, could look forward to many years guiding the Church through the turbulent new century. It did not necessarily mean that he would enjoy them.

Unlike his predecessors, Pagiano was a progressive liberal and daring thinker, prepared to take firm action to tackle some of the thornier social problems facing the Church, even when such action contravened established dogma, to the consternation of many conservative elements within the Curia. Born and educated in Milan, Pagiano obtained a doctorate in Canon Law and studied at the University of Rome La Sapienza for his PhD in Theological Philosophy. In 1980, he was appointed to the Secretariat of State where he served until 1987. After a stint at the Commission for Extraordinary Affairs, he went home as Archbishop of Milan. In 2002, he returned to the Vatican and was instrumental in expanding access to the Vatican Secret Archives. His theological writings were meager but no one doubted his sincerity when he spoke of badly needed reforms within and outside the Church and its duty to care for the poor of the world. Charity, he said, should be seen to be practiced, not merely sermonized. With the passing of Benedict XVI, although not seen as a favorite, Cardinal Pagiano surprised many when he emerged from the conclave as pontiff. Albani owed his appointment as Archivist to the new pope and considered him a friend. There was something he needed to remember. His friend was now the Supreme Pontiff, not Cardinal Pagiano, and these were two different people.

Shafts of yellow light slanted through tall windows, making bright pools on the wooden floor. Apart from one floor-to-ceiling bookshelf filled with bound leather volumes, the small room empty. The new pontiff disliked the air of splendor and majesty that had surrounded the papacy and took steps to eliminate unnecessary protocol and pompous ceremonial as an outdated anachronism. Welcomed by younger progressive priests the move did nothing to endear him to diehards wedded to the dignity they insisted should surround his person. As he once remarked to Albani in a reflective mood, dignity is a state of mind, not a resplendent tiara. Besides, the diehards would soon die out and their objections with them. The world had no time for kings anymore.

"Come in, Gulio. Come in. Have a seat," Paul said pleasantly in a deep, confident voice and waved a muscular arm in greeting.

Albani walked quickly to the desk, leaned over the extended hand and kissed the offered ring seal.

"Thank you, Your Holiness," he replied and seated himself. "I appreciate you seeing me."

Dressed in a white cassock, looking fit and alert, the pontiff twitched his hand in dismissal. "Nonsense! I regret not doing it sooner, but preparations for my visit to Moscow next week kept me occupied."

"I understand," Albani said, and he did. He had taken official trips himself.

Pope Paul sat back in his chair and joined the fingers of his hands in a pyramid. "Amazing the arrangements needed for a simple visit. You'd think I was emigrating. God and governments, both work in mysterious ways."

"I wish you well in your talks with the Kremlin and the Russian Patriarchate."

"Thank you, but I suspect it will be easier dealing with the Kremlin than the Patriarchate."

"Can we dare hope to bring them around, Your Holiness? They have clung to the First Council of Constantinople version of the Creed since 381. I cannot see them abandoning their position now."

"We can argue that Pope Leo IX was wrong when he excommunicated the Patriarch of Constantinople over the *Filioque* heresy, and since 1054 the faith has been in schism. Perhaps it's time we looked beyond theological hairsplitting and argued on the intent of its meaning."

"A compromise?"

"To heal the rift between us, why not? Isn't my job to bring unity among all Christian Churches?"

"Not if it creates a rift within the Catholic Church."

"I'm spending all my time with ambassadors, movie stars, protocol and dogma, anyway. I might as well spend it on something worthwhile. I tell you, I sometimes wish I were an ordinary priest again, able to travel at will and talk to people openly. Impossible now, I'm afraid. You know, Gulio, I miss that. I miss having a parishioner argue with me, telling me exactly what he feels and the problems he faces. All I hear these days is rarefied discourse that hardly seems to have relevance to the Church or our duty. I read reports, analyses, figures and projections devoid of the human element. I fear, my friend, that somewhere, we have lost sight of our objective."

Startled by this frank admission, but not altogether surprised, Albani nodded, sympathizing fully. Closed within the Vatican's grim walls, the Curia issued rulings, held councils and gatherings, but none of them involved the common man on the street. They were merely somebody to talk down to, unthinking sheep. Hardly surprising then, that the Church was losing touch with its flock.

"Perhaps we *have* strayed, Your Holiness. Take me, for instance. I am no longer a priest, but an unfeeling bureaucrat operating under false colors. I sometimes look at my work and wonder how it benefits the faith or the ordinary churchgoer. Perhaps it's time we paused and connected with the people, uncluttered by centuries of irrelevancy and self-interest. We've forgotten how to reach out. In the confusion, the flock is dispersing, looking elsewhere for guidance we failed to provide."

The pontiff did not say anything for a moment and then sighed. "The problem is, Gulio, we have never connected with the people or provided guidance, only dictates. I'm supposed to have absolute power, yet in many ways, I am limited in what I can do. It's too big, too complex. Inertia is carrying all of us toward a dark destiny and I don't know how to prevent it. I thought I was the one with all the answers." He gave a sour chuckle and shook his head in helpless wonderment.

Disturbed, Albani stared hard at the pontiff. Some reflection was healthy, but not when it was soul destroying.

"Your Holiness, you are Peter! If you will it, it will be done!"

A wan smile lit Paul's chiseled features. "I once thought so. Now…"

"Trust in the faith and purity of our cause, not blind adherence to dogma in the misguided belief that they're one and the same, and people will follow you."

"Cleanse ourselves of the sins of our fathers, is that it?" Paul quipped with a grin.

"And sins of our own making, Your Holiness," Albani said softly, knowing he could not turn back now.

"Oh?"

"I had a purpose in seeing you, Your Holiness. I fear that Cardinal Belconi—"

"Belconi! What's he done now?"

"He has strayed and strayed badly. I don't have proof, but I believe he organized the deaths of Father Reoni, a scientist in the Conservation Laboratory, and Father Garbaldi, one of my senior researchers."

Paul gaped at him. "You can't be serious."

"Never more serious in my life."

"Incredible…Is that the same Garbaldi appointed to Cardinal Fontini's department?"

"That's him."

"I've read his work; controversial, but brilliant, although Cardinal Marati probably doesn't see it that way. Controversial perhaps, but something the Church will have to grapple with, and we need minds like that, not weed them out. What happened?"

"We may have to grapple with it sooner than you think, Your Holiness. Two months ago, we received a shipment of manuscripts from the Coptic Orthodox Patriarchate of Alexandria. Part of an exchange agreed to during the Commission for Theological Dialogue. Garbaldi was assigned to catalog and index the codices for appropriate storage. Although we cannot be certain, Monsignor Giacomo believes that in one of those codices, Garbaldi found a papyrus that stated Jesus was John the Baptist's disciple and the second Messiah."

"Go on," Paul prompted, showing no emotion at the revelation. Not exactly news, but not generally well known either.

"It could have been a plant by the Coptic Church to panic us, but I don't believe the Patriarchate were even aware of it."

"A ghost from our past comes to haunt us?"

"Very likely. Giacomo immediately reported the matter to me. I'm ashamed to say, Your Holiness, instead of handling it myself, I involved Marati."

Stefan Vučak

The pontiff pursed his lips. "Why didn't you simply talk to Father Garbaldi before doing anything?"

Albani squirmed with embarrassment, having failed in his duty for the second time by relying on Giacomo. It wasn't the Prefect's responsibility, but his!

"I wanted to! But when this surfaced, he was still on his sabbatical in Cairo. Giacomo left instructions for him to report in when he returned, but he never showed up. Yesterday, I received an email from the FBI informing me of Garbaldi's death by an unknown assailant. I can infer what happened. It is likely that Garbaldi took the tractate to the States to have it authenticated and Marati panicked, fearing disclosure. I always accepted the newspaper reports that Father Reoni was killed in a random robbery, but with Garbaldi dead, it was too much of a coincidence. When I talked to Marati about it, he as much as admitted that Belconi had them assassinated."

"To recover the papyrus and prevent it from becoming public?"

"Yes."

"And did he recover it?"

"I don't know, but I don't believe so. In his email, the FBI agent in charge of the case informed me that he intended handing the tractate to Harvard University."

The pontiff sat up with a jerk, his face suddenly pale and Albani knew what he was thinking among a riot of images flashing through his mind—all bad. Marati had erred in his approach, that was clear, and Belconi in his usual high-handed style thought that direct application of force solved most problems. In this case, it might have, had he succeeded. An unworthy thought and he would pray for forgiveness later.

"Revelation of the papyrus won't be a disaster, not exactly, but it *will* be a severe embarrassment for the Church," the pontiff mused pulling at his chin. "Still, we should weather it. However, I'm not so certain we can weather the revelation that The Entity sanctioned murder if the FBI breaks the case." Paul stared at Albani. "You replied to the FBI agent?"

"I asked him to return the tractate. Probably a futile gesture as our claim to the papyrus is tenuous at best."

Paul rubbed his eyes and sighed. "I agree and it probably is a futile gesture. Nevertheless, get in touch with the FBI Director and request his help in recovering it. If that doesn't work, I'll have a word with Cardinal Karpeli. The FBI might be more amenable to reason if the request comes from our Secretariat of State."

"Your Holiness, should Belconi prematurely learn that I have spoken to you…"

"Belconi…I don't know which is the greater evil, Gulio, maintaining our intelligence services or being without them. Don't worry. Karpeli knows how to keep secrets and we need that papyrus returned."

"Your Holiness—"

Paul lifted his hand, his eyes hard. "I can appreciate why it was done, but I can hardly condone that it *was* done. My problem right now, and that's obviously why you're here, is what do I do about Belconi."

Albani frowned. "Do? We call Inspector General Emanuo and have Belconi arrested!"

"Yes, but on what evidence?" Paul asked softly. "Your hearsay?"

"Then we simply leave it?" Albani looked horrified. "Your Holiness, if you allow this evil, then we're indeed being carried toward a dark destiny. You might as well call the Congregation for the Doctrine of the Faith by its true name, the Inquisition, and lump The Entity with it! That way, we won't have to pretend when we kill someone."

"You're overreaching yourself, Your Eminence!" the pontiff admonished sternly, clearly stung by the fire of Albani's words and the ring of truth they carried.

At any other time, Albani would have been shocked to dare dispute Authority like this, but he was not discussing points of theology now. He gave a small bow of apology, but when he looked up, his eyes were still defiant.

"Your Holiness, I respectfully submit it's Cardinal Belconi who has overreached himself. Doing nothing about curbing The Entity because action could damage the Church has been a flawed policy for far too long, and something that has already tarnished our credibility. Is expediency the same thing as truth? Why are we so afraid of truth, Holy Father?"

"Because a lie is easier to sell, my friend," Pope Paul VII murmured softly.

Albani's shoulders sagged as the realization tore at his heart.

* * *

Gazing absently through the tinted plate glass window at the sunlit King's Chapel across the street, Tom took another sip of coffee, not a Brazilian blend, but palatable enough. Nothing moved on School Street and only an occasional car whispered by along Tremont. Downtown would probably fill up later, but this early, people were either sleeping in, lying about or doing whatever people do on a warm, bright Sunday morning.

Parker's Restaurant not exactly crowded, but not empty either. Businessmen and tourists clustered in little groups, enjoying a sumptuous buffet breakfast before heading out for the day. He easily saw the difference between the two. The businessmen all wore dark conservative suits and sported somber looks like the fate of the world rested on their weary shoulders. The tourists were informal and boisterous, looking to have fun on a perfect day. Tom would not have minded a bit of fun himself, but doubted it would come his way. With a sore back and too much to drink, he hadn't slept well. Losing Peroni to a cheap diplomatic trick hadn't helped. Trying to think positive only made him feel gloomier. He had nothing to be positive about.

Eyeing the buffet layout, at least the hotel served great food, he had to give them that. The thought of stuffing himself only riled his stomach. Instead, he sipped his coffee, not in any hurry to face the world, not when it screwed him.

His cellphone went off and he flipped open the lid, ignoring automatic glances of curiosity from fellow guests.

"Meecham!"

"Well, crap! The sun's hardly up and you're already sore at life?"

Tom laughed, his black mood shredded by the cheerful voice. "I figure if I start off feeling mean, it can only get better."

"Yeah, I've had days like that myself. Cheer up, I came bearing gifts."

"Beware the Greeks, and I could certainly use a bit of cheering up right now."

"In that case, I'm your man. My Gulfstream will be touching down at Logan domestic in about forty minutes. Check out of whatever hole you're at and meet me at the Information Desk in the American Airlines domestic arrivals area."

"You're flying in? Christ! You didn't have to do that."

"Gift horses and all that, and you'll need a ride back to DC."

"I will?"

"Trust me."

"If you say so. Care to give me a hint?"

"And spoil the surprise? See you in a while."

Tom hung up, feeling more kindly disposed toward his rotten fellow human beings. Mark must have come through on his request for data on Wellard. At least he hoped so. He would certainly not be flying in simply to chat and share a coffee. Did he want to check out? If this was about Wellard, he would probably need to see the FBI Director before jumping on his boss. What with subsequent debriefs and sweeping up the fallout, the mess could drag on for a couple of days. So, checking out made sense.

With only a carry-on, packing did not take long.

Once out of the Ted Williams Tunnel, the General Edward Lawrence Logan International Airport opened into a sprawl of terminal buildings, hotels and maintenance hangars. Aircraft stood parked against loading ramps. Others moved slowly along taxiways, lining up for their shot at a runway.

The cab approached Terminal B and slowed as it neared the American Airlines entrance, maneuvering around cars, pedestrians and other cabs as it hunted for an empty slot. Not seeing anything, Tom told the driver to stop. Double-parked, he got out and winced at the pervasive blare of car horns, the crowded sidewalk, and the stink of gas mixed with the background smell of jet fuel. Where the hell were all these people going? He heaved his carry-on bag over his left shoulder and sauntered toward the entrance. A uniformed cop waved frantically at the cab to move on.

Inside the too-cold terminal, ignoring the noise, people and public address announcements, he made his way toward the Information Desk, past the AA help desk, hotel reservation displays and food venues. Not unexpectedly, a crowd waited for their turn at the two harried attendants behind the round counter. Looking at their patient expressions, Tom wondered how the girls did it. No sign of Mark, but he didn't hold it against him. It would probably take longer to taxi in and disembark than it took to get here—a contradiction of air travel.

To pass the time, he watched the antics of milling passengers, absently checked the hanging arrival/departure electronic boards and wondered what it would be like to take a flight to Hawaii or Alaska perhaps; do some swimming, fishing or nothing in particular where he wouldn't have to think about Peroni, Wellard or The Entity. Just when he considered getting a coffee or something, he saw Mark threading his way toward him and broke into a grin. Dressed in a dark suit, lean, hard featured, dark brown hair brushed back, he exuded competence and authority. His large violet eyes shone with friendliness.

Tom walked toward the taller man and held out his hand. "This is an unexpected level of service from the government."

Mark chuckled and they shook hands, his grip firm. "Unusual circumstances demand unusual measures. Hope you haven't been waiting long?"

"Admiring the scenery. So, what's so burning urgent that brings you to Boston?"

"Let's get out of here and I'll tell you all about it."

After flashing their IDs, clearing security took seconds. Mark led him down a deserted corridor dedicated for private and government flights. At one of the side doors they showed their IDs to another guard and were escorted to the tarmac and the parked Gulfstream V. Climbing up the extended stairs, Tom winced as his ribs gave a protesting twinge. A civilian flight attendant dressed in a white jacket stowed his bag, closed the hatch and the aircraft immediately began to move. After nine minutes crawling along a taxiway, they turned onto the active runway and the turbines spun up.

With a surge of power, the sleek jet accelerated past idling aircraft waiting patiently for their shot. The wheels came up with a thump and the pilot retracted the flaps. Below, Boston looked like a bright jigsaw puzzle picture. The aircraft banked and headed south, following the coastline.

Tom unbuckled his seatbelt, stretched his legs, shifted himself into a more comfortable position and beamed at Mark sitting opposite him.

"I could get used to this kind of service, you know."

"So could I," Mark deadpanned, unclipping his seatbelt, "if there was time to enjoy it. Mostly, I have to be satisfied with daily commuting through Washington's crush."

"I feel for you," Tom said with a straight face and Mark gave him the finger.

The flight attendant emerged from the rear cabin and made his way toward them.

"Drink, gentlemen? Coffee?"

"Coffee would be great," Tom said, despite the fact his stomach was already sloshing, and Mark indicated the same.

"Very good." The youngster nodded and walked back toward the rear kitchenette.

Mark leaned forward and peered closely at Tom. "Something wrong with your back? I couldn't help noticing the limp."

"A close encounter. It could have been worse."

"Obviously. After our chat yesterday, I took the trouble to read up on local events. There seems to have been a spike in homicides here. Reading between the lines and what you let slip, I figured it had to be your doing."

"Mostly The Entity's," Tom corrected, welcoming an opportunity to unburden himself. With Peroni out of the country, he had no reason to fear for Mark's safety now.

"The famed, or infamous, Vatican secret service, eh? Care to tell me what's going on?"

The smell of freshly brewed coffee permeated the cabin and Tom's saliva glands watered. The attendant emerged bearing a tray loaded with a glass carafe, cups and sundries. He unloaded everything onto a small table between them and poured two cups. Suddenly hungry, Tom reached for a warm apricot Danish and took a hefty bite. Chewing, he doubted they were picked up at a local corner bakery. Mixing in cream and sugar, he took an appreciative sip of the delicate brew.

"How's Washington?"

"Still steamy. Instead of coming here, I could have gone to Miami," Mark answered equitably, taking his black with one sugar. "I still might, but having to do your job—"

"Asshole."

"—has kept me back. When I saw the NSA material—"

"You got it?"

"—I knew you'd bitten off more than you can chew, my boy. Okay, let's have it, and don't spare the gory details."

Tom noted the command in Mark's voice. This was not his friend talking anymore, but Director, National Operations Center. Any way he looked at it, this was none of Department of Homeland Security's business, but Mark was not just anybody and he needed his CIA connections. Before this was over, he figured he would need all the help he could scrape up. He told it without embellishment, leaving nothing out. When he finished, he drained his cup, placed it down with a hollow click and sat back; the sound of jet engines a muted whisper in the cabin.

Mark pursed his lips and shook his head. "This Peroni character is some piece of work, all right. He had you outmaneuvered every step of the way. No reflection on your sterling performance, of course."

"Christ! Even you're screwing me!" Tom moaned and Mark laughed.

"Only kidding. Anyway, he sounds like somebody the CIA could use."

"They're welcome to him. Twenty-four hours and I'd have had him."

"Sometimes the other guy gets things right too. At least you tagged him with the die. That's something. Smart move that, by the way."

"Wasted if I can't grab him within the next five days."

"That's when the stuff wears off? Still, you have shots of his hand. The way I see it, everything hangs on the NSA coming up with a connection between Swens, Peroni, and somebody in The Entity who is presumably pulling the strings."

"That's about it," Tom agreed, "and he's the man I'm after. If Peroni hands over the fake papyrus and our guy handles it, *and* we get to scan him, I'll have him by the short and curlies."

"Such unholy thoughts. All this over some old dusty papyrus? I wish you luck. The whole thing hardly seems believable."

"I have five bodies at the morgue that makes it all too believable."

"Well, crap! We'll just have to go after them, then, won't we? But you'll need some high-powered help here if you want the Vatican to cooperate."

"I know. I'll have to run this by the Director."

"Not without something solid to back you up, you won't. If the papyrus is as toxic as you say it is, how much cooperation can you expect from Rome?"

"I'm betting The Entity is running this on its own, hoping to sweep things up before the papyrus surfaces. If I contact Karpeli, Cardinal Secretariat of State, I think he'll believe me. They might not like it, but they'll cooperate."

"Or get Peroni to finish the job on you."

"Yeah, there is always that."

"And if you're wrong?"

"I'll have to try something else. I *cannot* believe the whole Vatican Curia is behind this."

"If they are, it will make for a pretty rotten state of affairs. Say they believe you, they might not be keen to get involved. After all, you're kicking The Entity in the guts and that's always dangerous."

"You don't have to tell me. They'll want to be involved, if only to minimize the damage."

"Like I said, wish you luck. By the way, the CIA Rome Operations Section tailed Peroni from Fiumicino to Nomentano, one of Rome's northern suburbs. At least we now know where he lives. According to my source, Peroni hasn't left his apartment." Mark held out a piece of paper. "His address and the number of your CIA contact. You'll need both."

"Hey, that was great work!" Tom hooted, pleased that something had panned out and pocketed the note. "My thanks to the boys."

"I'll pass that along, but I wouldn't advertise how you got the information, if you understand what I mean. Not yet, anyway."

"A favor for a favor, eh? Got it."

"It's more than that. No one knows the number except the CIA team. If Peroni shoots through, it won't be because they leaked. When you're ready to go after him, call the watcher to confirm Peroni's location. You don't want to be waiting for him with cars and sirens all over the place. When the watcher on the shift asks you to identify yourself, answer 'Hawk'. Don't forget that."

"Hawk?"

Mark shrugged. "That's how the game is played. Don't worry about the tail getting spotted. The guys doing this are also pros, but they can't keep it up forever."

"Don't worry, I should get this wrapped up by Wednesday or not at all."

"Good enough." Mark reached down, dragged a briefcase from under the seat and placed it on his lap. Opening it to the sound of snapping clips, he handed Tom a stapled sheaf of papers.

"Talking about favors...data you wanted on Strand and Wellard. Say, that's an interesting decoration on your jacket. Another close encounter?"

"Our Italian friend," Tom muttered, flicking through the stack. "You know what's in it?"

"I've seen them."

Tom could hardly blame him for being curious. Going over the pages, he only saw routine phone and email transcripts, as expected. He never believed that Strand sold him out, but he wasn't about to make a foolish and basic blunder by not checking. He picked up the second stack and his heart beat faster.

The first two pages were ordinary phone calls and email messages. The following page caught his attention; copy of an email Wellard sent on Friday evening—transcript of his case file report.

The page showed an icon where the papyrus image was attached, but did not include the text itself. It didn't have to. The report contained a translation. He glanced at Mark, his face grim.

"Whoever sourced this at NSA, would they have read it?"

"Possibly. They know how to keep their mouths zipped."

"I bloody well hope so," Tom growled and turned to the next page, more routine messages.

Two pages down, an email of his case file update sent to the same destination not long after his less than warm conversation with Wellard yesterday morning. He placed the papers on the table and sat back.

"Son of a bitch!"

"There's no doubt that your boss hung you up to dry," Mark agreed with a thin smile. "But I've got something else that will make you feel all gooey." He pulled out a single sheet of paper from the briefcase and held it out. "In case you were wondering where Wellard sent his emails."

Looking at the paper with interest, at first, Tom didn't see it. Then his jaw dropped.

"Opus Dei? Christ!"

Two years ago, he handled a case where one of their Supernumeraries, a young woman with two small daughters, chose to leave the Order. Her husband killed her and his daughters, citing that she turned away from the true faith and poisoned the minds of his children. The episode caused Tom to learn more than he really cared to know about the Prelature of the Holy Cross.

The Order supposedly taught that all Catholics are called to holiness and life is merely a path to sanctity. Founded in Spain in 1928 by Josemaria Escriva, he gave the organization the name 'Opus Dei', meaning 'Work of God', and professed the Order was supernatural in character born out of a vision. In 1939, Escriva published *The Way*, a collection of 999 maxims concerning spirituality, which Tom saw as nothing more than an extremist right-wing manifesto, a form of Christian Masonry. Despite glowing internal propaganda, some former female Numeraries talked about slave-like treatment and sexual abuse from male members. In 1982, the pope made Opus Dei his personal prelature, which meant that its members fell under direct jurisdiction of the Order, wherever they were. In 2002, amidst raging controversy, Pope John Paul II made Escriva a saint, bypassing the canonization process. Go figure.

What Tom found particularly disquieting was the Order's demand that members practice flagellation and self-mortification as an offering to God, citing Christ's edict of 'let him deny himself, take up his cross daily and follow me'. Not surprisingly the Order disavowed any such practice, but nevertheless had come in for its share of criticism for alleged secretiveness, its standover recruiting methods, the rules governing member behavior, elitism, and right-wing policies.

During the ensuing trial, the husband broke down completely, confirming some of the worst practices perpetrated by the Order, but he never lived to be sentenced. Houston police found the man dead in his cell before the jury had a chance to deliver its verdict. Subsequent autopsy showed he died of a heroin overdose. How he managed to get heroin while in a cell never explained. The DA suspected the man's defense lawyer, but the case was dropped due to lack of admissible evidence.

Later, Tom managed to unearth an interesting fact; the lawyer was an Opus Dei appointee. The entire episode caused Opus Dei some embarrassment, but it blew over as new scandals crowded the channels.

But then, why should he be surprised that Wellard was an Opus Dei member? Louis Freeh, FBI Director until 2001, was said to be a member, as was Special Agent Robert Philip Hanssen who turned out to be spying for Russia. How many other skeletons rattled in the FBI's closet? With a former Supreme Court Justice Rodolfo Barra a member and Justice Antonin Scalia rumored to be one, was anything sacred? Despite the fact that its hierarchy came in for heavy criticism for being less than holy, the Order did do a lot of good pastoral work. Tom reminded himself that only the truly devout did the work, not the hierarchy. The parallel with Church activities did not escape him.

Expression grim, Mark pointed at the sheet. "The analyst at NSA used his head, knowing we'd want this link. It looks very much like Assistant Director Wellard is a member of that august gathering and an accessory to one count of murder and one of attempted murder, namely you, my reckless friend."

"I could strangle him." Tom snorted and shook his head. "I guess I don't have to worry about being suspended, not now. You saved my ass, Mark. I owe you a big one."

"Which I shall collect in due course."

"You're going to be lording this over me for the rest of my life?"

"That's my first plan, yes."

"Asshole!"

"And that's the thanks I get for helping out," Mark lamented with a sigh. "So, what are you going to do now?"

"I know Opus Dei has a checkered history, and some of its practices are perhaps less than savory, but resorting to murder? I still cannot believe he sold me down the river."

"Hard to figure sometime and something for the FBI to sort out. Better your problem than mine. However, from what you told me, it doesn't look like Opus Dei ran Peroni, but they probably passed Wellard's information to him."

Tom chewed that over. "Agreed. You were right about needing a ride to DC. Once I'm finished with my soon to be ex-boss, I've got another job for the NSA."

"Establish a connection between Opus Dei, Peroni and The Entity?"

"Might as well keep Johnston busy."

"That could be a tough ask, you know. Especially if Peroni scrambled his calls."

Tom shrugged. "NSA's got computers and cryptoanalysts. All I need is a phone number at the Vatican end. With that, I'll have my man, even if the conversation itself was scrambled."

"My CIA contact in Rome should be able to help you there. They're good at that kind of thing. Let me know when you get a number."

"Why are you doing this?" Tom demanded suddenly. "It's not exactly a Homeland Security problem."

"Well, crap! Who else will bail out your ass? Besides, I kind of like this case, it keeps my hand in."

Staring at his friend, Tom understood completely. Once a spook, always a spook, and it sure as hell broke doing office drudgery. Whatever the reason, he welcomed the help. He cocked his head at Mark's briefcase.

"What else you got?"

Mark grinned broadly. "The last item on your shopping list—data on The Entity."

"Anything juicy I should know?"

"The man you're probably after is Cardinal Avero Belconi, currently in charge of The Entity and the Vatican's counterespionage service, the *Sodalitium Pianum*. If he's your man, I'd start looking for a convenient hole to crawl into. He is a ruthless operator who lets nothing stand in his way."

"I found *that* out," Tom grated.

Mark held out the papers. "And you never saw this, okay?"

"Got it."

The top page stamped 'Restricted' in garish red, which meant that any enterprising Internet search would drag up the same stuff. Or perhaps not as Tom's efforts had not yielded much of anything substantive. He skimmed through the pages to get the feel of the contents.

Like Garbaldi said, his death still heavy on his conscience, the Holy Alliance, renamed The Entity in 1930, founded in 1566 by order of Pope Pius V. Its sister counterespionage service, the

Sodalitium Pianum, created in 1913 on direction of Pope Pius X. Carlo Castiglioni, historian and acknowledged expert on the papacy said, 'The triple crown worn by popes symbolizes the power they exercise in heaven, on Earth, and the underworld.' In heaven, the pope has God; on Earth, he rules; in the underworld, he has the Holy Alliance.

According to the report, forty-one popes have reigned since creation of the Holy Alliance, from Pius V to Benedict XVI. The popes set the objectives and the Holy Alliance carried them out, whatever it took. Up to the eighteenth century the Church faced liberalism, democracy and socialism. In recent times, the enemy was science, education, communism, totalitarianism, sexual liberalism and social atheism. At every turn the Church sought to neutralize these threats and destroy its enemies wherever they might be. Kings were killed, political factions supported and holocausts ignored. Terrorists were financed, as have South American dictators, Mafia money laundered and financial markets manipulated.

Tom was staggered to read that The Entity plotted against Elizabeth I and assassinated the Dutch prince William of Orange and the French king Henry IV. Directed by Pius XIII, The Entity went to bed with Hitler, exacting a promise that Germany would not bomb the Vatican or sack European churches in exchange for remaining silent while Jews were carted off to concentration camps. What Hitler wanted was Church approval of his regime to reassure the restive German people.

Worse still, after the war, The Entity was instrumental in smuggling numerous Nazis to South American havens, principally Argentina. Incredible! Pope John Paul II poured millions in support of Lech Walesa's Solidarity union movement against General Wojciech Jaruzelski, aided by the CIA. The pope being Polish himself, Tom understood the motive, but could not condone the action, historical precedents notwithstanding.

If that wasn't bad enough, the CIA claimed that in 1978 The Entity was complicit in the assassination of Pope John Paul I to prevent the pontiff from investigating criminal dealings by the Vatican Bank and its offshoot, Banco Ambrosiano. Tom stared at the page, not believing. If they could do this to a pope, swatting somebody like Garbaldi would not have raised a sweat.

With ascension of Pope Benedict XVI and Luigi Paggi's departure as head of the Vatican's intelligence services, Cardinal Belconi took over the spy network. With the pontiff's unexpected death from a stroke, Pope Paul VII ascended to the throne of Peter; a change of management perhaps, but it was business as usual for Belconi.

Tom put down the papers. "Is this shit for real?" he demanded and Mark's mouth twitched.

"Makes for interesting reading, eh?"

"Christ! They're worse than the CIA."

"Doesn't say much for either side, does it."

"Certainly throws a brick through my image of the Holy See."

"What did you expect, psalm-singing around a cozy fireplace and everyone wearing halos? You only have to look at any church anywhere to see them for what they are. It's all about property, money, economic, and political power directed at secular establishments to stop them from interfering. And the crummy part is, we went along with the charade and created laws to protect them. Why? Because they are guardians of heaven and you will never walk through those pearly gates unless you toe the line and bleed from the pocket. Never mind the quality, feel the width."

"I didn't know you were interested," Tom said, his gaze quizzical.

"Well, crap! It's not for nothing that priests wear black. In case you've forgotten, black is also the color of mourning. Remember the Bosnian war? I gave money to ease some of the misery there, as did millions around the world. What happened? Along the way, parish committees lined their own pockets, as did the priests who were supposed to control them; by no means all, but enough for the thing to stink. People cared, trusting the priests to send the money where needed. After all, if you can't trust your own priest, who can you trust? Funds were collected, banked and withdrawn without any audit or accounting oversight. You don't audit God's books. Sure, the priests read the usual Sunday balance sheet, but that meant nothing, as no one knew how much was actually collected. When some parishioners raised the matter with local bishops, and the thing quietly buried—for the good of the Church. Like they're trying to bury the children sex scandals now. What money did arrive in Zagreb or Split, you can guess what those responsible for its disbursement did with it. Despite millions that poured into that miserable country, the poor schmucks there got nothing, or at best a few cans of Spam or clothing that even the poor didn't want. These aren't anecdotal stories, but actual cases."

Surprised, Tom blanched and Mark smiled. "You don't believe me?"

"I'm afraid I do believe you."

"Then take this. I know a couple in Germany who used to drive a truck down to Zagreb loaded with clothing, food and fuel to be distributed by the diocese. They used to until one day they found some of their clothing in a local second-hand store. Don't that beat all? And you ask me if I'm interested? Frankly, I'm not. I've seen far worse in my time to be disillusioned or disappointed, but it still sucks when you see it happen. The Vatican has been running a con job on everybody for centuries. Why would I think that they would stop now? They've merely refined their technique. Priesthood isn't the second oldest profession for nothing. They have always been social parasites. You only have to look at our Southern evangelists and crowds like Hillsong and The Brethren. It is too bad that people stopped practicing the killing of priests and shamans when their prophecies turned out to be worthless."

Tom chuckled. "Ah, those were the good old days. Sometimes, though, it doesn't pay to think too much about these things, or I'd never sleep."

"Yeah, I know what you mean, and that's the reason they survive—social apathy. If people stood up and protested, things would change, but unless you have your nose rubbed in it, religion isn't one of the survival factors, not when you have your hands full holding down a job, a mortgage, and putting kids through college. I'm not being holier-than-thou either. Tell me. Would you have been this passionate if Peroni merely stole the papyrus and no one got hurt?"

Tom stared at Mark, startled by the question and the realization that he already had his answer.

"Funny, Strand asked me the same thing in a slightly different way."

"And?"

"I wouldn't have cared, but I'm not much of a Catholic either."

"I don't know. Perhaps you're one of those individuals who realized that whatever faith you might have, you don't need a Church to mediate for you."

"An interesting slant and not something I expected you to say."

"I've had my moments with religion." Mark picked up his cup and took a sip. "In my line of work, I ran across a lot of strange bedfellows—"

"And girls, no doubt."

"Well, crap! The CIA expects its people to make sacrifices."

"And you certainly made them, eh?"

Mark's face became dreamy. "There was one Mossad operative: black-haired, smoky almond eyes, willowy figure that made your eyes ache—"

"And other things too," Tom added with a broad grin.

"—and skin tingle. She thought I was a South African Secret Service courier and I thought she was gorgeous. Seeing her, I had no doubts how she got *her* information. She was passing nuclear reactor plans to Turkey using the South Africans as a go-between. I compromised her supply chain and she thought she had compromised me. We both got what we wanted. I tell you, Tom, her reactor safeties were *all* off. I thought I got terminal exposure."

Tom laughed, the image of Malena's curvy body entwined with his all too vivid in his mind.

"What I wanted to say before I got sidetracked," Mark went on, still wearing a wistful smile, "in my line of work, I've met the oddest people. In 2007, I had a run-in with a couple of Entity operators in Venezuela. Cold bastards, but very professional. Reminded me of Mossad stiffs. Both thought that God held his hand over them. The Venezuela spy service DISIP sent two women to Rome with a mission to entrap a prominent Venezuelan prelate and silence his opposition to President Chavez. The Entity agents tipped off the Italian military intelligence SISMI and the plot failed.

"This wasn't a joint CIA/Entity operation. Both sides were simply keeping an eye on Chavez. The President's left-wing tendencies had The Entity's antennas wiggling and they were stirring things up supporting the opposition. That's when I learned about the Vatican spy network and how the popes really run things, more than I bargained for. It didn't leave a pleasant taste in my mouth, I can tell you that."

"I wonder how many people know that the Vatican has a spy service and what they do," Tom mused. "I certainly didn't."

"Perhaps it's better they don't. Without some illusions, things could be a whole lot worse."

Glancing out the window, Tom saw a checkered landscape slowly creeping by with the Atlantic fading into haze as it merged with the horizon. After a moment, he lifted a white phone mounted on the bulkhead beside him—time to do more paid work. He tapped in numbers and waited. It only took a couple of rings.

"Strand."

"It's Tom. Sorry for the call—"

"What's up?"

"I have proof that Wellard is our leak and I'm flying back to Washington to see Marshal. I will also be asking Johnston to give the NSA another job. I have a feeling that I'll be sightseeing in Rome soon."

"Whom did Wellard talk to?"

"You won't believe it. He is Opus Dei."

"Shit! So he *did* pass on your reports."

"Looks like it. Call you when I have more. Hope I haven't spoiled your day."

"No peace for the wicked. Keep in touch," Strand ordered and hung up.

His next call was to Marshal's office. Even though a Sunday, Melissa was in, which typified their relationship. Both were slaves to their job. After an exchange of warmer than necessary pleasantries, she listened to his request, then told him to hold. Ignoring Mark's raised eyebrows, after enduring a few minutes of mindless background music, she came back saying the FBI Director would see him at eleven-thirty. Tom glanced at his watch, only 9:48. Plenty of time for a quick stop at his apartment and a change of suit.

* * *

Stepping out of the elevator into the subdued seventh floor interior that housed the executive offices, Tom twitched his jacket into place, wondering if his career would last long enough for him to ever get an office here. However pleasant the prospect, what worried him more was the neat furrow in the right shoulder padding of his jacket where Peroni's bullet missed him. The Gulf-stream V made it to Andrews with time to spare, but then they had to hold in a racetrack pattern while a flight of F-16s decided to jam the runways and play. When they eventually did get down and he snagged a cab, there wasn't any time left to run to his apartment and change. *Ah, to hell with it.* Marshal would probably be more interested in what he had to say than ogling a hole in his jacket. At least he hoped so. Office gossip said the Bureau chief was pretty easygoing, but he did enjoy tearing strips off some luckless agent now and then for relish.

Tom had met the fifty-eight-year-old director when he transferred from Houston and liked the man on sight. Although more a politician these days, having to handle Congress and the White House, Patrick Marshal was still an FBI agent at heart and understood operations. Born in Los Angeles, he did a stint in the New Orleans Division handling general crime and drugs. Along the way, he picked up a master's in Criminal Psychology. In 1990, he was posted to the LA Division as a Field Group Supervisor working on dismantling international drug trafficking organizations. Transferred to FBI headquarters in 2003 as Supervising Special Agent in the Special Operations Division, his career took off when in 2006, he was promoted to the Senior Executive Service as Associate Special Agent in Charge of New York's Drug Enforcement Task Force. In 2010, he returned to Washington as Executive Assistant Director for Criminal Investigations. When Robert S. Mueller retired, no one was surprised to see Marshal get the nod from the White House.

Admiring the tasteful wood paneling and soft indirect lighting, Tom's feet sank pleasantly into thick gray pile as he walked confidently toward the director's outer office. He opened the heavy solid door and Melissa looked up. She flashed him a smile and waved at a door opposite her desk.

"You can go right in, Mr. Meecham."

He walked to her desk and placed both hands on the gleaming surface. Apart from a flat computer screen, keyboard, and a switchboard phone, her desk clean. She liked things neat, she told him once. Long thick hair framed a delicate round face. There was only a hint of blue eye shadow and lipstick. Dressed in a yellow blouse and cream pants, the woman cut a striking figure. Her lavender perfume hovered around her like a cloud as he beamed at her, fighting an urge to nuzzle her.

"Mr. Meecham, is it? What happened to plain old Tom?"

"I'm on duty…sir," she explained and batted long eyelashes at him, which provoked a surge of desire from him. She saw his reaction and grinned. "But we could get more informal over dinner, if you're free, that is, since you didn't call me last night."

"Deal!" Tom agreed at once, pleased at the prospect of relaxing in her company. After the last few days, he could do with a bit of winding down. "Seven? I'll pick you up. Sorry about yesterday. I was tied up in Boston."

"What happened there?" she asked, pointing at his jacket, immediately concerned.

"Tell you tonight," he promised, blew her a kiss and marched toward the inner office door. He knocked once and walked in.

Facing Pennsylvania Avenue the office brightly lit, spacious without being huge. Shelving and cabinets filled the walls on either side of a large executive desk placed in front of narrow windows. The director shoved papers to one side and nodded as Tom closed the door behind him.

"Come in, Mr. Meecham. Have a seat." Marshal's voice even and rich without being deep. Tom was surprised to see him without a tie.

Noting his expression, Marshal chuckled. "As soon as you and I are done, I'm out of here. I want to spend what's left of my day on a golf course."

Tom blanched, chagrined at having to ruin his fun. "I'm afraid I'll probably be spoiling what's left of your day, sir."

"Well, it wouldn't be the first time I've had to live with disappointment. How do you like your Section? Settled into the job yet?"

"There is a lot to handle here, sir," Tom said truthfully, "but I like the challenge."

"Glad to hear it. The job's no good if it doesn't stretch you. Talking to Strand last night, you seem to have more than one challenge on your hands right now. Okay, what's this diplomatic nonsense with Peroni and the guff Melissa's been telling me about Wellard?"

Easing himself into a soft leather chair, Tom placed the blue case folder on his lap and took a deep breath. He had rehearsed this on the way downtown and the words came out smoothly, not at all overawed talking to Marshal. He had made presentations to bigwigs before. They were human...some of them.

He sketched out the background of his case in pithy sentences and finished with Mark's flight to Boston. Marshal looked thoughtful, presumably digesting the information. His poker face gave nothing away. After a while, he nodded.

"This Peroni character certainly gave you a hard time. At least you know where he is. That's useful. But Wellard? Who would have thought it? And I suppose that's the evidence?" he growled, pointing at the folder.

"Yes, sir." Tom stood up and placed the file before the director. "The Cyber Division and NSA emails are on top."

Marshal quickly scanned the pages and his scowl deepened. He closed the folder, shook his head and looked up.

"Opus Dei...After the scandal with Freeh, I thought we were done with that crowd. Apparently not, but that's not your concern. Father Garbaldi has definitely come up with something. When the papyrus becomes public, it's going to create a storm, but you knew that before you handed the thing to Harvard."

"Yes, sir," Tom said and waited for the axe to fall.

"You also knew that you were handing over evidence?"

"Yes, sir."

Marshal's eyes gave nothing away. "No explanations, no excuses?"

"I did what I considered appropriate, sir."

The director's clear blue eyes flickered at Tom's jacket. "Well, I might have done the same thing if I were in your place. As long as Harvard is prepared to produce the thing before a jury, I don't see that there is any harm done. It took balls to do what you did, son, and I like that in my agents. Before we can talk about a jury, you have to get your hands on Peroni first, and that's *your* problem. You were right about one thing, though. You'll need my help with the Vatican end if you want to get to the bottom of this, provided of course, that NSA comes through for you, but first things first," Marshal grated and pressed a button on his phone pad.

"Yes, sir?"

"Melissa, have security go to Assistant Director Wellard's office. If he's in, I want them to bring him to me. If he is not, they are to find him."

"Right away, sir."

"When you've done that, get me Torrent, will you please?"

"Of course, sir."

Tom showed no expression, but his pulse quickened. Torrent was Executive Assistant Director for Counterterrorism/Counterintelligence and Wellard's immediate boss. He could guess what the director was likely to tell him. Another spoiled day?

Satisfied, Marshal leaned back, crossed his arms and smiled. "Valero and now this. You seem to have a knack for getting yourself noticed."

"Believe me, sir, it was not by design," Tom protested in alarm at the thought he was kissing ass or seeking glory, but the Bureau chief merely nodded.

"Whatever, but you've done good work here, son. You planning on going back to Boston?"

"I'll be running this from here. Agent Johnston is quite capable of handling the technical end. I must point out, sir, that Mr. Strand was extremely cooperative during my stay over there."

"Good man, that. What do you want me to do?"

Tom blinked at this unexpected blank check, but it was more than that. The FBI Director had endorsed his actions, relieving him of a significant career worry. Handing the papyrus to Professor Norginson could easily have gone the other way.

"If I get the NSA data I need, I would like to discuss the case with Karpeli, Cardinal Secretariat of State."

Marshal looked thoughtful. "Why not Cardinal Albani? You've been in touch with him already and Garbaldi worked for him."

"That's the problem, sir. I'm not sure I can trust him."

"Mmm. Let me know when you want to call Karpeli."

"Thank you, sir."

The phone rang and Marshal pressed a button. "Yes, Melissa?"

"Executive Director Torrent, sir."

"Put him through…Wally?"

"What's up, Pat?"

"Can you come up to the office?"

"Now? It's Sunday for Crissakes, or haven't you heard?"

"You don't have to tell me it's Sunday, Wally. Just get your ass over here, okay?"

"Can't it wait until tomorrow? Justine and I—"

"I'm not exactly yachting either."

Torrent gave a long sigh and Tom sympathized. "Okay, half an hour."

The FBI Director cut contact and pursed his lips. "Hate to do this to him…"

The phone rang again. "Mr. Wellard is here, sir."

"Show him in and have security stand by."

"Very good, sir."

A knock and Wellard walked in, dressed correctly as always and clearly puzzled by the unexpected summons. When he saw Tom, his eyes widened in shock, but he recovered quickly. He cleared his throat and stopped before Marshal's desk.

"You wanted to see me, sir?"

The director glanced at Tom and waved his arm. "He's all yours."

Tom stood up and looked hard at his boss. "Sir, you're under arrest as an accessory to one count of murder and one count of attempted murder. You have the right to remain silent. Anything you say can and will be used against you in a court of law. You have the right to speak to an attorney. If you cannot afford an attorney, one will be appointed to you. Do you understand these rights as they were stated?"

Wellard glared, his expression contemptuous. "These charges are ridiculous. Accessory to whose murder?"

"Sir, do you understand your rights?"

"I understand already! Now, whose murder are you talking about?"

"Professor Vincent Renauld at Harvard's Center for Middle Eastern Studies, and attempted murder of me when you passed my case file to Opus Dei," Tom said quietly, enjoying seeing color fade from his boss' face. "And I have the NSA email records to prove it."

Ashen, Wellard stared at Tom and his shoulders sagged.

"Our talk yesterday, you weren't fooled at all," he whispered. "The gambit about the shooter breaking into your case file was only to throw me off. You were toying with me. But you're wrong if you think this is over. I regret the deaths, but I would gladly have pulled the trigger myself to keep the papyrus secret." He took a deep breath. "Did you end up giving the papyrus to Harvard?"

Tom scowled. "Unfortunately, the shooter stole the thing from my hotel room before I could do that."

Wellard's mouth twitched. "What I did then was worth it."

"Nothing was worth those five deaths, boss."

"I protected the Church!"

"You can explain it to a jury, Mr. Wellard," Marshal announced briskly. "Effective immediately, you're suspended, pending findings of a court. You will be held in remand until a hearing is convened. The Bureau will not oppose application for bail." Showing keen disappointment, he pressed a button on his phone pad.

"Yes, sir?"

"Send in security."

Two heavyset bruisers walked in and stood at attention. Marshal waved a hand at Wellard.

"The Assistant Director is under arrest. Place him in detention and have him processed. Supervising Special Agent Meecham will provide the necessary details. Mr. Wellard's office is to be locked and no one allowed in. He is not to access any Bureau files, computer systems or talk to anyone until legal representation has been made."

"Yes, sir!" The senior of the two turned to the silent figure. "Sir, I must ask you to accompany us."

Wellard straightened and took a deep breath. He glanced at Tom, made as if to say something, then changed his mind and walked out.

When the door closed, Tom sighed. "I thought I'd feel exultation or something at seeing the bastard get his, but I don't feel anything."

The FBI Director looked at Tom and slowly nodded. "I know. It's always like that. At least you have the pleasure knowing that he won't be endangering anybody else's life again."

"Seems a hollow victory nonetheless."

"Perhaps. One thing bothers me. Why did you tell Wellard the papyrus was stolen?"

"If he contacts Opus Dei…"

Marshal grinned. "Yes, of course. Very good, son. Very good indeed."

Stefan Vučak

Chapter Eight

After a slight wobble of wings as they rushed over the runway threshold, the Boeing 737 steadied and touched down with barely a bump. The pilot applied reverse thrust and the aircraft slowed quickly. Approaching the international terminal, it turned onto a taxiway and bumped over uneven joints in the concrete. Peroni glanced out at sharp tails of parked planes sticking up from terminal spokes and unclipped his seatbelt. The business class attendant reminded the nine passengers in the cabin to remain seated with their seatbelts firmly fastened until the aircraft came to a complete stop. Seeing that everybody always ignored the instructions, he wondered why the airlines bothered with the tiresome nonsense. Just covering their ass probably.

Once out of the aircraft, he walked steadily over hard blue carpeting past arrival/departure gates, food stands, and duty-free shops, glad to stretch his legs. The public address system requested that Mr. Hal Mahmoud and Raj Khalid please make their way immediately to Gate 9C as their aircraft was ready to depart. He could never figure out how people did it; arriving early to check in, then miss their flight, or worse still, delayed everybody else by lounging in a bar or getting that last minute bottle of perfume or whiskey. Must be either brainless or simply had no consideration for others.

There were enough people strolling, hurrying or simply gawking that he felt mild apprehension at the prospect of getting stuck in an Immigration line. When he reached the row of glass cubicles, he blanched at the snaking line of passengers waiting stoically to be processed. As he knew from personal experience, getting through the gauntlet could take some time, and after a lengthy journey, did nothing to welcome one home. Fiumicino had upgraded its facilities and provided two electronic passport processing booths. Peroni walked quickly past the lines and envious stares to one of the booths. Two people were in front of him and he didn't have to wait long to scan his passport. The gate light turned green and he walked through, striding toward the baggage claim area. With briefcase in hand and garment bag draped over his left shoulder, he handed his Customs declaration card to a bored attendant and he was done. He hardly bothered to look at baggage carousels and passengers standing around them like they were some sort of oracles. More mind-numbing waiting and seething frustration.

He did not hold the five-hour layover at Heathrow against Meecham. The man had simply bundled him off on a first available flight and probably didn't care what happened once Peroni was out of sight. The six-and-a-half hour flight to London comfortable enough, and the Virgin attendants pretty, courteous, and smiled like attendants everywhere. To them, he was just another classy passenger rather than a *persona non grata*, courtesy of Uncle Sam. Although his extraction was faultless, a sense of professional failure lingered at the back of his mind that Meecham still lived. Those were the breaks and he tried not to dwell on it. Nevertheless, recalling the cold look of steely determination on the FBI agent's face as he was escorted to the boarding bridge at Logan, Peroni wondered if they were fated to meet again, unlikely as that seemed. Meecham tried valiantly to contain his frustration as they parted, but Peroni knew he wasn't going to give up. If airport and hotel surveillance pictures were all the FBI could come up with, they had nothing, a cold case, and he had covered himself too well.

When Flight VS12 landed at Heathrow's Terminal 2, Peroni immediately walked to the Transfer desk and rebooked his flight to Rome. The attendant hardly raised an eyebrow at the routine transaction. Twenty minutes later, he was in the air again. All in all, not too shabby.

Bright sunshine greeted him as he walked out of the arrivals terminal, to be assaulted by the usual sights, sounds and smells of Rome's premier airport. He got a cab from the taxi station, threw in his briefcase and garment bag on the rear seat, settled into the cracked upholstery and directed the skinny bearded driver to take him to Nomentano. Staring at the driver's back as the cab threaded its way out of the airport toward the Autostrada Fiumicino-Roma highway, Peroni figured the man to be Tunisian, but he could have been anybody. Certainly an Arab, and judging by the scruffy beard, probably a Muslim. With every poor sorry slob fleeing Africa, seeking freedom and economic prosperity in the European Union, Italy had long ago become a funnel for legal and illegal immigrants. The country's security agencies were trying bravely to stem the tide, but they were fighting a hopeless cause. Simple logistics: too many illegals and not enough *polizia*.

Skirting the Vatican on their left, the cab crossed the Tiber and made its way north along Lungotevere Marzio. At Nomentano, hitting Viale della Trinita dei Monti, the cab turned left into a side parking area, the modern apartment condominiums protected by a soothing row of trees. Opposite the boulevard stretched parkland and open ground all the way to Plazza di Siena. Peroni told the driver to stop next to a gray four-story building, paid him and got out. Standing on the empty sidewalk, he watched the taxi speed off, then turned and walked to the thick, double glass doors. He tapped the access code into a wall-mounted security pad and the lock clicked. Pushing the door open with a stiff arm, he walked in and made for the stairs. He never used the elevator after buying his place since the stairs provided an excellent exercise machine.

On the top floor, he turned left and padded down a small corridor toward an entrance at its end. The smell of frying meatballs and bubbling spaghetti sauce permeated the corridor and Peroni licked his lips. Probably Rossi's wife doing their Sunday lunch. Right now, he would not have minded meatballs and spaghetti at all. He punched his six-digit code into the security pad and the lock cycled. Grasping the heavy bronze handle, he opened the door, crouched and peered carefully at a piece of felt-backed hard carpet that served as a mat. Unless someone deliberately stepped over it, it was impossible to get in without the mat slipping slightly on the polished floorboards. The carpet did not show the usual even five-millimeter gap from the doorframe. Peroni's mouth twitched as he straightened and walked in. The door clicked shut behind him, shutting off the inviting smells. He turned to the alarm pad mounted beside the door and typed in a ten-digit PIN. The red warning light stopped flashing. He stood there for a moment, only the sound of his breathing disturbing the silence.

It was good to be home again.

The first thing he did was open all the windows and start the air-conditioner. Although the apartment not exactly stuffy, he felt better having a light breeze stir the curtains. In the living room, he paused and gazed at the slim column in the center of Plazza del Popolo. On his left, he could make out the winding Tiber. In the distance the brown dome of St. Peter's shone beneath a blue sky. Despite its sometimes chaotic madness, whether he liked it or not, Rome was part of him and he was part of it. He could have done worse.

A quick check of carefully positioned items around the apartment didn't reveal any disturbance, but the doormat was a giveaway. Belconi's thugs searching for the tape of their deal, perhaps? Surely the cardinal didn't expect him to have something like that lying around the apartment. But then, people did the most odd things, even the smart ones. It didn't matter. Walking into the bedroom, he reminded himself to change his access and security PINs. Not that it would stop a professional, but he didn't want to make it too easy for them. Besides, next time they came calling, it would tell them he knew they were visiting.

After a refreshing shower, he changed clothes, threw his soiled stuff into the washer, and raided the fridge. Eyeing the leftover cold cuts and old rolls with distaste, he nevertheless piled the stuff onto the kitchen bench top and dragged out a plate. Although the two-and-a-half hour flight from London had not tired him, the accumulated kilometers had nonetheless taken their toll. Ordinarily, he preferred to eat out, but right now the thought of walking to Duegi's or Victoria House held little appeal. Perhaps for dinner. Cutting open a roll, a little dry, but still passable, he made a thick sandwich and stuck the plate under the broiler. While the thing worked, he poured himself a tall glass of assorted tropical fruits juice. The purple liquid cold and had a nice tangy taste he liked. He drank half and topped up. With the sandwich hot, he took the plate and glass into the lounge and switched on the small 108cm LED TV screen. The twelve o'clock news coverage had just started. He watched the latest domestic and international goings on and worked through his sandwich, not actually paying attention. Italian politics was like following an ongoing soap opera and about as exciting. European politics wasn't much better. The EU concept was sound, but Brussels' burgeoning bureaucracy and one rule fits all regulations were becoming a problem. You simply cannot switch off national interest, not after centuries of fighting over them. Basically, the EU was not a single, uniform economy, and trying to make it into one was clearly not working.

Finished, he clicked the multi-purpose remote that switched off the TV and surround system. With the remote in hand, he double-clicked the blue Pip Input key and the small LCD screen lit up as the nonlinear junction detector activated. Walking slowly around the room, he swept the ceiling, the lights, power points, and every piece of equipment. It took almost twenty minutes to check all the rooms, but the place was clean. It looked like his visitors were interested in something other than planting ordinary eavesdropping bugs. Eyeing the computer in the spare bedroom-cum-office, he lightly tapped a fingernail next to the keyboard and grinned when a narrow bar flickered across the detector's screen. He had to unscrew the board's back cover to find the button mike tucked into a corner. Holding the thing in his hand, it looked like a variant of a passive resonance cavity device. Being so small, it probably didn't have a transmit capability. That meant whoever planted it would have to remove it to analyze the contents. With a range of less than 400mm, the device useless for voice pickup, but it worked fine as a keystroke tracker. With the help of fairly standard software, the recovered bug would reveal all, enough to gain entry to his system. It gave a satisfying crunch beneath his heel and he dumped the bits into the dustbin.

After washing up, he returned to his office and powered up the computer. Typing in his twenty-digit BIOS password, he waited for Windows to come up. He was certain the intruder or intruders would have tried getting in, but without the BIOS password, the computer might as well have been a box of crackers. Logons can always be broken, but BIOS was the ultimate in access and hard drive security, especially when coupled with a limited retry function. Logging on to his email server with an alias he used as his 'professional' face, he quickly checked the entries.

He winced when he saw another invite from REPO Industries. A good, rough outfit, but he wasn't a front line soldier and had no interest fighting someone else's wars. A SISMI email caught his attention and he scanned it briefly. Did he want an assignment in Israel working with Mossad? He dismissed the idea outright. Tangling with Mossad was a good way of winding up in a body bag. Let them do their own murders. Sandline offered him 'a challenging assignment' in Northern Ireland. That meant a body job, something he might consider, but not right now. His regular email website had several bill statements and two personal messages. None of them required his reply.

Rummaging in a side drawer, he took out a spare SIM card and slipped it into the BlackBerry, then connected the cellphone to the computer. After uploading his data files and applications, he reinitialized the SIM, disconnected the phone and switched it on. When the dial tone sounded, he typed in his PIN and keyed in a special number. Every cellphone had a PIN facility, and modern variants like the BlackBerry supported real-time encryption, yet sadly, almost no one used it. For the sake of convenience, users left themselves open to remote eavesdropping, and modern smartphones with add-on software made that even easier. For him, using these functions was automatic as brushing teeth. His protection not completely foolproof, but it made life for the opposition a bit tougher. After four rings the connection was made and he tapped the mike pickup twice. There was a single answering tap and he hung up. With his source reassured that he was still alive and to continue sitting on his tapes, he powered down the computer.

With administration done, he went back to the living room and sprawled on the dark suede sofa. Adjusting the cushion just right, he locked his fingers behind his head and stared at the small crystal—glass really—chandelier hanging from the three-point-three-meter ceiling, allowing his thoughts to wander.

First thing in the morning, he would pick up his FedEx package from the central post office, within easy walking distance, and see Belconi. Working with Swens had definitely soured his taste for more of the same and he wanted to tidy up the last of this sordid assignment promptly. No more work from The Entity, not for a long while. Perhaps taking some time off would be advisable. He always wanted to visit Peru, walk the Inca Trail and see Machu Picchu. Maybe do one of the Amazon jungle tours at the same time. However attractive, the idea of more lengthy flying made him wince. He could go to Switzerland instead, much closer, hang around Zermatt and climb the Matterhorn. The more he thought about it, the better he liked it.

After a while, his eyes closed.

* * *

Without showing any emotion the Swiss security officer, dressed in a plain gray suit, slowly ran the metal detector wand up and down Peroni's body. When the wand beeped, he asked him to empty his pockets on the small table beside them. After picking through the contents, face still expressionless, the guard stepped back.

"Thank you, sir. That will be all."

Peroni pocketed his wallet, key ring, some change and picked up the opened FedEx package, having left the tape cassette in his bank's security box. He straightened and waited for the guard to open the door. After a few seconds of tense silence the guard got the idea, pursed his lips and obliged. Peroni shook his head and pushed through. He didn't blame the guard for this lame intrusion. Belconi probably wanted to trap him carrying a pocket recorder, but he didn't need a recorder, not now with his job done. He already had what he wanted.

After escorting him to Belconi's office, the guard knocked once and opened the door.

"Mr. Peroni, Sister."

The same dried-up matron he had met before looked up from her computer screen and her severe features hardened even further. She jerked her head and the guard closed the door as Peroni walked in, his face equally hard. He stopped in front of her desk and stood there. After giving him a stern glare of disapproval, she pressed a button on her phone.

"Mr. Peroni is here, Your Eminence."

"Show him in, will you, Sister?"

Her mouth a tight line, she shot him another glare and opened the heavy door beside her desk. Ignoring her completely, he walked through, figuring that any Christian compassion left in her must have dried up long ago. She and her boss were well suited to each other. Belconi looked up from his spacious desk and waved at one of two ornately carved French chairs. Tall windows opened onto the papal gardens.

"Ah, the prodigal returns. Please sit down, my son. Did you have a good flight?"

"Good enough, Your Eminence," Peroni said softly.

"Since you're here, the Italian Embassy has clearly done their job."

"That was quick work and much appreciated." Peroni stepped to the desk and held out the slim package. Eyes glittering in anticipation, Belconi hesitated and then reached for the proffered parcel. Peroni sat down and waited.

The cardinal noted the rectangle of paper torn from the package that contained the address and smiled. The look told Peroni everything. The cardinal probably already knew all his alternate identities.

"Your Eminence, I must inform you that I was not successful at eliminating the FBI agent."

Belconi's smile faded. "He is still alive?"

"He was wearing protection."

"Mmm. Yes…he anticipated your move. Do you see this as a problem?"

"I don't. With the papyrus recovered, the FBI have nothing, and what they do have is circumstantial only. They could have charged me with theft, but thanks to your intervention the matter was dropped."

"No harm done, then." Glancing at the package, Belconi shook his head. "You actually dared use something like FedEx to *mail* a priceless artifact? Unbelievable."

"I could hardly carry it with me, Your Eminence."

"No, I don't suppose you could. You brought it and that's all that counts."

Belconi reached for a letter opener stuck in a glass jar among pens, pencils and color markers. About to slash open the seal, he apparently noted the already cut flap, and slowly reached inside. Removing the bubble wrap, cardboard packing and felt wrapper, he hissed and stared at the revealed tractate. He ran his fingers lingeringly down the brown, faded text. Peroni could see that the script had no meaning for him. The man was marveling that a single, seemingly innocent document, harbored so much potential for turmoil and destruction.

"Well done, my son," Belconi said softly, opened a side drawer and held up a large color photocopy. He placed the copy next to the papyrus and carefully examined both documents. After a moment, he looked up and grinned. "I took the liberty of printing an image of the tractate from an email your FBI friend sent to Cardinal Albani."

Peroni didn't begrudge the cardinal his caution, but faking the papyrus was something way outside his means, even if he knew how to go about it. It would take vast resources and sophisticated technology to do, something not readily available to an ordinary individual. Besides, there was no reason for him to do it. A tiny suspicion tickled the back of his head, but he dismissed it as fanciful thinking.

"You're satisfied the papyrus is authentic?"

"Oh, the papyrus is authentic, without a doubt. I've seen similar documents before."

"In that case, Your Eminence, my work here is done."

Belconi's look cold, but Peroni returned it with indifference. There was no love lost between them, but they needed each other.

"Payment of the bonus will be made immediately. However, since you were not able to eliminate the FBI agent, balance of that payment cannot be made."

Stefan Vučak

"Understood," Peroni said, wishing to be out of here, wishing to cleanse himself of the unholy scent that permeated the office. Only one thing left to do, and he wondered if the cardinal would raise the matter.

Tucking the papyrus and the copy into a drawer, Belconi pushed the empty package to one side, relaxed and looked up.

Peroni stared at him with a face of stone.

"The recording you made of our agreement, I want the tape," Belconi demanded without preliminaries. "There cannot be any trace of what transpired, which you should appreciate."

Peroni stared at the old cardinal, allowing the silence to build until it began to get strained.

"In view of what Swens attempted to do, Your Eminence, I would say my prudence was justified."

"I will not be blackmailed!" Belconi bellowed and crashed his fist against the desk.

"Blackmail? I considered it insurance. I'm aware that you can make me disappear, but if I am to disappear, I want to do it on my own terms. You engaged me to do a job and I carried it out. As far as I'm concerned, that's the end of it…unless you choose otherwise." Peroni did not raise his voice or felt perturbed by Belconi's veiled threat.

The cardinal could indeed have him snuffed like a smoldering candle, provided he was prepared to accept the ensuing unpleasantness. When Belconi relaxed and sat back, although clearly not happy, he knew he had won. In the end, The Entity head was a pragmatist and knew how to cut his losses, but it was like having a rattler in one's bed. You did not dare make any sudden moves.

Capitulating, Belconi nodded. "We both have a Damocles sword hanging over us, but it hangs from a relatively heavy chain. I have a sophisticated organization behind me, with many government resources. If I choose, life could become extremely uncomfortable for you. I don't want to do that. You're smart and you would immediately suspect betrayal at any covert retaliation on my part, however well disguised. No, regardless of how much I desire to crush you, it simply isn't worth the effort…or risk. I might need you again, and competent freelance professionals are not easy to find. I guess your tape is as much a threat to you as it is to me. Very well, we shall say no more about it. Go with God, my son," he grated and extended his ringed hand.

Ignoring the gesture, Peroni stood up, nodded and walked out. The door clicked shut behind him.

* * *

Furious at such impertinence, Belconi clamped his mouth shut and glared at the closed door. After a moment, he recognized the ridiculous futility of his indignation and chuckled. As long as the man served Church, it was not necessary to like the tools he used.

Opening the drawer again, he lifted out the papyrus and laid it on the desk. To think that someone wrote those words who actually might have known Jesus or the apostles. He had read the translation and knew how dangerous this innocuous piece of history was, but that didn't stop him from feeling awe at being connected to the root of his faith. It mattered little whether the words were true or not, the connection made it important. He had proof undeniable that Jesus lived. Everything else was historical manipulation and contrived dogma. Staring at the papyrus, he thought he understood something of what Garbaldi must have felt when he saw the tractate for the first time. Almost reverently, he stroked the layered strands and gently replaced the document in the drawer.

Throwing the FedEx package into the wastebasket, he picked up the phone and dialed an extension. He didn't have to wait long.

"Cardinal Marati."

"It's Avero. I've got it."

Marati gave a sharp hiss and Belconi could clearly picture the look of startled surprise and probably no small amount of relief on his friend's face. Both had been chewing their knuckles for a while, expecting to see the tractate's text plastered across the world's media. It was finished and they can rest easy now, secure in the knowledge they had protected the Church.

"I'll be right over."

Belconi replaced the receiver, then turned his attention to a pile of paperwork and began to read, jotting an occasional note in the margins. Absorbed, his head jerked up when the door opened after a firm knock.

"Cardinal Marati, Your Eminence."

"Thank you, Sister…Come in Renaro."

Marati nodded to Sister Treeza and walked in. Without waiting for an invitation, he lowered himself into a chair.

"Show me," he demanded.

Wearing a satisfied grin, Belconi reached into the drawer and held out the papyrus. Marati leaned forward and hesitated before taking the ancient tractate, almost as if he feared it would burn him if he touched it. Holding it, his eyes slowly moved over the text.

Belconi allowed him a few moments of reflection.

Looking bemused, Marati sighed and slid the papyrus across the desk. "Doesn't look like much to have caused all this grief. Then again, I guess two sacrifices was a cheap price to pay to get it back. What about the FBI?"

Regarding his friend, Belconi chose not to correct him on the death count. It would not have served any purpose and Marati could become difficult when his sensibilities were threatened.

"Without the tractate, they're stuck. Father Garbaldi's rash act of rebellion has failed and we have done our duty to the Church."

"Our duty," Marati murmured. "Necessary, I suppose. That doesn't exactly salve my conscience, though."

Belconi frowned, disappointed at this belated surge of repentance. "You came to me, Renaro, and you knew what that meant when you did it. Remember that when your conscience starts to bother you. I know what my job is and what the Curia thinks of my department and me. Like a garbage collector, you're all happy enough for me to clean up your messes as long as you don't have to see how it's done, all the while decrying my methods. I would have thought that you, of all people, would have known better. I can put up with hypocrisy from the others, but I will not tolerate it from you."

Marati smiled without humor. "I'm not being holier-than-thou, Avero. We're hatchet men, you and I. In my case, I prefer to see myself as a gardener, having to sometimes prune a twig or branch in order that the tree remains healthy."

"And I'm your weed killer, is that it?" Belconi added dryly, amused by the analogy.

"That too is part of gardening," Marati agreed, his eyes twinkling. "So far, I don't think either of us has done too badly." He stood and stared at Belconi. "What now?"

"Simple. You give the papyrus to Albani and have him bury the thing somewhere in the Archives. We then move on to pruning the next branch, of course."

* * *

Cup in hand, Tom closed the door to his small office, paused and looked around. Windowless, bare, a bookshelf jammed against the right wall and a gray desk pushed into the left corner, the cheerless cubicle had only one redeeming feature. However humble, it was his, far preferable to being stuck in one of the open bullpen holes outside. Here, he could think, scratch and yawn without being subject to instant gossip from the morbidly curious. He was subject to gossip like everybody else, but at least he didn't have to see it being done. At any rate, there would be enough gossip to satisfy everyone once the old grapevine started twitching about Wellard's demise. He figured that by lunchtime the floor would be buzzing. Only mildly interested, he wondered who would step into his old boss' shoes. As long as it wasn't some bean counter or stickler for regulations, he would handle it.

After hanging up the jacket, he rolled out his chair and powered up the PC, reminding himself to ask Marsha about claiming for the two ruined suits. The round blue FBI logo came up and he quickly logged on. A red-flagged email from Wellard sent yesterday morning caught his eye. He read the subject line and shook his head, 'Coordination report'. As far as his boss was concerned, Boston may have been an interesting diversion for his supervising agent, but that report was his real work. Regardless of how much Tom wanted to press the delete button on the damned thing, he admitted that his ex-boss was right. The report constituted an important review of the Counterterrorism Analysis section's procedures and he would have to finish it sometime. Besides, it would be his operational rulebook, if adopted.

Following his principle of getting the pain out of the way as soon as possible, he resolved to peck at it. He didn't have far to go with it anyway. The other messages were more mundane, but still demanded attention. His teams required guidance and wanted him to make decisions. Casework went on, whether he was around or not. Now back on deck, he had to do his bit. Well, he wanted authority and responsibility. No use bitching now that he had gotten it. He didn't need to have it explained why Mark sought to keep his hand in. He understood all too well. At least his team leaders' meeting wasn't until tomorrow, giving him plenty of time to pick up the threads.

A solid hour later, trawling through emails and shooting off replies, he sighed when finished with the last one and sat back.

As usual, his half empty cup had gone cold, forgotten as he concentrated on the task at hand. Wellard had remarked on that after waiting two minutes in the doorway to be noticed. Staring at a spot on the wall, Tom beamed, happy, and it had nothing to do with work.

The Blue Duck Tavern at Georgetown's West End had subdued oak paneling, discrete lighting, unobtrusive waiters, candlelit tables and soft conversation. Guests enclosed in private glass booths, combined with good food and good company, it provided everything one could want to close a day off on a high. Last night, he closed off one of his better days. With Melissa across the table and lobster on his plate, he couldn't ask for more. She wore a low cut black dress, hair piled high, eyes sparkling, mincing her way through a great sirloin steak more suited for a lumberjack, but it hadn't fazed her at all. He had come to stand in awe of her appetite, wondering not for the first time how she managed to keep her trim figure. He asked her once and she simply laughed. Probably exercised all night. Absently, he speculated on the kind of exercise she indulged in, and with whom, for it damn well was not with him. *Patience, my boy,* he told himself. *Patience.* He saw depth in this woman and didn't want to blow his chances by being fixated on a promise of her alluring body.

And she did have depth. Apart from holding an MBA, she was learning the ropes acting as Marshal's executive assistant, she confided, before her talents were more gainfully employed. She dabbled in old English literature, loved South American folk music and adored the Smithsonian. He could understand everything else, but the Smithsonian? Refinement was wasted on a brute like him, she chided him once, then dragged him through two of the magnificent buildings, not exactly kicking and screaming, being with her more than made up for any unpleasantness in between. To his surprise, he enjoyed the aerospace exhibitions much more than he expected. The sight of the suspended Wright Brothers actual machine and a genuine Apollo capsule made him want more. His last visit explored early American history.

But last night, he explored Melissa's history, at least as much as she was willing to part with. She had a relaxed style that made it easy being with her, and she wasn't shy challenging male chauvinistic dogma, as she termed it, namely his pigheaded views. Which hurt a bit, as he considered himself progressive and liberal minded. But then, women had their own views on that. They clashed wills and ideas, neither seeking to dominate. She appreciated that from him and he appreciated her willingness to be open with him. On the steps of her Glover Park terrace, under stars that had to be there even though he couldn't see them through the streetlights, he kissed her good night. It lasted longer than strict protocol demanded, but she didn't seem to mind. With a lingering smile and a flutter of delicate fingers, she walked inside, hips swinging.

It had definitely been one of his better days.

Grinning at the memories, he leaned over the keyboard and sent her a single line message, 'Thank you'.

Getting himself a fresh cup of coffee, he called Peters and thanked him profusely for the papyrus, offering to pay for a night out with Dr. Riley. The forensic specialist merely laughed it off and hung up.

Feeling better, Tom pulled out his notes and settled down to hammering out the remaining part of his coordination report. Staring at the screen, he frowned when the phone rang. Without taking his eyes off the last paragraph, he groped for the receiver.

"Meecham!"

"Is that any way to greet somebody who's bringing you good news?" Johnston demanded good-naturedly and Tom brightened.

"Sorry about that. I'm trying to finish something I never wanted to start to begin with."

"Been there myself. Strand told me that you wanted to settle a personal issue with your boss. Hence your sudden return to DC."

"It worked out well, but I felt bad about leaving you stuck with the case."

"No problem. Now, about that good news. Forensics came up empty on Peroni's belongings and we haven't found his Hi-Point C9 either."

"And that's your idea of good news?"

"It gets better. We did find a jacket with a neat little hole in a dumpster behind the Ames Hotel. He had a room there on Saturday. Not a bad coat either, but I doubt it'll do us much good. It's been washed in some stuff, coffee and detergent by the smell. Forensics will check it out, but I wouldn't wait for any DNA."

"Any more good news?"

"Loads. Peroni stayed at the Sheraton Commander Hotel at Somerville on Thursday and Friday. That's only a stone's throw from Professor Renauld's place and we have a positive ID from hotel reception."

"That gives us a verified movement pattern, but hardly enough to nail him. Without his gun, it's still all circumstantial."

"Maybe this will help. The NSA sent me a nice email this morning. Swens' phone calls. I just emailed you a copy. It's all encrypted, but they're working on that. And here's the good part. We got—"

"Phone numbers! My man!"

"You can encrypt a conversation, but you got to type in a number to get connected. You can't encrypt that, not with a land-line number anyway."

"You traced them?"

"I think our boy Swens had a team working for him. It's being looked into. But get this. He received calls from two numbers originating in Italy. One of them is a silent number in the Vatican.

Colt Telecom over there identified the other as a cellphone number belonging to one Feranti Sontiri, registered to a PO box at Piazza san Silvestro, Rome's central post office. Swens' log shows he took a call from that number on Wednesday, July 20 at 12:08."

"Peroni finalizing their meeting, eh?"

"The interesting part, that same number was used to place several calls from Boston to—"

"The Vatican number," Tom finished for him, his voice filled with quiet satisfaction. They were getting somewhere now.

"Also to the cellphone number. We're having it traced."

"That was damn fine work, Brent. I'm only sorry to have ruined your weekend by loading you up like that."

"My old lady was having her hair done and glad to see the back of me," Johnston said equitably. "Besides, if I'm at the office, I couldn't very well do that lawn, now could I?"

Tom laughed. "Guess not."

"I've got one more juicy item left for you. That Vatican line number? A call was placed to it from New York on Friday evening. It came from the Opus Dei headquarters."

"Christ!"

Johnston chuckled. "I thought that would perk you up."

"Yeah, but I don't know if this will do us much good. They could have called to say hello."

"You still want the NSA to decode those transcripts? That should nail it down one way or another."

"Absolutely. Having those numbers is good, but actual records of conversations will hang our guys out to dry beyond any doubt. By the way, send your NSA contact a well done."

"The Vatican numbers—"

"Leave them with me. And Brent? Pack a bag. I think we might be going to Rome soon."

"Hoping to catch the big guy himself, eh?"

"You got it. Your passport in order?"

"I'll need to get it out of my bank's safety deposit box, but I'm good to go."

"Great. I'll arrange all bookings in case Strand asks who's footing the bill. And thanks again."

"He might not want me to go, Tom. I have other cases on my plate."

"Leave him to me. Just get packed."

"If you say so. We'll keep looking for that handgun, but I wouldn't be talking to Lieutenant Marsh anytime soon. He doesn't think much of you using his men to trawl drains."

"Christ! Like I'm worried." Tom hung up and then pumped his right arm. "Yes!"

Having put up with an unbroken string of frustrations, it felt grand having things break his way at last. Taking a sip of his room temperature coffee, he opened Johnston's email, did a quick scan and picked up the phone.

"Mark Price."

"And a good morning to you, Mr. Price."

"Well, crap! If it isn't the Assistant Director himself calling."

"Not yet, but I'm working on it. For your information, sir, Wellard is toast."

"Good move. Judging by your bubbly mood on this fine morning—"

"It's fine out there? I can't see anything. They've got me cooped up in a bunker."

"How you must suffer. Anyway, you have a number?"

"Two numbers, a landline and a cellular. Ready to copy?"

"Shoot."

Tom rattled off the digits.

"Give me an hour or so to check them out. You still planning going over there?"

"If you can confirm those numbers, that's all I need to call Cardinal Karpeli and give him a heads-up. Before I see him, I'll want to pick up Peroni first and start the extradition process. I don't want him spooked and have him disappear."

"Looks like you have everything organized. Be calling you."

As soon as Tom put down the phone, it rang.

"Meecham."

"I had a lovely time, Tom," Melissa gushed warmly. "And I wouldn't mind doing it again sometime. While you're thinking about that, Director Marshal wants to see you right away."

"Marshal? Tell him I'm on my way up." His visits to the director had not gone unnoticed, and the rumor mill was already grinding away.

Feeling good at the world, he logged off and slipped on his jacket. The bullpen outside noisy and busy with the usual Monday morning rush to pick up the week's workload. Waving down Greenfield's aborted attempt to hijack him, Tom made for the elevators. He would have to do something about Greenfield and soon. The man just didn't fit in. After three hectic days in Boston, he still found it strange being back in Washington. Missing out on a weekend and with his ribs still sore, he was not exactly overcome with nostalgic emotion.

When he got up, Melissa smiled at him and inclined her head at Marshal's door. "You can go right in."

"Do you know what he wants?"

"I'm just taking messages, Mr. Meecham."

Tom grinned at that. "And I got *your* message…soon."

He knocked on the heavy door, waited for a muffled 'Come in' and pulled down the handle.

"Ah, Tom. Make yourself comfortable," Marshal invited and waved at a visitor chair.

Tom sat down and folded his hands in his lap.

The FBI Director sat back and frowned. "This Boston case of yours is giving me a headache. Now, don't get me wrong. I'm not blaming you. No one could have foreseen Peroni pulling that embassy gag. You also cost me an Assistant Director, but Wellard did it to himself. That papyrus, on the other hand, is something else. We may yet regret giving it to Harvard. The fact that you were the one who gave it to them is a technicality. You represented the FBI, and as its director, I am ultimately responsible. The Vatican is sufficiently irritated that Cardinal Albani gave me a personal call, demanding its return."

"Sir, if you're ordering me to—"

Marshal raised his hand. "I won't order you to do something you will only refuse. That would make you insubordinate and I'd be forced to take disciplinary action. Not in anyone's best interest. It's too late anyway, but we do have a situation."

Tom relaxed, vastly relieved. For a minute there, he thought the FBI Director would play the politician, and that would have made him very unhappy—probably cost him his job too.

"I don't see it that way, sir. The Vatican's claim to the papyrus is nonsense. They can bluster, but that's about all. Professor Norginson wouldn't have touched the thing if Harvard faced a potential legal liability."

"The Church has a very long arm, son, as Harvard may find out to its grief. Their problem, I guess. My concern is what to do about Cardinal Albani's request."

"The fact that he wants the thing back suggests he doesn't know about Peroni."

"Perhaps not, but he knows about the fake."

"What! How?"

"This morning, Cardinal Marati walked into his office, handed him the papyrus and ordered him to bury it in the Secret Archives. Relieved to see the matter closed, although contrite at the loss of Father Garbaldi, he took the thing to their lab for routine processing and that was that."

"How many people know that it's a fake?"

"The senior researcher who made the check and he's been sworn to secrecy."

"Well, that's something at least. What do you want me to do?"

"I'm going to trust you to deal with it. The FBI will not be asking Harvard to return the papyrus. We're beyond that and the thing is still material evidence in case you manage to bring Peroni to trial. A thin argument, I admit, but you'll just have to make the most of it. Call Cardinal Albani and tell him why he can't have the real one back. And son, try not to piss him off, okay? I don't want this to escalate into a diplomatic incident."

Tom nodded, appreciating the director's support, but not altogether relishing the feeling of a breeze being out on that limb. Then it hit him. Marshal *was* playing the politician. If he screwed up, the director could still step in and smooth down the Vatican's ruffled feathers, or is it cassocks? Tom would get the chop, the Vatican would probably get the papyrus back if serious political pressure were brought to bear on Harvard, and smiles all around. As for the dead, they were beyond caring.

"I'll talk to Cardinal Albani, sir," Tom said heavily, not so hot on the idea anymore, "but I still don't know if I can trust him. If he is working with The Entity and I tell him that Harvard has the papyrus, we could have more Peronis on our hands. I *could* use the evidence angle and stall him. What I want to do is neutralize The Entity. Until that's done, no one is safe. That means going through Cardinal Karpeli on the assumption that he's an honest broker. If he's not, things will become a little more challenging."

"Hell of a thing when you can't trust a cardinal of the Church," Marshal growled. "But we're not dealing with a simple confession here and you're wise to be cautious. With Albani's demand, it occurs to me that you may have another problem. Having so many people handle the papyrus, they've muddied the trail for you."

"I don't think so, sir. I know that Peroni handled it. I only need to establish that someone in The Entity also handled it and I'll have my man."

"It could be Cardinal Marati for all you know. As Prefect for the Congregation for the Doctrine of the Faith, he is more than an interested party."

"He is definitely implicated, I agree, but I doubt that he ran Peroni. He doesn't have the necessary machinery behind him."

"What will you tell Cardinal Albani?"

"Honestly? I don't know, sir. Depends on what he has to say, but I'll tell him this. Should The Entity attempt anything, the papyrus will be published before he can say a Hail Mary."

Marshal smiled. "It's your case. Deal with it, and keep me posted."

On the way to his office, Tom stopped by Marsha's desk and asked her to place a call to Cardinal Albani at the Vatican Secret Archives, then route the call to him when she gets through. She raised an inquiring eyebrow at this unusual request, but he had no time to indulge her curiosity.

He snagged a fresh cup of coffee and barely got comfortable when she called.

"I have Cardinal Albani's assistant on the line."

"Thank you. Put me through, will you?"

"Cardinal Albani's office. Sister Angela speaking," a pleasant contralto voice answered with a mild accent.

"Good afternoon, Sister. This is Thomas Meecham, Supervising Special Agent, FBI. I would appreciate a few moments of Cardinal Albani's time if he is available."

"His Eminence is expecting your call, sir. Just a moment." Slow hymn music provided a few seconds of interesting diversion. The line clicked again. "Go ahead, sir."

"Your Eminence?"

"Cardinal Albani, Mr. Meecham, and I am pleased that you called so quickly," he said in good English. "I gather Director Marshal has spoken to you?"

"Your request places me in a most difficult position, Your Eminence. There are mitigating factors to be considered."

"I would have thought the request simple. The Church is merely seeking return of its property."

"Nothing is simple about this case, and the papyrus is not Church property. Before he died, Father Garbaldi told me how he happened to find the tractate."

"The circumstances surrounding Father Garbaldi's death are tragic and deplorable, but you must also appreciate the horrendous harm to the Church should the papyrus become public. Regardless of how it came to be in Father Garbaldi's possession, the document was sent to the Vatican."

"And the Church sanctioned five deaths to retrieve it, Your Eminence, and two attempts on me," Tom retorted harshly, the whole sequence crashing on him again, and he heard a startled gasp, clearly not feigned.

"Five deaths? Dear God." Albani clearly sounded stunned. "What happened?"

"Your intelligence service hired an assassin to recover the papyrus and kill everyone who had knowledge of it. Father Garbaldi's wasn't the only death, Your Eminence."

"It's not possible!" Albani protested weakly.

"I'm afraid it's only too possible. Since you established that the papyrus Cardinal Marati gave you is a fake, you must then suspect why I had it planted. You must also realize that you're now in a position to potentially undermine my entire investigation."

"Mr. Meecham, are you insinuating that I had something to do with this monstrous deed?"

"I have no way of knowing anything, Your Eminence."

"You don't know whom to trust. Ironic, isn't it? Forgive my outburst, but I'm still in shock."

"What happened is not exactly what I expected from the Church either."

"No, I suppose not. Mr. Meecham, I give you my word. I had nothing to do with Father Garbaldi's death, but I may have inadvertently caused it when I first spoke to Cardinal Marati, which obviously triggered the subsequent chain of events. You must understand. I only wanted to protect the Church."

Tom sensed that Albani knew more than he was telling, not altogether surprising. "But you had to know where this could lead."

"And I am burning in a hell of my own making because of it. More so now. Five deaths…"

For a moment, Tom felt sorry for him, until he remembered the deaths. The person witnessing a murder and doing nothing is equally guilty as the one who pulled the trigger.

"Your Eminence, until I apprehend the assassin and identify the person within The Entity responsible for hiring him—"

"It's Cardinal Belconi," Albani whispered in a dejected voice. "I'm telling you this now because you will probably find out soon enough anyway."

"You have proof?" Tom demanded and Albani gave a sour chuckle.

"Nothing that would stand up in a court of law."

"I guess it's up to me, then. I must advise you, Your Eminence, once I have my proof, I will act, regardless of any embarrassment to the Church."

"That's your affair. You need to know that I have updated His Holiness on this entire matter. Don't be alarmed. We shall not take any action regarding Cardinal Belconi without prior consultation with you."

"Thank you. That will be most helpful."

"Tell me, Mr. Meecham, did you give the papyrus to Harvard as you said you would?"

"I can tell you this, Your Eminence. The papyrus is safe, beyond the reach of the Church or The Entity."

"Do you intend to publish?"

"Can you give me one reason why I should not?"

"You know the reason yourself, my son."

"Perhaps, except for one thing. The Church chose to murder to recover the papyrus. How can it justify standing above its own commandments?"

"That's hardly fair. You cannot hold the entire Church accountable for the evils of one man."

"Am I my brother's keeper, is that it? If this was done by Cardinal Belconi's hand, he acted under a policy that condoned such action. If the papyrus is truth, the Church has been living a lie, and perhaps you should confess. If it isn't, you have nothing to worry about."

"Surely you cannot hold such simple ideas. You *must* realize what publication of the tractate will do."

"And because you also realized, you took the action you did."

Silence gathered and became thick. Tom wondered if Albani had hung up, then he heard a heavy sigh.

"Perhaps we do need to atone for the sins of our fathers and for the sins we committed. Is there nothing I can say to change your mind?"

"Whatever you wanted to say, Your Eminence, you should have said it to Father Garbaldi."

"Then the seventh angel shall indeed sound his horn. You have my blessing, my son."

The line went dead and Tom listened to the dial tone for a long time before replacing the receiver. They chose to kill, he kept telling himself.

He logged on, opened the Word file of his coordination report and stared at the screen. The words meant nothing; hollow, empty things. Images of the end of days kept running through his head. After a while, disgusted, he clicked on Internet Explorer and typed in a search for Revelations. When he finished reading, he sat back, deep in thought.

Everything Albani had said dealt with protecting the Church from scandal. It had nothing to do with faith, nothing. They merely wanted to perpetuate their comfortable lives. After a while, he firmed his mouth and nodded. If the seventh angel is fated to sound his horn, then let the trumpets begin. The other thing, Albani had given in too easily. This was not the end of it. He picked up his cold cup and walked out.

Christ!

Steaming coffee in hand, he took a thirsty sip and sat down. As though it had waited for him to settle in, the phone rang.

"Meecham!"

"You sore at the world again, Tom? That didn't take long."

"Sore at a couple of square miles in Rome, Mark."

"Ah. What happened?"

"I just had a chat with Cardinal Albani. He knows about the fake papyrus and wants back the real thing."

"Well, crap! How did he find out?"

"Peroni must have given the fake to Cardinal Belconi, who gave it to Cardinal Marati—"

"Who in turn gave it to Albani to bury and he had the thing checked."

"That's it."

"You're not planning to hand over the real one, are you?"

"You kidding? We're past that and I think everybody knows it. Albani was merely a ranging shot and I expect a broadside coming my way at any time."

Mark chuckled. "I like your optimism. You mentioned Belconi…"

"Actually, Cardinal Albani did. Looks like he's the man I'm after."

Stefan Vučak

"And I think he's right. Those numbers you gave me? The landline is one of his private lines and the other is a cellphone registered in his name."

Tom broke into a huge grin, relief flooding through him. "You just made my day, Mark."

"Ruined if Albani tips off the others."

"I think not. Our cardinal has a bad case of guilty conscience."

"Guilty conscience or not, given what's at stake here, he still might blow the whistle on you."

"It doesn't matter. I'm having the NSA decrypt calls made between Belconi, Peroni, and Swens. Once I have those transcripts, I'll be knocking on his door."

"Not much good if they've flown the coop. Still, it's amazing what twenty-four hours will do, eh? I've got to run. Let me know if I can help with anything else, okay?"

"Mark, thanks for everything. I mean it."

"Any time, my boy."

Tom hung up, wondering if Albani would actually tip off Belconi. That might be inconvenient for his investigation in the short term, but the cardinal would be a marked man with every law enforcement agency in the world after him, and for the Church, perhaps an even bigger scandal. He would simply have to wait and see how things developed.

If in fact it was a nice day outside, perhaps Melissa would care to have lunch with him. It would certainly top off what had so far been a great morning. Well, almost great. He still needed those NSA transcripts. Hesitating, he picked up the phone and dialed her extension.

"FBI Director's office. Gloria Black speaking."

"Hi, Gloria. It's Tom. Is Melissa around?"

"Oh, hi, Tom. She won't be back until two, a working lunch presentation to all Executive Directors. You want me to take a message?"

"No, that's fine, thanks." He hung up and frowned. An executive presentation? It looked like his girl was definitely moving up in the world.

Disappointed at missing out having lunch with her, he went down to the canteen and got himself a hot pastrami on rye and a bottle of mixed tropical fruit juice. He was drinking too much coffee and ought to cut down. Still in the mood with creative juices flowing, he took his sandwich upstairs and got stuck into the report. He wanted to get everything down and be done with it in case he had to fly off to Rome. Polishing grammar would be the easy part.

Staring at the completed executive summary section, he stretched his arms and winced at a protesting stab of pain from his back. He stood up and groaned, feeling sixty years old. After some loosening up exercises, his back's protests subsided to a dull ache. He needed to return to a solid workout regimen. If he kept going like this, too much chair parade would ruin him and he hated the idea of going flabby, dragging a belly around, and running out of breath picking up a cup. Systematic tightening up, that was the order of the day—and he would start first thing tomorrow. His inner self sneered, reminding him that the Bureau had an excellent gym downstairs.

Christ! Even his conscience was against him.

He glanced at the time display on the PC and his eyes widened: 3:12. No wonder his body had stiffened up. Perhaps wandering down to the gym might not be a bad idea at that. Clear the cobwebs and oil the hinges.

The phone rang and he picked up. "Meecham."

"Hi, Tom, it's Brent."

"More good news, I hope?"

"NSA came through for us. I'm just going over the phone transcripts. The big guy you're after? It's Cardinal Belconi. The transcripts don't say who he is, but must be someone high up the tree."

"They don't come any higher."

"You mean he runs The Entity?"

"That Vatican number you gave me? It's from his office. The other is his cellular. Sorry, I can't tell you how I found out."

"I won't pry, but I can guess. Anyway, we've got it all, a call from Belconi to Swens and several from Peroni to Belconi on both numbers. That Opus Dei chat? The NSA weenie who handled this noted that the speaker was Bishop Anthony Rodriguez."

"Rodriguez! I've had the pleasure. What did you do to get the NSA on this so quickly? Pay somebody off?"

Johnston laughed. "Strand talked to someone over there and greased the wheels. Anyway, you should have my email by now. You still want me to pack?"

"Definitely. I'll see if I can get us a flight for tomorrow. Take enough for two days. Marsha, that's our office gofer, will send you the e-ticket and itinerary details."

"Thanks for having me on board, Tom. You could have kept all this for yourself, you know."

"Hell, you did most of the work and deserve some of the fun." Tom hung up and stood up.

Johnston was a good man. Dour and a bit cheerless, but he knew his stuff. Nothing like a buzz one gets when the cuffs snap on a quarry. With Peroni, he would let Johnston have him. Belconi, he would keep for himself. He relished the thought of looking the man in the eye when the Vatican police came. Rome was a long way off and the case wasn't wrapped up yet. Plenty of things could still go wrong and he would have to think about the Opus Dei aspect.

He strode to Marsha's desk and waited. She looked up from her screen and flashed him a quick smile. In her fifties, no one quite knew her exact age, peppery hair, unassuming and very efficient, she was the person who got things done when the system refused to work.

"Yes, Tom?"

"I need you to book two tickets for Rome, departing tomorrow. One is for me and the other is for Agent Brent Johnston, Boston Division. I want us flying out together."

"Rome? A bit of sightseeing on Bureau time?"

"I wish! Once you have confirmation, send Brent the details."

"How long will you be staying?"

"Two days, and we'll want a hotel."

"I'll try to get you a flight from Boston, otherwise it will have to be from JFK—"

"No problem. Johnston and I can meet there if necessary."

"I will need authorization, Mr. Meecham."

"I just gave it to you."

She raised an eyebrow, thinking about it. "I guess it'll be all right."

Tom nodded to her and walked to his office. He could hear the phone going before he opened the door. He rushed in and picked up. Can't a guy have even a few minutes of peace?

"Meecham."

"It's Melissa, Tom. Can you come up? The Director wants to see you."

"Again?"

"He must like you."

"Yeah. How was the presentation?"

"I wowed them. Gloria said you called."

"Oh, I wondered if we could have lunch, but I had to be satisfied with my own company instead."

"You poor thing. Maybe tomorrow. Anyway, you better come up or both of us will be pounding the beat."

Tempted to say that tomorrow was probably out, he refrained. She wouldn't blab, but he would be remiss in his duty by telling her.

"On my way."

Upstairs, he beamed at her, knocked on Marshal's door and walked in.

"You wanted to see me, sir?"

"Sit down, Tom," Marshal ordered, his hand hovering over the phone keypad. "I've got Cardinal Karpeli holding on the line. It looks like the big guns are being brought to bear after you shortchanged Albani. Karpeli and I've been talking while waiting for you."

"Sir, am I in some sort of trouble?"

"Not from me you're not," Marshal growled and pressed a button. "Your Eminence, I have Supervising Special Agent Thomas Meecham with me."

"Mr. Meecham, I've been hearing a lot about you lately," a strong voice came from the conference speaker.

Tom had an immediate image of a powerful man: tall, dignified and polished, someone confident, used to getting his own way. This character was no lightweight, and he wondered if Marshal had thrown him into the deep end, or just thrown him.

"I trust it's been favorable, Your Eminence."

Karpeli chuckled. "Not as far as Cardinal Albani is concerned."

"I regret if I caused him any inconvenience, but if this is about the papyrus, my position hasn't changed."

"Mr. Meecham, under different circumstances, I would gladly engage you in a debate to challenge your position, but I don't have that luxury or the time. The Church is faced with a potential crisis and I must take whatever action is required to avoid it."

"By giving Cardinal Belconi a free hand to finish what he started?"

Marshal glared at him, but Tom didn't give a damn. He'd had enough of moral pontificating, especially from those purporting to be moral, but in reality wore it like a convenient cloak, to be discarded when it got too warm.

"My son, your reaction is understandable, and given what has transpired, natural. Although I stand in God's shadow, I'm only a man faced with a real world problem. Accordingly, I must use earthly tools to resolve it. Mr. Meecham, I shall dispense with sermonizing, since that did not work with Cardinal Albani, and I shall be blunt. If you gave the papyrus to Harvard University, as I suspect you did, publishing the tractate will result in a multi-million dollar suit that will cripple them. You may think that once the papyrus is published, the Church will be otherwise engaged. You would be mistaken. The Church will endure and the faithful multitude will endure. Will Harvard if that multitude turns on it? I do not condone violence in any form, but at the same time, I cannot control what some extremist elements out there might do. Do you want that on your conscience? I have read the translation, Mr. Meecham. It is a falsehood, but a dangerous falsehood, one that can only aid and abet the forces of evil. There is enough serious trouble in the world without you adding to it with this mischief."

Tom wanted to reach through the phone and strangle the two-faced smoothie. Abhorring violence, yet quite prepared to incite riot to achieve his objective. At least Belconi didn't pretend.

"I appreciate your frankness, Your Eminence. Allow me to be frank in turn. If the papyrus is a falsehood, and I'm not in a position to say, the Church has nothing to worry about. Publication may generate a few days of unpleasant publicity and get theologians engaged in some lively debates, but scandals of the rich and famous, tabloid sensationalism, and worry about how to pay off the mortgage should stifle any concern over a moot point whether Jesus was the first or second Messiah. It seems to me that your threat of punitive action may be out of proportion to the potential damage caused, however momentarily satisfying to the evangelical reactionaries. As for that vast multitude, I suggest that such violent expression will only serve to affirm the tractate's validity. What I do, I do with a clear conscience. Isn't there a proverb that says we should keep God's commandments?"

Karpeli was silent for several seconds. "Proverbs 3:1. You argue your position eloquently, my son, and your reference is apt. Because the Church has not kept the commandments, we deserve the Lord's wrath, is that it?"

"I'm not a philosopher, Your Eminence. I am an FBI law officer. Cardinal Belconi and the assassin he engaged to kill on American soil have broken the law. My job is to bring them before the courts and see justice done. Nothing else. I owe Father Garbaldi at least that much."

"Then you should confine your activities toward that end and not to be carried away by Father Garbaldi's schoolboy idealism."

"With respect, Cardinal Belconi didn't consider it schoolboy idealism."

"Forgive me. A poor choice of words on my part, and you're right, of course."

"Your Eminence, the Church is supposed to be a pillar of moral standing within our social fabric. Sadly, as we both know, it has fallen far short of its responsibility."

"I am not discussing history, Mr. Meecham, but current events."

"So am I."

"Then let us do so. Did you give the papyrus to Harvard?"

"So that you can initiate a preemptive strike?"

Karpeli laughed with genuine humor. "Despite your claim to the contrary, I would enjoy debating philosophy with you, Mr. Meecham. One day, perhaps we will, and you belittle your skills. My son, what Cardinal Belconi did cannot be condoned under any circumstance. If this is what the Church does, then indeed we do not deserve to be saved. I don't intend to follow in his footsteps, but I do have other tools at my disposal, and I will use them all. We both have a job to do. As for your job, Cardinal

Albani told me of the fake papyrus and the likely reason why you allowed the assassin to take it. I presume you have means to detect whoever handled it?"

Expecting a more vigorous argument to return the papyrus, Tom was thrown off the track. "That's correct, Your Eminence. I already established that the assassin has handled it. It is almost certain that Cardinal Belconi did as well. What I need is confirmation."

"Even if you confirm that Belconi handled the papyrus, that's not evidence of duplicity to engage an assassin and kill Father Garbaldi."

"Not conclusively no, but it does provide an important link in a chain of more substantial evidence."

"Oh? You have further proof?"

"The FBI has obtained phone transcripts of calls made between Cardinal Belconi, the assassin and a member of the Jesuit Order in Boston who provided the weapons."

Marshal looked sharply at Tom; then closed his mouth with a snap, having answered his own question.

"The Jesuits? My God. Then he really did it," Karpeli whispered. "I never actually thought…What are you going to do?"

"I meant to call you to discuss this. I'm organizing a flight to Rome and expect to be there on Wednesday. I'll advise your office once I have the details. This is where I will need your help, Your Eminence. I would like you to arrange for me to see Cardinal Belconi and Cardinal Marati. Please provide a portable UV scanner. When I am there, I will hand over the phone transcripts to you to take whatever action is required under Italian law. As for the assassin, the Department of Justice will petition the Italian government to have him extradited for proceedings here."

"You realize, Mr. Meecham, those proceedings could be even more damaging to the Church than publication of the papyrus."

"Only if the Church attempts to manipulate the situation."

331

Karpeli chuckled. "Bury it under the carpet, you mean? Rest assured, my son, however uncomfortable exposing The Entity's activities might be, justice will not only be done, but will be seen to be done."

"Thank you, Your Eminence. That means a great deal. I must advise you, though, the Italian State Police will also have all the evidence against Cardinal Belconi."

"I should be offended, but I understand the reason for your skepticism and caution. You have my blessing, my son. Director Marshal, do you endorse Mr. Meecham's actions?"

"I'm only interested in seeing the guilty apprehended, Your Eminence. As for the papyrus, it's evidence to murder. I'm not in a position to involve the Bureau beyond that."

"I see. Very well. I will help you in apprehending Cardinal Belconi. What he did was evil, but that won't stop me from keeping the papyrus out of the public domain."

"We all have to do what we consider is right, Your Eminence."

"Indeed. I look forward to seeing you, Mr. Meecham," Karpeli said gravely and the line went dead.

The FBI Director shook his head, a rueful smile on his face. "Wily old devil, but you handled that well, Tom."

"Thank you, sir. And I appreciate your support."

"The papyrus? Some may split hairs over legal ownership and your decision to give it away, but that was your call and I stand by it. Did you actually get the phone transcripts?"

"Johnston forwarded me the NSA email before I came up. I haven't had a chance to look at them yet, but he has read them. I need to advise you, sir, that one of the phone transcripts connects Cardinal Belconi with Bishop Rodriguez, Prelate of Opus Dei."

"Not unexpected, but we'll look into it anyway. The old Bishop may have opened himself to possible prosecution as an accessory before the fact. You also mentioned the Italian State

Police. That means getting in touch the Director General of Public Security to let him know that you're coming."

"I'll need his help to arrest Peroni, sir."

"I'll see to it." Marshal said briskly and glanced at his watch. "Too late to call him now, but I'll leave a message that I'll be in touch to arrange a meeting with you."

"That would be good, sir."

"You realize, of course, you won't be able to actually arrest Peroni. Only the State Police can do that."

Tom grinned in anticipation. "I only want to see him cuffed and I don't care who does it. He was good, but he underestimated the NSA."

Marshal shook his head. "No, he underestimated you. Send me Johnston's email and I'll get Justice to start on the extradition paperwork."

Tom sat up in alarm. "I'm happy to send you the email, but with respect, sir, I'd prefer to hold off on Justice."

"Oh? And why is that? I'd have thought you would want Peroni here as soon as possible."

"I'd like nothing better, but what if Belconi or Peroni get wind of what I'm up to before I act? They could both disappear and we'd have nothing."

"Mmm. Except for five bodies, but you have a point. It's a worry when you can't trust your own government. On the other hand, if Karpeli or Albani tip them off, all you'll have to show for your trip are some postcards and a hefty bill for the Bureau."

"Look at it this way, sir. My trip will stimulate the American economy."

The FBI Director laughed, apparently enjoying Tom's irreverent attitude. "It won't be stimulating when the auditors start looking at your expense report."

"I may already be in a jam over my Boston trip, but we were never going to be pals anyway. If you agree, I'll call you when I have Peroni in custody. You can start the extradition process then. I'm sure he won't mind a few days of rest in an Italian jail."

Marshal smiled and tapped the desk with long fingers. "Despite a connecting string of photos and the NSA transcripts, you don't have any direct evidence that Peroni actually committed the murders. A smart lawyer could still get him off."

"I know, but I can't worry about that. My job is to bring him to court with the evidence we have. I can only hope we've got a DA who knows his stuff. If I get a confession from Belconi, Peroni will sing a different tune."

Chapter Nine

Patchy clouds covered the city as Delta Air Lines flight DL246 descended toward Fiumicino airport. His face pressed close to the small scratched window, Johnston gazed raptly at Rome sliding beneath him.

"Hey! I can see St. Peter's and the Colosseum!"

"That's great," Tom mumbled, sleeping shades covering his eyes, and shifted under the thin tan blanket.

The Boeing 777 banked and the fasten seatbelt chime went off. His back hardly gave a twinge. A lush voice interrupted the last of his fitful sleep with landing instructions, customs and quarantine formality reminders, and transfer details for transiting passengers. Reluctantly, he pulled off his shades and sighed. Blinking, he got his seat into an upright position and glanced at Johnston, but the man was in a different dimension, wrapped up in playing the tourist. Tom figured if he had a window seat, he might have done the same thing.

He crumpled the blanket and pushed it down beside his feet. After wriggling his toes, he removed the in-flight socks and slid his feet into black loafers. He gave a big yawn to make his ears pop and rubbed his eyes, not interested in St. Peter's or the Colosseum. Not right now. The overnight flight from JFK okay, only eight-and-a-half hours, but he'd had a long day even before the flight started. The curvy Delta flight attendants with their ready plastic smiles made the trip pleasant, but he suspected that for them, it was probably just another day at the office, as it was for him. At least the arrival schedule had not screwed up his body clock too much, but a brisk shower right now would be good.

Yesterday morning, coffee in hand, padding through the al-most deserted floor, he hardly opened his office door when the phone rang. It was Melissa telling him to come up. The director was after him and only seven-thirty! Didn't the guy ever sleep? What the hell was going on with everybody these days? He dumped his carry-on in a corner behind his desk and hung the garment bag in the narrow closet, then glanced wistfully at the steaming cup on his desk and walked out. Having a 3:34 p.m. flight to JFK that connected with a 5:50 to Rome, his day would be full. He would have preferred a direct flight from Boston, but there weren't any seats available and he did not want to dally. With a return flight on Friday, he hoped to have an uninterrupted weekend for a change. He wondered vaguely if he could skip the in between bits and jump straight to the weekend part.

With a smile and a nod at Melissa, he walked into Marshal's office. The FBI Director looked up and waved at a chair. Tom made himself comfortable and waited. After pushing aside some papers, Marshal cleared his throat and sat back.

"All packed and ready to go?"

"Yes, sir. I just need to catch up on some last minute details with my teams."

"Good. You'll be pleased to know that everything is squared away with Director General Framanti. The man you'll be working with is Captain Renzo Fabrini, supposed to be one of his top men. I told him we'd email him Peroni's mug shots and address. They want to run a check on him and stake out his place. Get the stuff to Melissa and she'll take care of it."

Tom squirmed at the idea of fumbling Italian police giving the game away. Marshal saw his reaction and raised his hand.

"I know what you're going to say, Tom. It's their turf and they are doing us a favor."

"I'm simply not comfortable with the possibility of them blowing it, sir. Not when we're so close to wrapping this up."

"It's the price we pay for cooperation."

Marshal was right, but Tom didn't have to like it. He would just have to swallow it and hope that Fabrini knows what he was doing.

"Yes, sir."

"There has been another development. It doesn't affect what you're doing, but I thought you would like to know."

"Sir?"

"It looks like Cardinal Karpeli didn't much care for what you had to say and raised the ante. He must have talked to the Pope, because the Pope called the President, asking his help to recover the papyrus. Caught flat-footed, the President couldn't say much except promise to look into it."

Tom allowed himself a slow grin. "The Pope himself? I guess they're serious about getting the thing back."

"After I gave the President your story, he told me to handle it and he wasn't going to interfere."

"President Walters is Catholic, isn't he? If the Vatican leaks that he did nothing to stop publication, it could get nasty for him."

"He is well aware of the political dimension, but he also understands due process. Besides, he doesn't have the authority to demand that Harvard give up the papyrus."

"Technically true, but he could still make it tough for them if he wanted to."

"I suppose, but he doesn't, regardless of any possible consequences later. Besides, given the current Israel and Iran thing on his plate, the papyrus will be a mere distraction."

"I somehow doubt that, sir. What happens now?"

"As far as you're concerned, nothing has changed. The Pope will just have to get used to the idea that he couldn't bully the President."

"With this setback, will Karpeli still cooperate?"

"I don't see that he has any choice. Belconi committed a crime. That's not something he can cover up, not with the FBI involved."

Leaving Marshal's office, Tom figured the news could have been worse, but he still didn't relish the idea of Italian police stomping around spooking Peroni. Having to beg off on lunch with Melissa also bad, and she called him a pig when he refused to explain why, but he simply had too much to do, regardless of how badly he wanted her company. He would probably not be back until Monday and he needed to make sure his team leaders were able to handle everything until then. Tempted to call off his nine-thirty meeting, he decided to go ahead; it gave him a perfect opportunity to clue everybody in. They might wonder what he did with himself all week, but they would just have to handle the load by themselves.

The aircraft came in on the main north-south runway and squatted down with a light bump. After releasing reverse thrust, it turned onto a taxiway and jolted toward the terminal. Tom absently wondered why they couldn't make smooth taxiways. He heard overhead lockers bang open as coach passengers behind him scrambled to retrieve their belongings. In the business class cabin, the atmosphere more subdued. No need to rush, and anyway, he didn't carry much. That would avoid the mind-numbing wait at baggage claim for a suitcase to be regurgitated, but he still didn't look forward to clearing Immigration. Some evils clearly had to be endured. Glancing at his watch, only 8:42, they were down pretty much on time.

As the aircraft approached the terminal, two flight attendants walked briskly down the aisles and clipped on the curtain separating the economy cabin. Finally at full stop, Tom retrieved his carry-on from the overhead compartment and an attendant handed him the garment bag. The first class passengers got out quickly, then a male attendant nodded for the business class to alight. There were more nods, smiles and hollow goodbyes at the hatch. Bright light and a blast of warm air washed over him as he stepped into the boarding bridge.

Tom paused when he eased up into the departure gate and waited for Johnston to catch up. Looking around, he could have been at any airport: people everywhere, loud announcements, bright ad boards, glittering shops, and food stands. Standing beside him, Johnston nudged his arm and Tom turned. A young man dressed in a blue lightweight suit looked anxiously at emerging passengers, a cardboard card in his hand with Tom's name printed in large block letters. He glanced at Johnston and walked to the youngster.

"I'm Tom Meecham."

"Ah, Mr. Meecham! Welcome to Rome, sir," the man gushed with relief and stuck out his hand. "I am Detective Tiliari, State Police. I'll be looking after you."

Tom shook his hand and introduced Johnston. "You speak very good English, Mr. Tiliari."

The Italian shrugged. "Mandatory these days, I'm afraid. And it's just Antonio, sir. Now, if you will kindly come with me, I'll steer you through the formalities. Do you have any other luggage?"

"Only what we're carrying."

"Excellent. This shouldn't take long, then. We'll stop by your hotel first and you can freshen up. Afterward, I'll drive you to headquarters where you'll meet Captain Renzo Fabrini, who will be working with you."

"And what is your role here, Antonio?"

"I was only ordered to pick you up. That's all I know about anything. Now, if I can have the name of your hotel?"

Tom gave him the details as they walked down the long corridor with crowded gates on either side. Steering them through a bottleneck of duty-free shops, Tiliari led them past lines of passengers waiting their turn at a row of Immigration cubicles and ushered them into a small side room. Two pleasant officials quickly checked their passports, and after a superficial look at their bags, they were on their way. Tom appreciated the efficient service. Outside the terminal, Tiliari walked hastily to a light blue BMW police sedan. A white stripe ran the length of the car, with POLIZIA painted in large black letters beneath it. Assaulted by traffic and aircraft noises, Tom and Johnston piled their bags into the trunk and took the rear seat. Their guide got up front and shot instructions in rapid Italian to the uniformed driver. The cruiser pulled away from the curb and merged with the traffic stream.

Staring out the right side window, Tom figured the moving scenery looked like any other city suburbia. The major difference were the cars; mostly small, more compact than the gas guzzlers he was used to. As the police cruiser exited the highway and turned left, he nudged Johnston and pointed. On their right, managing to tower above lesser buildings, St. Peter's brown dome commanded the surrounds. As they neared the Vatican, he caught glimpses of the old city wall and history spoke loud to him in a cacophony of images from books and movies. By comparison, America's three hundred years paled into insignificance.

Following the ancient wall, the cruiser turned right and slowed. On the sidewalk beside them, a long line of people waited stoically to enter the Vatican museums. It could not have been very comfortable out there in the rising heat. The driver did a quick U-turn and stopped beside a non-descript yellow stone building.

"Hotel Alimani, Mr. Meecham," Tiliari announced brightly, got out and opened the trunk.

Tom followed him, not impressed, hoping Marsha had not dumped them in some hole. A doorman, dressed in a dark burgundy outfit that would have fitted in during the '30s, hurried from the entrance and gathered up the bags.

"I'll wait here, sir, until you come down," Tiliari announced and got back into the air-conditioned car.

Tom took it in stride and made for the entrance, not complaining about the VIP service. The hotel exterior may have looked drab, but the posh, subdued interior more than made up for it. The check-in formalities were handled quickly and the bellman took them upstairs to their rooms. Tom gave him a five Euro note after the man switched on all the lights and showed him the bathroom's gadgets.

Johnston popped his head in and beamed. "Not a bad setup, eh?"

Looking around the room, Tom had to agree. Soft beige carpeting, wide bed, old-fashioned lamp stands, a large LED TV mounted on the wall, the room spacious and comfortable. He could get used to such living, wondering vaguely how much they charged per night.

"We'll admire it later. Grab a quick shower and shave. We don't want to keep Antonio waiting."

Despite the unique surroundings, they were here on business, not a tourist jaunt. If they managed to wrap things up quickly, there might be time for a look around. He wouldn't mind seeing the inside of St. Peter's at all, since he was already here…

Changed into a lightweight somber suit, feeling refreshed, Tom pulled out his cellphone and punched in the CIA contact number. Someone picked up after a single ring.

"Identify yourself."

"Hawk."

"Subject is in residence. Note, there is a stakeout around the place. Presumably the State Police." The line went dead.

Tom stared at the cellphone and cursed. Exactly what he feared. If the CIA watcher team could spot a stakeout, it was likely that Peroni would also make them out. Frustrated that things might be falling apart, he locked his room and banged on Johnston's door. Brent walked out twitching his jacket into place and both marched toward the elevators. Downstairs, they handed in their keycards and were out. Piling quickly into the waiting police car, the cruiser pulled away and accelerated down the busy street.

Not much to see on their way to the Questra Di Roma Centralino: old yellow stone structures, narrow streets, cars and scooters everywhere, traffic noise and pedestrians trying to stay alive as they dared the intersection crossings. The street suddenly opened onto a large square and on his right, Tom saw the Colosseum for the first time. Only a fleeting glimpse before they shot into another narrow street, but the image of the imposing structure burned in his mind. He wondered how the thing might have looked in its heyday. After a quick run down Via Nazionale, they turned left, then right onto Via Di San Vitale. The only thing distinguishing the State Police headquarters from other square buildings around them, were the parked blue police cars, powerful motorcycles, and men in light blue uniforms. No one paid them any attention as the three of them walked into the cool interior.

Tiliari guided his guests into an elevator and they rode to the fourth floor in silence. When the doors opened, Tom could have been in any modern office building; open floor plan, manned desks, computers and filing cabinets, cubicles hugging the walls with people being busy, uniformed and civilian. Tiliari walked purposefully down the hard gray-carpeted strip hugging the wall toward an end office. He knocked once and opened the door. After an exchange of quick Italian, he stood aside and nodded to his guests to go in.

Perhaps thirty-five, around five feet seven, wearing a dark gray suit, Captain Fabrini stood behind his wide desk waiting to greet his visitors. A neat black mustache stretched to cover a broad grin.

"Come in, gentlemen. Welcome to *Roma*," he gushed in smooth English and extended his hand.

The office small and cluttered with steel filing cabinets and stacked folders, but had a cozy informal atmosphere. Tom stepped to the desk and grasped the proffered hand. For a short man, Fabrini's clasp firm and strong.

"Thomas Meecham, sir. And my associate—"

"Agent Johnston, no? Please, make yourselves comfortable. Can I get you anything? Coffee, soft drink?"

Tom eased himself into one of the visitor chairs, feeling comfortable, sensing a friendly rapport with the Italian cop.

"Thank you, sir. Nothing." He was still getting over the in-flight service coffee he had accumulated during breakfast.

"Please! Just Renzo. We are fellow law officers, no? Formality only gets in the way of business. Don't you agree?"

"It can work out that way," Tom said with a smile, liking the man even more. "For you, having us here must seem like very strange business."

"When Director General Framanti told me what you two were about, I did think it pretty strange. I've handled some odd cases in my time and nothing fazes me anymore. This has to be the same for you, no? Especially after that Valero incident." Noting Tom's surprise, Fabrini chuckled. "We do have newspapers, you know."

"And I hate to think what was in them," Tom moaned with feeling, which generated a laugh from the Italian.

"Always unpredictable, the papers, and not generally a reliable source of information. That must be true in your own country, no?"

"Unfortunately, it is."

"In your case, Tom, I had a more dependable source. We can reminisce later. Now we get serious. I was told to cooperate with you in apprehending this Mercurio Peroni. *Direttore Generale's* brief was sketchy, but he told me enough to know that going after Cardinal Belconi will cause a national scandal when the news breaks. Still, we Romans are used to scandals, especially when they are Vatican scandals. We love them and they only confirm what everybody already knows, that they're all crooks. Belconi has to be one to do what he did. We've been after him and his shady operatives for a while, but never came close to bagging him. Don't look so surprised, my friend. Italy thrives on corruption at all levels. Why should we be surprised that the Vatican is also corrupt? They're just men, no?"

"I must admit to being taken aback by your attitude, Renzo," Tom said cautiously. "As an Italian, I expected hostility at the thought that I came here to tarnish the Church."

Fabrini laughed a full-bellied expression of mirth. "Going after the venerable Entity, you added zest to what otherwise would have been merely another mundane day of handling petty crime. As for tarnishing the Church, that was done long ago. Being Roman, I get to hear things not generally known outside."

Looking at the Italian, Tom doubted that Fabrini handled anything petty. The man exuded too much competence for that. He reached into his jacket pocket, pulled out a long brown envelope, and slid it across the desk.

"NSA transcripts of phone and cellphone conversations made between Cardinal Belconi, Peroni, and a character called Swens in Boston. This constitutes incontestable proof that Belconi orchestrated the murders. Once we have Peroni, we're going to pay the Cardinal a little visit."

Fabrini took the envelope and negligently tapped it against the desk. "I hope you're right about the evidence, my friend. It is always dangerous stalking a cobra. We shall see what happens, no? *Direttore Generale* Framanti discussed the case with Cardinal Karpeli and Inspector General Giovani Emanuo of the Vatican City State police gave the *Polizia di Stato* jurisdiction. The Cardinal is expecting us at three this afternoon to carry out the arrests."

Tom looked sharply at Fabrini. "I hope the Inspector General has Belconi and Marati under surveillance."

"Rest assured, Tom, neither of them are going anywhere."

"Good. I'd hate it if Belconi were to pull a fast one on us."

"Pull a fast one? I like that. Pull a fast one…But before we talk about our Vatican friend, how do you want to handle Peroni?"

"I understand that you have a stakeout on him. I need to tell you they've been made."

"Ah, your CIA brethren, perhaps? Don't be alarmed; I am not offended. We have long ago come to accept the murky goings on from friendly, and sometimes not so friendly, intelligence arms. After all, we're doing the same thing to them. You think Peroni also has them made?"

"It's possible. I'm told he is still in his apartment, but the sooner we get this done the better."

"Before he disappears, I agree. My men are good, but we cannot afford to underestimate Peroni. We don't want cars and uniforms all over the place, not for a man like that. Too many ways he could slip through our fingers. I took a drive past his apartment building last night to check the layout, as you say in America. Discreetly, of course. Your friend likes to live the high life. Wish I had an apartment in Nomentano."

"I wouldn't want a frontal assault either. One car for backup, with two men along with us, should do it," Tom suggested. "We wait until they gain entry into the building and we move in on him. You managed to find out his apartment number?"

"He's on the fourth floor," Fabrini said absently and bit his lower lip. "A single backup, eh? It could work, but I'll take the precaution of alerting the stakeout team in case Peroni manages to slip past us."

"That's reasonable."

"Then let's go and get him!"

"I appreciate your cooperation, Renzo. Peroni has given the FBI quite a run and I want him to get his."

"My pleasure, Tom. After reviewing his SISMI and *Arma dei Carabinieri* files, that kind of man is a danger to all of us, and the

Polizia di Stato is happy to oblige. A private contractor is always bad news, especially when he's not working for us," he added with a wry chuckle.

Tom blinked, not sure if Renzo was serious or only having fun pulling his leg. He didn't care how the State Police played their games as long as he got Peroni.

"One thing, if I may. When you arrest him, I would like Agent Johnston to cuff him."

Johnston glanced sharply at Tom and Fabrini nodded, a faint grin lighting his face. "You Americans, so sentimental. I understand and you will have your wish. You'll also need these," he said, then pulled open a drawer and held out two Beretta 92 semi-automatics.

Tom took one, ejected the clip and pulled back the slide. The chamber was empty. He replaced the clip, chambered a round and flicked on the safety. Johnston checked his the same way.

Fabrini watched the whole thing with vast amusement. "Nice to be working with professionals," he commented dryly and picked up the phone.

Tom only caught the street name and Nomentano from the torrent of Italian. Finished, Fabrini stood, his eyes bright, clearly looking forward to the coming action.

"They will let me know when the backup is ready to make the entry. In the meantime, let's take a drive over there, pick a café and I'll treat you both to a genuine Italian cappuccino. And I know just the place. I had one there last night."

"Sounds good to me," Tom said and stood up.

The short drive across town was spent with Captain Fabrini pointing out the few visible sights they could see between the stone buildings. They hit the vast Plazza del Popolo with its towering central column, and after some tricky traffic negotiation, entered Viale Babuino. Three blocks down, they turned left into a narrow street and parked in a little parking lot of the Osteria

Margutta café. According to Fabrini, Peroni lived on the other side of Viale Margutta.

No one paid them any attention as they walked into the spacious, brightly lit interior and grabbed a table by the tall plate glass window overlooking the street. Enough traffic went past to make it not feel lonely. The place smelled of ice cream, cakes, and freshly brewed coffee. A pretty little thing dressed in a light brown skirt and matching T-shirt took Fabrini's order. Apart from everything written in Italian and a young couple smoking at a corner table, heads close together, Tom could have been anywhere. He knew this was business, but the atmosphere that Rome generated weighed heavily on him.

The waitress quickly brought their coffees and he spooned in some brown sugar crystals from a porcelain bowl. The chocolate powder sprinkled over the white froth smelled divine. He took a sip and raised his eyebrows in appreciation. The brew wasn't too milky like some he'd had, allowing the flavor of the coffee to dominate.

"How do you like your cappuccino, Mr. Johnston?" Fabrini asked over the rim of his cup, his mustache smeared with froth.

"It's just great, sir," Brent said seriously, sipping his with relish.

"Very delicate," Tom added. "I've tasted some that were far too bitter. You had to drown them in sugar to make it palatable."

"It can happen here also," Fabrini agreed after a short laugh, "but the better places generally serve good coffee. How long will you be staying in Rome?"

"If everything goes all right, we have a direct flight to Boston on Friday morning. I'll be taking a local shuttle to Washington from there."

"You'll have a chance to do some sightseeing, then."

"I don't know, but I would like to look around if I can. If we do get Peroni, my time will probably be spent at our Embassy. They know we're here and are ready for us, but I've never done an international extradition before and I'm somewhat daunted by the likely paperwork involved."

Fabrini nodded in sympathy. "If it weren't for the paperwork, we could actually enjoy our work, no?"

"Once the wheels do turn, Brent will almost certainly be back to pick him up."

"Ah, we'll have to make your next stay more interesting, Brent."

Johnston glanced at Tom and smiled. "I don't know about coming back, that's up to my boss, but I wouldn't mind seeing more of Rome."

Fabrini's cellphone went off and he dug it out of his pocket. "*Sì?*" He listened for a while and nodded. "*Grazia.*" Pocketing the cellphone, he glanced at Tom. "My men are at the apartment block and about to enter the building." He raised his arm and the waitress came over with the check.

"Let's make sure that Peroni is still inside," Tom said and pulled out his own cellphone. After identifying himself, he listened and then hung up. "Still in."

About to add that the CIA contact thought the State Police stiffs should have worn something casual instead of parading around in their Sunday best, then thought better of it. Fabrini was genial enough, but no one liked having his men trashed by a stranger. Besides, who gave a shit how they were dressed as long as they did their job.

Fabrini called his stakeout team, told them to move in and cover the building exits, then left fifteen Euros on the table and they filed out. It only took a couple of minutes to get onto Viale della Trinita dei Monti. Fabrini spotted an unmarked black BMW parked in a side area that fronted the building and pulled in beside it. The two plainclothes detectives inside the apartment building opened the front door for them. Taking the elevator to the fourth floor, everyone reached for their gun. The elevator doors opened and they turned left into a short corridor just as their target emerged from his apartment.

Tom could see Peroni's startled look, but before anyone could get off a shot, he jumped back and slammed the door shut. In that fleeting second, Tom saw bewilderment and dismay on Peroni's face. All his careful planning, meticulous attention to detail, and what he thought was flawless execution, seemed now undone. Perhaps he wondered if Belconi had betrayed him.

One of Fabrini's men ran to the door and put two bullets into the lock, the shots deafening in the narrow corridor. The other man jumped and hurled himself at the door. The lock splintered and the door burst open. Fabrini stepped in and immediately crouched, gun held in an extended two-hand grip. Peroni had the kitchen window open and right foot on the sill, ready to jump. Fabrini's shot rang out and Peroni grunted as his left leg gave way under him. He fell back on the floor tiles with a cry and clutched his thigh.

Holding his weapon ready, Tom walked in and looked down at the prone figure. "Going somewhere? I told you I'd be seeing you," he said softly and watched something fade in Peroni's anguished eyes. Acceptance maybe, or perhaps merely a pause until an opportunity presented itself to get him out of this.

Holstering his weapon, Fabrini stepped to the open window and looked out. "Fire escape." Shaking his head, he crouched beside Peroni, roughly pushed aside his hands, checked the wound and glanced at Tom.

"The bullet went clean through the fleshy part. He'll recover to stand trial."

He barked an order to one of his men, who disappeared, only to come back carrying a bathroom towel. The other detective kept back curious, babbling tenants, wanting to know what all the shooting was about. With Peroni's leg roughly bandaged, Fabrini pulled out his cellphone and punched in numbers. When he finished speaking, he looked down.

"*Non ti preoccupare*, we'll get you to a hospital soon. You might as well enjoy resting and get used to the feeling, as you'll probably get a lot of it before you're done," he said in English, then spoke rapidly in Italian, presumably reading him his rights and charges.

Finished, he barked another order to his detective, who saluted and walked out. Fabrini produced a set of cuffs from his jacket pocket and handed them to Johnston. Looking determined, Johnston slid his gun into his trousers and looked Peroni in the eye.

"Your hands."

Johnston ignored the wince of pain on Peroni's face and snapped on the cuffs.

A siren wailed outside, growing louder, then whined down. Moments later, two black uniformed paramedics walked in, guided by a plainclothes detective. Fabrini pointed at Peroni and stepped aside. The medics removed the blood-soaked towel, ripped open the trouser leg, quickly applied pressure patches on the entry and exit wounds and tied on a fresh bandage. One of the medics plunged a needle into the thigh and stood up.

Fabrini issued orders and the two plainclothes detectives followed the medics as they helped Peroni hobble away. Moments later a uniformed cop appeared in the doorway and looked at everybody, as if not quite sure what was going on or what to do about it. He appeared to recognize Fabrini, because he stiffened and saluted. Fabrini spoke to him, then nodded to Tom.

"We're done here, my friend. The apartment will be guarded and the forensics team will have plenty of time to check it out. My men will be with Peroni at all times to make sure he doesn't try to, as you say, pull a fast one."

Tom grinned, reached out and touched Fabrini's arm. "Excellent work, Renzo. You realize there cannot be any media reporting. One word—"

"Don't worry. My men will keep it quiet long enough for us to take care of Cardinal Belconi."

Outside, they got into their car, attracting inquisitive glances from the few passers by. However, none were anxious to draw attention from the prowling police. Watching the ambulance pull away, siren wailing, Tom called his CIA contact and thanked his team for the service. He got a curt, 'You're welcome. I enjoyed the excitement,' and that was it. He figured once back in DC, he would have to do something nice for Mark. This must have cost his friend a whole raft of favors.

As the BMW headed back toward the police headquarters, he sat back against the upholstery and allowed himself to relax. A quick, clean snatch, and he felt quiet contentment that at least half his job was done. The fact that Peroni got shot, he considered to be only poetic justice. Whatever happened next, he had Garbaldi's killer and the nights would not haunt him anymore.

You can rest easy now, Paulini.

In Fabrini's office, Tom wound down, feeling the adrenalin rush ebb. "To be honest, Renzo, I never thought we'd get this far. Last Saturday night, I was at a dead end toasting my misery."

Fabrini sympathized fully. "I've also had moments like that. In our line of work, we have to expect some disappointments, no? Sometimes a case remains such a mystery that it would leave even the famed Sherlock Holmes scratching his head, sucking a pipe."

Tom agreed completely, glad that things had turned out differently this time.

"I would love to have you gentlemen as my guests for lunch," Fabrini said apologetically, "but I have to report to Director Framanti. To make up for being a bad host, we'll do our celebrating tonight. I'll pick you up at seven, if that's okay?"

Tom nodded. "I'm looking forward to it."

"Excellent. Then you can tell me all about this fascinating case of yours. Tiliari will take you to your hotel now and I'll meet you there at two-forty-five. It's only a short drive from there into the Vatican."

"We'll be waiting for you out front. And thanks again for helping out."

* * *

Clad in a black cassock, the short taciturn individual opened the dark polished door, bowed slightly and extended his arm in invitation. Tom walked through and looked around the huge room in fascinated amazement.

On his right, ceiling-high windows overlooked immaculate gardens. Two intricate tapestries adorned the left wall, showing white robed warriors storming what looked like a Crusader fort, judging by the banners and clad figures. The wall on either side of the door held glassed-in bookshelves filled with dark bound volumes. An intricate chandelier hung suspended, set in the middle of an elaborate pastoral painting with two angels holding the heavy chain. A wide desk stood centered in front of him, framed against a background of the largest world map he had ever seen.

Standing behind the desk, wearing a broad red belt and red cap, the tall, powerful man smiled as everybody entered. Large dark eyes, sunk deep beneath prominent white eyebrows, shone with energy that seemed to envelop the entire sleek face. Thick white hair topped a high, broad forehead. Tom's impression of the cardinal was right on. This man was used to power and knew how to wield it, but he had not expected a lightweight either.

"Mr. Meecham, Mr. Johnston and Captain Fabrini, Your Eminence," their reserved guide announced gravely and quietly closed the door.

"Welcome to the Vatican, gentlemen," Cardinal Karpeli declared warmly in a strong voice and waved a hand at old French chairs arrayed on either side of the desk.

"Thank you, Your Eminence," Tom said soberly, slightly repelled by the opulent surroundings. "I only wish it were under more congenial circumstances."

"You're just as I pictured you, Mr. Meecham," Karpeli said, smoothly sidestepping the awkward purpose of their visit like the polished diplomat he was. "Your first time in Italy, Mr. Johnston?"

"It is, Your Eminence," Johnston said, his eyes roving over the paintings and frescoes adorning the walls.

"Good. Hopefully you'll be back to see more of it."

"I would certainly like that. It's all very fascinating."

"Rome is all that. And how have you been, Captain Fabrini?" Karpeli demanded and glanced at Tom. "The Captain and I are old acquaintances."

"Doing God's work in my own small way, Your Eminence," Fabrini said simply as he eased himself into a chair.

"And necessary work it is too. I wish it were otherwise, but if men everywhere followed in the Lord's footsteps, I would be out of a job."

"One day, perhaps," Fabrini quipped dryly and Karpeli laughed.

"Touché! Well said. Until that day, we do the best we can. And for you, Mr. Meecham, that best has been very good indeed, very good. You can hardly understand what impact your visit here will have on the Church."

"Every house needs an occasional airing, Your Eminence," Tom said easily, not intimidated by Karpeli's powerful presence, and made himself comfortable. For a two-hundred-year-old chair, it was well sprung.

Karpeli smiled. "However, this particular airing is being forced on the Church under the most unusual circumstances."

"Perhaps, but you're attributing too much credit to me," Tom added. "Agent Johnston deserves most of it."

"And you're gracious to say so. But then, both of you were only doing your job. I can hardly fault you for *that*."

The thinly veiled reference to the papyrus wasn't lost on Tom and he smiled, starting to get the cardinal's measure. He

Stefan Vučak

wouldn't mind debating the old boy at all, but doubted that an opportunity would come his way. Karpeli was a senior Vatican minister, equivalent to the American Secretary of State. A person like that would hardly be bothered with a minnow like him.

"One does not always know how these things will turn out, Your Eminence. I can only be thankful that in this case, faiths have smiled on us."

Karpeli nodded slowly. "Or God has, Mr. Meecham. Your work is not quite finished, yes? I shall not attempt to sway you from what you're about to do with what you might consider empty rhetoric. What you're doing is wrong, but nonetheless, I recognize that you're a man of principle. With a cynical outlook on life perhaps, but that's doubtless a byproduct of your profession. Who am I to say that such an outlook is not more realistic of life. It is certainly closer to the pulse of human existence than mine, cloistered as I am within the glittering walls of my sumptuous office. No?" He glanced at Fabrini. "I assume you're here in your official capacity, Captain?"

"By necessity only, Your Eminence. I need to advise you that you have twenty-four hours to hand over Cardinal Belconi and Cardinal Marati on charges of conspiracy to murder."

Karpeli sighed and nodded. "Thank you for the grace period, Captain. We have questions of our own they need to answer before the *Corpo della Gendarmeria* can hand them over to you."

"I shall be here tomorrow at three to pick them up."

"To have this happen…regrettable. Most regrettable, and an incalculable blow for the Church."

Tom reached into his pocket, pulled out a brown envelope and stood up. He walked to the desk and placed the thing in front of the cardinal.

"Transcripts of Cardinal Belconi's calls, Your Eminence."

Karpeli looked down at the envelope, but didn't touch it. "Damned by his own words," he murmured. "Very well, let's get this done." He leaned left and pressed a button on his phone keypad.

"Yes, Your Eminence?"

"Have them escorted in."

"Yes, Your Eminence."

Tom remained standing as the cardinal bent down and produced a small hand-held UV scanner and a digital camera.

"As you requested, Mr. Meecham, and I preempted your need for a camera. This isn't really necessary, is it? You wanted me to see this for myself, did you not?"

Tom was not surprised that the old boy had worked it out. He would have been surprised if Karpeli hadn't worked it out. The transcripts constituted irrefutable evidence, but they were dry and impersonal. There was nothing like a visual impact of guilt, being trapped, followed by admission, to generate maximum effect. He wanted to see all these on Belconi's face and remember it for Garbaldi and the others.

"You do want to see this for yourself, Your Eminence," he said softly, but there was force and resolve behind his quiet words.

A knock and the door opened. Two cardinals walked in, one short and chunky, the other tall and corpulent. Both wore an air of authority gathered after years of wielding power, at the moment tinged with wary curiosity. A muscular, dark haired individual dressed in an elegant blue pinstriped suit followed them in. Seeing Fabrini, the taller cardinal blanched and his step faltered.

Karpeli nodded to the priest at the door, who bowed and closed it, then stood up and walked around the desk. Looking at his visitors, mouth hard, he turned to Tom and extended his arm.

"On your right, Cardinal Belconi, head of the Vatican's intelligence services. Beside him, Cardinal Marati, Prefect for the Congregation for the Doctrine of the Faith, and lastly, Giovani Emanuo, Inspector General of the Vatican City State police force." He then introduced Tom and Johnston.

Belconi glared at Fabrini. "Tell me one thing. Has Peroni betrayed me? Because there is nowhere to flee from The Entity's reach, no matter where or how long it takes me to find him."

Fabrini grinned at him. "Both of you will have plenty of time to plot your revenge—in jail!"

Marati placed his hands on his hips. "Your Eminence, what's going on? Whatever you might think, I have carried out God's work."

"As I am carrying it out now," Karpeli said, then turned to Tom and nodded. "If you would, Mr. Meecham."

Tom saw Belconi's dismay and felt a surge of intense fulfillment. This was right and no amount of Hail Mary's would save his black soul. He picked up the scanner, glanced at Johnston and stopped before Marati, wanting Belconi to stew a while longer.

"Your Eminence, please show me your hands, palms up."

Marati shot a dark look at Karpeli and slowly lifted his hands, not understanding what was going on, but it couldn't be anything good for him.

Tom switched on the scanner and played the beam over the extended hands. Johnston took two quick snaps. Everyone should be wearing protective glasses, but he shut off the beam after only a couple of seconds. Those seconds were enough. They all saw the ruby glow on the open hands. Marati hissed in consternation and leveled an accusing stare at Belconi.

Holding the scanner like a gun, Tom advanced on Belconi. He stopped before the old cardinal and stared into his eyes. It was all there: apprehension, resignation, contempt, and something else—defiance. With disaster about to befall him, he was still defiant. No matter. Tom had gotten what he came for.

"Your hands," he ordered, his voice coming out more harshly than he intended. This man would not deal out death in God's name anymore.

Belconi pursed his lips, glared and thrust out his arms. His right thumb and fingers glowed bright in the beam, as did the palm of his left hand. Johnston took more shots and extracted the memory card from the camera. Tom switched off the scanner, walked to Karpeli's desk, and put it down. He glanced at Fabrini and nodded.

"Cardinal Marati, you're under arrest as an accessory to five counts of murder, committed by one Mercurio Peroni. Cardinal Belconi, you're under arrest for conspiracy to five counts of murder committed by Peroni under your instruction." Fabrini turned to the Inspector General. "Sir, these men must be confined and held in custody until their release to the State Police tomorrow."

Giovani Emanuo gave Marati and Belconi a long look and nodded slowly. "It will be done."

"That count should really be six, Captain," Karpeli added in a hollow voice. "We don't want to forget Father Estonio Reoni."

Marati gasped. "Six deaths? Dear Lord!" Face crimson, he turned to Belconi. "You deceived me!"

"Shut your mouth, you fool!" Belconi grated. He took a step toward Karpeli and pushed out his jaw in defiance. "Your Eminence! These charges are ridiculous and Mr. Meecham's light show a theatrical scam."

"Was it?" Karpeli smiled faintly and shook his head. "I know everything, Avero. Father Garbaldi, the papyrus, Peroni, Swens…You see, the papyrus Peroni stole from Mr. Meecham is a fake, doped to contaminate anyone who touched it, as you saw for yourself. I also have NSA transcripts of your conversations with Peroni and Swens. You didn't have to do it like this. And neither did you, Renaro. Not like this!" he thundered indignantly.

"Vitorio—" Marati started, but Karpeli cut him off.

"Cardinal Secretariat of State to you!"

Marati blanched under Karpeli's fury. "We've known each other for over fifteen years, but you're looking at me like I'm an enemy. What I did, I did it all to protect the faith, to protect the Church. I *have* done the right thing!"

"You have defiled the Church!" Karpeli announced with finality and pointed at the Inspector General. "Take them out of my sight."

Defiant, Marati turned and walked out, barely noticing the police chief holding the door open for him.

Belconi whirled and shot Meecham a look of naked wrath. "If the FBI thinks this is the end of it, you're all monumentally mistaken. I will never see the inside of a courtroom. Whatever evidence you can bring to bear, including your pitiful NSA transcripts, I can discredit everything. The FBI is flirting with the power of The Entity. *My* power, and that's always done at considerable risk."

Rubbing his contaminated hand against his robes, he stormed out. Two Vatican security guards paced him.

With a glance at Tom, the Inspector General nodded to Karpeli, walked out stiffly and softly closed the door after him.

Karpeli strode to his desk and sat down heavily, suddenly weary. He looked at Meecham and allowed himself a small smile.

"Did you get what you came for, my son?"

Noting the cardinal's wry expression, Tom almost felt sorry for him. "Believe it or not, Your Eminence, I did not come here seeking revenge, but justice."

"Do not demand justice, for you too shall be judged," Karpeli quoted.

"For allowing the papyrus to be published? Then I am ready to receive judgment."

"As shall we all, whether here on Earth or by the Lord's hand."

"Give unto Caesar…" Tom started and Karpeli smiled.

"But who is the Caesar here, my son?" He stood and extended his hand for the ring to be kissed, then pulled it back. "Forgive me. You probably consider this to be hollow ritual. Perhaps it is, and perhaps that's part of our problem. The Church is filled with too much hollow ritual and the faithful have become contemptuous. Don't look so surprised that I'm telling you this, Mr. Meecham. It's only the truth. Ceremony and pomp might have been necessary to impress the poor and the ignorant in centuries past, but it only serves to mock today's much more sophisticated believers. Like yourself. Substance is needed now, not robes and incense. Something to discuss with the Holy Father, perhaps?"

Tom *was* surprised to hear this from the cardinal. "Since we're talking about truth, Your Eminence, is the Church still bent on recovering the papyrus?"

"That, my son, is something yet to be determined. You're returning to America immediately?"

"On Friday," Tom said, relieved that it had ended, and not at all troubled by problems Karpeli would undoubtedly face in the days and weeks to come. They had sown the seeds of their own harvest and should not complain what their efforts had gained them.

"Enjoy your stay in Rome. See St. Peter's if you can. You will be impressed."

Tom cast a meaningful glance around the room. "The birds don't live in gilded nests, Your Eminence, yet God still provides for them."

"And what the Church has built are gilded cages? I will think about your words, Mr. Meecham and I would still enjoy discussing philosophy with you sometime. Go with God, my son…Mr. Johnston. I'll see you tomorrow, Captain."

"I shall be here, Your Eminence," Fabrini said woodenly, bowed and walked out.

Tom took one last look at the gilded cage Karpeli lived in, shook his head sadly and followed.

I am coming, Melissa.

About the author

Stefan Vučak has written twenty-one novels, which include eight SF books in the Shadow Gods Saga. His *Cry of Eagles* won the coveted Readers' Favorite silver medal award, and his *All the Evils* was the prestigious Eric Hoffer contest finalist and Readers' Favorite silver medal winner. *Strike for Honor* won the gold medal.

Stefan leveraged a successful career in the Information Technology industry, which took him to the Middle East working on cellphone systems. Writing has been a road of discovery, helping him broaden his horizons. He also spends time as an editor and book reviewer. Stefan lives in Melbourne, Australia.

To learn more about Stefan, visit his:
Website: www.stefanvucak.com
Facebook: www.facebook.com/StefanVucakAuthor
Twitter: @stefanvucak

More Books by Stefan Vučak

https://www.stefanvucak.com/Books/

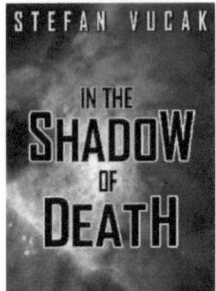  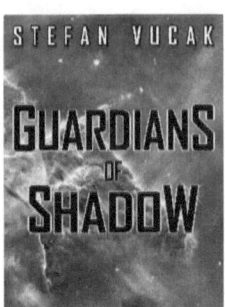

www.ingramcontent.com/pod-product-compliance
Lightning Source LLC
Chambersburg PA
CBHW030653120726
47905CB00001B/195